HONOR UNDER SIEGE

2-65

What Reviewers Say About Radclyffe's Books

A Matter of Trust is..."a sexy, powerful love story filled with angst, discovery and passion that captures the uncertainty of first love and its discovery." – *Just About Write*

Shield of Justice is a "... well-plotted...lovely romance...I couldn't turn the pages fast enough!" – Ann Bannon, author of *The Beebo Brinker Chronicles*

"The author's brisk mix of political intrigue, fast-paced action, and frequent interludes of lesbian sex and love...in *Honor Reclaimed*...sure does make for great escapist reading." – *Q Syndicate*

Change of Pace..."is contemporary, yet timeless, not only about sex, but also about love, longing, lust, surprises, chance meetings, planned meetings, fulfilling wild fantasies, and trust." – *Midwest Book Review*

"Radclyffe has once again pulled together all the ingredients of a genuine page-turner, this time adding some new spices into the mix. *shadowland* is sure to please – in part because Radclyffe never loses sight of the fact that she is telling a love story, and a compelling one at that." – Cameron Abbott, author of *To The Edge* and *An Inexpressible State of Grace*

Lammy winner..."*Stolen Moments* is a collection of steamy stories about women who just couldn't wait. It's sex when desire overrides reason, and it's incredibly hot!" – *On Our Backs*

"With ample angst, realistic and exciting medical emergencies, winsome secondary characters, and a sprinkling of humor, *Fated Love* turns out to be a terrific romance. It's one of the best I have read in the last three years." – *Midwest Book Review*

"*Innocent Hearts*...illustrates that our struggles for acceptance of women loving women is as old as time - only the setting changes. The romance is sweet, sensual, and touching." – *Just About Write*

Lammy winner..."*Distant Shores, Silent Thunder* weaves an intricate tapestry about passion and commitment between lovers. The story explores the fragile nature of trust and the sanctuary provided by loving relationships." – *Sapphic Reader*

In *When Dreams Tremble* the "...focus on character development is meticulous and comprehensive, filled with angst, regret, and longing, building to the ultimate climax." – *Just About Write*

Visit us at www.boldstrokesbooks.com

HONOR UNDER SIEGE

by

RADCLY*f*FE

2007

HONOR UNDER SIEGE

ISBN10: 1-933110-80-5
ISBN13: 978-1-933110-80-6

THIS TRADE PAPERBACK IS PUBLISHED BY
BOLD STROKES BOOKS, INC.
NEW YORK, USA

FIRST EDITION, JUNE 2007

CREDITS
EDITORS: JENNIFER KNIGHT, RUTH STERNGLANTZ AND J. B. GREYSTONE
PRODUCTION DESIGN: J. B. GREYSTONE
COVER GRAPHIC: SHERI (graphicartist2020@hotmail.com)

By the Author

Romances

Innocent Hearts

Love's Melody Lost

Love's Tender Warriors

Tomorrow's Promise

Passion's Bright Fury

Love's Masquerade

shadowland

Fated Love

Turn Back Time

Promising Hearts

When Dreams Tremble

The Provincetown Tales

Safe Harbor

Beyond the Breakwater

Distant Shores, Silent Thunder

Storms of Change

Honor Series

Above All, Honor

Honor Bound

Love & Honor

Honor Guards

Honor Reclaimed

Honor Under Siege

Justice Series

A Matter of Trust (prequel)

Shield of Justice

In Pursuit of Justice

Justice in the Shadows

Justice Served

Erotic Interludes: *Change Of Pace*
(A Short Story Collection)

Erotic Interludes 2: *Stolen Moments*
Stacia Seaman and Radclyffe, eds.

Erotic Interludes 3: *Lessons in Love*
Stacia Seaman and Radclyffe, eds.

Erotic Interludes 4: *Extreme Passions*
Stacia Seaman and Radclyffe, eds.

Erotic Interludes 5: *Road Games*
Stacia Seaman and Radclyffe, eds.

Author's Notes

Above All, Honor was the first book I published that really provoked many messages asking for a sequel. *Safe Harbor* was the second. Many of you recall me saying I wasn't going to write more of either one. This year I will publish number six in the Honor series and number five in the Provincetown Tales. Obviously, what do I know? I've discovered that writing multiple works in a universe of characters I and the reader are familiar with forces me to stretch as a writer in ways that stand-alones don't. Each has its unique challenges – neither is easier or harder or more rewarding. Just different. A series demands both continuity and new directions – consistency and change. We want to see more of the characters we love, but we also demand that they grow and evolve in the face of their personal struggles and in relationship to others.

Thank you to the readers who assured me that they really did want to read more of these characters and the world they inhabit. I have learned a great deal in the telling.

My thanks also go to my first readers: Diane, Eva, Jane, Paula, and RB for insightful comments and unfailing faith; to the editors who brought their special talents to making this a better book: Jennifer Knight, Ruth Sternglantz, and J.B. Greystone; and to the generous proofreaders at Bold Strokes Books for their painstaking devotion to duty. All the credit goes to these dedicated individuals and the responsibility for any shortcomings to me.

Sheri, as always, says it all and constantly says it better with every cover.

To Lee, for never ever saying write it later – *Amo te.*

DEDICATION

For Lee
To The Last Word

CHAPTER ONE

Monday, October 8

B lair Powell walked along the ocean's edge just after dawn, watching the sky segue through a palette of colors she had yet to capture on canvas. Thankfully, she wasn't a landscape artist, because she feared she would be doomed to an eternity of frustration and disappointment. Her life held more than enough challenge as it was, especially now, less than a month after the terrorist attacks on New York City and Washington, DC. Less than a month after four men she'd never met had tried to kill her.

Sliding her hands into the pockets of her dark navy windbreaker, Blair sheltered in the shadow of a tall, windswept dune and let the cold sea breeze and the force of nature's power drive the lingering melancholy away. Crisp, salty air filled her chest, and for an instant, she felt only the promise of a new season and the inner contentment of being in love. Despite the horror of the last month, she'd just spent one of the best weeks she could remember in seclusion on Whitley Island. At least two Secret Service agents followed her everywhere she went on the remote, sparsely populated island off the coast of Massachusetts, but she was out of the public eye and nearly alone with her lover. She cherished this rare privacy and feared that pleasure was about to change.

As much as she loved the island, she couldn't just disappear. And after the events of the last few weeks, she discovered to her surprise that she didn't want to. All her life she'd sought anonymity. Being her father's daughter had forced upon her a notoriety she had not chosen, and she had done all she could to escape the constraints it imposed. Yet sometime in the last year, that wild, furious need to break away had all but vanished. She wondered how much that sea change was due to the woman who walked toward her in the gathering sunlight.

Secret Service agent Cameron Roberts, Blair's one time chief of security and now her lover, was a few inches taller, dark-haired, lean and handsome. Her jaw was a little broader, her nose a little stronger, and the hollows below her cheekbones a little deeper than the dictates of classic beauty demanded, but what Blair saw when she looked at her went beyond beauty. She saw strength and passion, and above all, honor.

"You're supposed to be in bed," she chided as Cam approached. *Recovering.*

Cam grinned. "Bed was cold."

"It's a hell of a lot colder out here." Blair wrapped her arms around Cam's neck and kissed her, ruffling the short, almost wavy black hair that ended just above her collar. The almost casual brush of mouth on mouth turned unexpectedly more fervent. She stroked her tongue along the inside of Cam's lip, and delved deeper for an instant before leaning back. "Whew. Just got warmer."

"Let's see if we can get it up to August." Cam slid one arm around Blair's waist and underneath her jacket. She stroked Blair's back and nuzzled her neck. "Although, we probably shouldn't tamper with Greg and Hara's body temperatures quite so much."

Blair jerked and pushed away. "God, I can't believe I forgot about them. I *never* forget about them." She peered over her shoulder toward the dunes where two of her first team security agents stood with their hands at their sides, facing out toward the ocean as if she and Cam were not there. Of course, they had seen everything while continuously scanning the length of beach, the water, and the air.

"I'd say that little lapse is a very good sign." Cam brushed a strand of damp blond hair away from Blair's cheek and resisted the urge to kiss her again. Blair's deep blue eyes were shadow free, a rare occurrence, and even though she'd been up before dawn, she'd slept through the night. That, too, was unusual since the armed assault on Blair in her penthouse apartment. Cam loved to see Blair so relaxed and secure that she forgot she was being watched. She wished she could keep that from ever changing.

"When your eyes go from gray to black like that," Blair murmured, "I know you're thinking serious thoughts."

Cam shook her head. "No." She tugged Blair against her side and started to walk, keeping her arm around Blair's waist. "Just thinking I love you."

"That sounds serious." Blair slipped her hand into the back pocket of Cam's jeans and squeezed her ass. "In fact, we should probably do something about it ASAP."

"Okay."

Blair laughed. "You're too easy."

"I thought you liked me that way."

Blair caught Cam's hands and turned to walk backwards, swinging their joined arms lazily between them. The wind whipped her hair around her face, and her cheeks burned with the cold. She felt wonderful. "I like you every way you come, Commander. Hard and fast, slow and easy. Any way at all."

"Jesus, Blair. Have a heart." Cam tilted her head in the direction of the agents who followed along the invisible perimeter of their protection zone. "They can't hear us, but they'll have a hard time pretending not to notice if I throw you down on the beach."

"I thought you had better control than that," Blair teased.

"So did I," Cam muttered darkly. Everything she'd thought she'd known about herself had abruptly changed slightly less than a year before when she'd been assigned to protect the first daughter of the United States. Cam had fallen in love with her the first instant she'd seen her, her blond hair damp from the shower, her sapphire eyes sparking with anger, her sensual body blatantly seductive. Blair hadn't wanted protection, and she'd done everything she possibly could to avoid the constraints of twenty-four hour a day observation. She'd been wild and willful, a beautiful feral creature who defied taming. Cam had fought her desire, but ultimately, she had surrendered to her heart. "You changed all that."

"Funny," Blair said, returning to Cam's side and snuggling against her again. "I was just thinking the same thing about you."

"I love you."

"I love you." Blair kissed the edge of Cam's jaw. "Your throat sounds better. Does it still hurt?"

"No," Cam said quickly. Her voice still became hoarse when she talked for more than a few minutes, and swallowing was an exercise in masochism. But she didn't want to remind Blair of the injuries she'd sustained during an armed confrontation that she'd promised she wouldn't take part in.

Abruptly, Blair stopped walking and stepped slightly away. "Why do we constantly have to cover old ground? You know I can always tell when you're trying to protect me from something."

Cam winced. "Sorry. You're right. I need more practice at disclosure."

"Apparently." Blair sighed. "I suppose we both do. It's just that the very things I love about you make me crazy, too."

"Ditto." Cam laughed and then started to cough. It hurt, and she couldn't hide it. The finger marks on her throat had faded, but the bruising inside persisted. "Damn. The cold air is getting to me."

"I *told* you not to come out here," Blair snapped. "Damn it, Cameron." She hated it when Cam hurt. She hated feeling helpless under any circumstances, but it was worse when it was Cam and she couldn't do anything. She picked up her pace. "Let's get you inside. I'll make some tea or something."

"Tea?" Cam rasped, trying desperately not to laugh again.

Blair's glower could not hide her smile. "Well, something."

They climbed through the dunes toward the multi-level glass and wood house where they'd been staying for the past few weeks, the two Secret Service agents keeping pace behind them. Blair stiffened at the sight of a woman hurrying down to meet them.

"Hi, Paula," she greeted her new chief of security. Paula Stark was an athletic, dark haired, dark-eyed woman close to her own age. She had proven herself capable of protecting Blair in dire circumstances more than once, and Blair trusted her. More than that, she cared for her. That kind of affection probably wasn't wise; she was not supposed to form personal attachments to her security agents. But Blair never did anything simply because it was prudent. She spent more time with the four members of her first team than she did with anyone else in her life, and she couldn't help but care about them. Just the same, she preferred not to see Paula right now. It could only mean one thing. Her brief respite had come to an end. "What's up?"

"Your father wants to talk to you." Paula nodded to Cam. "Commander."

"Chief," Cam said. Technically, she wasn't the commander anymore, since she'd been replaced as Blair's chief of security by

Stark, but she couldn't seem to get any of the agents to stop calling her that. She wanted to ask if there was a problem, but she was trying to be respectful of Stark's new position. Security chiefs were circumspect by nature and rarely shared any more information than necessary with anyone, including the protectees and their families. *Especially* with the protectees and their families. Part of a security agent's job was to make the lives of those they guarded seem as normal as possible under the most abnormal of circumstances.

"Is my father all right?" Blair asked as they reached the rear deck of the house.

"I have no reason to think otherwise," Stark said in her official voice. "Lucinda Washburn put the call through. She said there was no urgency, but the president would like to speak to you at your earliest convenience."

Blair rolled her eyes. *At your earliest convenience* was Lucinda-speak for call immediately. Lucinda Washburn was President Andrew Powell's chief of staff, as well as his lifelong friend and adviser. No one was closer to him, not even Blair. Lucinda had helped him win the governorship of New York, the vice presidency, and finally the presidency. She was an astute politician and managed far more than the day-to-day workings of the White House staff. If someone wanted the ear of the president, they needed to court Lucinda Washburn first.

"Lucinda wants something." Blair glanced at Cam, who smiled ruefully. Lucinda did not make social calls. She also was not the president's secretary, which meant that she probably had an agenda of her own. "Give me a few minutes to have a cup of coffee, Paula, and then I'll call her back."

"I'll be in the command center." Paula kept her voice neutral and her face expressionless. The makeshift command center was actually part of the first floor of the smaller guest house that sat partway between the main house and the beach. Her scaled-down security team stayed there when they were off shift. Right now there were only three other agents with her—Greg Wozinski, Patrice Hara, and Felicia Davis. There was also one other inhabitant, her FBI agent lover Renée Savard, who was recuperating from a bullet wound. She and Cam had sustained their injuries during the same action. "Please call me when you're ready, and I'll scramble a line for you."

Blair halted with her hand on the handle of the back door and regarded Paula quizzically. "Is something wrong?"

"No ma'am."

"Am I supposed to guess why you suddenly sound like an android?"

Paula smiled. "Sorry. I was asleep when the call came in and I haven't had time to recharge my batteries. I'm running on auxiliary backup packs."

"Ha ha. Come inside and have some coffee, then."

Paula checked in with a quick glance at Cam, who signaled for her to follow them into the house.

"I'm going to grab a quick shower," Cam said, heading in the direction of the staircase leading to the second floor. "Be right down."

Blair led Paula through to the kitchen, while Patrice Hara took up a position just inside the rear door and Greg Wozinski walked through to the front of the house. "How's Renée doing?" she asked casually as she began to assemble the morning coffee.

"Restless." Paula settled into a chair at the rectangular oak table in the center of the room.

"Tell me about it." Blair turned on the automatic coffee pot, put a kettle of water on for tea, and sat down next to her. "Renée is just like Cam—neither of them is happy unless they're working." She touched Paula's wrist lightly. "You should understand that. You're all the same, really."

There had been a time when the slightest touch from Blair would have made Paula blush. She could not believe that eight months had passed since the few ill-advised hours she'd spent in the intimate company of the first daughter. The lapse was one of a potentially career destroying magnitude, and although she regretted her irresponsible behavior, she did not regret the private moments they had shared. Now, it seemed like the interlude had taken place in another lifetime, when she had been another woman. In the few scant months since then, she'd seen Cameron Roberts almost die, Blair narrowly escape assassination, and the nation that the entire world had considered unassailable become the victim of terrorism. She didn't blush.

"I do understand. But the doctor said she needed another few days before she could start walking, and the inactivity is wearing on her."

Blair knew the problem was more than just inactivity. Renée, along with many of the New York based FBI and Secret Service field agents, had been in the World Trade Center at the time the towers had been hit. She'd seen the devastation and horror firsthand. "It's going to take some time, Paula. She'll heal."

Paula's eyes revealed what she couldn't say. Wouldn't say, out of respect for her lover's privacy. "I know."

"She has the one thing she needs most of all," Blair said gently. "You."

"Oh, man," Paula said softly. "I hope that's enough." She wished she could feel certain, but she feared that something in Renée's soul had been irreparably broken and neither time nor love would heal it.

Blair stood. "Trust me, it is." She set a mug of tea at an empty place for Cam. "I think right now the people we care about might be all that matter."

"I...uh...how are *you* doing?" Paula asked as Blair poured their coffees.

Everyone knew how private Blair was, and it wasn't really her place to ask personal questions. But since September 11, the world as they knew it was gone and some of the old rules no longer seemed to apply. Paula understood the necessity for viewing the subjects she protected as critically valuable individuals, while at the same time avoiding any kind of personal involvement, even friendship. But they'd all been through so much together that the usual professional detachment seemed impossible, especially when Blair had been the object of a nearly successful assassination attempt in her own heavily-fortified home. What was once considered inconceivable now fell within the realm of the probable. It could happen again, and Paula had to see that it didn't.

"Sometimes I still can't believe that any of it really happened," Blair said quietly.

"I know." Paula took a deep breath. She was still trying to understand her new role as Blair's security chief and what the boundaries were. Most of the time when she wasn't certain, she followed her heart. That probably wasn't the way the commander did things, but she would never be the commander. "We weren't prepared for what happened in the Aerie, but we will be now. They failed, which just shows you how good your security was, even against the unexpected. Now it will be even better because we know the game has changed."

The game has changed.

Blair suppressed a shudder. Yes, the rules of engagement had definitely changed, and she was an unwilling player in a game where the stakes were higher than she'd ever imagined. She glanced toward the door as Cam walked in. Her black hair was wet and slicked back, making the sharp planes of her face stand out even more. Even in a loose black T-shirt and blue jeans, her body looked taut and fighting ready. Blair could tell from the set of her jaw that she'd heard the last part of the conversation; she had that intense, hard expression she always got when the subject of Blair's vulnerability came up.

"I'm not worried." Blair said, "We have the winning team."

Cam leaned down and brushed a kiss over her cheek, then regarded the tea with a raised eyebrow. "Is that for me?"

"Yes," Blair said with exaggerated seriousness. "And there's honey on the counter. Put some in. It will help your throat."

"I think coffee will do fine."

"Cameron." Blair's eyes glittered dangerously.

"But tea is probably better," Cam amended as she retrieved the jar of honey.

Paula watched the exchange with apparent interest, then looked quickly away as Cam gave her a pointed stare. She rose without finishing her coffee. "I'll be in the command center."

"Wait, Paula." Blair kept her gaze on Cam, thinking how much she loved going to sleep with her every night and waking up with her in the morning and having her around during the day. Just being with her. Not being guarded by her, not being worried over. Just being in her company. But this week had been an anomaly, and they both knew it. Softly, she said, "Ready?"

Cam nodded.

"Paula," Blair said. "I think we better make that call."

CHAPTER TWO

I just sent a transport plane to Lexington for you." In her usual rapid-fire fashion, Lucinda Washburn continued, "It should be there in two hours. Come on over to the office when you get in."

"Hi, Luce," Blair said sarcastically. "How's *your* day going?"

"About the way they've all been going for the last month."

Blair was surprised by the weariness in Lucinda's voice. She couldn't remember ever seeing her tired. In fact, she wasn't certain she'd ever known Lucinda to actually sleep. "Is everything all right?"

"As all right as can be expected." A small, impatient sigh filtered down the phone line. "Come home. We'll talk."

Home. The White House would never feel like home to Blair, because it wasn't, even though her father and Lucinda were there. True, she had no other family home. Her father had sold the house she had grown up in when her mother died. Blair was twelve at the time, and after that she had lived in the governor's mansion or whatever other house came with her father's political position. Lucinda had always been like family. She'd been a close friend of both Blair's parents before Blair's mother died, and she'd been a constant figure in Blair's life ever since. Not a mother figure, but strong and capable and comforting, for all her demands. But Blair's *home* was her loft in Manhattan, and that had been nearly destroyed in an attack that had come at the same time as the devastation at the World Trade Center. She didn't have a home now, and the memories of terror and death chilled her. She glanced at Cam, who watched her pensively. Cam. Cam was home.

Blair pushed the images of loss away. "It will take us a while to arrange transportation to the airport."

"I can get State Troopers to escort you."

"God, no," Blair said with barely suppressed horror. "I've got all the protection I need. Just tell the pilot he may have to wait."

"All right then. I'll see you this afternoon."

Blair ended the call and handed the phone back to Paula. "We're leaving."

"I'll let the teams know," Paula said.

"I'll call Tanner and arrange for drivers." Cam hesitated, casting a questioning look in Stark's direction. "If that's all right with you."

"It's fine. Thanks," Stark answered on her way out the back door.

Cam set her tea aside and slid her arms around Blair's waist. "What's up?"

"I don't know." Blair kissed the tip of Cam's chin. "But Lucinda wants to talk."

"Uh-oh."

Blair sighed. "I know." She rocked her hips lightly against Cam's. "Have you heard anything from Stewart?"

Cam shook her head. Assistant Director Stewart Carlisle was her immediate superior in the Department of the Treasury, but since she'd most recently been on special assignment reporting directly to the president, she hadn't been under Stewart's command for some time. "I don't actually know who I'm reporting to anymore." She glanced through the back door to the guest house visible partway down the slope to the beach. Blair's security team was there. The nerve center of all that went into protecting Blair was there. And she wasn't. "Especially since I'm not on your security team anymore."

Blair leaned back, hooking her thumbs in the loops of Cam's jeans. "It bothers you, doesn't it. That Stark is in charge now."

"Stark's a good agent."

Blair laughed. "Cameron. Don't even try."

Cam forced herself to unclench her jaw. "Yes, it bothers me. I didn't want to be switched from investigation to protection when they first assigned me to your team last year. But you know what?" She kissed Blair lightly. "I'm good at it. And I'm motivated. I like..." She shrugged. "...looking after you."

"Oh, darling," Blair murmured. "You do look after me. In all the ways that mean the most to me. You love me, and that's what I really need. I don't need you throwing yourself in front of me if some crazy person decides they don't like the color of my dress."

"I know that's not what you need." Cam ran a hand through her hair. "But it's kind of what I need."

"I know." Blair hugged her tightly. It was rare that she could touch Cam without being aroused, for which she was pleased and grateful. She hoped that never changed. She couldn't imagine not wanting her. Just at the moment, though, she wanted to comfort her because it was so unusual for Cam to be unsure about anything. And she could sense Cam's unease and uncertainty. "We all need time to get adjusted to the changes, Cam. But I'm always going to need you."

Cam smiled and rested her forehead against Blair's. "And I'm always going to need you."

❖

Paula hurried down the twisting path to the guesthouse. Under other circumstances she would have taken a second to appreciate the unseasonably warm early October morning, but her mind was totally consumed with the myriad details of her job. She felt the full weight of her new responsibilities intensely, but beneath the low-level hum of nerves, she was also aware of the surge of excitement that always accompanied any operation when Egret, as Blair was officially called, was on the move.

"Listen up," she said as she pushed through the front door into the living room. "Egret is flying." She shed the windbreaker she'd grabbed earlier on her way down to the beach and rolled up the sleeves of her white button-down collar shirt. She headed straight for the dining room where they'd set up their computers and communication equipment. "I'm going to call DC to arrange ground transport."

Felicia Davis, a statuesque African-American with features that suggested she might be descended from an ancient Egyptian queen, sat in a rattan chair sipping coffee. "Shall I arrange accommodations?"

"Yes. The usual hotel. At least for a night until the commander— until I determine Egret's immediate schedule."

Pushing numbers on her cell phone, Felicia rose and walked to the French doors leading to a wide deck with a view of the beach.

"What about me?" Renée Savard reclined on a sofa with her left leg propped up on an overstuffed hassock. A blue fabric knee immobilizer with wide white Velcro straps was wrapped around her knee. "Can I tag along?"

Paula held up one finger as she spoke into the phone and

simultaneously entered information into the computer. A minute passed, then she disconnected and returned to the living room to sit next to Renée. She skimmed her fingers through her lover's shoulder length golden-brown hair. "How's your leg?"

"Other than the fact that it feels as heavy as a tree trunk, and about as functional, it's fine," Renée said edgily. Her blue eyes narrowed. "It would feel a hell of a lot better without this immobilizer."

"Just for a few more days."

Renée waved her away. "Go take care of what you have to take care of. How soon are you leaving?"

"ASAP."

"Well then, don't waste time asking me about my stupid leg."

Paula kept her expression neutral. She knew Renée's leg hurt, and she knew that her bad temper was more than pain. "Do you want to hang out here while we're gone? I can get Tanner to arrange a private car to take you back to Manhattan if you don't."

Tanner Whitley, heir to the Whitley corporate dynasty and the owner of Whitley Island, was one of Blair's oldest friends from prep school. She also had one of the best private security forces in the country. Her crew had been providing perimeter protection during Blair's stay, ensuring that no one approached the house from the main road that bisected the island. Stark trusted Tanner completely.

"I don't want to go back to Manhattan." Renée sounded un-characteristically petulant. "Not when I can't work. Not when you're not there." She leaned back and stared at the ceiling. "Jesus, listen to me. I'm pathetic. I'm sure you don't want me underfoot while you're working."

"I don't know how long we'll be in DC, or where we'll be going after that," Paula said. "But—"

"Just go, Paula. I'll call Tanner later and arrange my own—"

"But," Paula continued as if she hadn't been interrupted, "if it turns out we're not staying in DC, it's just as easy for you to head back to Manhattan from there as from here. Come with us."

A crooked smile broke the smooth caramel plains of Renée's cheeks. "Sometimes I wish you weren't so sweet when I'm being cranky. It makes me feel guilty, which just makes me crankier."

"I'd be cranky too," Paula whispered. "I'm sorry it's so hard for you right now."

Renée's eyes filled with tears and she looked away. "Jesus. I need to do something. If I sit around much longer, I'm going to really be crazy."

"Officially you're still part of the commander's team, even though you're on sick leave," Paula said with conviction. "So, you're coming with us. You need help packing?"

Renée grabbed the crutches that leaned against the sofa next to her. "No. I can manage. You go take care of things, Chief."

"Yeah, okay," Paula said, unable to keep her face from flushing. Chief. It sounded good.

❖

Blair left her suitcases by the front door and walked outside to take a last look at the ocean. She wasn't sure when she'd be able to come back to the island and she already missed it. The solitude was good for her art. She'd been able to paint here, despite everything that had happened to her and the rest of the world. She had asked Tanner to investigate the possibility of her purchasing the house; the current owners only used it as a rental property. The location was perfect— isolated, easy to defend, and close to Tanner, whom she missed and never managed to visit enough. It was also near enough to Manhattan that Diane Bleeker, her art agent and best friend, could easily visit.

She sat down on the top step of the rear deck and punched in a number on the disposable cell phone Cam insisted she use. She was half surprised when the call was answered.

"Hi, where are you?"

"Still in Manhattan," Diane replied. "How about you?"

"About to head south." There was no reason to think that her calls were being monitored, but after the constant admonishments of her various security teams, Blair had reluctantly accepted the necessity of caution. She avoided mentioning the specifics of her travel plans in phone conversations. Diane was used to filling in the blanks.

"Ah," Diane said, "back to the real world."

"Yes. Do you have the gallery open?"

"I've postponed the next show at the artist's request. He didn't think it was the best time, and I tend to agree with him. It will take a while until it's business as usual back here."

"So are you going to take a trip?" Blair asked lightly, although she waited for the answer with a sense of misgiving. Diane had recently become romantically involved with a CIA agent who had disappeared under mysterious circumstances, and Blair worried that Diane was somehow going to try to find her. In all the years they'd known one another, Blair had never seen Diane truly in love before. Now that Diane had fallen hard, only to be left just as abruptly, she was suffering. It pained Blair to know that her friend was hurting.

"I haven't decided yet. I'm waiting for…inspiration."

She's waiting for Valerie to contact her, Blair mentally translated. "Well if that occurs, you'll be sure to let me know."

A beat of silence ensued. "Of course."

"I mean it."

"How about that other matter we were discussing?" Diane said, overtly changing the subject. "The celebration I'm going to be planning."

Blair smiled, thinking about the wedding. Her wedding. Hers and Cam's. Something she'd never anticipated wanting. A commitment to one woman for life. A formal commitment, a statement to the world. The idea had once seemed intimidating. But now, when the world had proved itself to be untrustworthy, capable of shifting dangerously at any moment, now more than ever she wanted that commitment. "I'm going to discuss that later on today. I'll get back to you with a timetable."

Diane laughed. "I wish I was going to be there to hear it."

The wind had died down and Blair was warm in the sun. She shrugged out of the black leather blazer she'd pulled on over a scooped neck navy T-shirt and jeans. "You could come down for a few days. I should stay for a while once I get there, and I could use the company."

"Really?"

"Yeah," Blair said softly. She wanted to say more, that right now it felt good to be surrounded by the people she loved and who loved her, but she couldn't. She didn't want to remind Diane that Valerie was gone, not when she knew how hard Diane was trying to hold on to the belief that Valerie still cared for her. That Valerie hadn't simply abandoned her after a short, convenient affair. Worse, that Valerie hadn't used her as part of her cover story. "Say you'll come down."

"I'm not staying…you know where."

The White House. Blair laughed. "Oh, believe me, neither am I.

We'll stay with a friend." *With Cam.*

"Oh goody," Diane said, sounding like her old self for the first time. "Sooner or later, I'm going to get to watch."

"You just keep on dreaming, honey. Everyone needs a dream."

After a pause, Diane said, "I know. I just discovered that."

❖

Five hours later, the Air Force jet that Blair and the others had boarded at Lexington Air Force Base northwest of Boston began its descent to Andrews Air Force Base in Prince George's County, Maryland, a few miles southwest of DC. Ordinarily Blair and her team traveled by corporate jet, but with the heightened security, Lucinda had dispatched the same transport usually reserved for the president, the vice president, high-ranking dignitaries, and other VIPs. It was another change in Blair's life that didn't make her particularly happy, but she understood the need for it.

"How long do you think we'll be at priority one," Blair asked, leaning against Cam's shoulder.

Cam took Blair's hand and drew it into her lap. "Indefinitely would be my guess."

"That's what I was afraid of." Blair sighed. "I detest military escorts. Do you think they're going to restrict my travel?"

"Are you planning on going somewhere?"

Blair laughed. "Well, I was hoping for a honeymoon."

"Ah. That."

"You're not backing out are you?" Blair shifted on the seat and studied Cam intently, the barest hint of worry in her eyes.

Cam held her gaze. "Absolutely not. I told you. Name the time and place, and I'll be there."

"You don't think we should wait, because of everything that's happened?"

"I think the best way for any of us, all of us, to let the world know that we won't be terrorized is to continue to live. No, I don't think we should wait."

"Thank you," Blair said.

Cam brushed a kiss over her fingers. "Did you think I'd change my mind?"

"You *have* hit your head a couple of times recently." Blair leaned over and kissed the corner of Cam's mouth. "It might have been enough to make you forget how much I'd hurt you if you did."

"Just let me know when you plan to drop this little bomb on Lucinda," Cam said. "I'd like to be somewhere else."

"Coward."

Cam grinned. "Guilty as charged."

"Excuse me," Paula Stark said as she made her way down the center aisle. "We'll be on the ground in a few minutes. Ground transport will meet us on the tarmac. You'll exit once we've cleared the area, Ms. Powell."

"Thank you, Paula. I know the drill."

"Yes ma'am."

"Sorry." Blair sighed, already feeling the claustrophobic atmosphere of priority one security. "Paula, I'll be staying at Cam's after we finish at the White House."

Paula nodded, her expression never changing. "Yes ma'am."

When Stark had moved back toward the front of the plane, stopping partway to confer with her team, Cam whispered, "It would be easier if we stayed at the White House."

"Easier for whom?"

Cam laughed. "Your security team."

"I don't like to make love in those antique beds."

"Have plans, do you?"

"Oh yes," Blair whispered. "I most definitely have plans."

Cam settled back for the landing, Blair's hand still in hers. "Well, then, the security team will just have to make adjustments."

CHAPTER THREE

Paula exited the plane first, followed by Hara and Wozinski. Felicia Davis waited just inside the open door to accompany Blair. Two late-model black Suburbans idled at the edge of the tarmac, each with a driver behind the wheel and an agent standing near the open rear door. The ground transport teams were Washington-based Secret Service field agents who were called upon to provide backup support for the first family and visiting dignitaries upon the protectee's arrival in DC.

Hara and Wozinski stopped at the bottom of the flight stairs while Paula crossed to the vehicles. She checked the IDs of every agent, scanned the front and rear compartments of both vehicles, and then took a slow visual survey of everything with a sight line to the path Blair would take from the plane to the Suburban—other vehicles, rooftops, communication towers. Everything she did was SOP, but it would never be routine again. Blair's security had been breached. They had all learned a lesson at a nearly inconceivable price.

"Ms. Powell will ride with you," Paula said, leaning down to the open driver's window of the first vehicle. "I'll advise as to route once we're in motion."

"Yes ma'am," the driver, a fresh-faced blond with a military style haircut, said sharply.

Paula walked back to the plane. When she'd contacted the Washington team, she'd outlined three potential motorcade routes from the air force base to the White House. Blair was vulnerable on the road in any type of vehicle, even with bulletproof glass and armored plating. Something as simple as a suicide driver in a tanker truck loaded with gasoline could kill her.

Once again, this was standard operating procedure, but Paula was uncomfortably aware of not totally trusting anyone outside of her immediate team. She did not welcome the feeling that no one, even those she should be able to trust implicitly, was above suspicion any longer, and she feared the situation was the new status quo.

With a nod to Hara and Wozinski, she started up the stairs to the plane. The pilots had not powered down the engines, remaining prepared to take flight again on her word if anything appeared amiss.

"Clear to disembark," she reported to the marine who had accompanied them in flight. He saluted and went forward to advise the pilot and copilot while she waited on the narrow platform at the top of the stairs, shielding the door and any view of Blair with her body.

Inside the cabin, Felicia stepped to one side so that Blair and Cam could pass. She then moved up behind Blair.

"You should let Renée go down first, Paula," Blair said, halting at the top of the stairs. "She's going to have trouble on the stairs with those crutches."

"Let's proceed to your vehicle, Ms. Powell," Paula said. "Hara can give Agent Savard a hand in a moment."

Blair started to protest, then felt a gentle touch on the base of her spine just as Cam whispered, "You're not secure here. Let's go."

"God, now I've got *two* of you ordering me around," Blair muttered, but she started down behind Paula. As soon as she reached the ground, Hara and Wozinski closed in on either side, and with Felicia behind, the agents formed a protective ring around Blair and Cam as Paula led the way to the first vehicle. An agent Blair didn't recognize opened the rear door and she and Cam climbed in.

"We're in the middle of a United States Air Force base," Blair griped. "The marine unit that protects my father and the White House is stationed here. What in God's name could happen to me walking from the plane?"

"It doesn't matter where we are," Cam said quietly. "We're at priority one."

Blair sighed. "And I'm sure Stark realizes you're watching her every move. I'll be lucky if she lets me take a breath without permission."

"I'm not watching her every move," Cam said. "I already know that Stark knows what needs to be done. And she knows that too."

"Sorry." Blair peered out through the smoked bulletproof glass. Felicia had apparently returned to the plane after Blair was secure in the vehicle, and she and Hara crossed the tarmac toward the second car with Renée between them. Paula and Wozinski headed toward their vehicle. "I'm edgy."

Cam took her hand. "I know. It's okay."

Paula climbed into the rear, Wozinski into the front.

"Would you still like to go directly to the White House, Ms. Powell?" Paula asked.

"Yes, thank you."

Paula keyed her transmitter to contact the drivers of both vehicles. "Destination Alpha, route Delta."

The Suburban accelerated smoothly and quickly away from the runway, and Blair settled back for the familiar ride.

❖

"Are you okay?" Cam asked.

Across from them, Stark looked out the window, her expression remote. Cam knew from experience that she could hear their conversation, but by means of some unconscious filter cultivated by most Secret Service agents for their own comfort as well as that of their protectees, she would not register the meaning of the words.

"I just want to find out what onerous chore Luce has planned for me now. It's been a while since I've had a command performance, so I imagine she needs a visible White House presence somewhere."

Cam wasn't happy with that thought. Ordinarily, Lucinda tapped Blair when the White House wanted to make a statement, the kind of declaration that the president couldn't make himself for political reasons—such as offering support for a pro-choice charitable organization or attendance at a fundraiser for a beleaguered political ally. Sometimes, the White House just needed a presence at a media-worthy event, and Blair was always popular. She was beautiful, well-educated, and personable. She was a great stand-in for her father. And her status made her a great target.

"Now isn't exactly the time to be parading you out in public," Cam observed.

"What?" Blair focused on Cam, aware of the tight thread of disapproval in her tone. "Do you want me to sit in a dark room somewhere for the rest of my father's presidency?"

"That might not be a bad idea."

In the past they would have fought about it. As it was, Blair struggled with her temper and her overwhelming need not to be controlled. She'd spent all her life resisting the efforts of others to safeguard her at the cost of her independence. She'd resisted Cam, too, for months, even as she tried to seduce her. She'd wanted to prove that she didn't need to be protected, and she'd wanted to undercut Cam's authority over her. Unfortunately, her plan hadn't worked. She'd fallen in love, and although she hadn't realized what that meant at first, she did now. Loving, being loved, was a responsibility. The decisions she made now didn't just affect her, they affected Cam's life, too. So she took a breath and listened to what Cam *hadn't* said. Cam was worried for her.

"Remember you said yourself we couldn't stop living," Blair said. "We can't let whoever tried to destroy us think they've frightened me into hiding."

A pulse pounded in Cam's neck. "I wasn't talking about putting you on display somewhere when I said that."

"You don't know that's what Lucinda wants."

"She's gearing up for your father's reelection campaign. She's not going to put that on hold no matter what's happening on the international scene." Cam consciously relaxed her hands, which had tightened into fists. "And you're going to be a great campaign asset."

"Darling, I've never been a great campaign asset. I'm the wild child, remember?" Blair laughed, thinking of the international debacle that would have resulted if her affair the year before with the French ambassador's wife had come to light. "My security chiefs spent half their time trying to keep me *out* of the press, not in it."

"Not anymore." Cam trailed her fingers down Blair's cheek. "You're as close to a first lady as this country has. And the public loves you."

"Let's just wait and see what she wants," Blair said, but she had an uneasy feeling that Cam might be right. She'd taken a back seat during her father's run for the presidency, but she wouldn't be able to do that again. She wanted him to be reelected. The country needed him. And if *he* needed *her*, she might have to get used to campaigning. She found Cam's hand and squeezed it. "I'm not the first lady. I'm just your lady."

"When did you figure out just what I needed to hear?" Cam murmured, kissing Blair's temple.

"I've been practicing."

"You're doing well."

Blair smiled. "Yeah? How well?"

"Want to keep Lucinda waiting for an hour or two?"

"Yes." Blair leaned closer to Cam. Dropping her voice, she whispered, "You're not the only one who's been suffering while you recuperated."

"Then it's probably going to take me more than two hours to make it up to you. It might take me all night."

"Then I guess I'll just have to suffer a little while longer." With a satisfied expression, Blair leaned back and closed her eyes. "Because I don't intend to hurry."

❖

When Emilio, assistant to the White House Chief of Staff, directed Blair and Cam into Lucinda Washburn's office, Lucinda was on the phone. Blair waved to the commanding looking woman with the stylishly coiffed, silver-streaked black hair. As usual, Lucinda wore a conservatively styled jacket and skirt, plum colored this time, offset by burnished gold jewelry at her ears and throat. A single large, square cut emerald in a plain gold setting adorned the ring finger of her right hand. That, Blair noted, was new.

Lucinda paced in front of a wide walnut desk covered with neat stacks of folders and memoranda. When she caught Blair's eye, she mouthed *coffee* and pointed to a credenza against one wall.

Blair signed, *you too?* and at Lucinda's nod, proceeded to pour coffee into three China cups. She handed one to Lucinda and then carried the others to the sofa across from Lucinda's desk, where Cam was waiting. They sipped in silence as Lucinda expertly pressured whoever was on the phone.

Her tone was even and unmistakably edged with flint. "Listen Tom, I really don't care if Charlie has to walk all the way from Chicago. He owes us that vote and I expect him to be here tomorrow morning for roll call." With a faint smile, she concluded, "Either that, or he'll find himself pushing that school tax referendum up a long steep hill all by himself."

Lucinda listened for another few seconds, said, "Wonderful," and hung up. Then she crossed the room and settled into one of the brocade Chippendale chairs facing Blair and Cam. "Good flight?"

"Military transport isn't known for luxury," Blair said.

"True," Lucinda conceded. "But they're reliable."

"Well, I'm here now, so what do you need?"

"I'd forgotten how much you enjoy small talk." Lucinda turned to Cam. "How are you feeling?"

"Better every day."

"Judicious answer."

"Luce," Blair said impatiently. "I was having a really nice morning when you called. A walk on the beach, and then I was planning on going back to bed. Once there, I intended to sedu—"

"You can probably skip those details, Blair," Cam interjected, brushing her hand down Blair's arm.

Lucinda laughed. "I wouldn't put it past you to tell me all the details, Blair, just to make me suffer. Considering that I haven't been out of this office before 2 a.m. the last month, I haven't exactly been getting—"

Blair held up her hands. "I don't want to know what you do in your spare time."

"Truce then." Lucinda's expression softened for an instant. "You look rested, both of you, as much as can be expected. Doing all right?"

Both Blair and Cam nodded.

"Good." Lucinda drained her coffee cup and set it carefully on a low cherrywood Federal table. "We have a slight problem that I think you can help us with."

Blair stiffened. Cam remained completely still, but her eyes sharpened as she studied Lucinda's face.

"The Company has lost an important asset, and they'd rather not inform their counterparts in the other divisions. Such a lapse is embarrassing, especially these days when everyone is a little unsure of who will remain top dog in the security world."

"Is this conversation being taped?" Blair asked casually.

"Of course not."

"No video cameras in here?"

"No."

"Then do you think it would be possible," Blair said, emphasizing each word, "for us to speak English, Lucinda?"

"The CIA has lost a deep cover operative and they don't want the FBI or the Department of Defense to know about it."

"Valerie Lawrence," Cam said.

Lucinda regarded her steadily. "Yes, and I don't think *we'd* even know about it except someone at Langley let a bit of a memo regarding the lost contact slip into the daily security briefing report. Averill Jensen picked it up."

Blair knew Jensen well. He was her father's hand-picked security adviser, and before her father's presidency, Averill had been attorney general. He'd also been her father's college roommate. She said, "Averill would. He never misses anything."

"Yes, and when he followed up, the lid slammed shut." Lucinda lifted her shoulder. "I suspect the operative responsible for the information leak has been transferred someplace where the nights are long and dark."

"So Valerie is out in the cold somewhere," Cam said. "Are they trying to bring her in?"

"We don't know. But we'd like to find her ourselves." Lucinda crossed her legs and folded her hands loosely in her lap. Relaxed. Friendly. "You know her, Cam. That could be useful."

"I don't think I like where this is going," Blair said. "Cam and Valerie—"

"Have a history, yes I know." Lucinda's gaze never wavered from Cam, even when Blair stood abruptly.

"History, Luce. History. As in past." Blair wanted to pace but the room wasn't quite big enough for it. Instead she walked to Lucinda's desk and stood there with her back to the others. She looked out the French doors that opened to the esplanade running along one side of the West Wing until the red haze of anger cleared from her brain, then she turned back. Cam and Valerie had once been lovers when Cam had thought that Valerie was a high-priced Washington call girl. "Cam doesn't know anything."

"Blair," Cam said gently. "That's not why we're here."

"I don't understand." Blair looked from Lucinda to Cam. "God damn it, I hate this."

"It's Diane," Cam said, watching Lucinda. "Isn't it?"

"Oh no. No, no, no." Blair stalked back to the sitting area but did not sit. She slammed her hands onto her hips to hide the fact that they were shaking. "Diane is not part of this. She was never part of this. She doesn't know—"

"We haven't been able to access very much information," Lucinda went on in her conversational tone. "Averill wouldn't have pushed at all except Lawrence's name came up in association with the raid in Tennessee. That's getting close to home."

"So you want to know what Valerie knows," Cam said, thinking out loud. She reached up and pulled Blair down beside her. "It's okay. Let's just talk for a few minutes."

"Actually, we want to know *who* Valerie knows," Lucinda replied. "Because someone tipped Matheson about the raid. He's disappeared."

Cam straightened in surprise. Matheson was the head of a paramilitary organization that had direct ties with the men who had staged the assault on Blair in the Aerie. Possibly even with the men who had orchestrated the World Trade Center attacks. When Cam's team uncovered his identity, she, Renée, and a hand-picked cadre of covert military operatives, had stormed the compound. Matheson had not been there. "I thought the Company had him."

Lucinda shook her head. "As far as we know, no one has him."

"And someone thinks Valerie tipped him off?" Cam asked tightly.

"We don't know anything. We would very much like to speak to Valerie Lawrence."

"Who's *we*?" Blair snapped.

Lucinda rose. "Have you two had lunch? I was about to ring for something."

Blair closed her eyes and counted to ten. "This is one of those times when my father doesn't know anything, right? Even when he does?"

"Turkey clubs okay?" Lucinda inquired with the phone in her hand.

"Yes, fine," Blair said. "I still don't understand why we're here."

Lucinda gave her order to the kitchen, then hung up. "As I said, we—well, Averill—was able to access some of the information about Valerie Lawrence before the door slammed shut. They had tapes. Phone records. We have reason to believe she's going to contact, or already has contacted, Diane Bleeker."

"Diane doesn't know anything about this," Blair repeated insistently.

"No, she probably doesn't," Lucinda said. "All we need to know is where Valerie is. When she contacts Diane, we'll know."

Blair laughed harshly. "Diane will never tell you that."

"No," Lucinda said. "But she'll tell you."

Cam slid her arm around Blair's shoulders. Blair pulled away.

"I won't do it. I won't do it for you, Luce, I won't do it for my father, I won't do it for anyone. I love Diane. She's my friend. I won't spy on her."

"I understand," Lucinda said. "Just think about it."

"There's nothing to think about. Nothing at all." Blair jumped to her feet. "I'm going for a walk."

Cam stood but Blair shook her head, insisting, "No, I'm going by myself."

"Blair." Cam tried to catch her hand but Blair sidestepped. "Baby, let's—"

"No. Just—no."

Cam watched her go, a sinking feeling in her chest. She reached for her radio to call the team, and then realized she didn't have it. She didn't have it because she wasn't part of the team. "God *damn* it." She started toward the door.

"They'll pick her up right outside the office," Lucinda said. "Give her some time, Cam. It's been a difficult month."

It took everything Cam had not to go after Blair. To trust that someone else would. That someone would keep her safe.

"Besides," Lucinda said. "It will give us time to talk."

CHAPTER FOUR

B lair yanked out the clip that held her hair at the back of her neck, letting her thick, unruly waves fall free around her face. She was aware of Paula Stark falling in behind her as she hurried from Lucinda's corner office in the West Wing through the labyrinth of hallways and into the lobby. Once outside, she skirted around the circular drive toward the northwest gate.

"Ms. Powell," Paula said, slightly breathless as she fell into step. "It would be better if we took the vehicle. If you let me know your destina—"

"I'm walking," Blair snapped.

"Uh, yes, I can see that, but with all respect, we're not prepared for street surveillance."

"If you and your minions weren't tagging along behind me in your shiny blue suits with your big-ass gas-guzzling black car, no one would even notice me. Go away."

"I can't go away. I'm sorry." Paula was well aware that Blair could go unnoticed in street clothes. She had followed her into enough bars, and seen her pick up women who had no idea who she was enough times, to be convinced of that. Nevertheless, she wasn't comforted by the knowledge that people might not recognize Blair when she wasn't at an official function or dressed for a political affair. It was just as possible that unfriendlies were routinely watching the comings and goings at the White House, and right now, Paula didn't have enough personnel to guard Blair out in the open. "Ma'am, this is not advisable."

"I just need some air." Blair slowed and met Paula's worried gaze. "Please. Just give me a few minutes."

"If you wouldn't mind waiting, I can have another team here in two minutes." Paula glanced over her shoulder and saw the Suburban following slowly behind them on 17th St. She held a hand behind her with two fingers extended and heard car doors open and close. Hara and Wozinski should be on the ground now too. Unfortunately, it was late afternoon and would be dark soon. They were also heading toward the Mall, which was exactly where she did not want to be at night.

"Can we compromise?" she urged. "Can you just sit somewhere, and I promise we'll disappear."

Blair laughed abruptly and looked past her to Hara and Wozinski. "The three of you would stand out in a crowd, no matter what you were wearing. Out here, you might as well be waving a sign saying 'we're government agents.'"

Paula pointed to a bench. "There's a great spot right by the reflecting pool."

"And with three people, you can easily watch my back and flanks, and unless the creature from the Black Lagoon comes up out of the pool, you don't have to worry about a frontal approach." Blair recited the tactics flatly as she quickened her pace. She sat down on the white stone bench, gripped the cold edges with her fingers, and closed her eyes. She wasn't angry with Paula. Making Paula's job harder wasn't going to ease the hurt and fury that stormed with equal measure inside her.

She couldn't believe that Lucinda had summoned her to Washington to ask her to spy on Diane. No, actually she *could* believe it. She'd seen people in power compromise their principles often enough, but she hated to think that the people she loved, Lucinda and her father, would sacrifice trust and fidelity to achieve their goals. Maybe that's why she'd fallen in love with Cam. Because Cam was always so clear about which side of the line she stood on. Cam did not compromise.

"Paula?" Blair said softly as the sun went down.

"Yes ma'am?" The reply came from somewhere behind her.

"Would you call Cam and tell her you're with me. She'll worry."

"Right away." After a moment's silence, Paula added, "Can I tell her when we might be back?"

"In a little while," Blair murmured.

She should go back. Cam wouldn't be satisfied with a phone call. It didn't matter that she knew Paula was capable. It didn't matter that she knew Blair was safe. She needed to see that for herself. Blair sensed that Cam already felt powerless with Paula in command and that she was having trouble adjusting to the change in their relationship. She loved Cam for wanting to protect her and care for her, even though that wasn't why she'd fallen in love with her or even what she needed most from her. Trying to change that about Cam would be denying what made her who she was. And making her needlessly uncomfortable was just unkind. She could be furious at her father and Lucinda just as easily at Cam's condo.

"Paula?"

"Yes ma'am?"

"Would you ask her to walk down to meet us?"

"I don't think she'll be able to, ma'am. She's in a meeting with the president."

Blair's stomach tightened. So there was more. Of course there was. Lucinda didn't fly her down here just to solicit a little snooping between girlfriends. Cam was a trained investigator. Cam had been Valerie's lover. Cam was talking to her father. Alone.

Cam never turned down an assignment, never stepped away from her duty, never put her own safety first.

Blair stood abruptly and strode from the park, Paula and the other agents close behind.

Cam had given enough. And so had she.

❖

Sybil Gretzky, the personal secretary to Andrew Powell, smiled at Blair as she entered the anteroom to the oval office. "Hello Blair."

"Is my lover still with my father?"

Sybil's smile never faltered. "Agent Roberts is with the president, yes. Would you like me to ring through?"

"Sorry," Blair said, realizing she'd been saying that all day. She wasn't just edgy, she needed to pound something. "Yes, please."

She walked to the wide windows and looked out into the Rose Garden. It was so beautiful in the spring, with everything in bloom, but so desolate in the fall. Cold and a little barren.

"Let me take you in," Sybil said.

"Thanks."

Her father stood to greet her when she came in and kissed her cheek.

"You feel cold," Andrew Powell said.

"I've been out walking." Blair settled onto an antique sofa and glanced at Cam, who sat in a chair opposite her father on the other side of a low coffee table. "Hi."

"Hi," Cam rose and walked around the table to sit next to Blair. "Okay?" She touched her fingertips briefly to Blair's leg, then put her hand back in her lap.

"Sure." Blair regarded her father. "I know there are some things we can't talk about, but Cam is my partner. She almost died ten days ago. What more can you ask of her?"

Andrew Powell, in his early fifties but looking a decade younger, with thick wavy hair and blue eyes the exact color of Blair's, regarded her with an expression that might have been sympathy or regret. "We need good people, Blair, especially now. And Cam is one of them."

Blair shook her head. "How many times? Is there a quota on bullet holes? Concussions? Because she's had her share. More than her share."

"Blair," Cam murmured. "Let's hear what the president has to say."

"I'm not talking to the president," Blair retorted. "I'm talking to my father. That counts for something, doesn't it, Dad? Just a little?"

"I'm your father," the president said. "It means everything."

"But you're still going to ask her, aren't you? For whatever job needs doing, no matter what it might cost."

Andrew Powell shifted his gaze to Cam. "You can say no, no questions asked. No one will think less of you."

Blair snorted. "That's because the people giving the orders are sitting safe behind some desk somewhere. They don't have the balls for anything else."

Cam waited.

"Three weeks ago," Powell said, "I established the Office of Homeland Security. I expect within a year the office will become a Cabinet department. We're drawing from all sectors of domestic and foreign security to fill the critical positions."

"Field posts or administrative?" Cam asked.

"Both."

"Answering to whom?"

"For now, to the Director of Homeland Security—who answers to me."

"Anti-terrorism?" Cam asked, very aware that she was interrogating the president, and he was allowing it. She wondered how much that had to do with her relationship with Blair. Quite a lot, she imagined.

"That and border security. Possibly Customs. We'll work those things out as we finalize the Cabinet level responsibilities."

"Why can't the security agencies we already have handle anti-terrorism?" Blair asked. "The CIA, the FBI, the military security divisions. God, how many are there?"

"A lot, and that's part of the problem," the president said. "We obviously need to centralize and oversee intelligence gathering, analysis, projections—the whole thing. And we need to be able to respond with effective, organized force."

Cam leaned forward. "On domestic soil?"

Powell's face hardened. "If need be."

"It's going to take some doing to get the FBI, CIA, DOJ, and military intelligence to play together," Cam observed.

"I know that. And time is something we don't have." He stood and walked to his desk, then returned to his seat with a thick folder. "We're organizing a number of special teams immediately, drawing from personnel across security divisions. I'd like you to head one, Cam."

"On behalf of the Secret Service?" Cam asked.

The president shook his head. "Obviously, all of this is for your ears only, but I expect we'll move the Secret Service completely into Homeland Security within the next few months. I want you as one of the new deputy directors of the OHS."

"In what capacity?" She quelled the quick surge of excitement. The balance of power within the intelligence community was shifting, and she was being offered a premier seat.

"Counterintelligence."

Cam looked at Blair, and her focus instantly shifted from exhilaration to concern. Blair was pale, and the shadows beneath her eyes were back. "I can't give you an answer right now, Mr. President. Blair and I need to talk."

"I understand. Once you've decided, we can discuss specifics."

"Thank you, sir," Cam said, standing and extending her hand.

Powell rose to return the handshake. "I couldn't discuss this with you beforehand, Blair. With either of you. It's a matter of national security."

"Of course," Blair said dully. "It always is."

❖

Stark approached as Cam and Blair stepped into the lobby.

"We'll be going directly to my apartment, Chief," Cam said.

"Very well." Stark murmured a few words into her radio. "The vehicle's right outside."

"Thank you."

Blair was silent on the walk to the Suburban and remained that way for the cross-town ride. When they reached Cam's building, Blair automatically took her position between Stark and Hara, with Cam and the third agent slightly behind her as they entered the lobby and crossed to the elevator.

"Hara, you're on radio backup. Wozinski, you'll take the lobby this shift." Stark glanced at Blair. "Will you be going out this evening?"

"I don't know," Blair said as she stepped into the elevator ahead of Cam and Stark.

"You can reach me on my cell should you decide—"

"I know that."

When the elevator doors opened, Stark checked the hall before allowing Blair to exit. There were only two apartments per floor with doors opening off each end of a spacious, carpeted foyer and small seating area. The short hallway and the alcove next to the elevator were empty.

Cam removed her keys from her pocket. "I'll check the apartment, if you want to wait here with Ms. Powell."

Blair made no objection, and when Cam emerged from the apartment a moment later and held the door open, Blair walked past her with no comment. Cam followed her inside and closed the door.

"Hungry?"

Blair glanced at her watch. "Diane should be here soon. Let's wait." She checked her phone, then pushed a button. "I'll see where she is. We can order pizza."

"Okay. Let me have your jacket." Cam held out her hand for Blair's leather blazer. She hung it in the closet next to her own, listening as Blair spoke with Diane.

"Where are you?...Do you need a ride? Are you sure?...Okay. See you soon."

Honor Under Siege

"She's on the train?" Cam asked.

"Yes. She'll be here in about an hour."

Cam crossed the room, took Blair's hand, and drew her to the sofa in front of the windows. "Let's talk."

Blair leaned against Cam's shoulder. "Why? It never changes anything."

"I didn't see this coming," Cam said. She eased her arm around Blair's shoulders and drew Blair against her side. She leaned her cheek against Blair's hair. "I didn't give much thought to this homeland security business when I first heard about it. It's going to be a huge bureaucratic snafu with all the security agencies struggling to protect their turf. That's not my style."

"My father wants you to head a special team." Blair said. "That always means outside normal channels. *That's* your style."

"I admit that's a little more appealing. I've never had a desk job. I don't want one."

"I know. You're a field agent. But we're not talking about chasing counterfeiters, Cam. Special teams for homeland security means terrorists. It means something dangerous."

"Not necessarily. Most of the time special teams are assembled just because they're more efficient at gathering information. It's still mostly desk work."

Blair tilted her head up. "That's bullshit."

Cam smiled. "We don't know what your father wants me to do."

"You can't possibly think it's a coincidence that Lucinda brought up Valerie Lawrence right before my father asked you to head up a special counterintelligence team. Do you?"

"No," Cam said quietly. "I don't."

"My father can't talk about those kinds of operations, but Lucinda can, which is why she met with us first." Abruptly, Blair stood up, walked to the windows, and spoke with her back to Cam. "They want Valerie, and they'll use me and my friendship with Diane if I let them. And they'll use you, because you..." She raised her hand, then let it fall. "Because you were in love with her."

Cam crossed to Blair and rested her hands on Blair's shoulders, drawing her gently back until their bodies connected. "You know that's not true. What happened between us was limited to a few disconnected

• 45 •

hours. It had nothing to do with the rest of our lives. And I *didn't* know she was a counterintelligence operative. Jesus, I thought she was a prostitute."

"I know all that. And I know you had feelings for her. I've told you before, it's okay." Blair shrugged, her back still to Cam. "Well, *mostly* okay. Except now and then when I let myself notice how beautiful she is."

Cam nuzzled Blair's hair. "I was never in love with her."

"She was special, though. She had to be, for you to care for her." Blair half turned so she could see Cam's face. "Do you trust her?"

"That's part of what I'm going to have to decide. Because if I undertake this assignment, and it's Valerie they want me to find, I have to know who I'm going after."

Blair turned completely and threaded her arms around Cam's waist. "*If* you take the assignment?"

"I won't do it if you don't want me to."

Blair pulled away. "I *hate* when you do this."

"Do what?"

"Make me be part of the decision. It was easier when you just did what you wanted. Then I could be angry with you for doing it."

"You're losing me." Cam caught Blair's hand again. "If I've learned anything about being with you, it's that I'm supposed to talk about things with you. Don't confuse me."

Blair grabbed Cam's shoulders, jerked her close, and kissed her. Hard. "How would you feel about me if I said no. I don't want you to do it."

"I love you."

"I can't stand worrying about you. I can't take one more phone call telling me you're hurt."

"I won't do it."

"I want you to take a supervisory position in homeland security. You know how to run teams. You can do it without being on the street."

"Okay."

Blair squeezed Cam's shoulders, felt the hard muscles ripple under her fingers. She flashed on an image of Cam naked, her body toned and tight. Her body scarred. Her body battle ready. She kissed her again, tasting the heat of her mouth, feeling the strength in her arms as they came around her and held her tightly. "I love you so much."

"Blair." Cam whispered, sliding her fingers down over Blair's chest to cradle her breast. She kissed Blair's throat as Blair's nipple hardened against her palm. "I never want to hurt you."

"I know," Blair breathed, arching her back and exposing herself to Cam's mouth, offering the vulnerable vessels in her neck to the glide of teeth and tongue. She covered Cam's hand where it held her breast and pressed down, moaning at the ache of pleasure that shimmered through her. "Do what you have to do."

Cam splayed her hand over Blair's back and pulled Blair's shirt from her jeans. She kissed down Blair's throat to the hollow between her collarbones. "What are you saying?"

Blair leaned away and pulled off her top, then swiftly released her bra and dropped it to the floor. She arched her back, breasts lifting in invitation while she fumbled at her jeans. "Hurry. We don't have much time."

Swiftly, Cam pushed Blair down onto the wide leather sofa and knelt to pull off her boots. Grabbing the top of her jeans, she stripped the denim and silk away in one long wrenching pull until Blair was nude.

"Lie down," Cam ordered. Easing between Blair's legs, she braced an arm by Blair's shoulders and kissed her. While she stroked inside Blair's mouth, she cupped her sex. Blair was wet, swollen, already opening for her. Blair's hands came into her hair and Cam slid into her. Blair jolted and cried out.

"I never want to hurt you," Cam said desperately, her breath tearing from her chest as she pushed deeper.

"You aren't. You can't. Not when you lo—oh, god." Blair gripped Cam's forearm as Cam thrust between her legs. She drove her pelvis up to meet Cam plunging down, the pressure building, burning, blinding. "Cam, I…"

"Blair, Blair," Cam groaned against Blair's mouth. "Come, baby. Oh Jesus, please let me feel you come."

"Oh now," Blair cried, her nails digging into Cam's arm. Her abdomen tightened and she jerked upright, clutching Cam as her orgasm spilled from her. "Hold me. Hold me. God, please hold me."

Cam gripped Blair tightly and as Blair's body sagged, she eased her back onto the sofa, shifting until she could lie beside Blair and hold her in her arms. "Okay? Baby, you okay?"

Blair pressed her face to Cam's chest, listening to her heart thunder. "God. You make me come like nobody's business."

Laughing, Cam stroked her hair. "Is that right."

"Mmm." Blair stretched and eased her thigh between Cam's legs. "You sound hoarse again. Is your throat okay?"

"Everything feels fabulous."

Blair nudged Cam's crotch. "How 'bout this?"

"Fabulously horny."

"Thought so." Blair gripped the button on Cam's fly.

Cam stopped her. "Uh-uh. Not now. I'll last."

"Since when?"

"Since Diane's going to be here any minute."

"Darling," Blair said in a reasonable voice. "I can make you come in under thirty seconds."

Cam kissed Blair lightly. "That's true. But I want you to take a lot longer."

Blair sighed. "If that's what you want, I suppose I can be patient."

"So," Cam shifted onto her back so that Blair lay partially upon her, "you want to explain what you said back then just as my mind was melting?"

Blair skimmed her hand back and forth over Cam's chest. "I told you the truth. I don't want you to be in danger. I want you to be safe." She met Cam's questioning gaze. "But I don't want my love to keep you from being who you are. Or doing what you have to do. So you have to promise me, on your word of honor, that you won't let anything happen to you. Swear it."

"I swear," Cam whispered, stroking Blair's cheek. "I swear I will love you with my whole heart every day for the rest of my life."

Blair blinked back tears. "That's not what I asked."

"I know. I'll be careful."

Blair settled down again and pressed her face to Cam's neck. "So noted, Commander."

CHAPTER FIVE

"There!" Diane Bleeker leaned forward over the front seat of the cab and pointed to a building on the right side of the street. "That's it—1202."

When the cabbie swerved toward the curb, a horn blared behind them, making Diane jump. She peered out the street-side window in time to see a black sedan rocket by. The cabdriver muttered an expletive as he parked and climbed out to retrieve Diane's luggage from the trunk.

Diane handed him a ten after he'd set her suitcases on the sidewalk outside Cam's building. The door opened as she hauled her luggage toward it, and she smiled in recognition at the burly blond who stood just inside. Agent Wozinski made some linebackers look small.

"Hi, Greg."

"Ms. Bleeker."

Diane shook her head. She'd given up trying to get him to call her Diane even though she'd once spent a week with Blair and had seen him every day during that time. In the fifteen years that she'd been friends with Blair, she'd grown used to the presence of security agents. But it had never been like this. So many, keeping such a close watch. She was surprised that Blair didn't break out more often. *She* would have.

"Okay to go up?" she asked.

"Yes, ma'am. I'll call up and announce you."

"It's 501, isn't it?"

"That's right."

The elevator was efficient, and Diane suspected that she arrived outside Cam's door seconds after Wozinski called. When she rang the bell, Blair immediately answered.

"Hi." Blair pulled her into a hug. "I'm so glad you came."

Diane hugged her back, surprised at the intensity of Blair's embrace. She leaned back, her arms clasped loosely around Blair's waist, and studied her. Blair looked more rested than when she'd seen her ten days ago, but she could hardly look worse than she had the day after both Cam and Renée had been injured. Still, there was something in Blair's eyes that telegraphed worry. Worry and...regret?

"Are you okay?" Diane looked past Blair into the expansive living room beyond. Cam, who stood behind a small bar tucked into the far corner of the room, nodded in greeting. As usual, Diane could tell nothing from her expression. She waved and returned her attention to Blair. "Did Lucinda give you a terrible task?"

"The usual," Blair said, trying to inject lightness into her tone. "I don't have all the details yet." She grasped the larger of Diane's suitcases. "Come on, let me show you where the guest room is."

Diane hesitated. "Are you sure? I can stay at a hotel and give you two some privacy. I don't need to stay here."

Blair shook her head. "No, I want you to stay here." She followed the direction of Diane's gaze. "Cam is fine with it. Really." She laughed without much humor. "And God knows, we're used to having people around all the time. At least with you, it's by choice."

"You're sure?" Diane realized that she really wanted to stay with Blair. She'd been lonely almost beyond bearing in a city still in the throes of grief.

"Positive." Blair took Diane's free hand and tugged her into the apartment. "So this is the living room, bathroom's over there, and the guest room is down this hallway." She nodded to the opposite side of the living room. "Our bedroom is over there."

Diane glanced back over her shoulder as she followed Blair. "Well, hell, I won't even be able to listen."

Blair laughed. "Like you haven't heard it all before. Well, at least me."

"That's true," Diane said as they both set her luggage down in the guest room. "But we were sixteen."

"Cam is opening some wine." Blair took in Diane's dark brown Tahari pantsuit and ivory silk shell. "Why don't you change into something sloppy and comfortable and join us in the living room. We ordered pizza."

"God, that sounds fabulous." Diane removed her raincoat and draped it over the chair that sat in front of a narrow writing desk, kicked off her Jimmy Choos, and flopped backwards onto the bed. She patted the space beside her as she curled on her side. "Stay for a minute first."

Blair climbed onto the bed and propped her head in the palm of her hand, facing Diane. As usual, Diane looked beautiful. Her shoulder length hair was more gold than Blair's honeyed tones, and nearly straight, framing a dramatic oval face with ice blue eyes. Katherine Hepburn in blond. "I feel like we're back in prep school."

"Sometimes I wish we were." Diane smiled wanly. She looked tired. Who didn't? Her eyes grew distant. "No, on second thought, maybe not. Because if we went back, I'd still be trying to seduce you, and you'd still be breaking my heart."

"As I recall," Blair said fondly, "you *did* seduce me."

"I dragged you into bed when you were stoned. Plus, you'd been coming on to me all night, so that doesn't count." Diane laughed at the memory. "It was good sex though, wasn't it?"

"We were fifteen. Of course it was." Blair sighed. "I do love you, you know."

"I know." Diane stroked Blair's arm. "So what's wrong?"

Blair shook her head. She couldn't tell Diane about the situation with Valerie, not until she'd had time to talk to Cam some more. Not until she'd had a chance to decide what she'd do if Cam sided with Lucinda and her father. Her mind rebelled at the possibility, because she wasn't sure what she would do if she had to fight everyone she cared about. She wasn't sure she could stand being at odds with Cam over something like this.

"God, you look sad, honey." Diane slid her hand to the back of Blair's neck and massaged her gently. "Is something wrong with Cam? Is she in trouble over what happened at the compound?"

"No," Blair said quickly. "I'm just tired. And the last thing I wanted was to be dragged back here."

"Are you going to tell me what's going on? Because I'm probably the only person in the world besides Cam who can tell when you're upset and trying not to show it."

"I will," Blair said, realizing there was no point in denying what Diane already knew. "As soon as I can."

Diane sat up and slipped off her jacket, then laid it on the bed beside her. "Do you think Cam can find out where Valerie is?"

Blair caught her breath, glad that Diane wasn't looking at her. She took an extra second to be sure her voice was steady. "I don't know. Why?"

Diane stood, unbuttoned her slacks, and slipped them off. Wearing just her blouse and panties, she opened her suitcase and lifted out a pair of soft, faded jeans. She pulled them on and zipped them, then lifted off the shell and placed it with her suit. "Because I thought I'd hear from her by now, and I haven't. And I don't know how to go about finding her."

"Maybe it would be better if you didn't find her," Blair said carefully.

"You mean you think her disappearing act was just her way of dumping me?" Diane donned a pale blue cotton shirt and buttoned it, turning partially away from the bed so that Blair wouldn't see her hands shaking. She knew what Blair was trying to say, and she had considered that obvious explanation every day since Valerie had vanished one morning before dawn. They'd had an affair and now it was over and she was a fool not to simply accept it. "You think I should just let her go?"

"I don't know, Diane," Blair said gently. "But it's complicated with Valerie. There's no way of knowing if she left because she wanted to or because she had to. But either way, she left without explaining, so I can't imagine she wants you to go looking for her."

"She *did* call me." Diane referred to the brief call the morning that Valerie had disappeared. The morning of the raid on the mountain stronghold of a group of paramilitary fanatics. "That must mean something. If she was...moving on, why call?"

Blair agreed, but was afraid to say so. She wasn't sure it was safe for Diane to have anything to do with Valerie now. Not when it seemed like half the country was looking for her. "You know she's an agent, and the whole national security system is in an uproar now. It's going to take time for everything to settle down. Weeks. Months maybe."

"I don't want to wait months to talk to her. To see her again." Diane turned her back and walked to the window. She wrapped her arms around herself. "I miss her. God, I miss her."

"Oh, hey," Blair said, hating the pain in Diane's voice. She scrambled off the bed and crossed to Diane, hugging her from behind.

"Maybe Cam could just get a message to her from me. Just so she knows—" Diane struggled with tears. "Just so she knows I haven't given up."

"I'll do what I can," Blair whispered.

Diane leaned back in Blair's arms and rested her cheek against Blair's. "Thanks."

Blair held her tightly, wondering what she'd just promised. And how she could keep her word to one woman she loved without betraying another.

❖

The elevator jerked to a stop and Paula opened her eyes. For a few dizzying seconds, she wasn't sure where she was. Two women and a man, all in business suits, stood talking to her left, ignoring her as she leaned against the wall in the corner. She blinked at the number panel. 10th floor. A glossy picture of a restaurant on the far wall advertised the Veranda at the Wyndham Washington, DC. She was at the hotel where the team stayed when on temporary assignment in the Capitol. She remembered Hara dropping her off out front before he took the Suburban around to a special reserved parking slot. Then what?

Jesus, was it possible she'd fallen asleep standing up?

"Excuse me." Flushing with embarrassment, she pushed away from the wall and jumped between the elevator doors as they started to close. Some Secret Service agent. She'd completely lost track of her surroundings. It didn't matter that she wasn't on duty. It was her job to be observant.

She slid the plastic card key from her pocket as she strode quickly down the hallway, hoping to leave her discomfiture behind. She let herself into room 1020. It was dark and still inside, and for an instant, she thought she was in the wrong place.

"Renée?" Unconsciously, she swept her blazer back and rested her hand on the grip of the Sig Sauer holstered on her right hip. "Babe?"

"I'm here," Renée Savard replied.

Paula felt on the wall for the switch, then hesitated. "Can I turn on the light?"

"Just a second."

Paula heard the squeak of springs, then the bedside lamp came on. Renée, still in the clothes she had traveled in, lay on top of the covers on the queen sized bed. Renée's holstered service weapon rested on the bedside table next to a prescription medicine bottle. Paula's stomach tightened, but she forced a smile as she crossed the room and leaned down to kiss her lover. She brushed her hand over Renée's cheek.

"Taking a nap?"

"Trying to."

Paula settled gingerly on the side of the bed and tapped the immobilizer encircling Renée's leg. "Is your knee bothering you?"

"It's fine," Renée said sharply, then just as quickly caught Paula's hand as Paula started to get up. "I'm sorry. Yeah, it's a little bit sore." She gestured toward the medicine bottle on the table. "I'm trying not to take those things, but my whole body aches from not being able to move around much. This fucking immobilizer—" She trailed off, looking disgusted. "Christ, you've been on your feet working since dawn, and I'm complaining."

Renée closed her eyes and turned her head away.

"Since I'm here now and can wait on you," Paula said lightly as she released the Velcro straps on the stiff wraparound brace, "why don't we take this off. The doctor didn't say you couldn't bend your knee, just that you couldn't weight-bear. No wonder it hurts, being squeezed in this thing for hours. You want me to lock up your weapon, too?"

"You should. I was going to wait until you got here to set the combination on the safe."

"I'll take care of it in a minute," Paula said, enormously relieved. She should know better than to think Renée would even consider...she couldn't even complete the thought. Unexpectedly, she felt tears prick at her eyes and she blinked hard, her jaws clamped tight.

"What?" Renée studied her through narrowed eyes.

"Nothing," Paula said hoarsely. "Just tired."

Renée glanced from Paula to the bedside table, and she breathed in sharply. "You didn't think? Oh, sweetie, never."

"I know," Paula said, cradling Renée's hand in both of hers. "I know. Just for a minute there, when I walked in, it all felt so strange. Then I saw—" she shook her head. "Everything is changing so fast, sometimes I just feel confused."

"Where's Blair?"

"At the commander's," Paula said, unconcerned by the apparent switch in topic. Nothing happened in her life, or for the last few months, in Renée's, until what really mattered was squared away. And that was Blair Powell's security. "She should be in for the night. Greg is there now, and Hara will take the overnight watch. I'll pick her up in the morning, unless she calls to tell me she's going out."

"Good. Secure our weapons and change into something comfortable. Then, come lie down with me."

"Should I order us something to eat?"

Renée carefully drew her legs up and pulled the covers aside. She opened her jeans and started to push them down over her hips. "In a little while."

"Okay." Paula picked up Renée's weapon and unholstered her own. She crossed to the closet and, after setting the combination on the in-room safe, stored them away. Then she closed the drapes, stripped down, and folded her clothes over the arm of the reading chair in front of the windows. "I could probably use a shower."

"Let's talk for a second. Then we can order dinner and shower while we wait for it to get here."

Paula lifted the covers and slid into bed. She turned on her side and kissed Renée softly. "I missed you today." Carefully, she slid her arm around Renée's shoulders and eased onto her back with Renée in her arms.

"What's going on with Blair needing to come back here, do you know?" Renée rested her cheek against Paula's breasts with a sigh.

Paula hesitated. It was an innocent enough question, but she felt protective of Blair in a way she hadn't before, even though she had been prepared to protect her at the cost of her own life for more than a year.

"Never mind," Renée said flatly into the silence. "That was out of line."

"No," Paula said. "It wasn't. You've been part of the team in one way or another for months."

"But?"

Paula sighed. "I'm not sure."

Renée kissed the soft, smooth skin of Paula's breast. "It's different, being her security chief, isn't it?"

"You know, I owe you an apology," Paula whispered.

"What?" Renée raised her head, her expression concerned. "What are you talking about?"

"I never asked you how you felt about me accepting this assignment. I'm sorry."

Renée inched away and leaned on her elbow, trailing the fingers of her other hand absently up and down Paula's stomach. "Sweetie, you got a promotion that you deserved. I'm really proud of you. Don't you know that? Because if I didn't let you know that—"

"No," Paula said quickly. "I mean, I never gave you a chance to say you didn't want me to do it."

Renée's eyes darkened. "Is that how I make you feel? That I don't want you to be Blair's security chief?"

"No," Paula said, frustrated. "But it means I'll be traveling more, and working more, and probably…I don't know, distracted. And that affects us." She cupped Renée's jaw and traced her thumb over Renée's cheek. "I don't want anything to come between us."

"You're a secret service agent, Paula," Renée said matter-of-factly. "Just like I'm an FBI agent. At least, I was."

"Hey. You still are."

"Yeah, maybe. First my shoulder, now my leg. If I don't rehab a hundred percent they're going to pull me out of the field." Renée looked away. "We're not talking about me. We're talking about you." She glanced back to Paula, her eyes intent. "I understand what your job requires. I'm okay with it. I'm proud of you. I'm just…things are tough right now, but it's not you." She leaned down and kissed Paula hard. "Sweetie, it's not you."

Paula drew Renée into her arms again and returned her kiss. "I hate for you to be unhappy."

"I just need to figure out what I'm going to do if they transfer me to a desk job somewhere." Renée closed her eyes. "I don't think I can take that."

Paula tightened her hold, frightened more by the despondency in Renée's voice than the thought that her lover might be transferred across the country. "It'll be okay. Your leg will be fine and you'll be back to duty before you know it."

"I'm not going to accept a post somewhere if it means I'm never going to be able to see you." Renée caressed Paula's chest, then circled lower, unconsciously tracing the line of muscles down to the base of her belly. "Not after everything that's happened."

Paula tried to focus on being supportive, but Renée's persistent caresses were starting to sap her concentration. Casually, she covered Renée's questing hand and drew it away from the trigger zone that was dangerously close to igniting. "I know. I feel the same."

"We haven't made love since I got shot," Renée observed softly, extracting her hand from Paula's grip. She cupped Paula very lightly between the legs. "Miss it?"

"Oh, geez," Paula choked, her legs starting to quiver. "Yeah."

Renée squeezed gently. "Have you been taking many solo flights?"

"Not many." Paula flushed as she felt a flood of wetness between her thighs. "Oh."

"Mmm. You *did* miss me, didn't you?" Renée gripped a little harder and jiggled her hand.

"Stop." Paula slammed her hand down over Renée's, effectively preventing her from moving her fingers. "Honest. Don't. I'll get really excited, and we can't until your leg's better."

Renée laughed. "My leg might keep me from working, sweetie, but it doesn't keep me from taking care of the important business." She lowered her head and licked Paula's nipple into rapid attention. When Paula shivered and moaned softly, she worried the small, hard knot tenderly with her teeth. "So I think you should hold very still." She sucked until Paula moaned again. "While I make you come."

"Renée," Paula said hoarsely. "We should wait."

Renée shifted and guided Paula's face to her breast. "No. Waiting is the last thing we should do." She hissed in a breath as Paula's mouth closed over her nipple. Delicately, she traced the hard prominence of Paula's clitoris with her fingertip. When Paula jerked and started to pull back, she gripped her between thumb and forefinger and squeezed. "We're here together right now, Paula. Feel me now, sweetie. Feel me."

Unable to resist the persistent caresses, Paula closed her eyes as Renée fondled her in just the right spot with just the right pressure to make her come. Spinning toward orgasm, she whispered the one thing of which she was totally certain in a suddenly uncertain world. "I love you."

CHAPTER SIX

"D iane was quiet tonight," Cam said as she sat on the side of the bed and pulled off her shoes. She unbuckled her belt, lifted her hips, and shed her trousers. Across the room, Blair undressed, tossing her blue jeans and T-shirt into the laundry basket in the bedroom closet. The circles that had surfaced beneath her eyes earlier in the day had deepened, giving her a haunted look.

"Things are still pretty awful in Manhattan," Blair said. "She closed the gallery for a while."

"It's going to take some time before people and businesses recover." Cam gave a mirthless laugh as she removed her shirt. "I guess *recover* is an optimistic word."

"Adjust to a new reality is more like it." Naked, Blair brushed her fingertips over Cam's chest as she slid past her and into bed. "I guess we're just catching up to the rest of the world."

Cam removed the rest of her clothes, turned off the light, and got into bed. She turned on her side and circled Blair with one arm, easing close to her in the dark. "You should go back to Whitley Point for a while. Take Diane."

"Turn the light on."

Wordlessly, Cam complied.

"Go back to Whitley Point and stay out of the way?" Blair asked edgily.

"I don't believe I said that." Cam traced a fingertip along the rigid arc of Blair's jaw. "I was thinking that twenty-four hours ago you *almost* looked relaxed." She smoothed her thumb over the crest of Blair's cheekbone. "Now you're looking a little weary."

Blair snatched Cam's hand away from her face and bit her thumb hard enough to make Cam wince. "Don't try to distract me with your slick moves."

"Ow."

"Let me guess what you're going to be doing while I'm painting pretty pictures on a remote island. And Diane is doing…cross-stitch."

Cam smothered a grin. Blair had been pale moments before. Now she was flushed and her eyes were bright. Anger looked good on her, but then, it always had.

"You'll be playing super sleuth in Washington or New York or God knows where, chasing down maniacs who would be happy to kill you, and themselves, and anyone in the vicinity." Blair pushed at Cam's shoulder. "I already know you're going to take my father's offer. Just what else do you have planned?"

"I'm not sure. I've been out of the intel loop since the raid. I've got to assemble a team and do some catching up." Cam risked diving in for a quick kiss. "And it's possible I'll need to travel."

Blair sat up and wrapped her arms around her knees. "Where? And don't you dare say anywhere in the Middle East." She focused on Cam, her face set. "I mean it. If someone has to go there, fine. That's why we have the CIA and all the other spies." She fisted her hands so tightly Cam thought her fingers must be getting numb. "I've never asked you not to do something, Cameron. But I'm asking this."

"That's not where I meant," Cam said, prying Blair's clenched hands open and clasping her fingers. "I was thinking Paris."

"Paris?" Blair echoed. "Why?"

"Because Foster made more than a few trips there in the ten months before the assault on you. Maybe there's a connection." Cam shrugged, frustrated. "I don't know. That's the problem—none of us know, because none of us expected anything like what happened."

"Do you think Valerie's in Paris?"

"Valerie?" Cam circled Blair's shoulders and tugged her down onto the bed. She stroked Blair's hair even though she could feel Blair resist her caress. This wasn't anger. This was fear. Fear and something else she couldn't quite get a sense of. "I suppose it's possible. She knows as much as I know about what happened in the attack at the Aerie and who might be behind it. That's part of the problem. She's knows as much as I do, or more, and she's one step ahead of us."

"You're taking this assignment with OHS to find Valerie, aren't you?" Blair asked.

"No," Cam said. "I'm taking this assignment because Stark

doesn't need me, and neither do you, not professionally. And there's no way I'm going back to providing security for presidential hopefuls or visiting diplomats, and I'm sure as hell not going to chase bad money, even if it *is* funding drug cartels. There are bigger threats than drugs to worry about now."

"And of course, you want to go after the biggest and baddest." Blair rolled on top of Cam and braced herself on her elbows. She very gently touched Cam's face. "I'm surprised you're not in the military. You're such a patriot."

Cam smiled and kissed the tips of Blair's fingers. "I thought about it when I was younger, but I don't take orders all that well." At Blair's snort of derision, she shook her head. "No, I don't. Not really. I understand the chain of command and I respect it. But I need the freedom to call my own shots in my day-to-day work."

"You avoided my question about Valerie. You do want to find her, don't you?" Blair was aware of treading carefully. She did want to know what Cam planned to do. As much as Cam could tell her. Cam was her lover, and she needed to know what mattered to her, what drove her—what danger she would put herself in and why. But she didn't want anything that Cam might tell her to be an unwitting betrayal of their trust.

"I want to find her," Cam agreed, "and I *need* to find her. She's either in danger or a potential danger to others. Either way, she's not safe out there alone."

"I'm not going to use Diane to help you." Blair didn't know why she was surprised that the words came so easily. There had never been any doubt about what she would do. Or wouldn't do.

Blair started to sit up, but Cam held her close. "I never thought that you would. You know I wouldn't ask you to, right?"

Silently, Blair nodded.

"But just hear me out, okay?"

"You might not *ask* me to, but you might want me to." Blair rested her head on Cam's chest. "I don't want to…disappoint you."

"Disappoint—" Cam tilted Blair's chin and met her eyes. They were cloudy and troubled. She hated that her lover had been caught in the tangled web of divided loyalties. "Baby, it's *my* job. Not yours. Lucinda was wrong to ask you to get involved."

"What about national security?"

"We'll have no national security—or any other kind—if we resort to spying on our friends." Cam shook her head. "I trust you'll tell me if Diane gets into any trouble."

"I will."

"And you have to stay out of it." Cam held Blair's jaw more firmly, delving into the blue eyes that glimmered with anticipated resistance. "Okay?"

"Okay." Blair hesitated. "Can you tell me why you think Valerie might be in danger? Diane really loves her, Cam."

"Ah, Jesus," Cam breathed. "What a mess."

"Love tends to get that way," Blair murmured, kissing Cam's throat. "You mess me up."

Stroking the back of Blair's neck, Cam sorted her thoughts. "Until a few hours before the raid, the only people who knew Matheson's identity were Valerie, Stark, Savard, and Davis. If Matheson disappeared from the compound—or never showed up there to begin with because someone tipped him off—there are only a limited number of explanations. I know it wasn't any of my people and not likely to be anyone on the assault team. So, either Valerie warned him or someone Valerie *told* warned him."

"Valerie must report to someone inside the Company, Cam," Blair said.

"Of course. Whoever ordered her to infiltrate our team to begin with."

Blair closed her eyes. "Then that means they'll know that you're looking for her. Jesus, this is a nightmare. And you're going to be right in the middle of it."

"If Valerie *wasn't* responsible for the leak, once she got wind of Matheson disappearing, she'd know she was the weak link. She'd have to disappear because she'd know whoever tipped Matheson would be coming after her."

"So you're telling me that Valerie isn't safe, and I should help you find her."

"That's one way of looking at it," Cam said. "Right now, I'm not sure. And because I'm not sure, I don't want you to do anything."

"Except hide out with Tanner and Diane at Whitley Point."

"That would be my wish." Cam kissed the tip of Blair's chin. "Any chance?"

"I don't know, maybe," Blair said. "Not because I want to hide, but because I don't want to stay here. And I can't go back to Manhattan, because I don't have any place to go back to."

"This is sounding good," Cam said.

"But—"

"Uh-oh."

Blair smiled. "I'm not going without you."

Cam frowned. "I'm going to be pretty busy, Blair. I've got to put a team together, for one thing. Then who knows what I'll find once I start digging into this whole Valerie situation."

"Are you telling me you're going to direct the investigation from some office in DC somewhere? Where anyone could access your files or monitor your activities?" Blair made a face. "Even *I* know that's not very smart. If you even suspect that there's someone high enough up to get Matheson's name from Valerie's intelligence reports and warn him, then nothing is secure." She grinned. "Unless you're going to work out of Lucinda's office."

Cam groaned. "You make it sound *so* appealing. But we're talking about a big operation here, baby."

"You found Matheson working from Whitley Point. That was a big operation, too."

"Yeah, and someone ferried Valerie off right under our noses."

"Good point, except Valerie helped them from the inside." Blair saw the anger and betrayal flicker across Cam's face, knowing nothing she might say could lessen it. Only the truth could do that. "You've got to admit, it's going to be more secure there than almost any place around here."

"I'll think about it. At least for a base of operations. Hell," Cam mused, "we used to do all of our advance surveillance and intelligence right out of the Aerie. That was a damn big operation, too."

"I'll talk to Tanner tomorrow about speeding up the property purchase. I'm sure she can make it happen. Besides," Blair said softly, "I love it there, and we need a place to live."

Cam brushed her fingers through Blair's hair, then drew her head down and kissed her. She murmured against her lips, "We do, don't we."

"Is it all right with you?"

"Are *you* going to be okay having a base of operations where we live?"

Blair laughed shortly. "Cameron, I've always had some kind of base where I live. Look at the Aerie. I'm used to it."

"If you're sure. Right now, I'd feel a hell of a lot better if you were back there."

"I'm going to talk to Lucinda tomorrow about our plans," Blair said.

Cam rolled her over and settled one thigh between her legs. "You're not going to make me go with you, are you?"

"I can't believe you're afraid of Lucinda." Blair curled her leg around the back of Cam's thigh and nestled her center against Cam's crotch. "It'll cost you."

"Anything." Cam slowly rotated her hips between Blair's legs. "Just name it."

"Let's see how many times you can make me come," Blair whispered, "while I think about it."

Cam laughed. "Tough duty."

❖

"Hello?" Diane said distractedly, expecting a wrong number.

"Hi. Did I wake you?"

Diane sat up abruptly, the sheet falling away unheeded. The sliver of moon and the glow from the surrounding city cast the room in dim, gray light. She hadn't been sleeping, even though it was the middle of the night. "No. I was thinking about you."

An indrawn breath and a beat of silence followed. Diane almost said her name, but knew instinctively not to. She waited, the seconds interminable.

"Are you home?"

"Actually I'm…" Diane thought of all the conversations she'd had over the years with Blair and how they'd always been careful, even when there was probably no need to be. Now, with Valerie, there surely was. "I'm visiting friends."

"Ah. Anyone I know?"

"Yes." Diane's heart pounded and she strained to hear every nuance in Valerie's voice. "How's your trip going?"

"I shouldn't have called, but I missed you."

Diane caught her breath. "Can I join you? I'm in a bit of a hiatus myself right now."

"That's not a good idea."

"Why not? I miss you, too. Terribly."

"I'm not very good company right now."

Diane heard the warning beneath the words but refused to be deterred. "Shouldn't I be the one to decide that?"

"Trust me, it might not be all that...pleasant."

"To be with you?" Diane said lightly while mentally translating, *It's not safe.*

"Yes."

"Then that's all the more reason to let me come and prove you wrong." Diane raised her knees and pressed her forehead to them. She closed her eyes, trying to shut out every other sensation except the sound of Valerie's voice.

A sigh came through the line. "And that's why I've stayed away."

"I'm sure our friends could help cheer you up."

"I'm not so sure of that."

Diane hesitated. Blair was the one person in her life whom she trusted completely. But there was no reason that Valerie should. But what about Cam? Didn't Valerie trust her? Cam would help Valerie, if she were in trouble. Wouldn't she?

Would she? Cam's allegiance was never in doubt. Blair first. Country second. And friendship? Diane had no doubt that Cam would risk her life for Stark or Savard or any of the others. Didn't Valerie, Cam's ex-lover and colleague, fall into the same category?

But then, she didn't really understand anything that had happened. She didn't understand why Valerie had left, why she'd stayed away, and why she was obviously afraid to talk to her now. She wouldn't understand until Valerie explained it, and she desperately needed to know. "I want to see you."

"Diane—"

"No one will know. Please."

Another endless pause, not even the sound of breathing on the line.

Diane forced herself not to say anything more than she already had. She had never begged a woman for anything in her life, not even

Blair when they had been younger and she'd been desperately in love with her. Blair had never known the depth of her feelings, perhaps because she had already learned to shield her emotions behind casual nonchalance. It hadn't taken many disappointments before she had also learned not to make herself vulnerable by asking for things she couldn't have. Valerie had effortlessly changed all that. And now, if she didn't sense that begging would somehow endanger Valerie, she would gladly beg. Anything to break this unwilling isolation.

"How long will you be there?" Valerie finally asked.

"How long *should* I be?" Diane countered.

"A few days would be good."

"I'll try." Diane opened her eyes. The moon had gone behind a cloud and the room was black. "Don't be afraid."

Valerie laughed thinly. "Of you?"

"For me," Diane whispered.

"I don't think I can promise that."

Diane smiled. "And I feel the same. I'll be waiting."

"Goodbye," Valerie whispered.

Diane sat in the silent darkness for a few more minutes, fixing the sound of Valerie's voice in her mind. Then she pulled up the last number on her call log and called it.

I'm sorry. The number you're trying to reach is no longer in service.

CHAPTER SEVEN

Tuesday

B lair paused halfway across the living room and groaned in appreciation as she smelled coffee. She turned toward the seating area in front of the windows and caught a glimpse of the first streaks of a hazy orange sunrise outside the windows. Diane sat curled up in one corner of the sofa in burgundy satin pj's, her blond hair loose and partially shielding her face, a mug clasped in both hands.

"Hi," Blair said. "Mind company?"

"No, of course not."

Blair continued into the adjoining galley kitchen, poured coffee, and returned. She settled onto the sofa and mirrored Diane's pose, legs drawn beneath her, partially turned so she could face her friend. "Early morning or late night?"

Diane smiled ruefully. "Both. Funny, I never used to mind sleeping alone."

"It's one thing to sleep alone because you prefer to," Blair said half to herself. "But once you've gotten used to someone and then they're not there, it's a bitch."

"I'd forgotten it's not all that easy for you and Cam most of the time, either. Sorry."

Blair stroked Diane's shoulder. "I just meant I understand."

"I know you do." Diane was certain that Blair understood all of it—the reluctance to trust, the self-made barriers to protect against heartbreak and disappointment, and the terrible joy of letting someone inside at last. Blair had lived it, just as she had. And because Blair knew—knew her, knew what she hoped and feared, knew what it was to fight for what she wanted—Diane felt some of the desolation lift from her heart. "Valerie called."

"Is she all right?" Blair held her breath and strained to hear the sound of the shower running in the master bathroom. She didn't want Cam walking in on this conversation and hearing something she would feel duty bound to act on.

"I don't know," Diane said, her voice shaking slightly. "It was a tense conversation. She didn't say that she wasn't all right, but obviously something's wrong." She searched Blair's eyes. "Do you know what's going on?"

"Oh God," Blair murmured. "I don't, honey. Honest, not really. And I…" she glanced over her shoulder toward the hallway on the far side of the room.

"Cam's involved somehow, isn't she? And I'm putting you in the middle. I should go."

"No," Blair said sharply, grasping Diane's arm to prevent her rising. "You should *not* go. No one knows anything, including Cam, other than Valerie snuck off in the middle of the night and doesn't want anyone to know where she is."

"You make it sound like she's a criminal."

Blair shook her head. "No one is saying that." She wasn't exactly certain that was true. She imagined that if Valerie hadn't warned Matheson herself of the impending capture, then whoever *had* told him would point to her disappearance as evidence of her guilt. "But the way she left is suspicious, and the fact that she's hiding doesn't help clear things up at all." Her grip softened and she clasped Diane's fingers. "You *know* Cam, Di. She doesn't jump to conclusions, and she never settles for easy answers. Valerie needs to talk to her."

"I'm scared," Diane whispered. "I'm scared that every phone call will be the last one. That I'll never see her again and I'll never know why."

Blair leaned closer. "I know you want to protect her. So would I. But she needs help. Can you try to get her to talk to Cam?"

Diane's eyes were moist, the blue misted to gray with sadness. "How can I if I don't know how to reach her?"

"Something tells me she'll find you." Blair heard the sound of the bedroom door closing and footsteps approaching, then Cam passed behind them on her way to the kitchen. "Morning, darling."

"Hi," Cam replied.

Diane called a greeting then lowered her voice. "I have to think about it. For now, can we keep it between us?"

"Yes," Blair said, knowing that Diane wouldn't be pushed into making a decision any more than she would. "I'm going to talk to Lucinda this morning. After that, let's just get out of here for a while. Walk around, shop, do something mindless."

Some of the tension eased from Diane's face. "I think that's a great idea. After all, we have a wedding to plan."

"We certainly do." Blair glanced across the room to where Cam stood in the doorway of the kitchen. She'd dressed for work for the first time in almost two weeks, and the pale blue shirt, dark raw silk slacks, and black Italian loafers gave her a cool, sleek look. She wasn't wearing her shoulder holster, but she would be, along with a blazer, when she went out. The image of confidence and strength Cam projected was more than just appearance, and it surprised Blair how right it felt to see her lover preparing to do what she did so well. "We can't stop living, can we?"

"No," Diane said with a shadow of a smile. "We can't."

❖

Blair stepped from the shower, wrapped a towel around her chest, and used another to dry her hair. She finger-combed the thick waves and finished drying her body. She paused at a knock on the bathroom door.

"Yes?"

"Want a fresh cup of coffee?"

Smiling, Blair pulled open the door that connected to their bedroom. "Special delivery?"

"At your service." Cam slipped inside and set the cup down on the vanity. "Stark's here."

Blair frowned. "What time is it?"

"0700."

"God, she's eager."

"She's just doing her job," Cam said, smiling.

"Yeah, yeah." Blair tossed the towel aside and wrapped her arms around Cam's neck. "So what are you going to do while I'm with Lucinda?"

Cam brushed both hands down Blair's back and cupped her buttocks. "Probably be thinking about this."

Blair grinned and nipped at Cam's lower lip. "Smooth."

"You're getting my shirt wet," Cam murmured, nuzzling Blair's throat.

"Just your shirt?" Blair whispered in Cam's ear and bumped her pelvis into Cam's crotch.

Cam groaned. "Cut it out."

Blair laughed, kissed her hard, and then let her go. Cam's shirtfront showed the wet impressions of Blair's breasts. "Uh-oh. You need a new shirt."

"At the least."

"So what *are* you doing this morning, Commander?" Blair followed Cam into the bedroom and sorted through the clothing she kept at Cam's for occasions when she stayed over..

"I'm hoping to meet with your father's security adviser about this new Office of Homeland Security," Cam said as she changed her shirt.

"And your new job," Blair said casually. Even though she'd known from the second her father offered the position that Cam would take it, the reality made her stomach tighten. She paused in the middle of buttoning her blouse. "I understand now why you wanted to be in charge of my security detail, even when I didn't want you to be."

"What do you mean?" Cam tucked in her shirt, but her eyes never left Blair's face.

Blair slipped into her slacks and regarded her shoe choices. "I like having you where I can see you. Even though it doesn't mean you'll be safe, it feels less scary."

"Hey," Cam said, gently resting her hands on Blair's shoulders. "It's not that kind of job, okay?"

"Yeah, yeah." Blair sighed. "I hate being this shaky about things."

"We're all off balance." Cam kissed her forehead. "Give yourself a break."

"I'll try." Blair smiled. "I'd better go take care of Stark."

Cam rolled her eyes. "Be gentle."

Laughing, Blair skimmed her fingertips up the inside of Cam's thigh. "Always."

With a muttered curse, Cam followed Blair down the hallway.

In the living room, Paula pivoted away from the window where she'd been waiting. "Good morning." She nodded to Cam before getting down to business. "I wanted to review your plans for the day, Ms. Powell."

"After breakfast, I'm going to call Lucinda and see when she can fit me in," Blair said. "This afternoon, Diane and I are going shopping."

Blair was aware of both Cam and Paula stiffening. She wasn't surprised. Neither of them would want her out and about. "I'm not staying locked up inside."

"You didn't mention a shopping trip." Cam followed Blair into the kitchen.

"I just did," Blair said, peering into the refrigerator. "There's nothing in here to eat."

"You know what I mean."

Blair closed the door. "I figured there was no point in dealing with your objections and then Stark's. This way, I get it all taken care of at once."

Cam grinned but her eyes were serious. "The things I love about you make me crazy."

"Funny how that works." Blair kissed her. "Let's gather the troops and go out to breakfast. Then let's go to the White House."

❖

"Thanks for seeing me, Luce," Blair said. While she'd been waiting, she'd counted two senators, three deputy directors, the White House press secretary, and a handful of lobbyists pass in and out of Lucinda's office. "Things look hectic."

"It's never a problem to meet with you." Lucinda relaxed into a chair in the seating area as if she had all the time in the world.

Blair was instantly on guard. "I wanted to clear up a few things about yesterday and inform you of some new plans."

"All right. Would you like something to drink? Pastry?"

"No," Blair said carefully, trying to read what was behind Lucinda's calm façade. She'd never been able to, and she still couldn't. "We just had breakfast. Thanks."

"Oh, that's right. Cam's here too, isn't she. Meeting with Averill."

Blair didn't see that the statement required an answer. Lucinda knew everything that was happening in the White House. In the country for that matter. Hell, most likely in the entire world. So she obviously knew that Cam was meeting with the presidential security adviser. "I suppose you know all the details there."

Lucinda nodded, without actually acknowledging anything.

"I'm not going to help you with Diane."

"You've forgotten that I know Diane," Lucinda said evenly. "I've known her almost as long as I've known you." She held Blair's eyes. "She could be in trouble."

"Don't use my friends to blackmail me into doing something I know is wrong," Blair said sharply.

"But I expect that Cam will explain all that to you."

"*Or* my lover."

Lucinda sighed. "Blair, next to your father, you're my favorite person in the world. But you really can be a right pain in the ass sometimes."

Blair smiled. "I'm not going to suggest how I come by that trait—considering my role models."

"I'm not exaggerating when I say that Diane may be in danger. If *I* know that she was involved with Valerie Lawrence, other people do too. Other people may think she can help them find Valerie."

"She's with me, and for the time being, I intend to keep her with me."

"That might be a good idea," Lucinda mused. "If she's with you, she'll be under surveillance by our people."

"She'll be *safe*," Blair snapped. She jumped up, too agitated to continue to sit and pretend they were having an ordinary conversation. "God, Lucinda! Is this what it costs to keep my father in office? People you know, people you love, become pawns?"

A hint of color flared on Lucinda's cheeks. "Sometimes it costs a great deal more than that, Blair. It goes without saying that being under surveillance by the best security team in the world will keep her safe. It also might help us, and I'd be a fool, or worse, to suggest otherwise."

Blair closed her eyes for an instant, and when she opened them again, she gave Lucinda an apologetic look. "I'm sorry. I couldn't do what you do, and I know how necessary it is." She sat down again. "As soon as Cam settles whatever she needs to do in this new position, I'm taking the whole team and Diane back to where we've been staying for the last month."

Lucinda raised an eyebrow. "Cameron intends to go back with you?" She held up a hand. "Never mind. I'm sure Averill will discuss that with me." She crossed her legs, her black skirt rising to reveal the barest hint of shapely thighs. "Let me give it some thought, but that just might be an excellent plan. Of course, you're going to have to tell me where it is."

"Just you?"

"For now."

"Whitley Point."

"Tanner Whitley's place?"

Blair nodded.

Lucinda laughed. "Oh my God, you and Diane and Tanner together? I feel for your security team."

"Tanner's married," Blair said, grinning. Lucinda had been around for most of her wild prep school years and was aware of some of the trouble the three of them had gotten into. Of course, most of the time they'd been successful in pulling off their fairly frequent disappearing acts. "Which brings me to the other thing I wanted to discuss with you."

"Oh?"

"Cam and I intend to get married this fall."

"That may be problematic, since same-sex marriages aren't legally recognized anywhere in the United States."

"Neither is my sexual orientation," Blair said, "but that hasn't stopped me, and it never will. We won't have any difficulty finding someone to perform the ceremony, legal or not."

"That will be difficult to keep quiet," Lucinda said.

"It wasn't my intention to keep it quiet." At Lucinda's look of surprise, Blair went on, "I'm not planning on taking out an ad in the New York Times, but I'm not going to sneak around with this either."

"The first person outside of your immediate circle who gets a hint of this will go straight to the papers with it. A caterer, a dressmaker, even someone you think is a friend…this is going to be news, Blair, and people will pay for this kind of information."

Blair flushed. She hated the thought that her life was tabloid material. "I can't stop that. I've never been able to."

"Well, at least consider the timing." Lucinda sat forward. "We'll be facing midterm elections soon and then swinging directly into the presidential reelection campaign. Your timing couldn't be worse for something like this."

"Something like this," Blair said flatly. "Something like this would be my *life*, Lucinda."

"I know," Lucinda said gently. "I know, and I know how much of your life has been overshadowed by your father's career. I'm not going to apologize for that, but I do know."

Blair rubbed her forehead. "Don't switch sides on me now, Lucinda. Just stick with the hard-ass routine."

Lucinda smiled. "You're going to expose your personal life to international scrutiny. To say nothing of fueling every right wing fanatic in this country. Do you really want that?"

"What I want is to do what feels right for myself and my lover and our relationship without worrying about the politics of it." Blair sighed. "Don't tell me you can't figure out a way to spin it."

"Probably. At least give me time to work on that."

"I'll postpone hiring a float."

"Thank you." Lucinda glanced at her watch and then rose. "I've got a budget meeting, so I'll get back to you on this."

"I'll let you know before I leave town."

"Good. By the way, there's a fundraiser in Boston this weekend that I need you to attend."

"I can't do it, Luce. There's just too much going on right now."

"I understand." Lucinda walked back to her desk, sat down, and drew a file toward her. "It's for stem cell research. One of the primary investigators at Harvard will be there, and I just thought you might want to show your support."

"Damn it." Blair had no doubt that proponents of stem cell research, including major pharmaceutical companies, were lobbying hard in Washington to prevent legislation aimed at restricting the source of tissues used for the studies. Her father couldn't publicly issue a statement in favor of the research, but *she* could, as the daughter of a woman who died of breast cancer. Her presence at the fundraiser would send a clear message as to the White House's position. Despite the fact that she didn't like to be used as a White House front person, she happened to believe in this research. She yanked open the door. "I'll be there. E-mail me the details."

"That's wonderful. Thank you."

Blair closed the door without answering. As usual after leaving Lucinda, she was never certain if she'd won or lost the skirmish. She walked briskly past Paula and Felicia and pulled out her cell phone.

"How's it going?" she asked when Cam answered.

"I'm going to be here most of the day. You?"

"Bloodied, but unbowed."

Cam laughed. "What about the rest of your plans? Any changes?"

"No. And you don't have to say it. I'll be careful."

"Thanks. I'll see you later, then."

"All right. I love you."

"I love you too."

Blair closed her phone, smiling. She wondered what the national security chief thought about *that*.

CHAPTER EIGHT

A re you ready for some serious shopping?" Blair held up Diane's coat. She hoped that the diversion would take Diane's mind off Valerie, but knew it wouldn't. She'd been there too many times herself, not knowing what was happening with someone she loved, not being able to help or protect them.

Diane smiled, but it didn't reach her eyes. Her smooth, milky complexion was even paler than normal, and lines of tension marred the sleek planes of her face. Diane was ordinarily so poised and kept her emotions so tightly reined that to see those cracks in her composure made Blair's heart ache. It also made her angry. Angry at Valerie for involving Diane when she must have known something like this could happen, at the political system that so effortlessly ignored the human consequences of its policies, and even at herself, for not knowing the best way to help her friend.

"The Shops at Georgetown?" Blair suggested.

"Let's start on M Street and finish up inside."

"Done." Blair grinned when she heard Stark muffle a groan. Many of the trendy boutiques on M Street in Georgetown fronted a portion of the four-story mall that housed over seventy shops and restaurants. It was the best shopping in DC. She hooked her arm through Diane's as they stepped out into the foyer and pushed the button for the elevator. "I'm glad you're here."

"So am I," Diane whispered.

Paula slid into the elevator next to them. "I don't suppose you could think of a slightly less crowded place for your retail therapy?"

"What, and take all the fun out of it?" Blair feigned shock. She knew from experience that her security agents hated it when she went to large, crowded places where it was impossible for them to set up advance surveillance. But if she let that dictate her movements, she'd never go to a movie or a street fair or a shopping mall. Until the recent attacks, outings such as this had been more an inconvenience than a serious security issue, and that was all the more reason for her *not* to change her behavior now.

"Fun," Paula muttered. "More like hell."

"You never know." Blair laughed as the elevator opened and they all stepped out. "You might end up enjoying it."

Paula, busy alerting Hara in the vehicle idling at the curb that they were exiting, didn't bother to object.

"Oh, goody," Blair said as Felicia moved up beside her, "girls' day out."

"We didn't think Greg would mind if I took his shift this afternoon," Felicia said. "Hi Diane."

"It's good to see you again," Diane said, as she climbed into the rear of the Suburban next to Blair. "How's Mac doing?"

Felicia's smile widened. "He's out of the hospital and doing very well."

"I suppose he's chafing to get back to work."

"He's like the rest of us. If we're not working, we tend to get into trouble." Felicia glanced at Stark. "I know he misses being part of the team."

"The team misses him," Stark said.

"Hopefully, he'll be back soon," Blair said, wondering if Mac would resume his duties as second-in-command and communications officer. That would be up to Paula now. Felicia had taken over Mac's responsibilities when he was shot during the assassination attempt at the Aerie, but her real expertise was intelligence and data analysis. "Tell him I said hi."

"I will," Felicia replied. "Where are we headed?"

"Georgetown Park," Paula said with a grimace.

Felicia's eyes widened. "Oh, I should be getting hazard pay. To be surrounded by all that trendy glitter and not be able to window shop. That's harsh."

Blair laughed. Even though she loved Mac and enjoyed Greg Wozinski's dry humor and subtle sensitivity, if she had to have close surveillance twenty-four hours a day, it was so nice to have female agents. They understood about shopping.

Nevertheless, three hours later, Blair found that even Paula was as grumpy as any of the male agents who had ever accompanied her on a shopping excursion.

"I'm just going to try on these dresses." She gave Paula a winning smile. "I need something for the fundraiser this weekend."

"It feels like divine punishment that we're shopping at a place called the White House," Paula said with a sigh.

"Maybe it's cosmic destiny," Blair said as she carried another stack of clothing into the dressing room. "If you see Diane, tell her I'm in here. She went to check out the shoes."

"Fine. Great." Paula turned her back to the dressing room door and folded her arms. It wasn't that she minded shopping so much, she just didn't like to do it for hours on end. And when she went shopping, it was always with something specific in mind—a new pair of shoes or a suit to replace one that got torn up or soiled during work. It was never just to check out the latest styles. She scanned the dress department, automatically reviewing the faces to see if any seemed familiar from other stores, other departments. She didn't recognize anyone and was comfortable that they were not being followed. Felicia, posted in the aisle between the dresses and accessories, was doing the same thing. Hara had drawn the short straw and stayed with the vehicle.

Idly, Paula watched a woman pull a white halter dress from a rack and hold it up in front of her body. The unexpected mental picture of Renée in that dress stirred a hum of arousal in the pit of her stomach, and she swiftly looked away. Felicia was right. Shopping was dangerous duty.

❖

Diane lifted a Louboutin black lace and suede pump with a peep toe, thinking it would go well with the dress she was planning to wear to the fundraiser Blair had invited her to. Ordinarily, she would have looked forward to a gala event, but it was hard to be excited about a night out now.

"Would you like to try those on?" a saleswoman asked with a polite smile.

"Yes I—" Diane caught her breath as she glimpsed a figure slip from view on the opposite side of the room. She went on hurriedly, "Not just yet, thank you."

"Of course. Just let me know."

Diane dropped the shoe back onto the rack and walked quickly across the seating area toward the sign marked exit. She pushed through the fire door and into the stairwell.

Valerie stood on the landing.

"Oh my God," Diane breathed. She extended one hand, but didn't touch her. "I wasn't sure—I thought I saw you once earlier, but I told myself it was just my imagination." She let her fingertips drift down Valerie's cheek. "It is you, isn't it?"

Valerie caught Diane's hand and kissed her palm. "Yes."

"How did you know where I was?"

"I called the gallery and asked for you. They know me as an art dealer, remember?" Valerie kept hold of Diane's hand, stroking the top with her thumb. "They told me you were in DC, and it wasn't hard for me to figure out where."

"But how did you know I would be *here*?"

Valerie smiled softly. "The Suburban is hard to miss. I've just been waiting until you weren't with Blair."

Diane touched the loose curls at the base of Valerie's neck. "You've cut your hair." She fingered the soft blond strands. "It's nice." She was used to seeing Valerie in stylish slacks, silk blouses, and designer jackets. Today she wore a navy T-shirt, low-cut Levi's, and scuffed brown boots. Her worn brown leather jacket was over-sized, hiding her full breasts and slender torso. She looked younger. And she looked very tired. "Are you all right?"

"Yes." Valerie drew a shaky breath. "God, I want to kiss you."

Diane smiled. "That's good, because I feel the same way. Do you think we could get out of the stairwell?"

Valerie shook her head. "I shouldn't even be here, but I just had—I just wanted to see you."

"You're in trouble, aren't you?"

"I'm not sure." Valerie leaned forward and brushed her lips over Diane's. "I'm so sorry."

"For what?" Diane gently caressed Valerie's face again, then drew closer and kissed her softly. She'd left her coat in the car, and the heat of Valerie's body penetrated her silk blouse and slacks as if they weren't even there. Diane's nipples tightened instantly and she moaned softly. "Oh, I've missed you. Where are you staying? Can I come to you?"

Valerie shook her head. "No. You can't right now."

Diane slid her hand inside Valerie's jacket and clasped her waist. "Then come to me. We need to talk. I need to understand what's happening." She kissed her again, harder. "I need you. Please."

Valerie skimmed her fingers into Diane's hair, her body trembling. "You can't. It might be dangerous, and I won't have you hurt."

"Being away from you hurts me," Diane whispered. "Not knowing what's happening to you is driving me mad. Please. Give me a number to call, somewhere to meet you."

"I'm using disposable phones. I'll call you." Valerie curled her hand behind Diane's neck and pulled her close. Her tongue slid possessively into Diane's open mouth. She groaned, the sound mingling with Diane's echoing moan. When she pulled away, her ice blue eyes sparkled with tears. "I love you. No matter what happens, I want you to know that."

Diane pressed her fingertips to Valerie's mouth. "There won't be any goodbyes. Whatever has happened, Cam can help you. You know how to reach her. Call her."

Valerie shook her head. "Not yet. Not until I know more."

"You can trust her," Diane said insistently. "I know you can. *You* know you can."

"Cam can't control everything, Diane," Valerie said wearily. "There are powerful people involved. Dangerous people."

"And that's all the more reason for you to have help. You can't do this alone." Diane kept both arms around Valerie's waist, afraid that she would bolt and disappear. "I don't want you to be alone."

"I've always been alone," Valerie whispered, "until you."

"And I'm not going to let you go," Diane said urgently. "I'll only be here a few more days. Let me come to you."

"Are you going back to Manhattan?"

"I don't know. I'm probably going…" Out of years of habit, Diane hesitated mentioning anything about Blair.

Valerie stiffened. "Never mind. You don't have to tell me."

Diane shook her head. "It's not what you think."

"You don't have any reason to trust me." Valerie gently disengaged Diane's hold on her and backed away. "I should apologize for ever involving you."

"Don't you say that," Diane shot back. "This isn't just about you, and what you need and what you're afraid of. I'm in this too, because I chose to be." She closed the distance that Valerie had created. "I chose to be with you."

"How can you choose when you don't even know what's going on?"

Diane's heart clenched at the uncertainty in Valerie's voice and the tormented look in her eyes. She sensed Valerie struggling not to pull away and risked sliding her hand inside her jacket again. When she rested her fingertips against Valerie's side, Valerie trembled.

"Oh, don't," Diane breathed. "Don't hurt so much, my darling. Help me understand. Tell me, so that when I say I love you, you can trust me."

"I can't seem to think straight when you're near me," Valerie murmured before kissing her again. When the door behind them opened, she spun Diane to the wall, shielding Diane's body with her own, and pushed her hand into her jacket pocket. "Keep your head down."

Diane held her breath, her heart jumping in her chest. Valerie's face had gone completely still, her blue eyes intently focused, and her body coiled as if it were poised to explode. Footsteps passed behind them and started down the stairs, clattering loudly in the enclosed space. Diane's breath whooshed out. "God."

"Do you understand now." Valerie backed away until their bodies didn't touch. "That's what you're asking me to bring into your life. I can't."

Diane's gaze dropped to the bulge in Valerie's jacket pocket, which she now realized was a gun. Having been around Blair since they were teenagers, she'd seen men and women with guns before. But she'd never sensed the lethal menace of one as acutely as she did now. "Are you saying that someone wants to kill you?"

"I don't know." Valerie moved to the stairs leading down. "And until I do, you can't be anywhere near me."

Diane followed her and grasped her jacket tightly. "I'm not going to let you walk away from me so easily again, Valerie."

"I'll come back," Valerie said, her voice choked. "I have to. I can't get you out of my head."

Diane kissed her, hard and long. Then, though it wrenched her heart so badly she felt like she was bleeding inside, she let go of Valerie's jacket. "Come soon."

"I'll try. I promise."

Then Valerie turned and hurtled down the stairs until all that remained was the distant echo of her footsteps.

❖

"Hey!" Blair said. "You missed the fashion show."

"Sorry," Diane said breathlessly. "I got...lost in the shoes."

"So what do you think." Blair held up a strapless black silk chiffon dress.

"Nice," Diane said, running her fingers over the sheer fabric.

Blair frowned and cast a glance in Paula's direction. Paula appeared not to be watching them, although Blair knew she was. She lowered her voice. "You're shaking. What's wrong?"

"Nothing."

"Of course," Blair said, loud enough for Paula to hear, "now I have an excuse to buy more shoes." She moved closer to Diane. "Bullshit. What happened?"

"I just saw Valerie."

Blair slipped one arm around Diane's waist and draped the dress over her free arm as she guided Diane through the dress department and out of hearing range of her security team. "Here? When?"

"Yes. Just a few minutes ago."

"You talked to her?"

"Briefly. She's scared, Blair." Diane's voice broke. "She scared, and she's alone."

"What did she say?"

Diane shook her head. "Not much. It was only a couple of minutes." She laughed unsteadily. "And I was kissing her about half the time."

Blair rolled her eyes. "Why am I not surprised. Jesus, Diane. You have to be careful." When Diane started to pull away, Blair tightened her grip. "I'm sorry, I know you love her. And I love you. And if she's in trouble, you could get hurt." Blair felt Diane shiver. "What? What happened?"

"Nothing," Diane said quickly. "Really. It's just..."

"What?"

"Someone came into the stairwell while we were together, and Valerie acted as if she expected someone to try to hurt her. She was armed and—"

"That's it," Blair snapped. "You have to talk to Cam."

"I don't *have to* do anything until I'm certain Valerie will be protected."

"You don't trust Cam?"

"Shh," Diane warned, aware that Paula and Felicia had closed the distance behind them. "I don't know who to trust, all right? I trust *you*. Just let me have a few days. Please."

Blair bit back another angry retort, thinking that she would probably behave the same way in Diane's position. Still, she wasn't certain she trusted Valerie, not just with her best friend's heart, but possibly with her life.

CHAPTER NINE

It's Cameron Roberts," Cam said in response to the question called through the door. The thunk of the lock disengaging was followed by the door opening, and she was face to face with a panicked-looking Renée Savard.

"Is Paula okay?" Savard asked, her voice tight.

"Yes," Cam said immediately. "She's fine. Sorry, I shouldn't have come by unannounced. I wanted to talk to you."

"That's okay," Savard said, running her fingers quickly through her hair as she stepped back.

"Thanks," Cam said. A quick visual sweep of the dimly lit room revealed closed drapes, an unmade bed, and a room service cart just inside the door. The food on the uncovered plate was mostly uneaten. The three bottles of Beck's were empty.

Savard grabbed the cart. "Here, let me get rid of this."

"I've got it." Cam held the door open with one hand as she pulled the cart out into the hall. Then she followed Savard toward the two chairs and small table that comprised the sitting area. She noticed Savard's limp first and then registered that she wasn't wearing her knee immobilizer over her navy FBI sweatpants. The loose wrinkled white T-shirt was also FBI issue. Savard's initial panicked expression had changed to one that Cam recognized as weary resignation. "How's the leg?"

"Fine," Savard avoided her eyes. She eased into one of the chairs without bending her knee.

"Going a little stir-crazy?"

Savard grimaced. "Been there and back."

"How did you like being assigned to counterterrorism?" Cam asked as she took the chair opposite Savard at the little round table.

Savard blinked, then her body seemed suddenly infused with energy. She sat forward, her elbows on the table, her eyes fixed intently on Cam's face. "Before 9/11 it used to bug me a little bit, how much time I had to spend at the desk on the computer, sifting through bits of data and chunks of memos, screening crazy tips from civilians about strange looking characters in their neighborhood." She shrugged. "Still, when we identified persons of interest or traced messages to potential cells, I felt like I was doing something."

"What about now? You said *before* 9/11."

Savard averted her gaze again and slumped back in her chair. "I fucked up."

"*You* did? You personally?" Cam had seen Savard close to coming apart when Stark had been hospitalized following exposure to a possibly lethal biological agent. Even as bad as it was then, Savard hadn't looked or sounded like this. As if she'd somehow already given up on everything. "How do you figure that?"

"I was there, Commander. Not just in New York City, but right in the goddamn building that they hit. What kind of an agent sits in the target zone and doesn't even have a clue about what's coming?"

"I was in the Aerie," Cam said, "and my only job—*my number one priority*—was to see that no one got close to Egret. I failed."

"That's not true," Renée said sharply. "Blair's alive because of you and your team. No one could have anticipated that kind of assault in the middle of Manhattan. Jesus, Foster was one of us."

"That's really the point, isn't it? No one anticipated either of those events, which makes us all equally responsible." Cam didn't point out the very real differences between her degree of culpability and Savard's. It had not been Renée Savard's responsibility to anticipate disaster scenarios on a worldwide scale, but safeguarding the first daughter against any conceivable attack had been Cam's. No amount of rationalization would change that.

"I know in my head what you're saying is true," Savard whispered. "But I still feel guilty."

"Are things better or worse than a month ago?"

"It's different. Then, I was just so angry. Now I feel...helpless."

"Are you seeing anyone about it?"

Savard flushed. "Yes. Couple times a week, we're talking on the phone."

"Good," Cam said briskly. "Then the only thing left to do is get you back to work."

"I'm due for my final med check in a couple of days. Once I get cleared, I'm going to call the SAC where I was last assigned and try to find out if I've still got a job there."

"I've got another suggestion."

Savard's eyes brightened. "What?"

"How would you like to work with me in homeland security?"

"You're moving over?"

Cam nodded. "Officially as of today."

"In what capacity?"

With a sigh, Cam confessed to the title she'd rather not use, but understood was part of the package. "Deputy director of counterterrorism."

"Oh man," Savard whispered. "And you can take me with you?"

"I've got the green light to handpick my core agents." Cam grinned. "Kind of a special ops thing."

"Yes. I'm in."

Cam laughed. "I haven't outlined what you'll be doing."

"I don't care. When can I start?"

"How does tomorrow sound?" Cam stood. "0700, room B-12 in the West Wing." At Savard's look of surprise, she said, "Temporary quarters, just until we get organized."

"Looks like I need to get some clothes." Savard glanced down at her sweats. "I just brought hanging-around stuff. I guess Paula will have to take me shopping tonight."

"Since that's what she's been doing all afternoon with Blair and Diane," Cam said with a straight face, "I'm sure she'll be eager to do a little more."

Savard smiled, some of the pain lifting from her eyes. "She'll probably hate it, but she won't complain."

"Better woman than me," Cam muttered as she started toward the door. Turning, before she exited, she said, "See you in the morning, Agent Savard. And welcome aboard."

"Thank you, Director Roberts."

"Make it Cam."

"Yes ma'am. Commander."

With a shake of her head, Cam walked out into the hall. She had a few more people to talk to, a few calls to make, and then she could go home. Home to Blair. She smiled, liking the sound of it.

❖

The phone rang in a room two floors below Stark and Savard's. A broad-chested, trim-waisted man with an upright, military bearing strode across the room and picked up the receiver. His dark button-down collar shirt and black pants were pressed and wrinkle-free. On some men the clothes would have appeared casual. On him, they were a uniform.

"You're right on time. I hope you have something useful to report."

"Nothing yet, I'm afraid."

The general smiled thinly. "How is it that one of your own people, someone *you* presumably control, can evade you so successfully?"

"Lawrence is a chameleon. She was trained to be elusive and is very good at it. But we'll find her. For now, I have someone watching the girlfriend."

"We don't even know that Lawrence is trying to make contact with her."

"We have reasonable intel that they're lovers. That's not her pattern with women, so I suspect she'll try to contact her."

His smile disappeared. "It's a long shot, but I suppose it's the best we have at the moment. It's your job to improve those odds. I want her silenced before the rest of our operation is compromised."

"Yes, sir. I'm tracking her through every known alias and attempting to set up a meet, but I obviously can't go through channels. It's slowing me down."

The general's jaw tightened. He hadn't been prepared for the attack on his compound because he hadn't expected anyone on the government's payroll to uncover his connection to Foster and the assault team—certainly not as quickly as Roberts had managed. The warning from his contact within the CIA that his mountain camp was about to be raided had barely come in time for him to escape. He'd slipped their net but at the cost of revealing that he had sources within the Company. He preferred not to sacrifice those sources, but if he couldn't find the one person who might expose the link, then he might be forced to take other action. "I'm not interested in excuses. You have someone on Bleeker?"

"Yes sir, but close surveillance is out of the question. She's with... her *friend*, sir, and security there is very tight, especially after...New York."

"Yes, your percentages have been poor lately." The general rolled the hotel pen idly between his fingers. His mission had come so close to succeeding. His men, his handpicked boys, had nearly succeeded in eliminating their prime target. "I'm not impressed."

"We're confident Lawrence will attempt contact eventually, and then we can eliminate any chance of compromise."

"Let's hope the bait is sweet enough." Matheson drew a circle on a notepad next to the phone and then placed a precise X through the center. When he turned the pad, the X looked like the crosshairs of a gun sight. "Perhaps this time we can sweep the board. In memory of *our* fallen friends."

There was a moment of silence, then, "Yes, sir. And may God bless America."

"May He indeed. You know where to reach me if anything changes before our next scheduled communication. Let's take care of these loose ends quickly, agent."

The general broke the connection, then pushed the extension for valet parking and requested that his vehicle be brought to the front of the hotel. He clipped a holster with his Glock to his belt and selected a dark overcoat. It was time to take another drive through the city, past the White House and Cameron Roberts's apartment building.

The time was rapidly approaching when he would have to take care of unfinished business personally.

❖

Cam stepped off the elevator and, with a quick rush of relief, nodded to Greg Wozinski, who stood just outside her apartment door. For the first time in almost a year, she hadn't sat in on the morning briefing with Blair's security team. She hadn't been advised of the shift schedule or known from one minute to the next where Blair was. She had been uneasy all day.

"You can spell Hara in the lobby now that I'm here," Cam said, appreciating the close surveillance but knowing that it spread Stark's team thin. "I may not be official, but I still know the ropes."

Wozinski grinned. "I'll check with the chief."

"Absolutely. Whatever Stark says." Cam let herself into the apartment and closed the door behind her. The first thing she noticed was that the living room was empty, and the second was an amazingly good smell coming from the direction of the kitchen. She followed it, to discover Blair and Diane cooking together.

Cam eyed the stir-fry concoction that Diane tossed in a large skillet. "Chinese?"

"Thai," Blair said. She slipped both arms around Cam's neck and kissed her hello. "Wine?"

Cam encircled Blair's waist. "Sounds great. Let me change, and I'll give you two a hand."

"I'll help," Blair said, grinning at Diane's snort. "I'll be right back, Di."

"Sure," Diane said good-naturedly. "I won't time you, but don't be too long because this will be done soon."

"Promise," Blair said, tugging Cam by the hand across the living room and into the hallway to the bedroom.

"How was your day?" Cam asked as she followed Blair into the bedroom. She hung up her blazer and removed her weapon and holster. She secured them on the top shelf in the closet and unbuckled her belt.

"It was fun," Blair said, sliding Cam's belt through the belt loops and draping it over the rack on the back of the closet door. "I'd forgotten what it felt like to just have fun, even though Stark seemed to be in serious pain."

Cam laughed. "She's in for some more, I'm afraid. I saw Savard this afternoon, and she said something about Stark taking her shopping for work clothes."

"You saw Renée?" Blair asked as she unzipped Cam's trousers and pulled her shirt free, then began working on the buttons. "How come?"

"I recruited her for my team."

"Oh."

Cam covered Blair's hands with one of hers and tilted Blair's chin up with the other. "And Felicia."

"That's good. They're good people."

"But?"

Blair shook her head. "Nothing. It's just…" She smiled a little crookedly. "Goddamn it! I'd gotten used to you and the rest of them being on my detail. Now I'm not going to know what you're doing, and they will."

Cam sensed Blair's real concern that in this new position there were things they would not be able to discuss. They'd worked hard to overcome the twin obstacles to communication between them—Cam's natural reluctance to share professional and personal information, even when it wouldn't violate procedure or protocol, and Blair's deep-seated need to safeguard her privacy, even from those she loved. Now, Cam's job was reconstructing those barricades, and this time she would be taking some of the important people in Blair's life behind those walls with her.

Cam eased away and shed her trousers, exchanging them for a pair of sweatpants. She finished unbuttoning her shirt, placed it on the pile to go to the dry cleaners, and pulled on a T-shirt. Then she drew Blair with her to the side of the bed, sat down, and guided Blair onto her lap. She clasped her loosely around the waist and kissed her throat.

"It's going to take some getting used to, but we'll manage." She rubbed her cheek over the valley between Blair's breasts, inhaling the lingering scent of her perfume on the silk T. "I promise to tell you as much as I can, but right now there really isn't much to tell."

Blair combed her fingers through Cam's hair, then tilted Cam's head back and kissed her. "Did you meet with my father today?"

"No, just with his security adviser. The president doesn't really get involved with the specifics of these things."

"That's a very subtle way of saying he needs to disavow all knowledge."

Cam lifted her shoulder. "It's important to insulate him."

"Insulate," Blair mused, remembering how it always seemed as if her father had a shield between him and everyone else, even her. "Yes, that's a civilized word for it, I guess."

"Baby," Cam heard the unspoken fear, "I won't let that happen to us."

"When did you learn to read my mind so well?" Blair lifted Cam's T-shirt and stroked her abdomen.

"Still learning," Cam said, her voice thickening as Blair untied the string to her sweatpants and slid her hand lower. "Blair. Don't go there."

Laughing softly, Blair caught Cam's earlobe between her teeth and nipped it gently. "Since when?"

"Since Diane's in the kitchen, and if you make me come, she'll know just from looking at me."

"So? She can always tell when you make *me* come, and you don't seem to mind." Blair cupped her hand between Cam's legs and teased her with one finger.

"She's *your* friend." Cam gasped, and yanked Blair's hand out of her sweatpants.

"Okay," Blair murmured, sucking lightly on Cam's neck. "But only because dinner's almost ready, and I think Diane could use the company."

"How is she doing?" Cam noted the fact that Blair had not asked if the issue of Valerie's disappearance had come up during her discussions with the president's security adviser.

"As well as can be expected, I suppose. I've never seen her hurting so much and so much in love at the same time." Blair sighed. "I don't want her to feel like she's alone in this."

"She's not."

"I know, but she's afraid to talk to anyone about..." Blair hesitated, realizing they were venturing onto dangerous ground. She wished desperately that Diane would talk to Cam.

Cam felt Blair stiffen and leaned back to study her face. "Did something happen today that she needs to talk about?"

Blair stroked Cam's shoulder and kissed her quickly. "Let's go eat."

"Blair," Cam caught Blair's hand as she rose and tried to move away. "What happened today?"

"We agreed we wouldn't talk about—"

"What we agreed," Cam said dangerously, "is that what went on between Diane and Valerie was Diane's business unless she got into trouble."

"Right." Blair centered herself, dropped one leg back and rotated her arm in a quick, tight circle, breaking Cam's grip. It was a standard self-defense move, and if Cam had been expecting it, Blair wouldn't have been able to break her hold.

Cam's face darkened, but she didn't try to stop Blair as Blair started toward the bedroom door. "What we *didn't* agree on," she said to Blair's back, "and something I didn't think we'd have to discuss, is what would happen if Valerie involved you in any way. I didn't think I'd have to ask you to tell me."

"I'm not involved."

"Then tell me nothing happened today when you were anywhere around."

Blair hesitated with her hand on the doorknob. "Don't, Cam. Please."

Cam let her go, because she was so angry that anything else she said would likely drive Blair into the streets, which is where she usually went when she felt threatened or cornered. Better she left than Blair. Cam laced her running shoes, grabbed a windbreaker, and stalked through the living room and out the door. She didn't bother with the elevator, but descended the stairs two at a time. When she shouldered through the door into the lobby, she didn't even slow down as she passed Wozinski, who stared at her in surprise. "If Egret goes out, don't lose her. If you do, you'll answer to me."

"Yes ma'am," Wozinski said smartly.

❖

Diane turned to Blair at the sound of the door slamming. "What happened?"

Blair drained her wine glass and refilled it. "Nothing."

"It didn't sound like nothing." Diane turned off the burner and picked up her own glass. "Are you fighting about me?"

"No," Blair snapped. "We're fighting about what we've always fought about."

"And what's that?"

"Cam's goddamn job and the fact that she still wants to keep me tucked away somewhere. Safe and sound like some exotic animal in a fucking gilded cage."

"She loves you."

"That's not the point."

"Of course it is."

"I thought we were past this," Blair said sadly.

Diane picked up the bottle and her wine glass and gestured toward the living room. "Let's talk."

"I don't want to talk. Let's drink wine instead."

"Let's do both." Diane tucked the bottle under one arm and wrapped the other around Blair's waist. "We're too old to drown our sorrows. I always feel like crap the next morning."

"Are we too old to pick up strange girls in bars, too?" Blair said as she walked with Diane to the sofa.

"Sadly, I think we might be." Diane stood the bottle on the end table next to the sofa and settled into the corner. The drapes were open, the room lights off, the city aglow outside. "Is that what you want to do?"

Blair curled up next to Diane, their shoulders lightly touching. "When I'm this angry, fucking someone keeps me from punching walls."

"Not always. I seem to remember a couple of dents in our dorm room door, way back when."

Blair smiled thinly. "I wasn't as accomplished at picking up girls back then."

"If you want to go out," Diane said calmly, "I'll go with you. If you want to find a stranger to fuck your anger away on, I'll watch your back."

"I can't," Blair said softly. "Goddamn her. I can't."

Diane eased an arm around Blair's shoulders, drew her close, and kissed her cheek. "Then let's have some wine."

Blair closed her eyes and tried not to think about how desolate she felt when Cam walked out the door.

CHAPTER TEN

Cam ran, barely registering the driving rain as she pounded south toward the lights of Union Station. Her windbreaker had no hood, but she didn't mind the cold water whipping her face and barely registered the steady trickle down her collar, soaking her T-shirt. For the first few blocks, she ran through the nearly deserted streets without thinking, her mind hazy with anger and an undercurrent of sick fear. She hadn't been an investigator for more than a dozen years without learning how to ask questions that left no room for evasion.

Tell me that whatever went on between Diane and Valerie didn't happen anywhere near you.

Blair hadn't answered, because Blair wouldn't lie to her. And that was answer enough. It angered her that Blair would keep something like this from her, but even more it frightened her that Valerie had somehow made contact and Blair's security team hadn't detected it. Because if Stark *had* known, she would have informed Cam immediately. Cam was certain of that. The ramifications of the scenario were blood-chillingly clear—if Valerie was a target and someone tried to take her out of the picture when she was anywhere near Blair, Blair could become collateral damage. Blair had been unprotected. Blair had been vulnerable.

Cam's stomach rebelled at the images her mind projected in a relentless stream—a glimmer of movement on a rooftop before a bullet tore into her chest, a vehicle exploding into a lethal inferno, a firestorm of smoke and death outside the Aerie. Each time, Blair as the target.

"Goddamn it," she seethed. She felt as if she were always one step behind. How much longer could her luck hold up? How much longer could Blair's? Sooner or later, Blair would be caught in someone's crossfire, and Cam couldn't let that happen. The thought was beyond anything she could even allow into her consciousness. Blair would just have to understand that her safety was more important than her freedom.

Cam squinted in the steady downpour as she approached an intersection and automatically glanced to her right as she started across with the light. Headlights shimmered through a curtain of water halfway up the block, and it wasn't until she was in the middle of the street that she registered the sound of an engine accelerating. She looked right again and dove toward the far sidewalk as a vehicle barreled down on her. The next instant something solid grazed her right hip and she was airborne. She crashed down, rolling out of her fall as best she could while reaching for her weapon. Stunned by the impact, it took her a second to remember she didn't have her weapon or her cell phone or even her wallet. Like an idiot, she'd left the apartment with nothing but the clothes on her back. When she pushed herself to her knees, the vehicle had disappeared around the corner.

Stiffly, she got to her feet and swayed for a minute until she got her balance. It all happened so quickly, she could almost believe it *hadn't* happened except for the throbbing in her right shoulder and hip, which had taken the worst of the glancing blow. When she swiped at the moisture on her face she saw a streak of blood on her hand. She ignored it, thinking she must have scraped her hand when she hit the ground. Ignoring the pain shooting through her right side, she turned back the way she'd come and ran as fast as she could. By the time she reached her building and shoved through the glass doors into the lobby, she was gasping for breath and staggering from a cramp in her side.

Wozinski rushed toward her. "Commander!"

Cam braced one arm against the desk where the doorman usually sat and gasped, "I'm okay. Get...Stark here." Her voice cracked and she swallowed against the raw ache that accompanied every breath. Running in the cold air seemed to have exacerbated the swelling in her injured throat. "Savard, too." She glanced toward the elevators, almost terrified to ask. "Egret?"

"Upstairs, Commander."

The relief was so intense her legs nearly buckled, but she waved Wozinski away when he took another step toward her. "Just winded. Make the calls."

"Yes ma'am."

"No one else comes up," Cam rasped on her way to the elevator. Once inside, she pulled off her windbreaker and mopped up some of the water and grit from her hair and face. Glancing down as she crossed the foyer, she realized the right knee of her sweatpants was torn out. Grimacing, she tapped on her door. "Blair? Blair, it's Cam. I don't have my keys."

After a moment, Cam heard the sound of footsteps approaching. As soon as the door started to open, she held onto the handle so Blair couldn't see her. "I'm okay, but I took a little bit of a spill."

"A spill?" Blair pulled against the resistance from the other side, instantly attuned to the hoarseness in Cam's voice. "Sweetheart?"

Cam leaned against the doorjamb, pale and shivering. "Rough run."

"There's blood on your face and neck," Blair gasped, grasping Cam's shoulders. When Cam winced, Blair slid her arm down around her waist. "What happened?"

"Oh my God," Diane exclaimed from across the room. "Should I call an ambulance?"

"No." Cam struggled not to cough. "I just need to sit down a second."

"Put some coffee on, would you, Di." Blair switched on a nearby table lamp. "I'm going to help her get cleaned up."

"Stark and Savard are on their way. I need to—"

"Be quiet and let me look at you." Blair framed Cam's face and studied her eyes, some of her fear dissipating when she saw that they were clear. She gently touched a jagged scrape along the right side of Cam's jaw. "Where else are you hurt?"

"Bumps and bruises." Cam tried not to limp as she and Blair started down the hallway to the bedroom. "It's not serious, baby."

"What happened?" Blair repeated as soon as they were in the bedroom. She quickly got two large towels from the bathroom and tossed them onto the foot of the bed. Then she gently lifted Cam's T-shirt and guided it off over her head. After draping one of the towels around Cam's shoulders, she untied her sweatpants and eased them down and off. "Oh, sweetheart."

Gently, she brushed her fingertips over the discolored, swollen areas on Cam's shoulder and hip. "You didn't fall."

"Somebody tried to run me down," Cam said, slowly making her way to the bathroom. "I need to get a fast shower. Stark and Savard should be here in a minute."

Blair turned on the water, her motions sharp and angry. She needed the anger, because the thought of how much worse it might have been made her want to scream. "Who was it? Did you see?"

"No." Cam groaned softly as the hot water hit her rapidly stiffening back and hips. "Couldn't see a thing except headlights."

"It was deliberate?" Blair ran the towel through her hands over and over, wanting more than ever to hit something. To hurt—no, *annihilate*—whoever had attempted to kill her lover, to take someone precious from her. The pain of just thinking of it was so huge she shook.

"Yeah, I think so."

"Oh sweetheart, I'm sorry," Blair whispered. "If you hadn't been angry with me, you wouldn't have gone—"

"Bullshit, Blair," Cam said mildly, stepping out of the shower and accepting the towel Blair held out for her. "Baby, if it was anyone's fault, it was mine. I wasn't paying attention, and whoever it was probably followed me from here. I didn't have my weapon or my phone. Fucking idiot." Roughly, she toweled her hair until it was dry enough for her to finger comb it back out of her face. "Would you mind grabbing me some jeans and a shirt."

"Here," Blair said a moment later. She helped Cam with the buttons and zipper even though Cam didn't need her to, because she had to do something, other than slam doors and swear. "I'll get you some ibuprofen too. From the looks of those bruises, you're going to be sore."

When Blair started to turn away, Cam gently caught her by the shoulders and stopped her. "I'm okay. You've given me a worse thumping in the training ring."

Blair turned in the circle of Cam's arms. "I might have bloodied you, but I've never *tried* to hurt you." She rested her cheek against Cam's shoulder. "God, I can't believe someone tried to run you down. I shouldn't have let you go."

"I shouldn't have gone. I'm sorry."

"I was so pissed off at you for leaving." Blair was starting to shake as her anger dissipated. "You beat me to it."

"I'll make a deal with you. The next time we're pissed at each other, I won't walk if you won't."

Blair sighed and kissed Cam's throat. "I guess I have to agree, because I can't stand it when you're angry, and it's even worse when you're gone."

"We're going to have to talk about this with Stark and Savard. Diane too, a little later."

Blair met Cam's eyes. "Is this about Valerie?"

"I don't know, baby. But we have to find out." She kissed Blair carefully, slowly and tenderly. "Tonight was either a warning or they were just sloppy. Either way, they made a mistake. We're not waiting for whoever's out there to try again." Cam's eyes hardened. "We're going after *them* now."

❖

Diane placed a cup of coffee on the end table next to Cam and handed another cup to Blair. "There's more in the kitchen for when the others get here. I'll be in my room." Her eyes held an apology as they met Blair's. "Let me know if you need anything."

"Wait!" Blair caught up to Diane on the way to the guest room. "Are you okay?"

"Me?" Diane shook her head. "Forget about me. Is Cam okay? Are you?"

"She's banged up, but she'll be fine." Blair's voice trembled and she forced back a surge of anxiety. She squeezed Diane's hand. "I just wasn't expecting this here. It shook me for a minute."

"A minute!" Diane laughed shakily. "I thought I understood what your life was like all these years, but I was wrong. I've always loved you for your spirit and courage. Now even more." She lightly stroked Blair's cheek. "If I am the cause of any of this because of my relationship with Valerie, I'm leaving. You don't deserve to have more pain in your life because of your friends."

"Diane," Blair said gently. "Shut up."

Diane paused. "I'm serious."

"I know, and I love you for it. But you're not going anywhere right now. I'll talk to you as soon as I can."

When she returned to the living room, Cam was just opening the door to Paula and Renée. Blair guessed they had come directly from their shopping trip, because Renée's dark slacks, pale yellow blouse, and dark green blazer were clearly just out of the package. Paula, in jeans and a navy crewneck sweater, looked worried even before she zeroed in on Cam, and then her eyes widened in alarm and she immediately pivoted toward Blair. "Are you all right?"

"I'm fine. Just Cam was hurt." Blair stroked Cam's arm, needing the contact. "Someone tried to run her down."

"Do you have anything on the vehicle or driver?" Renée asked briskly.

"Nothing on either one," Cam said in disgust. "I was too busy kissing the pavement." She sat on the sofa and gestured toward the matching leather chairs opposite her. Blair settled beside her, and Cam briefly squeezed her hand before filling Stark and Savard in on the details of what had happened.

"Is there any chance you might've been mistaken for someone else?" Savard asked.

Cam shook her head. "Doubtful. The streets were pretty empty because of the weather, so I expect the vehicle followed me from here. I'm taller than Blair and I wasn't wearing a hat, so my face and hair were visible. It's unlikely anyone would mistake me for her."

"Even so, is there any specific reason that you think Ms. Powell might have been a possible target?" Stark asked carefully.

"None, other than all the usual reasons," Cam said grimly, pleased that Stark's focus was on Blair.

"What about yourself?" Savard interjected.

"Ordinarily," Cam said, "I'd say no. But there are other factors at play that you both need to be aware of." She shifted slightly and focused on Stark. "I assume you know that Savard is on my OHS team now."

"Yes." Stark smiled fleetingly. "I think it's terrific."

"So do I." She shot a quick glance at Savard before turning again to Stark. "I intended to brief Savard and Davis tomorrow on our prime mission, and you too, Chief, to the extent that circumstances involve Blair. What happened tonight has pushed up my timetable."

"Yes, ma'am," Stark said. "I appreciate you including me tonight."

"You have to be included." Cam could sense Blair's tension but she continued without hesitation. "As you know, Valerie Lawrence is missing and quite a number of people would like to find her. Not all of those people are friendly. We're not even completely certain that Valerie is still on our side."

"Cam." Blair abruptly withdrew her hand, which had been lightly clasping Cam's thigh.

Savard didn't seem to notice the whispered protest. "What do we know about her location since the raid on Matheson's compound?"

"Nothing. She's been completely out of contact." Cam placed her hand on Blair's knee, hoping to reassure her. "I'm not asking you to break any confidences, Blair, or to confirm anything, but Stark needs to know this. I strongly suspect that Valerie made contact with Diane Bleeker sometime during the shopping trip today."

Stark paled but kept her gaze on Cam's face. "I didn't see anyone who fits Valerie's description. No one reported anything unusual to me. If she was there…we missed her."

"There's no reason you should have been looking for Valerie, Paula." Abruptly, Blair stood and directed her next comment to Cam. "You don't seriously think *Valerie* tried to run you down tonight."

"No," Cam said, "I don't. I can't think of anything Valerie might gain by having me out of the way, especially since she doesn't know I plan on finding her."

"Even if she did," Blair said, "I can't believe she'd try to hurt you."

"I don't think so either," Cam said, "but we can't make assumptions. Until we have more information, all we know is that Valerie is missing, Matheson is missing, and *someone* tipped him off to the raid on his compound."

"If Valerie made contact today," Stark said, her voice low and tight, "then we had a serious breach in security. I'll need to report it."

Cam shook her head. "No, for two reasons. Number one, I don't want anything about Valerie reported to anyone except me. We don't know who's reading those reports. Number two, your priority and that of your team today was Blair. Valerie is an experienced operative, and I'm sure she simply waited until Diane was out of your surveillance zone before approaching her." At the set look on Stark's face, Cam leaned forward. "Now you know, Chief. Now you widen your perimeter. There was no breach today."

"What about my chain of command?" Stark asked stiffly. "A.D. Carlisle should probably be informed."

"I don't want to pull rank," Cam said, "but Homeland Security takes precedence."

"Yes ma'am." Stark said.

Cam looked at Blair. "After what happened tonight, I think you and Diane should head for Whitley Point tomorrow. I'll bring the rest of the team in a day or two."

"I'm not sure Diane will go," Blair said. "Not if Valerie is here somewhere."

"If Diane has contact with Valerie, she needs to get Valerie to come in. If Valerie's not responsible for the leak, she's in big trouble. Matheson is going to try to eliminate her."

"Commander," Savard said. "Someone helped Valerie disappear from Whitley Point. It's not a secure location anymore."

Cam nodded. "I agree that the site is no longer a secret. Despite that, Whitley Point is easy to secure, and with Tanner's private forces, we'll have plenty of personnel. It's the best place for Blair—"

"I'm not going without Diane," Blair said. "I understand what you're saying, and I'll go, but not without her. She'll be defenseless if we leave her."

"I'll put people on her," Cam said.

Blair shook her head. "I want *my* people." She glanced at Stark. "They're the best and you know it."

Cam sighed. "I'll talk to Diane. It's time that I did." She grasped Blair's hand and drew her back down to the sofa. "Okay?"

"Yes. I know it's time." Blair leaned gently against Cam's uninjured shoulder.

"Chief," Cam said to Stark, "you'll have complete control of Blair's security, but you'll report to me and not Carlisle until further notice."

"Understood," Stark responded smartly.

"Savard, you're second-in-command of my OHS team. Our first priority is to find Valerie Lawrence. And after that, we're going to find Matheson."

Savard's eyes sparkled and her fatigue seemed to drop away like a distant memory. "Yes ma'am, Commander. Will there be anyone else besides Felicia?"

"For now, no. Once we get a lead, we'll need someone in the field."

Savard looked as if she was about to say something, and then stopped herself. Nevertheless, Cam heard the message. "If and when you're ready for the field, I'll decide where I need you most. Can you work with that?"

"Absolutely," Savard said. "I serve at your command, with pleasure."

Cam stood, careful not to favor her aching hip. She didn't want Stark or Savard, and especially not Blair, to know how much it hurt. "Contact Felicia tonight and tell her we'll meet here at 0700, not in the West Wing. It's time to close our doors to any eyes and ears except our own."

Blair walked Stark and Savard to the door, then returned to Cam. "I know there wasn't much time before the briefing, but I wish you'd told me about leaving for Whitley Point earlier."

"I know. My timing has been off with everything tonight." Cam cupped Blair's cheek. "I'm sorry. It wasn't meant to blindside you."

Blair sighed. "You're forgiven."

"Thanks," Cam said, meaning it. She was in pain, she was facing enemies she couldn't identify, and she needed Blair now more than ever.

"Your hip hurts, doesn't it?" Blair said, resting her hands gently on Cam's waist.

"I thought I was doing a good job of hiding it." Cam laughed softly at Blair's expression. "It's getting stiff pretty fast."

"Let's get you to bed."

"In a minute. I need to talk to Diane."

"She's hurting, too, Cam," Blair said softly.

"I know. I'll do my best not to make it worse."

"Your best," Blair whispered, kissing her. "Yes, that will do."

"I know how much she means to you, and I'm very fond of her. I'm not going to let anything happen to her."

"Do you ever get tired, taking care of others?"

Cam frowned. "I don't know what you mean."

Blair smiled and kissed Cam again. "I know you don't, and that's another reason that I love you. I'll be waiting."

"And that," Cam whispered, "is just what I need."

Blair watched her walk away, knowing she was hiding her pain. She wanted to shield Cam and keep her safe, and knew Cam wanted the same for her. She feared it was a wish neither of them could fulfill.

CHAPTER ELEVEN

Diane, in royal blue silk pajamas, sat propped against the pillows, an open book in her lap. She smiled wanly at Cam. "I've been trying to read, but I can't remember a single sentence."

"I'm sorry to disturb you."

"Don't be silly. How do you feel?"

"I'm fine." Cam left the door open an inch and leaned against the wall, her arms loosely at her sides. "In light of what's happened, I'd like you and Blair to leave for Whitley Point tomorrow morning."

"I hadn't planned on leaving so soon."

Cam followed Diane's gaze as she glanced unconsciously at her cell phone on the table next to the bed. "If Valerie calls, she can reach you there as well as anywhere else."

"I know."

"But you're hoping to see her here, aren't you?" Cam asked gently.

Diane sighed. "Am I that transparent?"

"No. I'd feel the same way if I were you." Cam's chest tightened just thinking about Blair suddenly disappearing with no word. Perhaps forever. But she couldn't make command decisions based on what she felt, or how deeply she ached for Diane's pain. No one would be safe then.

"Sit down," Diane said, indicating the bed. "You've had a difficult night."

Cam grinned as she sat on the foot of the bed. "You saw her today, didn't you?"

"Is that why you and Blair were fighting?"

"Nice evasive maneuver," Cam murmured. Assuming that Blair wouldn't mind Diane knowing what had gone on between them, she answered honestly. "We were fighting because I thought she should have told me about Valerie showing up today and she didn't."

"I'm sorry."

"You don't need to be. Blair and I don't always see things the same way, but I understand why she made the decision she did."

Diane studied Cam curiously. "And that makes it all right?"

"No," Cam laughed. "But it usually means I don't stay angry very long."

"She's lucky."

"That works both ways."

"You're right. I did see Valerie. She was at The White House today." Diane smiled fleetingly at Cam's look of consternation. "It's a boutique in Georgetown. We talked for a few minutes."

"Did she say where she was staying?"

Diane shook her head.

"Phone number?"

Again, Diane shook her head.

"Did she say why she's hiding?"

"No. But I got the distinct impression that she was in trouble, serious trouble."

"What kind of trouble?"

Diane picked at the corner of the book in her lap, recalling Valerie's haunted look and the way she'd reacted when the stranger came into the stairwell. When she met Cam's calm gaze hers was cut through with anguish. "She acted as if someone was going to hurt her."

"I need to talk to her. You need to tell her that. Tell her if she meets with me, she can walk away no matter what she tells me."

"Do you really think she betrayed you? Or our country? After helping you in the first place?" Diane's voice trembled and she looked away, biting her lip. "How can you think that when you've held her?"

Cam's stomach churned, and for an instant she remembered the dark nights that might have been endless if it hadn't been for Valerie. *Claire*, as she knew her then. Claire's tenderness and her uncanny ability to absolve guilt without demanding explanations had kept her together when everything inside was breaking.

"They recruited her when she was a teenager," Cam said. "Part of the indoctrination is to isolate the recruits from everyone outside the system. Family, friends, everyone. Your handler becomes your primary point of contact for everything—he or she becomes your emotional and physical touchstone. Sometimes no one else even knows your name. Soon you forget you ever had another life."

"What are you saying?" Diane's expression verged on horror. "That she's been brainwashed?"

"No, only that she's been trained—relentlessly and expertly conditioned—to follow orders without question. How else do you think a woman like Valerie could have done the things she's done in the name of her country?"

"She didn't make love to you for her country."

Cam flinched but kept her eyes level on Diane's. "Maybe not after the first time."

"I'm sorry. I'm just so worried about her." Diane pushed her hair back from her face with an unsteady hand. "And I know that she needs your help or something terrible is going to happen to her. Please, Cam. Don't abandon her."

"I want to find her," Cam said vehemently. She leaned forward, her hand flat on the bed next to Diane's ankle. "Until we get the *real* people behind the attack on Blair at the Aerie, Valerie is in danger. And if Valerie is in danger, so are you—and so is Blair."

"Blair isn't in danger if I'm not with her." Diane swung her legs off the bed and jumped to her feet. "I'll leave now."

Cam rose and caught Diane's shoulders as she rushed toward the closet. "No. You're staying with us."

Diane spun around to face Cam and tried to push her away. "Let me go."

"Diane." Cam ignored the screaming pain in her shoulder as Diane fought her. "You're not alone. And neither is she."

"Oh," Diane gasped, tears filling her eyes. "I'm so frightened."

Cam gathered her close, stroking Diane's hair as Diane buried her face against her shoulder. "It's going to be okay."

After a moment of silent sobs, Diane leaned away from Cam and brushed at her cheeks. Shakily, she said, "I've always wondered what it would feel like for you to hold me."

"Overrated, probably."

Diane smiled. "No."

Cam eased her grip and stepped back. "If she calls you, tell her I'll bring you to her. Tell her…tell her to go to the first place she and I met."

"Why? Why would you do that? It has to be breaking some kind of rule or other."

"There are no rules anymore, Diane."

"I trust you."

"Thank you."

Diane wrapped her arms around herself. "Oh God, what if she doesn't call me? What if she doesn't trust *me*?"

Cam paused at the door. "If she risked exposure today to see you, she'll call, and soon. Give her my message. And then come and get me."

❖

"Do you really think Valerie's going to call her?" Blair asked after Cam described the conversation.

"I do. Probably tonight." Cam unzipped her jeans and pushed them down over her hips, letting them fall to the floor. She sat on the side of the bed and unbuttoned her shirt. Blair, in a threadbare T-shirt, was already under the covers.

"If she does, you're not going," Blair said, lifting the sheets.

Cam slipped underneath with a sigh. Turning onto her uninjured left side, she pillowed her head against her bent arm and smiled tiredly at Blair. "Let's get some sleep, baby."

Blair caressed Cam's cheek. "Yes. You need it. And you're still not going out if she calls."

"I love you."

"I love you too. And you're still not going."

"If I don't, Diane is either going to try to get to her herself, or Valerie's going to risk another rendezvous with Diane. Either way, they'll *both* be vulnerable if Valerie is a target."

"I hate it when you're reasonable."

Cam smiled. "I know. I do it just to make you crazy."

Blair kissed her. "It's working." She slid an arm beneath Cam's shoulder and drew her closer, pillowing Cam's head against her breast. "How are you feeling?"

"Not that bad. The ibuprofen finally kicked in."

"Why can't Valerie come here?"

"Because you're here," Cam mumbled. "Too hard to secure."

"Why can't she come to Whitley Point?"

"What?" Cam said, her mind fuzzy with near sleep.

"You said yourself Whitley Point is going to be far easier to defend."

Blair waited in the silence, caressing Cam's neck and shoulders. Eventually when she realized Cam was asleep, she turned off the light and closed her eyes. She drifted on the border between sleep and consciousness, some part of her needing to feel Cam in her arms, to know that she was safe. A knock sounded on the door, and she reluctantly slid from bed, uncertain how long she'd been asleep. When Cam did not wake up, Blair knew just how much the accident had taken out of her. She crossed the room stealthily and opened the door a crack.

"I'm sorry," Diane whispered from the hall. "I'm sorry, but I need to talk to Cam."

❖

"Scotch, please," Cam said as she eased onto a stool at the far end of the highly-polished mahogany bar in the nearly deserted Four Seasons Hotel lounge, just before 1:00 a.m. She was as certain as she could be that she hadn't been followed. Assuming that someone was watching her building, she had left by the rear service doors and walked to the nearest Metro stop. En route, she'd checked carefully for a tail and saw no indication of one, but while she waited for her drink, she scanned the room.

At first glance, the area appeared secure. Three business types, two men and a woman, sat around a cocktail table near the windows discussing market shares and margins just loudly enough for her to catch snippets of their conversation. A lone man in a rumpled suit talked on a cell phone while he peered at a laptop computer and tapped frantically on the keyboard with his free hand. A fortyish woman in jeans and a sweater sat hunched at the opposite end of the bar, scribbling in a notebook and sipping absently from a glass of white wine.

Cam, intending to appear like a late-night business traveler, had dressed in a cotton shirt and lightweight wool trousers beneath a casual leather jacket and had exchanged her usual shoulder harness for a hip holster. She nursed her Scotch and waited fifteen minutes before calling the bartender over.

"You know, I must've gotten my signals crossed. I just got in from the airport and I was supposed to meet a colleague here. We've got a big meeting in the morning…"

"A lot of people come through here," the stocky bartender said.

"We've never actually met in person. Only on the phone," Cam said, as reluctant to give a description as he was to disclose anything about patrons. She patted her pockets as if looking for something. "Hell, maybe I got the time wrong. I thought for sure Claire said—"

"Claire." The bartender smiled. "Yeah, she was here for a couple of minutes, but left when you didn't show. She said if anyone came looking, to tell them room 418."

"Thanks." Cam dropped a ten dollar bill on the bar as she rose. "You saved me a lot of embarrassment in the morning."

She took her time walking to the elevators, once again covertly observing those around her. Satisfied that no one was watching, she rode to the conference level and stepped off. She couldn't access the room floors without a keycard and hadn't planned to anyway. As expected, the foyer was empty in the middle of the night. She picked up a house phone and dialed 836.

"I'm here. Third floor."

"I'll come down."

Two minutes later the elevator stopped and Valerie stepped off. She immediately pushed the up button, shaking her head in irritation as if she'd forgotten something. She did not look at Cam, who stood nearby. An up-elevator stopped and they both stepped into the empty car. Valerie, in narrow, low heeled black boots, a black boatneck sweater with a wide band at the waist, and flaring black silk slacks, looked very much as she had the first time Cam had seen her. Her hair was shorter and, rather than platinum blond, was now shot through with red highlights. Her elegant near-patrician features were strained.

The door opened on the eighth floor and Cam followed Valerie to room 836. Once inside, Cam removed her leather jacket and laid it over the back of the antique desk chair. The room was typical for the Four Seasons, with a king size bed and a formal sitting area complete with sofa, end tables, coffee table, and a minibar.

"Scotch?" Valerie asked, her voice as rich and mellow as the whiskey she offered.

"A short one," Cam said as she walked into the sitting area.

Valerie poured an inch of the smoky liquor into two crystal rock glasses and offered one to Cam. "You didn't bring Diane."

Cam shook her head and drank off half the Scotch. "Did you think that I would?"

Valerie smiled softly. "No. I knew that you wouldn't, especially after giving her the message that you would meet me here."

"Sorry."

"You shouldn't be. I didn't want her to come. I was calling her to tell her that." Valerie sat on the sofa and sipped her Scotch, her expression distant. "I couldn't walk out twice without saying goodbye."

"Going somewhere?" Cam sat next to Valerie.

"What happened to your face?"

"Someone tried to run me down not far from my apartment tonight."

Valerie lightly touched one finger to Cam's chin, tilting her face toward the lamp. "Blair must be wild."

"Good deduction."

"If your face looks like this, I imagine the rest of you is pretty sore too."

"You would be right again," Cam said, aware that Valerie's hand was shaking. "How are you doing?"

"I've been more comfortable." Valerie dropped her hand into her lap. "You know it wasn't me."

"In the vehicle that tried to turn me into roadkill? I know. What I don't know is what else is going on."

"Neither do I." Valerie shifted until her knee lightly touched Cam's leg. "You remembered our system." She smiled almost wistfully. "The first time you called the service and I met you downstairs in the bar, I was surprised."

"About what," Cam asked gently. She was in no hurry. There was too much between them not to let Valerie say what she needed to say.

"You were gorgeous. I couldn't imagine that a woman like you would need to…"

"Pay for it?" Cam said with a sardonic shrug.

"Find comfort with strangers."

Cam smiled. "We're not strangers now."

Valerie rested her fingers lightly on Cam's forearm. "No, we're not. But you don't altogether trust me, do you?"

"I know you're a professional and I know that you'll follow orders. Your orders might be at odds with my mission."

"You want Matheson," Valerie said with certainty. "And so do I."

"Someone warned him before we could get to him."

"I know that. What I don't know is who."

"The leak had to come from you," Cam said mildly.

Valerie sighed. "Yes. I know."

"Your handler?"

Valerie looked pained. "I don't know. I hope not. I've known him fifteen years." She met Cam's gaze, an apology in her eyes. "I've told him a lot in those fifteen years."

Cam grimaced. "I've already come to terms with the fact that my private life isn't private and hasn't been for some time. What's his name?"

Valerie hesitated.

"Jesus, Valerie," Cam snapped. "If he's not dirty it won't matter. If he is, we need to know because he's probably not the only one. Do you seriously think that Matheson could pull off something like the assault on Blair with only one contact on the inside? For all we know, he's got a *network*. For all we know, he's going to try again."

Cam jumped to her feet, too wired to sit, and winced at the sudden surge of pain that sliced down her back and into her right leg. She barely bit back a groan.

Valerie grasped her hand. "Sit down, Cameron. You're in too much pain to stand."

"What's his name?" Cam looked down at Valerie and at their hands, still joined, remembering. She had held this woman in the night. She had come in her arms. She had found some semblance of peace in her touch during the darkest hours of her life. And she had loved her as much as she'd been able to then.

"Henry," Valerie said softly. "That's all I know."

"Fifteen years and you never tried to find out more?"

Valerie shook her head. "That's not the way things are done."

Cam gently released Valerie's hand and sat down again. "I know. Do you think he's the link?"

Pain flashed across Valerie's face and was quickly erased. "I don't know. And until I do, I can't contact him or anyone else on the inside."

"Where were you planning to go?"

"Just before 9/11 we began to see intelligence that there was an active cell in France, possibly Paris, working with other cells in Europe and the Middle East. They were rumored to be planning a coordinated attack here."

Cam swore and struggled to keep her temper in check. "Why didn't anyone *else* know this?"

"Cameron," Valerie said with a resigned sigh. "You know how every agency guards its intelligence. And certainly those of us in the field were never told anything. I didn't learn this until after everything happened."

"When they sent you to work with us," Cam said bitterly. She'd been used, and although it hadn't been the first time and in all likelihood wouldn't be the last, she resented it.

"Yes. They were hoping we might find a lead to the cell in Paris in the course of investigating Foster."

"What do you think you can do there on your own?"

Valerie shrugged, clearly frustrated. "I don't know. Possibly nothing. But if I don't find the link that ties Foster and Matheson and the Company together, I'm never going to be able to come in."

"Come in now, with me."

"I trust *you,* but you can't protect me once I'm visible. And we both know the easiest way to make this all go away is to eliminate me." Valerie drained her Scotch and set the glass carefully on the end table. "Whoever tried to run you down tonight probably knows about our relationship. Killing you would cut off one more avenue of escape for me."

"I came to the same conclusion," Cam said, hoping Blair hadn't.

"I'm sorry."

"For what?" Cam laughed wearily. "For believing in the Company line, or for meeting me in the bar that first night?"

"Certainly not the latter. I'm coming to regret the first. I'm already responsible for one attempt on your life. I don't want to be the cause of another."

"I'm your best shot, and you know it." Cam stood. "If you let me bring you in, I give you my word no one will know until we've identified Matheson's source. I'll personally guarantee that you are protected."

"I don't want to spend months, possibly years, in a safe house, Cam." Valerie laughed. "God knows, if I wanted to disappear and start over as someone else, I could. I'm tired of being someone else. I want out."

Cam made a decision based on everything she knew, and more importantly, on everything she believed. "Work with me and my team to find Matheson, and I'll get you out."

"I'm not sure even you can do that, Cameron." Rising, Valerie slid her hand to the back of Cam's neck and kissed her on the cheek. "I need to think about it."

"The longer you stay under, the worse it looks."

"I know."

"What about Diane?"

"I shouldn't have contacted her today. It was selfish." Valerie hooked her arm through Cam's as they walked toward the door. "I won't try to see her again."

Cam gave her a secure phone number as she shrugged into her jacket. "No one will know. You have my word."

"I won't be here in the morning, in case you were wondering."

"I won't come after you, not unless I have to."

"Thank you." Valerie smiled sadly. "Goodnight, Cameron."

Cam drew her into a gentle embrace. "Call me. Soon."

CHAPTER TWELVE

Wednesday

Thomas Jefferson Matheson picked up the phone on the first ring. If he hadn't been listening for it, he wouldn't have recognized the faint buzz emanating from the electronic jammer. He'd put his own people on surveillance duty as soon as he'd gotten word of where the bait had landed. Trusting an agent he couldn't directly control was not ideal, and he wanted his own back-up plan in place if he needed to settle matters himself. "Yes?"

"Nothing to report, sir."

"No activity during the night?"

"No sir. Everyone is still in the apartment."

"Really." Matheson swallowed a generous mouthful of steaming coffee, ignoring the burn in the back of his throat. He'd slept well, risen before dawn, and worked out vigorously in the hotel health club for an hour. And he'd had a most satisfactory evening. "No one in or out?"

"Well…" his man said hesitantly.

Matheson heard the rustle of papers.

"Routine movement reported at…ah…around 1900 yesterday. Roberts went for a run…several hours later security changed shift… uh, today…three subjects arrived at 0800, most likely for start of shift briefing. Nothing beyond that."

"You seem to be missing a few details in your report."

"Yes sir. What would that be, sir?"

Matheson smiled, picturing the man squirming. He was new. "At 1932 last night, Roberts was struck by a passing motorist and may have sustained substantial injuries." He still felt a surge of pleasure thinking about the flicker of shock on her face as he bore down on her. When he'd had the good fortune of passing by just as she exited the building, his only intention had been to follow her. But the longer he'd watched her pound through the streets as if she owned them while he hid like impotent prey, the more his anger had grown. She had destroyed his compound and killed some of his best boys, and now she stood in the way of him completing his mission. She needed to be neutralized. "Apparently your surveillance team didn't think it necessary to cover her."

To the man's credit, he defended his team. "I'm sure they felt it more important to watch for any contact between our critical target and those on site, sir."

"It's just as strong a possibility that Lawrence will contact Roberts. I expect Roberts will move her base today. It's what I would do after a pre-emptive strike. As soon as you have a new location, contact me. Bleeker is the bait, but Roberts is in command. Without her, they'll break ranks."

"Yes sir. I'll relay your orders."

"Be prepared to take action soon." Matheson felt his groin tingling as he considered a plan to turn the hunters into quarry. "I'm growing tired of this waiting game."

❖

"Are you sure you want me to come with you?" Diane asked as she packed her suitcase. "I know what Cam said, but—"

"If you weren't already here, we'd come and get you." Blair sat cross-legged on the bed in blue jeans and a long-sleeved navy T-shirt. Her hair was loose and she was barefoot. "I can't believe I let you go back to Manhattan alone in the first place."

"Who knew that these people…these maniacs…who tried to hurt you would keep coming? How can they possibly think they can gain power in this country? We aren't some third world dictatorship that's likely to topple at the slightest show of violence."

Blair shrugged. "They're fanatics. Look at all the paramilitary and right wing fundamentalist groups springing up across this country. *They* think they can change the order of things, and they're recruiting more people all the time who agree."

"God, it's like those zealots who shoot abortion doctors and think that's going to stop the pro-choice movement." Diane looked at Blair in confusion. "I can hardly believe it's real."

"I can't believe we didn't see it coming, and after what happened last month, I don't think it's going to stop." Chafing at the inactivity, Blair stood and started folding clothes. "Every psycho with an agenda is going to think they have a chance after 9/11."

Diane stopped what she was doing, her fingers digging into the sweater she held. "I'm ashamed to admit that part of me wishes your father wasn't president, because I hate to think of you or Cam in danger. I can only imagine how you must feel."

Blair smiled ruefully. "You know, for the first time in my life I'm honestly *glad* that my father's president, and I want him to be president for as long as he can be." She carefully placed a silk blouse into the suitcase. "Because these fuckers, whoever they are, wherever they are, have to learn that we won't be victims."

"I guess we'll have to keep that sexy dress you bought for the wedding in the closet a while longer."

"Why?"

Diane regarded her with surprise. "I can't imagine either you *or* Cam is going to want to think about wedding plans until all of this is resolved."

"We're not waiting for something that might never happen." Blair folded her arms, part defiance, part comfort. "And we're not putting our lives on hold until it does. I'm instructing Lucinda to slip a nice quiet statement out to the press today that Cameron and I intend to be married in a private ceremony before the end of the year."

"Oh boy."

Blair grinned. "And girls."

"Indeed." Diane kissed her cheek. "I think you're the bravest person I know."

"I wish I were," Blair said. "I'm terrified every day that something will happen to Cam. And if it did, I don't think I'd survive it."

"I would never have imagined you with her."

Blair lifted her shoulders. "We don't choose who to love."

"No. We don't." Diane smiled sadly. "Now I can't imagine you with anyone else."

"Neither can I." Blair stroked Diane's arm. She was already dressed to travel in a pale blue cashmere cowl-neck sweater and tan slacks. For the first time Blair realized that Diane, always slender, had lost weight. "How are you holding up?"

"It's so hard, knowing that Cam saw Valerie last night and I can't even speak to her."

"Have you thought maybe you should try to let her go?" Blair reached for Diane's hand. As hard as it was to ask, it was even harder to watch her suffer.

Diane twined her fingers through Blair's and squeezed lightly. "Cam didn't tell me very much about what went on. I understand that she can't. She wouldn't tell me exactly why Valerie is staying away, but I know it's partly because of me."

"She doesn't want you to be hurt."

Diane trembled and Blair drew her close. With a shaky breath, Diane continued, "Cam must trust her, because she didn't try to detain her. I love Valerie. I have to trust her as much as Cam does."

"You're really sure, aren't you?" Blair said.

Diane smiled almost shyly. "I really am. Nothing has felt as right since I met you."

"Then I'm on your side," Blair said, hugging Diane tightly. "And hers."

❖

"We'll travel in two groups to Whitley Point," Cam said, scribbling on a flip chart that she had dug out of the closet earlier. She couldn't find the stand, so she balanced the oversized pad of paper on her knees facing Stark, Savard, and Davis, who clustered around her in the living room. "Stark, you and your people will take Blair and Diane. You'll fly out of Andrews again at 1100 hours, but this time you'll land at Westover, Mass."

Stark frowned. "What's there?"

"It's an Air Force Reserve base, so it's relatively low profile. We'll have Tanner's people pick you up in three vehicles and take you the rest of the way, each vehicle following a different route."

"Who knows about the itinerary?"

"The flight plan was filed through Lucinda's office, but there's no attendant passenger list. Only Tanner knows the routes and final destination."

"You're putting a lot of faith in Tanner's people," Stark said mildly.

"My feeling is that we know more about her team than we could about anyone coming to us from inside the system right now. You're the security chief. What's your call?"

Stark took her time. "Until we find Valerie and Matheson, I don't want anyone new getting close to Blair."

"I agree." Cam blew out a breath. "Basically we'll handle Blair's security in the same way the Vice President's has been set up since the attacks. She'll be based in a secure location away from the White House known to as few people as possible, and she'll make very few and only essential public appearances. We can't keep her completely sequestered—first because she'd never allow it, secondly, because we can't make prisoners of our elected officials and their families, and finally because the public is going to be looking for her. She's too popular to just disappear."

"We're going to be thin on the ground," Stark said, "now that Davis has gone over to OHS."

Cam nodded as she drew a grid and added names. "You'll have to work with a smaller team than usual for the time being. Hara, Wozinski, yourself, and Tanner's people. Can you handle it?"

Stark didn't hesitate. "Yes, we can."

As satisfied with the security as she could be when all she really wanted to do was take Blair to some remote island for six months, Cam switched her attention to Savard. "We'll follow by ground as soon as you and Davis are happy that you've accessed all the data immediately available to us. You can use the computers in my office in the West Wing and wipe them when you're done."

"How long will you need, Felicia?" Savard asked, sitting with her injured leg straight out in front of her. The cane she'd used in lieu of her knee immobilizer rested against the arm of the chair. She looked focused and steady.

Davis smiled, her dark eyes glowing. "I want to make sure I look in everybody's closets and leave myself a backdoor before we leave. Say, three hours."

Cam checked her watch as she stood. "It's 0815 now. We should be leaving DC by 1200 hours, which puts us into Whitley Point around 2300."

Savard and Davis rose, and Savard asked, "Where will we rendezvous, Commander?"

"In case anyone is checking, I'll schedule you and Davis for a meeting at FBI headquarters at 1130 hours. On your way there, the meeting will be canceled and a vehicle will pick you up at 13th and Pennsylvania Avenue." Cam regarded Stark. "When would you like to depart here, Chief? If there's anyone following Blair, they'll lose the trail at Andrews."

"We'll have the vehicles out front at 0900 hours. I'll wait downstairs until then."

"Thanks," Cam said, appreciating the few moments of privacy she would have with Blair. After returning from her meeting with Valerie, she'd been up all night talking to Lucinda and the president's security adviser. She had yet to tell Blair the specifics of the plan, because she hadn't worked it out until shortly before Stark and her security team had arrived. She was sore and tired, but it felt good being in the field again. Working. Doing what she knew how to do.

When the others had left, Cam walked down the hall to Diane's bedroom and tapped on the door. "Can I talk to you a minute, Blair?"

"Sure," Blair said. After she'd finished helping Diane pack, she'd gone to the kitchen for more coffee and heard the murmur of voices in the living room. Although she knew Cam wouldn't exclude her from the discussions if she asked to sit in, she also knew that Cam and Stark were getting their first real test of working together in their new roles. She doubted that anyone in security or intelligence was going to like being overridden by agents from the new Homeland Security Office, not even Stark, not even when the agent in question was Cam. She decided her presence would only add to the tension. "When are we leaving?"

"About forty-five minutes."

Blair glanced over her shoulder at Diane. "I'll meet you in the living room in a few minutes, okay?"

"Yes. I've got some calls to make. I should let my gallery manager know how long I'll be away."

"Tell her three weeks for now." Cam rested her hand lightly on Blair's shoulder. The contact felt good. She had missed her the previous night, missed the way holding her through the night rejuvenated her.

Diane nodded. "All right, but I can't be away any longer than that.

Sooner or later, I have to go back to my life."

"I understand."

"Will I be able to call or give them a number where they can reach me?" Diane asked.

"Everyone will have temporary cells by tonight. Once we reach Whitley Point you can call them."

"Thank you." Diane squared her shoulders. "You two go ahead. I'm fine."

Blair slid her arm around Cam's waist. "Come on, darling. Better fill me in on what's going on."

❖

"Let me get this straight." Blair leaned against the dresser in the bedroom watching Cam pack this time. "I'm being spirited away to Whitley Point surrounded by armed guards, while you drive for twelve hours out in the open where anyone could follow you."

"We're not going to be followed."

"Then why can't I come with you?"

Cam passed Blair the extra suitcase. "You need to take anything?"

Blair dropped it on the bed. "Yes. I'll pack in a minute. Why can't I go with you?"

"If anyone is watching us they'll have a hard time following two separate groups. It buys us time."

"Bull. You don't want me with you in case someone comes after *you* again. In case someone…" Blair stalked across the room and pulled the shirt Cam was folding from her grasp. "Someone tried to kill you last night. And you think they might try again, don't you?"

"Blair—"

"Don't lie to me."

Cam cradled Blair's face between her hands and kissed her softly. "I won't. You know that."

"That's what you think, isn't it?"

"It's a consideration, especially in light of my past relationship with Valerie. Matheson might suspect that she would come to me and that I might be able to bring her in. If someone wants to prevent that, getting me out of the way is the logical step."

Blair forced herself to keep her expression neutral, even though the calm way that Cam discussed why someone would want to kill her chilled her to the core. If she wanted Cam to tell her the truth, she had to be able to handle the truth. No matter how much it terrified her. "Did you tell Valerie where we're going?"

"No, but she has a number to call me." She lowered her hands to Blair's shoulders and rubbed them softly. "I'll be okay. I've got good people with me and I know what I'm doing."

"Do you think Valerie will call?"

Cam sighed. "I don't know. When it comes right down to it, her training may win out. And she's been indoctrinated not to trust anyone."

"I don't like us being separated."

"Neither do I, but it's only for a few hours. I'll be there tonight, and we'll wake up together tomorrow."

Blair closed her eyes and wrapped her arms around Cam's waist. "You didn't sleep all night. You're hurt and tired. You're not at your best, Cam, and you need to be."

"Savard and Davis will be with me. They'll do the driving. I'll sleep."

Blair rubbed her cheek against Cam's shoulder. "I don't want other women taking care of you."

Cam laughed. "I think I'll be safe with them."

"What about the thing Saturday night I'm supposed to do for Lucinda?"

"I don't like it," Cam said, "but we all agree we can't keep you completely out of the public eye. Lucinda is arranging for a suite of rooms at the Copley for us and the rest of the team for the weekend. I'll be your escort, and Savard will accompany Diane."

"Oh, Stark's going to love that."

Cam grinned. "It's all in the line of duty."

Blair leaned back, a glint in her eyes. "Is it, now? Then you'd better pack something besides work clothes. Like a tux."

"That's what rental places are for."

"And you better make sure you sleep in the car," Blair murmured, running her fingers along Cam's collarbone and down over her chest. "I missed you last night."

"Me too."

"What about your hip and shoulder?"

"I'm stiff and sore, but functional." Cam kissed Blair, taking her time, because it would be hours before they saw each other again and despite her words of confidence to Blair, she knew that anything could happen in the interim. "Besides, massage therapy will be good for them."

"Then I'll put you on my schedule for the morning."

"I'll be there."

Blair held her tightly, unable to imagine any other possibility.

CHAPTER THIRTEEN

"Paula," Blair said with quiet intensity, just the slightest bit of edge in her voice.

"Yes?" Stark said solemnly.

"If you had a round robin, why didn't you bid more?"

Diane snorted and, despite the fact that it had been dark for over three hours and it was impossible to see the beach, Wozinski seemed to find something fascinating happening out the window. Stark hastily squinted at her cheat sheet, obviously at a loss.

"A king and queen in every suit. I would've taken the bid if I'd known you had that much meld," Blair said.

"I didn't see it," Stark said bleakly. "I was so excited about the pinochle—"

"Never mind. It doesn't matter." Blair abruptly pushed back her chair, strode across the kitchen, and slammed out the door.

The room was silent for a moment and then Diane rose. "It's freezing out there. She doesn't have a jacket."

Wozinski glanced at Stark. "Should I go with her, Chief? I can take her jacket."

Stark shook her head. "Hara is out back and Tanner stationed a team in a vehicle on the street. She's covered."

"I'll take her jacket," Diane said, patting Wozinski's shoulder as she passed behind his chair. "But thank you."

"Yes ma'am." Wozinski flushed. "Pleasure."

It took less than thirty seconds for Diane to reach the back deck after grabbing Blair's jacket, but she saw only a single figure standing at the railing, facing toward the ocean—shorter than either herself or Blair by several inches and more slender than Stark. Hara. Not Blair. For an instant, her heart twisted with an overriding sense of dread, as if Blair too had walked out the door and simply vanished. Just like the

RADCLY*f*FE

morning she had awakened in the guesthouse in a still room beneath a silent dawn and realized that Valerie had disappeared while she'd slept. "Where's Blair?"

Hara did not turn, and even in the darkness, Diane knew that she was watching Blair. The cloud cover was so dense even the light from the full moon barely penetrated the inky sky.

"Sitting on top of a dune, fifteen yards down the path and ten feet off to the right."

"It feels like thirty degrees out here, and you just let her go?" Diane snapped.

"Thirty-eight degrees."

"Never mind," Diane muttered, hurrying down the stairs to the path. A minute later she knelt beside Blair. "Put your jacket on."

"Thanks," Blair said, shrugging into it. "You don't need to stay."

With a sigh, Diane shifted around to sit facing the same direction as Blair and leaned against her. When Blair wrapped an arm around her, she snuggled closer and lightly rested her head on Blair's shoulder. "Couldn't you brood inside where we can have a fire?"

"It's a lot harder to do if you're comfortable." Blair pressed her cheek to Diane's hair. "Do you have any idea how much I hate waiting here, safe and sound and protected by armed guards, while Cam is out there somewhere with people who want to kill her?"

"I think I know," Diane whispered.

"Oh, honey, I'm sorry," Blair said. "Of course you do."

"Renée called Paula with an update," Diane pointed out gently. "She said everything was fine and that Cam was resting."

"I know." Blair sighed. "But that was three hours ago and they're not due here for another four at least. Anything can happen." She reached beside her and dug her fingers into the cold sand. "I just want to be able to protect her the way she protects me."

"I bet you already do."

Blair laughed harshly. "Hardly. Since everyone thinks I'm so important, I seem to be the one destined to wait, just like tonight."

"You are important—"

"I'm no more important than Cam or you or Stark or any of the others."

Diane wrapped both arms around Blair's waist and hugged her. "You, *Blair Powell*, may not be more important than the rest of us,

• 126 •

although I happen to think you're pretty special and I'm sure Cam does too, but it's not about Blair Powell."

"No, it's about the first daughter."

"Yes. And I imagine that makes it all the harder."

"There's a reason you're my best friend, you know," Blair said softly.

"Besides the fact that I'm smart, beautiful, and well-connected in the art world?"

"Those are definite pluses, but you might be the only person other than Tanner who's ever understood that having a famous father mostly just sucks."

"Yes, I never did think living in a mansion was all that cool when it came with a bunch of state troopers hanging out on the front porch." Diane tried not to shiver from the cold. She sensed Blair's mood beginning to lighten and wanted to keep her talking. "Tanner could relate, because she had to put up with a lot of the same thing. Not the bodyguards and everything, but having a lot expected of her because of who her father was."

"Mmm," Blair said, patting the sand she'd squeezed into a hard ball back into the ground. "Tanner understands. But she's not a girl, like you are. It's not the same."

"You mean you wouldn't snuggle with Tanner in the dark?" Diane teased.

"Snuggling is not what I had in mind with Tanner. Definitely not when we were teenagers." Blair thought back to how wild and drop-dead sexy Tanner had been then. "And I don't think I would, even now. After all, I've had a lot more practice resisting you."

"Thanks, I think." Diane kissed Blair's cheek. "We have to go inside, sweetie. I've officially frozen my ass off."

Blair reached for Diane's hand as they rose. "Thanks for coming out to get me and just for...getting it."

"Cam's going to be okay," Diane said gently. "She's amazingly good at what she does, and besides, Felicia and Renée are with her."

"I know." As they started back toward the house, Blair added, "Cam's going to figure out a way to help Valerie, too."

"That's what I keep telling myself. I have to believe it, because I can't stand to think of anything else."

"Sometimes it's better not to think." Blair stiffened. "Did you hear a car door slam just then?" She hurried up the stairs, tugging Diane behind her, and rushed past Hara into the kitchen. The room was empty. She raced toward the front of the house, Diane right behind her. "Paula, is someone here? Is Cam...oh my God!"

Blair skidded to a halt, barely stopping herself from throwing her arms around a beaming Mac Phillips. He was unnaturally pale, and whereas he'd always been slim and muscular, now he was simply thin. But his gaunt face was still handsome and his blue eyes bright and mercifully pain-free. She hadn't seen him for several weeks, and he had still been in the rehab center then, recovering from the gunshot wound that he had sustained while protecting her during the attack on the Aerie. "Oh my God. What are you doing here?"

Mac clasped Blair's hand, half shaking it, half holding it. "I got a call late this morning from the commander to pack my bags, and I'd barely finished when a Humvee with two of Tanner's people showed up, and...here I am."

"Did you know about this?" Blair asked Paula.

"No." Paula tried to look serious and in-charge, but she couldn't help grinning at their old team member. "Apparently it was arranged after we left DC." She carefully clasped Mac's shoulder. "How are you doing?"

"A hell of a lot better than I was yesterday. I'm officially cleared for light duty starting next week, but I've been sitting around all *this* week doing nothing but going crazy." He reached down for his suitcase but Wozinski grabbed it first.

"I have that, sir."

Mac raised an eyebrow. "Jesus, Greg. I'm not your boss."

Greg's face was totally serious. "No sir. Anything you need, just let me know, sir."

Mac looked perplexed, but Blair understood. Mac had almost died trying to save her, and when an agent was willing to make the ultimate sacrifice, other agents considered them heroes. The same thing had happened to Cam when Cam had been shot in the line of duty, and Cam was just as uncomfortable with the adulation as Mac seemed to be. Blair hooked her arm through Mac's and gave him a little hug. "Does Felicia know you're coming?"

"I'm not sure," Mac said, blushing and looking even more handsome. "She told me about her new posting with the commander." He met Paula's gaze. "And Renée's."

Paula nodded, realizing that they had more in common than ever. She and Mac were all that remained of the original team. They'd been together before the commander took over, and now they were the veterans. And they shared something else, something almost more critical...the women they loved were both part of the commander's OHS team. Renée and Felicia were involved in something potentially more dangerous than any of them had ever experienced. She squared her shoulders. "She's really happy about it, and I think it's exactly where she belongs."

"Yeah." Mac nodded. "Felicia too."

"Come on back to the kitchen," Blair said. "Are you hungry?"

"I could—" Mac broke off at the sound of footsteps on the front porch, and both he and Paula automatically stepped between Blair and the door, their shoulders touching, shielding her.

"It's Tanner," a voice called as a knock sounded.

Paula opened the door just enough to check outside, blocking the view into the room. After a second, she swung the door open and Tanner Whitley strode in with her characteristic saunter, a strikingly beautiful blonde in a naval uniform by her side.

"Mac," Tanner said. "I trust the trip went all right?" Without waiting for an answer, she kissed Blair soundly on the mouth. "You look terrific."

"You don't look too shabby either," Blair said, thinking that with her windblown dark hair, piercing dark eyes, and muscular build Tanner looked every inch the playgirl she had once been, rather than the head of a huge corporate conglomerate and the owner of Whitley Island. As usual, she was dressed in casual pants, an open collar shirt, and well-worn black boots. Blair smiled at the blonde who held Tanner's hand. Adrienne was more than a decade older than Tanner, and Blair had only to see Tanner with Adrienne to know that the new peace in Tanner's eyes was entirely due to Adrienne's presence in her life. The gold wedding bands they wore only affirmed what was obvious from seeing them together.

"Hello, Adrienne. How are you?" The last time Blair had seen Adrienne had been immediately after 9/11. Adrienne had been spending almost all of her time at the nearby naval base where she was stationed.

"Slightly less crazy than last time we met."

"I wish we weren't always dropping in on you quite so unexpectedly."

Adrienne's calm blue eyes held Blair's. "We're happy to have you, anytime, under any circumstances."

Blair was certain that Cam would not have confided any of the details surrounding their precipitous return to Whitley Point to Tanner, and she knew that Tanner would not have asked, but she understood Adrienne's message. Without even knowing the circumstances, Adrienne and Tanner would be there for them, whenever they were needed. To her horror, Blair felt her eyes sting with tears. "Thank you."

"Tanner, darling," Diane said, kissing Tanner's cheek. "Thank you for the wine and other essentials in the guest house." She extended her hand to Adrienne. "Thanks for taking such good care of us."

"If you need anything else that our security people can't get for you, just let us know. We'll see to it."

"How are you at pinochle?" Blair asked.

Stark groaned. Adrienne smiled.

❖

Just after midnight, the door to Blair's bedroom opened slowly and a thin shaft of pale yellow light slashed across the room.

"Cam?"

"Hi baby," Cam said. "Did I wake you?"

Blair rolled onto her side and turned on the bedside lamp. She canted the shade so that most of the light angled away from the bed and then sat up. "No. I wasn't sleeping. Are you all right?"

"Beat, but okay." Cam sighed as she crossed to the bed. "I'm going to take a shower and talk to Stark for a while, then I'll—"

"You don't have to shower and you can wait until tomorrow to talk to Stark. I want you to just come to bed."

Cam hesitated. "Okay. I'll wait until the morning briefing to check in with Stark. But the shower isn't optional."

"I like the way you smell," Blair said, folding back the covers and patting the bed beside her. "If you don't get in here soon, I'm going to think you're avoiding me."

"The only thing I've been thinking about for the last twelve hours is you." Cam kissed Blair, put her weapon in the top drawer of the bedside table, and undressed rapidly. "But I'm still going to shower. I'll be back in a few minutes."

Blair waited until she heard the shower running and then followed Cam into the bathroom. When Cam stepped out of the enclosure and reached for the towel that Blair held, Blair shook her head. "You just stand still. I'll do this."

"You know what I'd really like?" Cam said as Blair toweled her hair and then wiped her face and neck.

"No, darling, what?" Blair bit back a murmur of concern when she saw that the bruises on Cam's shoulder and hip had spread, darkening in the centers to almost black.

"I'd like that massage. I'm too damn tall to sleep in the back of an SUV."

Blair knew that if Cam was asking, she was more than stiff from sleeping in the car. She was hurting. "I think that can be arranged." She dried Cam's chest and stomach, then her back. Kneeling, she gently smoothed the towel over Cam's buttocks, down the outside of her legs, over her calves, and up her inner thighs. "Turn around, darling."

Slowly, Cam turned. She skimmed her fingers through Blair's hair and then over her cheek. "Feels good."

Tenderly, Blair dried Cam's thighs and hips, taking care with the bruise on the right side. "You're so beautiful."

"Let's go to bed," Cam said thickly.

Blair rose, her nipples tight beneath the T-shirt she had worn to bed. "Come on, I'm not done yet." She took Cam's hand and led her into the bedroom. "Lie on your stomach and get comfortable."

Cam complied, pillowing her head on her folded arms. When Blair knelt next to her, she said, "Aren't you getting undressed?"

"Not just yet." Blair decided it was safer if she kept her T-shirt and panties on. Although her only intention was to help Cam relax, she became aroused any time she touched her, for any reason. Starting at the back of Cam's neck, she worked her way down, pausing when she found the clusters of knotted muscles along the way and gently massaging them until they softened.

"Jesus," Cam muttered at one point, "that feels great."

Blair smiled. "Good. Now turn over."

Cam carefully flipped over. Her limbs felt loose, her mind more than a little hazy. She was also wet. Blair knelt beside her in a short T-shirt and skimpy panties, her hair down, her face void of any makeup. Her full breasts pressed against the thin cotton as she leaned forward, her hard nipples clearly visible. Cam swept her hand up Blair's side and cupped her breast.

"Stop that," Blair protested with more determination than she felt.

"I want to touch you," Cam murmured.

"Tonight is for you. Just relax."

Cam sighed but she felt so good she couldn't argue. She moved her hand to Blair's side and left it there as Blair worked.

Staying away from the bruise on Cam's right shoulder, Blair circled her thumbs along the muscles under her collarbone. Cam had a warrior's body—her sleek muscles long and tight, her breasts small and round. Her nipples were neat pink circles, as compact and hard as the rest of her body. Scars marked her chest and thigh—the gunshot wounds she had earned in battle. "I love you very much."

"Makes all the difference," Cam whispered.

Blair smiled. "I know." She stroked Cam's stomach, then worked her way down the front of Cam's legs. As she slowly skimmed her fingers along the insides of Cam's thighs, she felt a different kind of tension infuse her lover's body. She leaned down and kissed Cam's stomach, then rubbed her mouth over Cam's navel. "Feel good?"

Cam twisted her fingers in Blair's hair. She was so relaxed she could barely move, but every nerve was singing with arousal. "Not even close."

"That bad, huh?" Blair stretched out along Cam's uninjured side, resting her cheek in the center of Cam's stomach. She drew one leg up over Cam's and nestled her sex against Cam's calf. "If you promise to lie still, I'll see if I can make you feel better."

"You're hot," Cam whispered, drawing strands of Blair's hair through her fingers. "I can feel how hot you are against my leg."

"I am," Blair said, smoothing a fingertip up and down the cleft between Cam's thighs. "I'm very hot. And wet. That's what happens when I touch you."

Cam groaned softly. "Seems the same thing happens to me."

"Oh yeah?"

"See for yourself," Cam whispered, her fingers trembling as she caressed Blair's face.

"I love this," Blair said. "I love you. Now don't move."

Cam closed her eyes as Blair softly, ever so softly, massaged her clitoris until she climaxed. Blair moaned quietly, her mouth against Cam's stomach, her legs shaking as she rubbed against Cam's leg until she came.

"I didn't know it was possible to come without moving a muscle," Cam murmured, the last tendrils of tension bleeding away. "Jesus, I couldn't get up now if I had to."

"Good," Blair said lazily, turning on her back so she could reach the lamp to turn it off. She found the sheet and pulled it over them. "Because I'm not letting you get up. Maybe not for a couple of days." She turned on her side again and wrapped an arm around Cam's middle. "I'm so glad you're here."

Cam stroked Blair's hair and held her tightly. "I need to be here. I need you."

"I'm here. Go to sleep now, darling."

Morning would come soon enough, and when it did, the hunt would begin again. But for now, Cam accepted the peace that only Blair could bring her, and slept.

CHAPTER FOURTEEN

Thursday

M atheson smiled at the man who joined him on the steps of the Lincoln Memorial. He was much younger, a stocky redhead in neatly pressed work pants and a brown leather bomber jacket with an American flag patch stitched onto the sleeve. They shook hands and moved off to one side of the rotunda as a maintenance worker began polishing the stone floor with an electric buffer. The noise made conversation difficult, but it also provided excellent cover.

"How are things at the new compound, Colonel?" Matheson asked his freshly-promoted second-in-command.

"The men have nearly finished the barracks, sir."

"How is morale?" Matheson had lost some of his best officers during the Special Ops raid on his compound in Tennessee. Unfortunately, many of his ground troops were unseasoned volunteers who had never faced combat or even given any thought to what a real battle might be like. Now he needed to rebuild his paramilitary force and relocate his base, and some of the men—mostly truck drivers and other blue-collar workers—were beginning to realize that they weren't just playing at being weekend soldiers. There was a war on. And war meant casualties.

"We lost about twenty percent of our original force to desertion, in addition to those who were captured," the redhead reported. "But we're adding new men at twice the normal rate since 9/11. The patriots are rising across the nation in response to the attack."

As we predicted, Matheson thought. The only reason that he and his patriot brothers had been willing to aid the foreign insurgents was to further their own agenda. An attack on American soil was guaranteed to rally the loyal. Now, with more men joining them every day, he and his compatriots could consolidate their power base and expand their sphere of influence.

"The FBI will undoubtedly accelerate their attempts to infiltrate our ranks now, so be vigilant," Matheson said.

"Yes sir. We're screening carefully." The redhead hesitated. "Have we resolved the problem with the security breakdown here, sir?"

Matheson shook his head. "Not yet. Take this lesson to heart, my friend. Never rely too strongly on anyone but your most trusted brothers-in-arms." He clamped a hand on the younger man's shoulder. "But, despite the unreliability of dealing with bureaucrats and low-level informants, it's also useful to have sources inside the system. We may be able to deal with all our problems another way."

"Sir?"

"I was advised that the White House press secretary released an interesting tidbit last night," Matheson said. "Blair Powell and her deviant secret service guard intend to hold a so-called *wedding* ceremony. I imagine the papers will have that this morning."

The redhead grunted. "She's an embarrassment to the entire country."

"But the timing is good for us. If a morally outraged man—or woman—were to put a stop to them, we'd fulfill our mission to destabilize President Powell's administration, and we'd cut off a possible return route for our missing CIA agent."

"And *we* could disavow any involvement."

"Exactly. Let's call on our friends to activate someone, preferably a member of one of the splinter groups—someone expendable who won't be traceable to us or our Conservative Coalition allies."

"What should I tell them about the target, sir?"

"That we want both neutralized, but Roberts should be the priority."

"Do we have their location, sir?"

Matheson grimaced. "No, we've lost them temporarily, but Powell's official schedule of appearances is updated daily."

"A public assault is a suicide mission," the redhead said mildly.

"All the better, as long as he—or she—takes the targets out first."

"Yes sir."

The men shook hands.

"Godspeed, Colonel."

"God bless America, General."

❖

When Blair awoke, she was surprised to discover that Cam had gotten out of bed without waking her. Ordinarily she was a light sleeper, but she had lain awake for a long time the night before, after Cam had fallen asleep in her arms. Partly, she'd still been wound up from worrying about Cam all day, but it was more than that. Felicia and Renée were staying in the guesthouse, which had been transformed into an ad hoc office for the OHS. Her security team had relocated to the main house, and Mac was probably already setting up a command center in the dining room downstairs. Diane remained in the main house at Paula's suggestion, which made it easier to protect her as well. The new arrangements made it impossible to deny that she was living in a high security complex. And now her lover was a deputy director in a national security organization that had not existed two months before. Blair was faced with the cold hard realization that, even when her father was no longer president, her life was not suddenly going to be normal. This *was* normal, and it was what she'd been fighting to avoid all her life.

Blair rolled over and opened the bedside table. Cam's weapon wasn't there, because she was wearing it. Because even in this, their soon-to-be new home, they weren't entirely safe. She walked to the window to look out over the dunes to the ocean. There was no one in sight. Even the fishing trawlers were so far out to sea they were no more than dots on the horizon. She was as alone here as she had ever been, and she should have felt free, but she didn't. With a sigh, she pushed her melancholy aside and went to look for her lover.

She found Cam in the kitchen, leaning against the counter drinking coffee. She wore her casual work attire—chinos and a button-down collar shirt—and her weapon.

"Did you eat something?" Blair asked as she placed a hand in the center of Cam's stomach and kissed her. Then she sidled around her to pour her own cup of coffee.

"I had some toast. You want some?"

"No thanks." Blair kept her back turned. "I'll grab some later. How's your shoulder and hip?"

"Fine." Cam set her mug down and caught Blair's wrist before she could slip away. "What's the matter?"

Blair smiled and brushed her fingers over Cam's chest again. "Nothing."

Cam waited until Blair had sipped her coffee, then plucked the cup from her hand and deposited it next to hers on the counter. Then she threaded her arms around Blair's waist and pulled her gently against her body. She kissed Blair a little bit longer than her normal morning hello, and then studied Blair's eyes. "Something happen I should know about?"

"Just a case of the blahs," Blair said lightly. She nipped at Cam's chin. "Really. Go to work."

"You'll tell me when you're ready, right?" Cam murmured, placing another kiss gently on Blair's temple.

"Mmm hmm," Blair sighed.

"Ready now?"

Laughing, Blair pressed her mouth to the hollow at the base of Cam's throat. "I've forgotten how persistent you are. I was just thinking that what you do, what you all do, isn't confined to some office in a building in DC or Langley anymore. It's everywhere, wherever *you* are. Wherever we are. Even here."

Cam caressed Blair's back. "I wish I hadn't had to bring this into our home. I wish it didn't touch you, or us. As soon as I can, I'll move the team—"

Blair shushed her with a kiss, sliding her hands into Cam's hair and melding her body a little more tightly to Cam's. She felt Cam's heart beat against her breast and the muscles in Cam's stomach and thighs tighten. She felt the connection that held her secure no matter where she was, no matter what was happening, and realized that just as the danger was part of their life, no matter where they were, so was their love. And that mattered more to her than any place on Earth. She stroked Cam's neck as she leaned back in her arms. "That's not necessary. I'd rather you and the others work here if it's the most secure location." She pressed her hand to Cam's heart. "This is my safe place."

Cam's eyes darkened and she held Blair more tightly. The next kiss was rougher, longer, deeper.

"Cam," Blair said just a little breathlessly. "One word."

"What," Cam growled, sliding her hands under the back of Blair's T-shirt.

"Briefing."

Cam hesitated. "What?"

Blair laughed and bumped her pelvis into Cam's crotch. "I love to make you forget yourself, but…what time is your briefing with Felicia and Renée?"

"Hell," Cam muttered, tracing the edge of Blair's ear with her mouth. "How did you know I had one?"

"Because it's morning and you always brief in the morning." Blair murmured appreciatively and closed her eyes as Cam sucked her earlobe. Cam's breath was quick and hot against her neck. Nothing aroused her more than Cam's desire. "Careful."

"I was tired and sore when I got home last night," Cam whispered, kissing her way down the pulse that shimmered in Blair's throat. "I'm not anymore." She nipped at Blair's neck when Blair tilted her head back with a sigh. "And I didn't thank you yet for the massage."

Blair caught her breath as Cam skimmed her fingers around her sides and over her stomach. When Cam stroked higher, brushing the undersurfaces of her breasts, her nipples tightened in anticipation of a caress. She was dangerously close to not caring if Cam had a briefing or if Diane came looking for her any minute to take a walk on the beach, which was their habit. "You have two seconds to decide—either move your hands or be late for your briefing. Because if you get me any more excited, I'll have to come, and since you started it, I expect *you* to take care of that."

"You started it." Cam was seriously considering delaying the briefing when a discreet cough from the doorway caught her attention. She lifted her head from Blair's neck and found herself staring at Tanner Whitley.

"Sorry," Tanner said, grinning broadly, "but Stark said to come on back."

"Remind me to speak to her about that," Cam muttered.

Blair pushed Cam's hands away and spun around, leaning her back against Cam's front. "Tanner!"

"I was in the neighborhood."

"Ha ha. You live next door." Blair drew Cam's arms around her middle and folded hers over them. "What's up?"

"Well, I *was* wondering if you and Diane were up for a little trip to see what I've been doing at the marina." She slid her hands into the pockets of her khakis and rocked back and forth, still grinning. "But I get the feeling this isn't a good time."

"It's a great time," Blair said emphatically. She tilted her head back and kissed the side of Cam's jaw. "Cam has to go to work and I don't have anything planned until this afternoon. Once the light's a little better, I'm going to paint."

"I'll let Stark know so she can organize your teams," Cam said as she carefully loosened her hold on Blair. She would have preferred that Blair stay close to the compound, but that wasn't her call anymore. Plus, the whole team would be heading to Boston the next day for the fundraiser. Maybe if Blair had the opportunity to relax today she might not resent the upcoming restrictions so much.

She kissed Blair lightly. "Have fun. I'm heading down to the guesthouse."

"See you later, darling."

"You will," Cam murmured.

"Sorry about that," Tanner said after Cam had left. She strode across the kitchen and looked out the back door. A member of her private security force stood guard on the rear deck. "When Stark asked me to assign some of my security officers here, she requested the ones with military training. Combat troops." She turned to face Blair. "I know you can't tell me anything, but I just wanted you to know that Adrienne and I are prepared to do whatever you need us to do."

"You two have done enough. I'm not even sure we should have come back here." Blair loved the island and she loved this house. But part of what made the property so perfect for their needs was that it abutted Tanner's estate. They had no year-round neighbors to the north and Tanner's house, which occupied half of the island, was less than a mile down the beach—close by if they needed her, but far enough away for privacy. "I feel like I'm taking advantage of our friendship. And Adrienne shouldn't feel obligated—"

"Adrienne is a naval officer. Do you think I could convince her that it *wasn't* her duty to assist you in any way possible?"

"God, this is hard."

Tanner walked over to her and put her arms around her. "It is. But it would be harder if you didn't let us help."

Blair rested her forehead on Tanner's shoulders. "You're helping. Not just with your security people, but because you understand. Thank you."

"You're welcome. So, let's get Diane and go cruising."

Blair laughed at the line that Tanner had always used when they were planning to sneak out for a night of partying. She squeezed Tanner's hand, grateful that despite all the changes, the love that the three of them had forged had never faltered. "I'm afraid this time, we're not going to be able to duck security."

"No problem," Tanner said, grinning. "I've already pissed off your lover once today. I'm not about to push my luck."

❖

"So," Cam said, taking a chair across from Davis and Savard at the sleek glass and wood table that now served as their conference table. They had turned the first floor of the guesthouse into their base of operations. Davis had the computers up and running and networked. The dining room did duty as their file room. All things considered, it was a better working area than the converted storage closet they would have worked out of in the West Wing. "Let's prioritize."

No one took notes. Everyone understood that there would be no reports generated by their work, and the only files would be the ones they appropriated from other security agencies.

"First order of business is to find Matheson, because we have to assume that there will be another attack on Egret. He and his organization will lose credibility if a failed attempt is allowed to stand." Cam carefully kept her voice and face from showing her rage. "We can assume he will either establish a new paramilitary base of his own or join forces with another one. He'll need a network in order to reestablish himself."

"A guy like that won't give up control easily," Savard said. She wore jeans and a dark blue polo shirt. She'd pulled her hair back into a loose ponytail, and she looked more rested than Cam had seen her in weeks.

Cam nodded and pointed the pen she'd been rolling between her fingers at Davis. "He didn't do much to hide the compound in Tennessee because he didn't expect us to come after him. This time he'll take more precautions. Background him—his family by blood and marriage, the military academy and its faculty, donors to the school, previous graduates—anyone who might have purchased or inherited land. For now, I'd prefer a covert examination of the academy files, because anything else is going to tip him off." She shrugged. "But the academy is the logical place to start. We know he recruits there. If I have to, I'll confiscate every scrap of paper in the entire place."

"The FBI should have files on the other patriot organizations," Savard said, "and if he's ever so much as made a phone call to one of their leaders, there should be a record of it somewhere." She grimaced. "The biggest problem is the files are so decentralized it's practically impossible to search them."

"Try."

"Yes ma'am," Savard said smartly. "We might get something from the interrogations of his captured personnel too, if the Company hasn't buried the intel by now."

"See what you can find there," Cam said, pleased with Savard's natural instincts for counterintelligence. She'd need that kind of back-up from her second-in-command. "And that brings us to the problem of Valerie Lawrence. We need to know who her Company handler is and determine if there's a link to Matheson."

Davis took a breath. "Due respect, Commander, but there won't be any records of Lawrence's handler. It's not like they keep employment files."

"I know," Cam said, "and that's just one reason why we need to bring Valerie in."

"We don't know if Matheson only uses men he recruited from his military academy. She could be his mole," Davis said. "Just like Foster."

"She could be. I don't think she is." Cam expected her people to examine every option, and Davis's comment didn't bother her. "But until we've proven it one way or the other, she has to be considered potentially hostile."

"How do we find her?" Savard asked.

Cam sighed. "Our only link is Diane. We have to hope Valerie tries to meet with her again and that Diane trusts me enough to tell me. In the meantime, we've got Foster and the four dead commandos from the assault on the Aerie. We know they were all at Matheson's military academy. Maybe that's not their only connection."

"We really need someone who's an expert on these paramilitary organizations," Savard said. "I bet all of these guys know each other."

"I'll work on that." Absently, Cam rubbed her sore shoulder. "Blair is scheduled to make a public appearance Saturday night at a fundraiser in Boston. I'd like you two to assist with the security detail. I know it's not in your job description any longer, and Stark's doing a great job integrating Tanner's people, but I'll feel better if we had seasoned agents for this. It's her first solo appearance since 9/11."

"Of course," Savard said, joining Davis in accepting the assignment. "Do you think they'll try again so soon?"

"I don't know." Cam tried not to let her fury, or her seething sense of frustration, show. "But we can't afford to think they won't."

CHAPTER FIFTEEN

S o, what do you think of the place?" With a sweep of her arm Tanner indicated the world-class yachting marina tucked into a deep, narrow inlet on the ocean side of the island. Wrapping one arm around Blair's shoulders and the other around Diane's waist, she led the two women to the end of the longest pier. Sailboats and cruisers were moored in the slips along either side. The charterhouse and a luxury hotel completed the accommodations. "You like it?"

"It's amazing," Blair said. "Somehow you've managed to do all this and still keep the untamed feel of the rest of the island."

"It's great," Diane said, echoing Blair's sentiment. She hugged Tanner. "I admit, I never thought you'd settle down enough to run the family business, let alone do something like this. I figured you'd be lying out on some beach with a string of bored, horny cover girls—breaking their hearts—until you were fifty or so."

"I might have been." Tanner grinned, then her expression sobered. "Except I don't know that I would've made it to fifty. I was a little crazy before Adrienne."

Blair shook her head fondly. "God, she certainly has tamed you."

"Ah, look who's talking." Tanner hip-bumped Blair playfully. "Who would have guessed you'd pick a spooky to marry!"

"Yeah yeah," Blair said. "Come on, let's get off the pier. It's freezing in this wind."

"I have to run up to the charterhouse for a second to check something," Tanner said, "then I'll meet you at the car." She tossed Blair her keys. "Turn the heater on and warm her up for me. Kind of like old times."

"Your charm doesn't work on me, Whitley. So I'd watch your step." As Tanner laughed and hurried away, Blair grasped Diane's hand

and studied her worriedly. "You okay? Tanner and I rhapsodizing about the joys of settling down must be tough for you to hear right now."

Diane nodded. "I'm happy for you. Both of you."

"I know that. But these tears aren't from the wind." Blair gently brushed at the moisture on Diane's cheeks. "You look worn out."

"I'm okay. I'm just not sleeping very well."

"Or eating very well." Blair loosed an exasperated sigh as she keyed the remote to Tanner's SUV. She pointed for Diane to get into the front passenger seat as she got behind the wheel and started the engine. "It's not going to do anyone any good if you make yourself sick."

"It's hard not to think about it all the time," Diane whispered. "It's hard not to wonder where she is. Not to wonder if someone's hurt—" she looked away, her voice breaking.

"You don't have as much experience with this kind of waiting, of not knowing or understanding what's going on, as I have," Blair said emphatically. "And I'm glad. But now you've fallen in love with someone whose whole life has been a secret. She's always going to have secrets, Diane, and you can't let that eat you up."

Diane regarded Blair as if seeing her for the first time. "How do you handle it with Cam?"

"Not very well most of the time," Blair said, grinning sheepishly. "After a while you accept that there are parts of themselves they don't, or can't, let us see. And once you're done being pissed off by it, you understand that those are the parts that make them frighteningly good at what they do. Valerie has to be that kind of good to have ever fooled Cam."

Diane smiled weakly. "I guess the fact that my girlfriend and your girlfriend have a history makes some kind of cosmic sense, doesn't it?"

"That just might be the understatement of the year." Blair laughed briefly, thinking of the night she'd unexpectedly discovered Valerie at Cam's apartment in DC, and recognizing their connection, how much she had resented the place Valerie held in Cam's heart. Cam swore that there was nothing between them any longer, and Blair knew that Cam believed it. But she had seen something that Cam had not. There had been a sadness in Valerie's eyes that Blair understood with perfect clarity. Valerie had been deeply in love with Cam. Thinking about that sadness now, Blair found that she no longer resented what Valerie and

Cam had shared. Valerie had been there when Cam needed someone, and that was all that really mattered.

"She'll need you, Di. She'll need you, but she won't let you know." Blair reached for Diane's hand. "That's the hardest thing to remember—that the need is there, even though it's buried so deeply even she can't see it. It's a pain in the ass, but you'll just have to get used to it. I know you're strong enough, and stubborn enough, to do it."

"I don't feel very strong sometimes."

"Then that's when you come find me, and I'll remind you."

"It helps to be with you, and I usually love Whitley Point," Diane confessed, "but the quiet is driving me a little bit crazy right now. I've got too much time to think. Maybe I should go back to Manhattan."

Blair shook her head vehemently. "Not a chance. I want you to come to the fundraiser Saturday night. And if Paula can take it, we'll go shopping again."

"Okay." Diane laughed shakily as she glanced out the rear of the vehicle to where Stark and Hara sat in the Suburban. "If I have to suffer, I suppose she can too."

"There, see? You're sounding better already," Blair said, smiling. "Here comes Tanner. I'll get in the back."

As Blair stepped from the car, she caught sight of Tanner's expression and stopped. "What is it?"

Tanner handed her the Boston Globe. "I don't know how you put up with this shit all the time." She slid into the front seat and slammed the door.

Blair glanced down at the grainy picture of her in Paris with Cam standing just behind her. The caption read "President's daughter to marry lesbian lover—Anti-same sex marriage groups protest."

"Well," Blair said as she climbed into the backseat, "Boston is looking a lot more interesting."

She leaned her head back and closed her eyes, trying not to think about the crush of reporters sure to be waiting for her when she arrived at the fundraiser. She had wanted to go public, because any attempt *not* to would make her and her father appear like hypocrites when news of her plans inevitably leaked out. Nothing could be worse for a politician than the appearance of having one set of standards in public and another in private. She'd insisted on disclosure, but it was never easy exposing her personal life to public scrutiny.

"Let me see that," Diane said.

"Hey Tanner," Blair said, handing the newspaper to Diane as Tanner rocketed the SUV out of the parking lot and onto the narrow twisting road that hugged the ocean shoreline. Gravel spewed out behind them.

"What?" Tanner snapped.

"It's okay. It's just another day at the office."

"It sucks."

"Yeah, that, too." Blair leaned forward and squeezed Tanner's shoulder. "But try not to give Stark a heart attack and slow down a little."

Tanner half turned her head, a grin pulling at her mouth. Then she looked back to the road and eased off on the gas. "Sorry, force of habit. I'm used to you telling me to lose your spookies."

"Yes," Blair said softly. "How things have changed."

❖

Cam's jaw tightened as she scanned the newspaper. "Call Lucinda and tell her you're canceling for the fundraiser."

Blair braced both arms on the kitchen counter behind her and lifted herself up so that she was sitting on it. She still wore the blue jeans and red sweater she'd pulled on to go out with Tanner. Cam was in her work clothes and still wearing her weapon, and although Blair knew it was foolish, the additional height advantage made her feel better. "I wouldn't do that even if it would do any good, which it won't. Once Lucinda makes up her mind—"

"Lucinda is the president's chief of staff, not yours." Cam tossed the newspaper onto the oak table and started for the front of the house. "If you'd prefer, I'll tell Stark to call her."

"I'm sure Stark will appreciate that."

Cam turned, her eyes narrowing. "What is that supposed to mean?"

"I know about the whole rank thing, but she's still my chief of security. I don't imagine she'll appreciate being *told* anything. You never did."

"Stark understands the situation," Cam said, thinking about the briefing with Davis and Savard, and about Blair at a crowded cocktail reception where it would be impossible to control the guest list or secure the physical environment beyond the most basic measures. Thinking how exposed Blair would be. A ball of anger and anxiety filled her chest. "The timing is bad, especially after this newspaper article."

"We've already discussed this, Cameron. If it isn't this event, it will be some other one. We can't prevent a public response to anything we do."

"Why do you sound so calm?" Cam moved closer, but stopped two feet away. Just outside of touching distance.

"Because I know you're not, and I know you're worried." Blair kept her hands on the counter, because she wanted to reach out and pull Cam across the divide. It was odd how she hated distance between them now. Once she had wanted, *demanded*, nothing but distance between herself and anyone who had the potential to hurt her. Mostly she resisted the urge to draw Cam near because she needed to judge exactly how much of Cam's concern was her normal distrust of any public appearance and how much was a lover's less rational concern. If she touched her, her perspective would be gone. "Why are you so much more worried about this event?"

"Jesus, Blair! Maybe you've forgotten what happened—" Cam bit off the rest of the sentence, cursing herself inwardly when she saw Blair flinch. Of course Blair hadn't forgotten the assassination attempt at the Aerie. Blair would never be able to forget it, and bullying her with the memory instead of explaining her own unease was cowardly. And cruel. "I'm sorry, baby."

Blair took a long breath. "Don't apologize. Just trust me."

Cam fell silent and Blair watched her struggle, waiting.

"I don't feel like I've got a handle on anything right now, and I can't afford to be wrong when your safety is at stake." Cam took one step closer and rested her fingertips lightly on the outside of Blair's thighs. "No one knows what really happened in September. We don't know how much of the attack was orchestrated outside the country and what part insurgents inside the country might have played. But we know someone got very very close to you." She hesitated.

"Say it, Cameron. All of it." Blair pressed Cam's hands to her legs, covering them with her own. She'd been wrong about not being able to think when Cam touched her. As the distance dissipated she could hear her far more clearly.

"There's no reason to think they won't try again," Cam said. "Until we have Matheson, until we have Valerie, the risk is greater than I'm comfortable with."

"I'm not the only one at risk," Blair said softly. "Have you forgotten someone tried to run you down?"

"That might not even be related."

Blair gave her a look. "What does Stark say about Saturday?"

Irritation flared in Cam's dark eyes. "I haven't discussed it with her."

"Because…"

Cam grimaced. "Because I haven't managed the transition to her as your security chief very well."

"You take a lot on yourself, Commander."

"I love you," Cam whispered.

"Oh I know." Blair said. "What if you don't find either Matheson or Valerie?"

"We will."

"All right, *until* you find them, what do you suggest I do? It could be months. Years."

"Are you *trying* to make me say things that will piss you off?"

"Well, I do enjoy makeup sex." Blair lifted Cam's hand and kissed the top of it. "But I'm trying something new. I'm working on being reasonable and rational."

"I think maybe you're more dangerous this way than when you're flat-out furious," Cam grumbled. She eased forward until she was completely between Blair's legs, then wrapped her arms around Blair's waist and pulled her forward until Blair's crotch rested against her middle.

"I'm not ready for the makeup sex yet," Blair whispered, wrapping her arms around Cam's neck. "So don't get any closer."

Cam rested her forehead against Blair's. "You're calling the shots."

"Hardly," Blair murmured, running her fingers through Cam's hair. "I understand why you're not happy about the fundraiser, but it was scheduled months ago and if I cancel now, it will seem as if we're afraid. Add to that the newspaper headlines this morning, and it will also look like I'm ashamed of us. Neither of those things is true. It's not going to get any better, darling, because if it's not Matheson, there will be someone or something else that poses a threat."

"Unfortunately, you're right." Cam sighed. "Assuming we do this, there are going to be a lot more press than usual."

Blair grimaced. "I know."

"Have you given any thought to what you're going to say about the wedding?"

"Well, if it's all right with you, I was thinking that I'd say that I'm deeply in love with you and plan to spend the rest of my life with you, and since that's traditionally the situation when people get married, that's my plan, too." Blair nuzzled Cam's neck. "What are you going to say?"

Cam grinned and kissed Blair. "If it's all right with you, I just thought I'd say that I've never met anyone who was better in bed, so it seemed like marrying you was the smart thing to do."

"Really?" Blair skimmed her lips along the edge of Cam's jaw.

"Really." Cam dragged Blair another inch forward, her hands cupping Blair's butt.

"I think I like your reasoning," Blair whispered.

"And I think we need to finish this conversation in private."

Blair nibbled on Cam's neck, then bit her. "See, it's not so difficult for us to come to an agreement."

CHAPTER SIXTEEN

Saturday

You're not ready for field duty," Paula said.

Renée clipped her Sig Sauer to the waistband of her flaring black silk pants, settling the pistol at the middle of her back. Then she pulled a dark green, notched collared jacket on over her black shell and closed it loosely with a wide belt. She checked first that the lie of the jacket was smooth, concealing her holstered weapon, and then that she could draw unencumbered by any snag in her clothing. Satisfied that the short jacket covered her weapon but wasn't going to interfere with it, she checked her makeup in the mirror over the dresser. After slipping into black heels, high enough for a formal event but low enough to run in, she walked over to sit next to Paula on the sofa in their hotel room.

"I'm Diane's escort. It's not exactly field duty."

"You're splitting hairs. Just because you're wearing a fancy outfit," Paula said, smoothing her hand up and down Renée's thigh, "doesn't mean you're not providing protection."

"I know, sweetie." Renée caught Paula's hand and held it. "And I promise if all the standing around starts to get to me, I'll signal for help. But I can handle this. Really."

Paula sighed. "I'm not doubting you. I'm just a little worried."

"Of what?"

"Has it occurred to you that we're all operating off the radar ever since we left Washington?"

"You mean because we're not reporting to some desk jockey who doesn't know what it is that we do half the time anyway?"

Paula laughed. "Yeah, I think that's what I mean."

"Sweetie, we're on Cameron Roberts's radar. I'll take her being in charge over some SAC or deputy director I've never seen and who's never had my back in a firefight. What about you?"

"Yeah, me too."

Renée slipped her arm around Paula's waist and turned her lover's face toward hers with one finger on her chin. "I'm really okay. You know that, right?"

"You still looked tired," Paula said, adding quickly, "*but*, I can tell you're feeling better."

"Oh yeah?" Renée kissed her lightly on the lips. "How?"

Paula grinned. "You're sleeping better."

Renée kissed her again, a little more firmly. "Is that all?"

"You're walking better. No cane."

"Mmm-hmm," Renée said, trailing a line of kisses along the edge of Paula's jaw.

"Honey," Paula said just a little breathlessly. "We'll mess your makeup."

"Oh, like I care," Renée whispered.

"You know I can't have sex before a big game." Paula eased away. "It saps my strength and makes my brain sluggish."

Laughing, Savard skimmed her hand inside Paula's jacket and over her breasts. "Are you afraid you'll forget all the big plays and run toward the wrong end zone?"

Paula jumped up and backed away. "No fair touching when you're just teasing. You know I get excited."

Renée's eyes glittered. "Do you now?"

"Renée," Paula said, hearing her own voice rise with a combination of excitement and nerves. "I'm leaving now. I'm going to Wozinski's room for the briefing." She held out her arm, palm facing forward. "*Don't* get up."

"I know the schedule. You're not briefing for an hour, Chief."

"I want to review everything by myself, first."

Renée smiled. "Okay sweetie. I know you've got a lot on your mind." She rose and kissed Paula on the cheek. "But when we're back here tonight, I'm going to show you just how much I've recovered."

"I'll look forward to a demonstration. Be careful tonight."

"You too, sweetie."

❖

Cam tapped on the hotel room door, feeling like an interloper. Stark, in a smartly tailored navy blue suit and white shirt, answered.

"Do you mind if I sit in on your briefing, Chief?"

"No, come on in."

When Stark stepped aside, Cam nodded her thanks and entered the dimly lit suite. The drapes over the windows were closed and the overhead lights turned off, leaving only the scattered table lamps for illumination. The effect was oddly intimate. Cam strode directly to one of the empty chairs grouped around the coffee table in the seating area, nodding to Mac, Wozinski, and Hara as she sat down. Stark returned to the chair in the center of the group.

"We were just reviewing the exit routes, Commander."

"Go ahead," Cam said. "Sorry to interrupt."

"No problem," Stark said quickly and handed Cam a printout. "The timetable, shift assignments, and agent placements are all outlined there."

Cam glanced at it briefly. It was thorough and complete, as she anticipated it would be. It wasn't the things they planned for that concerned her. It was the threat of the unanticipated that had her pacing in the suite across the hall until Blair had strongly suggested that she ask to sit in on the pre-departure briefing. So now Cam found herself in the awkward position of being an observer.

She was on the verge of getting up and leaving when Stark pushed the papers aside and said, "Is there something in particular you wanted to review, Commander?"

Cam cleared her throat. "First of all, I just wanted everyone to be clear that I'm here because Blair threw me out, not because Stark needs any help."

Stark smiled and the other agents laughed.

"Well," Cam continued. "I'm definitely more use over here than across the hall right now." She addressed Stark. "I don't suppose metal detectors are feasible, considering that the reception is in the open mezzanine?"

"We could insist that everyone use one escalator and one bank of elevators, but I think we'd get a major logjam as a result. That kind of chaos sometimes makes it easier to overlook things."

"I tend to agree. Plus," Cam said with a sigh, "it rather defeats the purpose of having Blair make a public appearance if we ramp up the security measures to the point where it's obvious we're worried."

"I'm not worried, Commander," Stark said steadily. "As far as I'm concerned, every time Egret makes a public appearance, we have to assume she is a target. That's the only way to do the job."

After a moment of complete silence, Cam said, "You're absolutely right, Chief." She glanced at the others. "Perimeter coverage?"

"I get to sit this one out in the surveillance van," Mac said, unrolling a schematic and spreading it out facing Cam. He pointed to a red X with a circle around it. "Here. The other vehicle will be at the south entrance." He pointed to a blue X. "Here. One of Tanner's men will drive that vehicle."

He then opened another schematic of the ballroom. "Exits…here, here, here, and here. Also covered by Tanner's people."

"Are we using the local field agents?" Cam asked.

"No," Stark said. "I decided that Tanner's team has just as much experience, maybe more. And we're already used to working with them."

"Good call," Cam murmured. She was as certain as she could be that the local Secret Service agents were not compromised, but they also weren't as likely to fit seamlessly into their current team as Tanner's security personnel were. Under the circumstances, she would have made the same decision.

"Savard will be with Diane," Cam said. "We have to assume Diane is a potential target as well." She glanced at Stark. "But Savard still has mobility issues. She'll be fine at close range, but you're going to need mobile backup for her."

Stark never changed expression. "Already taken care of."

"Did anything turn up in the doctor's background?" Cam asked, referring to the keynote speaker. "Threats, angry protesters, anything that might spill over tonight?"

Stark nodded to Mac, who opened a file folder. "Emory Constantine. She's thirty-one years old, has been at the Johnson Institute for five years, and received a sizable federal grant matched by the Institute two years ago. Has a bunch of recent publications and is considered one of the front runners in stem cell research in the world."

"Young for that," Cam observed.

"Apparently she was one of the few to see the writing on the wall before anyone else. She did a lot of the preliminary work while she was still an undergraduate. A case of good timing and, from what I've been able to find out, a lot of brains."

"Personal life?"

"Not much there. Lives in Beacon Hill in the family residence with her mother, divorced, no children."

"Threat assessment?"

Hara spoke up. "There have been right-to-life protesters at the last three seminars where Constantine has been a headliner. This guy," she passed out photographs, "was arrested at the last one for physically threatening her as she left the podium. Alexander Frenkel. There's a restraining order on him now. If he shows up within five hundred feet of her, he goes to jail."

"Everyone has his picture," Stark said. "He's not registered at the hotel, at least not under that name."

"These four," Hara went on, fanning out another set of images like playing cards, "have been observed at two out of the last three locations where Constantine made a public appearance."

Cam frowned. "Affiliations?"

"Three belong to different groups, but the fourth doesn't appear to have any group connections at all," Hara replied. "Two are fetal rights activists, one is a pro-lifer, and the loner is an unknown commodity."

"Who's providing this intelligence?" Cam asked.

"Local FBI," Mac said. "They've kept a file on the doctor since another stem cell researcher—James Bennett—was attacked in a car park a year ago. The injuries kept him in the hospital for two months."

"Did the victim have any relationship to Constantine?"

"None other than the fact that they knew each other professionally," Mac said.

Stark said, "We anticipate the usual demonstrators tonight. We'll bring Egret in through the side entrance, because the protesters will most likely be out front where they'll get more press coverage. The hotel can legally bar them from entering, so once we're inside, she'll be in the clear from the majority of the organized dissenters."

"What do you have on local anti-gay factions?" Cam asked.

"A few religious groups, but they're mostly involved with debates over the church recognizing gay priests and performing same-sex marriages," Stark answered.

"None of them with a history of violence?"

"No."

"The press will be all over her tonight, and we're not going to keep them out of the banquet. It's a fundraiser, and I'm sure the PR people from the institute will want reporters present." Cam shook her head. "It's going to be a long night."

"There's one other issue, Commander," Stark said.

Cam gave her a questioning look.

"You were targeted this week, so we have to assume you're at risk. Wozinski will cover y—"

"No," Cam said flatly. "I appreciate it, Chief, but don't pull someone off Blair's detail for me. I don't need it."

"With respect—"

Cam stood. "I'm officially refusing, Stark. You already have two to cover—Blair as the primary and Diane as the secondary. You don't have the people to cover anyone else. Are we clear?"

"Yes ma'am," Stark said tightly.

"Thank you."

❖

"You ready for this?" Blair asked Diane, who sat across from her in the rear of the limo. Renée Savard sat next to her and anyone who didn't know better would think they made an amazing looking couple. Diane, slightly taller and more willowy than Renée, wore a fitted cobalt blue evening gown with a halter tie and keyhole openings in the bodice. Renée's jacket and pants were equally elegant. It was obvious to Blair that Renée walked just slightly ahead of Diane and scanned the surroundings with every step. Blair noticed the subtle surveillance because Cam always did the same thing.

Now Diane peered through the bulletproof, one-way glass as the armored limo, courtesy of the Boston Secret Service office, slowed at the side entrance of the Ritz-Carlton. "There are fewer press here than for one of your gallery openings." She smiled at Blair, but her eyes were sad. "I was hoping to get a chance to plug your next show."

Blair laughed, appreciating Diane's fortitude. She hoped that the evening would at least provide a diversion for her for a few hours. She settled her hand onto Cam's thigh, absently running her fingertips along the seam of the silk tuxedo pants. "Most of them are probably out front, don't you think?"

"Yes," Cam said. "But it won't take long for them to figure out where we are."

"Well, then," Blair pushed the door open as the limo stopped at the curb, "let's make them run for it."

With a muffled oath, Cam jumped out and surreptitiously grasped Blair's hand. "God damn it, Blair, wait."

Stark barreled out of the front and rushed to Blair's opposite side. Renée and Diane moved up behind them with Hara following.

"Sorry, darling," Blair said lightly, hooking her arm through Cam's. "We've got cameras on the left and people waving signs off to the right."

"I see them," Cam muttered, keeping her expression neutral as Blair smiled briefly in the direction of the photographers.

When several called out questions to Blair, she waved but didn't answer, pretending she hadn't heard them. She pointedly ignored those calling on God or whatever other powers they believed in to punish her for her sinful ways.

"Lovely," Diane said from close behind.

Cam reached for the hotel door and found Stark there before her.

"Go ahead please," Stark said. "The escalators to the mezzanine are directly to your right."

Cam hesitated for just a second, then moved through with Blair by her side.

"You're just my date, remember?" Blair murmured.

"Sorry," Cam muttered.

"Don't be."

Blair and Cam joined the crowd on the mezzanine and a moment later, a small, compact brunette in a black evening dress approached. Even in heels, she was of average height, but her dynamic expression and confident carriage made her presence seem larger.

"Ms. Powell." She extended her hand. "I'm so honored that you could come this evening. I'm Emory Constantine."

"Dr. Constantine," Blair said, taking the researcher's hand. "Thank you. My partner, Cameron Roberts, and my good friends Diane Bleeker and Renée Savard."

"Agent Roberts, a pleasure." Emory Constantine shook hands with Cam, then indicated the open doors to the banquet hall behind her. "Please, won't all of you join me at my table."

"Thank you," Blair said. "We'd love to."

"You should burn in hell," a male voice shouted from across the foyer. "The Bible says you are an abomination."

Cam instinctively stepped between Blair and the direction of the voice just as Stark did the same. Stark slid a hand under her jacket.

"Wozinski has him," she murmured just loud enough for Cam to hear.

"Good." Keeping between Blair and that side of the hallway, Cam took Blair's hand and said, "We're clear. Let's go inside."

Blair met Emory Constantine's concerned gaze. "I'm sorry for the disruption."

Emory smiled faintly. "I was about to say the same thing to you, Ms. Powell. I have a number of fairly vocal opponents."

"Then we have quite a bit in common," Blair said.

Emory's gaze flickered briefly to Cam and then to Diane and Renée. Then she grinned, her dark eyes sparkling. "It seems that we do."

CHAPTER SEVENTEEN

I'm sorry," Emory Constantine murmured, bending over Blair, who sat at the head table with Cam, Diane, Renée, and a number of notables from the scientific and financial world, "but would you mind posing for one more round of photos? The president of the Institute—"

"No, I don't mind," Blair said with a smile, even though she'd been photographed with and without her permission more times than she cared to count in the last three hours. She was used to the press and had expected more than her usual share of attention after all the events of the last few months and the recent announcement of her personal plans. Emory it seemed, also garnered a fair amount of media notice, so with the two of them sitting together, the questions and photos had been non-stop all evening. "I'll be right there."

As she rose, Cam did also. Out of the corner of her eye, Blair saw Paula wending her way through the tables toward her. When Blair followed Emory onto the stage and joined the small group waiting there, Cam and Paula took up positions off to each side. Randolph Sumter, the current president of the Johnson Institute, was middle-aged, handsome, and wore his power with subtle arrogance. He didn't try to hide his non-philanthropic interest as his gaze swept over Blair during their introduction.

"Ms. Powell," he said in a smooth baritone, "we'd love to have you tour the Institute. I think you'll find we are doing some remarkable work."

"Yes," Blair replied with polite reserve. "I've followed Dr. Constantine's research with interest. You must be very pleased to have her and her team on board."

To his credit, his smile never wavered. "Without a doubt. Please remember me to your father. The board was a staunch supporter during his last campaign."

"I certainly will." Blair took Cam's hand. "I don't believe you've met my partner, Cameron Roberts."

Sumter acknowledged Cam perfunctorily, signaled to the photographers, and positioned himself between Blair and Emory with a hand on each of their backs. Once the obligatory photo shoot was over, Blair drew Emory aside.

"I hope you don't mind, but I'm going to slip out a little early."

Emory shook her head. "Please, you don't need to explain." She glanced at a woman who pointed a camera in their direction. "They're hungry tonight, aren't they?"

"Tonight?" Blair laughed. "I'm really glad we got to meet. I thought your speech was dynamite. If there's ever anything I can do, just give me a call."

"Thank you." Emory walked Blair to the far side of the stage where the crowd on the floor was thinner. "I might just take you up on that someday."

Blair smiled. "Good. I'm serious."

"Congratulations on your upcoming wedding, too," Emory said, waiting until Cam was close enough to hear.

"Thank you," Cam and Blair said together.

"I'll walk out with you," Emory said, "and we can trade phone numbers." She looked over the several hundred people in the banquet room and sighed. "I've still got another hour's networking to go, and I could use a break."

"Come on, then." Blair grinned. "I'm an expert at sneaking out of things like this."

Cam motioned to Stark. "Let the team know we're ready to leave. I'll get Diane and Savard. We're still using the planned exit?"

"Yes. I'll have the cars move around now." Stark murmured instructions, then said to Blair, "Five minutes, Ms. Powell."

At the appointed time, the small group took the elevator at the rear of the building to the ground floor and headed briskly down the service corridor toward an exit used by the hotel staff. Blair couldn't see anyone in the alcoves and smaller hallways branching off the main corridor, but she was certain that members of the security team were stationed along the way. She leaned close to Emory.

"If you really want to break ranks, you can come back to the hotel with us for a drink."

Emory laughed. "God, don't tempt me. Unfortunately, fundraising is a necessary evil and I've got enough to worry about without adding money problems to my list."

"I can imagine," Blair said. "Don't worry too much about anti-stem cell research legislation. I can tell you my father does not support measures to restrict your work."

"Thank you. I—"

"Stark," Cam said sharply as a man in a three-piece suit rounded a corner twenty feet in front of them and strode rapidly toward them. Even as she spoke, she started to step toward Blair. He raised his arm.

"Gun!" someone shouted.

Blair barely heard the warning before the hallway erupted in gunfire and she was knocked to the floor. As she fell she grabbed for Cam but could not reach her. Then she was on the floor with a tremendous weight pinning her down. She pushed and struggled to get free but was only able to turn her head. She saw a hand and part of a sleeve stretched out on the floor a few yards away. Cam's hand. She screamed but couldn't get enough air to emit more than a choked sob. Someone groaned.

Then Blair was yanked to her feet, then *off* her feet, and propelled down the hallway by someone she couldn't see. Someone big. She finally twisted enough in the iron grip to make out the features. Wozinski.

"Cam," Blair gasped. "Where is she?"

Wozinski didn't answer as he shouldered his way out into a narrow service alley. The metal service door banged against the stone building façade with a sharp clang.

The limo idled directly in front of the exit with the back door open. Hara crouched beside it, her gun extended in both hands as she visually swept right and left. Blair jerked in Wozinski's grasp and almost wrenched free, but he dragged her across the sidewalk, pushed her head down, and shoved her into the backseat.

"Cam," Blair shouted, immediately trying to climb out of the vehicle. Diane's body blocked her way as she too was pushed inside. Savard followed, the door slammed, and the vehicle careened away.

Blair stared at Savard, whose face was bone white. Her own heart was racing so quickly her chest ached. She took a breath and then another and dug her fingers into the leather seat. "What do we know?"

"Nothing," Savard said tightly.

Beside her, Diane sat rigidly upright, her arms wrapped around her torso, her pupils dilated so much her blue eyes looked black. She said *my God, my God* over and over in a hushed voice.

Blair heard sirens, and then tires squealed behind them and she hastily knelt on the seat to stare out the rear window. Renée leaned across the space between the seats, grasped her shoulder, and gently pulled her back down.

"Please stay away from the windows."

"Where's Cam?" Blair took a shaky breath. "Where's Paula?"

"Paula…is down. I'm not sure about the commander," Renée said in a monotone.

For an instant, Blair couldn't decipher the meaning of what she had just heard. Paula is down. Down. *Shot?* Her mind veered away from the thought. Cam. Cam wasn't wearing a vest.

"Who's behind us?" Blair carefully enunciated each word and forced herself to think calmly. Her only hope of getting to Cam was to maintain, or take, control. She wasn't about to become an unwilling captive of her own security team ever again.

"Mac. I'm not sure who else."

"Call them," Blair demanded.

"Protocol is for radio silence," Renée said.

"I don't care. Call them now. Consider it an order, Agent Savard."

Savard stared at Blair for a long moment, then punched two numbers on her handy talky. "Status?"

Blair couldn't hear a response, but only a few seconds passed before Renée said, "We're secure," and slipped the radio back into an inside pocket of her jacket. At the sight of her hand trembling, Blair's stomach clenched into a painful knot.

"Report?" Blair asked.

"All present and accounted for."

"What…what does that mean?"

"It means no one was left at the scene. Stark and the commander are in the Suburban behind us."

"Are they—"

"I don't know," Renée said.

The tight fist around Blair's heart loosened enough for her to breathe without each movement feeling like a knife stabbing through her. "Diane, are you all right?"

Mutely, Diane nodded.

Blair concentrated on burying her panic. Cam was in the car behind her. That was all that mattered. "Where are we going?"

"If Paula…"

Renée shuddered and for just a second, Blair thought she was going to break down. Then she squared her shoulders and continued.

"Paula will let Mac know the exit route, and he'll communicate with our driver."

Blair looked out the window and saw that they were heading out of the city. The last thing she wanted was to end up in another safe house, but she realized that was one decision she couldn't impact. She closed her eyes and willed her mind to go blank. It didn't work, but it kept her from trying to break down the barrier between herself and whoever was driving and demanding to know where they were going. Just when she thought she couldn't stand it anymore, she felt the limo slow down. She jerked upright and saw a sign for Interstate 495 South flash by as the vehicle turned into a deserted truck weighing station by the side of the highway. "What's happening?"

Renée shook her head. "I don't know."

Blair reached for the handle, but Renée stopped her. She was about to protest when the door opened and Cam slid in. The limo immediately accelerated back onto the highway.

"Are you all right?" Cam slid her arm around Blair's shoulders and pulled her close.

"Am I?" Blair laughed shakily and pressed her palm to Cam's chest. "I was afraid…" She lost the words and just kissed Cam instead. "Are you?"

"Other than a few sore ribs from ending up under one of Tanner's security guards, I'm fine." Cam stroked Blair's hair and looked at Diane and Renée. "You both okay?"

"Yes," Renée reported, sitting tensely on the edge of the seat.

"Stark took a round in the chest," Cam said. "Her vest stopped it. She's in pain, but she's still in charge. She'll be okay."

Renée blinked and looked away. "Thank you."

"Was anyone else hurt?" Blair asked.

"Another one of Tanner's people took a shot to the vest in the process of shielding Emory Constantine."

"Emory!" Blair said, momentarily stunned. "My God, is she hurt?"

"She sprained her wrist, but she's tough and taking everything in stride." Cam glanced at Savard. "We brought Emory with us. She's in the Suburban."

"Smart call," Savard said. "What about the assailant?"

"He's dead. Stark left Wozinski behind temporarily to coordinate with the FBI and police." Cam coughed and winced.

"Are you sure you're not hurt?" Blair said immediately.

Cam shook her head. "Sore ribs. I got a quick look at the guy. He's one of the four on Emory Constantine's watch list."

"You mean *Emory* was the target?" Blair exclaimed.

"We're not sure, but it's possible." Cam shifted, obviously trying to get comfortable. "For now, we're not making any assumptions."

"How much of this can we keep out of the press?" Blair asked.

"Stark's already been on the line to Lucinda, who's spinning some story right now about Emory suddenly being taken ill to cover her leaving the banquet. Fortunately, the scene was contained immediately so we may be able to keep the real details out of the press."

"Good," Blair breathed. "The last thing I want is another story circulating about me being a target." She took Cam's hand. "You're sure you're okay?"

"Yes." Now she was, now that she'd seen Blair. Now that some of the helpless fury at not being able to reach her when she'd been in danger was dissipating. Despite the pain in her ribs, she held Blair more tightly.

"What?" Blair murmured, sliding her hand to the back of Cam's neck. "Darling?"

"Nothing," Cam whispered. The instant she'd seen the assailant, she'd tried to shield Blair, but Tanner's man had grabbed her from behind and thrown her down. If Stark hadn't been there, hadn't moved without the slightest hesitation, Blair could be dead. Cam closed her eyes, as if that could obliterate the image in her mind, and buried her face in Blair's hair.

Blair moved her mouth close to Cam's ear. "I'm all right. I'm right here."

Cam took a long breath, straightened, and directed her next comments to Savard again. "There's been no evidence of pursuit, and this has the feel of a lone gunman."

"I agree," Savard said. Her color was better and her eyes focused and intent. Beside her, Diane looked exhausted, but calm. "He was probably staying at the hotel or knew someone who was."

"But how did he know where we were?" Blair said. "Or that we were leaving?"

"He could have paid one or even several of the hotel employees to keep him informed," Cam said. "It's possible he had an accomplice who was a legitimate guest at the fundraiser. He might have been watching the limo from some vantage point within the hotel, but I think that's less likely. Once Wozinski and the rest of the on-site team backtrack his route, we'll know more."

"He didn't say anything, did he? I didn't hear anything before… the shots." Blair knew how to fire a gun. She'd had a license since her late teens and had been to the firing range fairly regularly since then. But the muffled pops of controlled gunfire in a firing booth bore no resemblance to the terrifying reverberation of gunshots echoing down a hotel corridor. She could still hear the shots, and the shouts, and her own silent screams. She found Cam's hand and held it. "I was wondering about the guy earlier—the one outside the banquet hall who was quoting scripture, or his version of it anyway."

"The gunman didn't say anything," Cam said. "His message was in his gun hand."

"Where are we going?" Blair asked.

Cam smiled for a second. "Home to Whitley Point. Lucinda will have someone take care of the hotel room and pick up our luggage."

"If it's all right with you, I'd rather not leave the island again for six months or so."

"I'll see what I can do," Cam said.

"Thank you." Blair knew it wasn't possible, but for just a little while, it felt good to dream.

Chapter Eighteen

Sunday

Tanner's here," Blair said as the limo pulled up behind the SUV parked in the circular drive in front of the beach house. She stiffened when three figures materialized out of the dark and approached the vehicle. Even in the middle of the night, with only streaks of moonlight to cut the inky blackness, she could make out the automatic rifles.

"They're Tanner's people," Cam said. "Stark probably called ahead once we were out of range of the city and filled Tanner in on what happened."

Despite Cam's assurances that the figures posed no threat, Cam and Savard got out of the limo first and closed the door, leaving Blair and Diane shielded inside.

"I don't know how you stand it," Diane said. "It's all so horrible."

Blair slid across the space between the facing seats and put an arm around her. "Try not to think about it right now, honey. We'll get you inside and once we're safe, you'll feel better."

Diane laughed harshly. "Safe? That's just an illusion, and I bet you've known that all along, haven't you?" She touched Blair's face as if seeing her for the very first time. "You've known you could never be safe, so there was no reason to let them pretend to protect you."

When the door opened and Cam leaned in, Blair didn't move but smiled over at her. "I'll be right out, darling."

"Go with her," Diane said. "I'm all right."

"No you're not. None of us are." Blair rubbed Diane's arm and rocked her gently as Cam moved away. "You're partly right, you know—about my being guarded. I used to think there was no real need for protection and I resented them for trying, especially when it meant having them in my life twenty-four hours a day. I still hate it—everything about it—but mostly I hate that one of them could be hurt trying to protect me. But they're very good and they've saved my life and I trust them with it, now. All of them." She took a deep breath. "And I know that I need them."

Diane shivered. "I saw Paula jump in front of you and I saw her get shot. Thank God, it was just a millisecond, but I saw her body jerk, and I'll never forget the shock on her face." She looked down at her hands which were clasped tightly in her lap. "All the way back here, I kept wondering if Valerie's already dead. If someone—"

"She's not, and you can't think that way." Blair took Diane's face between her hands. "You never give up. Okay? It's not allowed. We *will* win."

"God," Diane laughed unsteadily. "You're turning into one of them."

"Bite your tongue." Blair released Diane and opened the door. "Come on, let's go inside."

Tanner stood waiting with Cam next to the vehicle. As Blair and Diane slid out, she wrapped her arms around both of them. "Hey, you two okay?"

"Just shaky," Diane said.

"We've got a fire going and a nice bottle of wine waiting for you," Tanner said.

"I don't even want to think about why you need your security people," Blair whispered against Tanner's ear, "but I owe you for the rest of my life for them." She closed her eyes, trying to banish the sight of Cam lying on the floor. "Thank you so much."

"Don't even go there," Tanner said grimly. "I'm just sorry I wasn't there myself."

"You did exactly what we needed." Blair eased away from Tanner. "Is Emory inside already?"

"Yes, she volunteered to check out Stark and Tanner's security guard." Cam wrapped her arm around Blair's waist as they walked to the house. "Stark took a hard hit and I ordered her to stand down. I'm sorry, but I need to contact Wozinski to find out what's going on back there."

"I understand. Just promise me you'll try to get some sleep tonight, too." Blair held the door open and waited until everyone else disappeared inside before asking, "Do you need something for your ribs?"

"No, it's tolerable. I'll wrap this up just as soon as I can." Cam cupped the back of Blair's neck and kissed her gently. "I love you."

Blair kissed her back, far less gently. "I love you too."

"If that's a come on, I might be too tired to deliver tonight," Cam said.

"It is, but I think I'm too tired to accept delivery." Blair gave her a gentle push. "Go do what you have to do. There's always a shower to look forward to in a few hours."

❖

"Where's Diane?" Blair asked when she looked in on Adrienne and Felicia in the living room.

"She wanted to be alone," Adrienne said. "Do you think she's all right?"

"She will be," Blair said. "It's the first time she's ever been shot at."

"If she needs a little escape from all of this, she can stay with Tanner and me," Adrienne said. "The atmosphere around here might be a little intense for her the next few days."

"Tanner never mentioned you had such a knack for understatement."

"Speaking of my spouse," Adrienne said, rising, "I should find her and get her home before she decides to stand guard herself." She glanced at Blair. "She's more than willing, if you need her—"

Blair shook her head. "No. And you've both done enough. We're fine."

"We've got plenty of people to secure this location," Felicia added, setting her coffee aside and standing as well. "I'm going to check in with the commander."

"And I want to see Emory," Blair said.

She bade the others goodnight and walked down the hall to the bedroom the agents used when they were off-shift. As she knocked on the partially open door, it swung open before she could catch it, affording her a glimpse of Emory Constantine leaning over a semi-nude young woman stretched out on the bed. Steph Fletcher, one of Tanner's security guards.

"Sorry." Blair started to close the door.

"That's all right," Emory called. "We're done."

Blair stepped inside as Emory drew a sheet up to the shoulders of the wiry, short haired redhead. "I'm going to leave my cell number right here on the bedside table." Emory crossed to a small desk and scribbled something on a piece of paper that she then placed next to the redhead's holstered weapon. "Six hours of bed rest, minimum. If your chest pain gets worse, you develop a cough, or you feel lightheaded, call me immediately. Otherwise, I'll see you first thing in the morning."

"Look, thanks." Steph was already pushing herself up, clearly intent on returning to duty. "I really appreciate everything, but—"

"You know, Steph," Blair said conversationally. "I bet Tanner would put you right on the inactive list if she thought you weren't a hundred percent. Not that anyone would tell her..."

Steph groaned and flopped back down. "Okay. Okay, I got it. Roger on the six hours bed rest."

"Thank you." Emory followed Blair into the hall. "Is there someone who can give me a ride to a hotel?"

"We have plenty of room right here," Blair said as they returned to the living room. "You can stay here until Cam is sure that it's safe for you to go home."

"I don't know precisely what went on in that hallway, but I heard some of the conversation among the agents on the way here. That man...that man might have been trying to kill me. I certainly can't endanger you or—"

"No one is going to let you leave, Emory, and no one wants you to." Blair found a half-empty bottle of wine, refilled her glass, and poured another for Emory. "I'd be very grateful if you'd look at Cam later. She's been through a lot this past week and..." She realized her hand was trembling and put the glass down abruptly.

"Of course I'll look at her," Emory said.

"Thank you. Is there anyone you need to call? The White House will take care of devising some story for the press, but if there's someone who's going to be worried about where you are tonight—"

"No, there isn't." Emory reached for her wine. "Since my divorce last year, I've been living in the family home with my mother. She travels a lot, as do I, so it works out very well for both of us. Right now she's in Milan."

Blair curled up on the sofa and regarded Emory thoughtfully. "Well then, consider yourself our guest."

"All right. Of course." Emory gestured to her evening dress. "Do you have clothes I can borrow? One of the security guards gave me his jacket in the car, but I gave that back to him when we got here."

"Between Diane and me, I'm sure we can outfit you."

"In that case, I gratefully accept. I can e-mail my chief technician with instructions for the lab in the morning. This will give me a chance to check on Steph again, too."

"Is she badly hurt?"

Emory shook her head. "I don't think so, but blunt trauma to the chest can be tricky. I'd feel better if I could x-ray her and get a cardiogram, but that's out of the question."

"If you think it's necessary, Tanner is very good at making arrangements for that sort of thing without a lot of fuss."

"You mean no records?"

"Pretty much."

"Somehow I get the feeling none of this is new to you."

Blair sighed, kicked off her shoes, and propped her feet on a leather hassock. Sometime in the last year she'd gotten used to living with danger. Not just the vague and barely countenanced possibility of harassment or kidnapping that she'd grown up with, but the life and death reality of bombs and bullets. Her lover had almost died, her friends had been shot, and she had been exposed to a potentially lethal bioweapon. "No, it's not new." She smiled wearily at Emory. "And I don't think it's going to go away—ever."

❖

"What the hell went wrong?" Matheson barked into the cell phone as he paced in his motel room. The need to change locations frequently and the inability to easily access his funds were wearing on him.

"He wasn't a professional, sir, and the targets were very well covered," the colonel said. "We knew using a civilian might be a problem."

Matheson sighed. "It was still a good plan to use someone who would be seen as targeting Constantine, but relying on amateurs is too risky. We're going to have to handle this ourselves."

"It won't be easy without inside help, sir."

"According to my friend in the Company, they're most likely back on the island, and it's not impregnable. If Lawrence doesn't surface soon, we'll have to force her out."

"Sir?"

"We'll start eliminating her contacts." Matheson relaxed his grip on the phone. "One by one."

CHAPTER NINETEEN

"If we're going to shower together," Blair whispered in Cam's ear, "we have to get up now."

"Did you wake up with an urge?" Cam murmured.

"Mmm. A big one." Blair teased the rim of Cam's ear with the tip of her tongue and pressed her pelvis against the crest of Cam's hip. "I went to bed with one, and it just kept growing." She reached around Cam's body and caressed her breasts and abdomen. "Of course, if you're really tired, I could probably manage on my own for a while."

Cam rolled over onto her back and pulled Blair on top of her. "Who needs a shower."

Grinning, Blair sat up and straddled Cam's waist. Keeping her weight off Cam's bruised hip, she grasped the hem of her T-shirt and stripped it off over her head. She let it fall onto the floor beside the bed and skimmed her hands slowly over her chest and down her abdomen, watching Cam follow the movement of her hands on her own body. "How do you feel this morning?"

"Surprisingly okay."

Blair trailed her fingers along the inside of her thighs, her fingertips brushing Cam's abdomen as well as her own legs. When Cam's muscles tightened, she felt an answering tension between her legs. "Shoulder stiff?"

Cam raised both arms and cupped Blair's breasts. "Not at all."

Blair closed her eyes as her nipples hardened and her breasts swelled against Cam's palms. "Still, let's be sure you don't overdo it." She rocked her pelvis in a slow steady glide on Cam's stomach, pressing a little harder with each stroke as the delicious pressure built. She covered one of Cam's hands on her breast with her own, and with her other opened herself so she could rub more of her rapidly swelling sex over Cam's belly. Soon the steady pump and glide of her hips gave way to short, erratic thrusts and she moaned softly. "Oh God, you feel so good."

"Blair," Cam whispered. "Open your eyes, baby."

Smiling crookedly, Blair blinked and struggled to focus. "Sorry. I'm so close, I almost…" She took a shuddering breath. "I need to back off a minute."

When she started to lift herself away, Cam shook her head.

"No, don't move." Cam kept one hand closed around Blair's breast, the nipple vised between two fingers, and slid the other between Blair's legs, palm up. Her fingers slipped down the hot, wet valley until her fingertips dipped just inside. "Now make yourself come in my hand."

Blair caught her lip between her teeth and bent forward to wrap both hands around Cam's arm, just above her wrist. "Tell me…if I hurt you."

"You won't. I want to feel everything." Cam started a steady tug and squeeze on Blair's nipple. "Fill my hand. Come on, baby."

With a groan, Blair pushed hard against Cam's hand, circling herself over the smooth firm muscles at the base of the palm. Soon she was balanced on a razor's edge. Panting, she frantically sought Cam's gaze. "I'm going to come."

"Don't hold back," Cam urged hoarsely. "I need all of you. Everything."

"Push inside me," Blair gasped, her back arching. She jerked Cam's arm hard between her legs, trying to force Cam's fingers into her.

Cam buried her hand, her palm riding hard over Blair's clitoris again and again.

"Oh God, Cam," Blair cried, "there. Oh right there." The muscles in her stomach and thighs shook violently as she tightened inside, over and over. When she couldn't hold herself upright any longer, she tried to brace herself on one arm, but managed only to collapse on her side next to Cam, Cam's hand still inside her.

"All right, baby?" Cam kissed Blair's closed eyelids, then her mouth. "Blair?"

"Mmm, oh God, wonderful."

"Ready for that shower?"

Blair snuggled a little closer and smoothed her hand down Cam's stomach, smiling against Cam's throat as she felt her twitch at the touch. "In a minute," she murmured, caressing lightly. "Or maybe two, if you can behave that long."

"I'll do my best," Cam groaned.

"That should do nicely."

❖

Renée Savard stifled a groan and eased to the far side of the bed, trying desperately not to shake the mattress. Her knee was so stiff and swollen, she feared she might have to crawl to the other side of the room where she'd left her cane propped against a chair two days earlier. Only two days ago, when she'd actually been walking fairly comfortably unaided. Of course, that was before she'd thrown herself down on top of Diane Bleeker and then sprinted fifty feet down a hallway and hurled herself into the back seat of a limousine.

"Can you walk?" Paula whispered.

"I'm just taking it slow," Renée replied. "Go back to sleep, sweetie."

Paula pushed the covers aside and started to sit up. "I'll get your cane."

"Don't, Paula," Renée said more sharply than she had intended. Knowing she must sound angry, she turned onto her side and stroked her lover's arm. "Hey, I'm sorry. But you should stay in bed for a little while longer."

"Where are you going?" Paula caught Renée's hand and intertwined their fingers.

"It's already 0600. The commander will be briefing soon."

"And *I* need to brief the security team," Paula countered.

"The commander didn't take a bullet in the chest last night. You know you should take it easy today."

"I was wearing a vest. The commander took a bullet in the chest for real and that didn't keep her down for long."

"You're every bit as strong and dedicated as the commander." Renée pushed a pillow behind her back, drew Paula against her side, and kissed the top of her head. "The commander is amazing—I'd follow her anywhere, do anything she asked. But you're my lover, and I know what *you* did last night. I know what might have happened if he'd been using different ammo or you took that shot in the neck. Those few minutes in the limo last night…when I wasn't sure how badly you were hurt…that was the worst kind of hell. God, sweetie, I was scared."

"Hey, hey. I know." Paula rubbed her cheek against the side of Renée's breast. "I know what it was like thinking you were in one of the towers when they came down. I know, baby."

"So," Renée said shakily, "you get that I need you to take care of yourself for a little while."

"I'm sore," Paula admitted. "Every time I breathe it feels like someone's poking a sharp stick into my chest and out through my shoulder blades. But I'm not going to do anything except sit at a table and talk. I won't take a shift."

"And after the briefing you'll lie down again for three or four hours?"

"Two. Two hours and I won't mention to the commander that you're having trouble even standing."

Laughing, Renée tilted Paula's face up and kissed her. "I never realized you were so devious."

"I can't take you being hurt, either," Paula whispered, closing her eyes and pillowing her face between Renée's breasts. "Maybe you could just stay here for a few more minutes."

"Anything," Renée murmured. "Anything for you."

❖

Just before seven, Blair walked with Cam as far as the guesthouse. A light rain fell beneath a gray sky and in the distance the ocean was rough with angry chop.

"Winter's coming," Blair said, and for some reason, that made her feel melancholy.

Cam took her hand. "Let's get married at the Lodge in Colorado. We can call Doris today and make arrangements."

"What?" Blair gaped, then her eyes brightened with pleasure. "What brought that on?"

Cam brushed her thumb along the crest of Blair's cheek. "We haven't stopped moving for the last two months. I want a few days with you when all that matters is *being* with you."

"You do?" Blair glanced down the path to the guesthouse where the current office of the Deputy Director of Homeland Security was located, knowing that Cam's agents waited for her inside and that the work her lover was doing was critical to the nation's well-being. She also knew that the work was essential to *Cam's* well-being. The last thing she expected was for Cam to be thinking of anything *except* work.

"I'm sorry," Cam murmured as if reading her mind. "I'm sorry that I haven't made it clear to you how much I need you."

"Cameron." Blair skimmed her fingers through Cam's hair. "You made that perfectly clear not more than an hour ago."

Cam grinned briefly. "That too, but more than anything I need you..." Her eyes darkened and she touched her palm to her chest. "...in here."

Blair caught her breath. "Oh my God. You have to go right this minute or I'm going to have to drag you back to bed. You can't say things like that to me when we're standing out here and I can't have you."

"Is that a yes about Colorado?"

"I'll call Doris today. I know Tanner and Adrienne will love to see her again."

"Good." Cam kissed her. "I might be a while."

"I know. Do what you have to do. I love you."

"Be careful today."

"I will be." Blair asked the question lurking in the back of her mind. "Have you learned anything?"

"On the surface it looks like the shooter was targeting Emory."

"On the surface?"

"He's on her watch list, but some of these groups have multiple agendas. It's not a stretch for an anti-fetal research zealot to also be anti-gay."

"So it might've been us he was after."

"Possibly."

"But?"

Cam sighed. "We can't discount the remote possibility that this might be related to the previous assault on you."

"And you."

"So our safest course of action," Cam said, "is to assume all three are probable and investigate accordingly. The local FBI is putting together a file on the anti-stem cell research groups, and we'll continue to focus on connections to Matheson."

Blair caressed Cam's ribs lightly, wishing fervently that she could heal them. "What about Valerie?"

"If she doesn't contact either Diane or myself, our chances of finding her are remote. Given enough time, we might, but time is something we don't have much of." Cam ran her fingers through Blair's hair. "I'm working on something that might draw her in."

"Is it classified?"

"No, but it does involve Lucinda."

"Uh-oh. Do I even want to know?"

"You'll find out later." Cam kissed Blair's forehead. After a second she said, "No questions?"

"I'll wait for you to tell me about the briefing. Perhaps I'll go down to the marina in a while to see Tanner."

"Take three people..." Cam grimaced. "I'm sure Stark will take care of that."

Blair smiled. "I never mind you looking out for me. Stark doesn't have to know."

"Thanks, baby." Cam kissed her again, then turned and strode briskly away.

Blair waited until Cam disappeared inside, then continued down the winding path to the beach. As she turned north, tucking her hands in the pockets of her windbreaker and walking quickly to keep warm in the brisk wind, she was peripherally aware of the two figures shadowing her. They had been there, of course, the entire time that she and Cam had stood on the path sharing something so intimate she still felt like crying. Those who had watched would of course never acknowledge in any way what they had witnessed, and during those moments, she hadn't been aware of anyone except Cam. She stopped and pulled out her cell phone and speed-dialed.

A moment later, Cam answered. "Are you all right?"

"I'm sorry, I know you're briefing. I just want you to know that I'd love to go to Colorado to get married."

"All right," Cam said probingly. "And?"

"And this morning in bed was wonderful, but the only thing I really need is for you to look at me like you just did for the rest of my life."

"You can count on that."

"I love you," Blair said quietly. "I'll see you later."

Blair closed the phone, slid it into her pocket, and turned her face up to the rain. It was cold and sharp against her skin and she felt unbelievably alive.

❖

When Blair let herself into the kitchen forty-five minutes later, Diane was waiting for her. She was without makeup, in loose cotton slacks and a pale blue cotton blouse, and she didn't look like she'd slept at all the night before. Her freshly washed hair was loose and unstyled. She looked vulnerable and young, and Blair's heart ached. Diane had finally fallen in love and instead of being able to immerse herself in the joy of it, she might lose Valerie and never know why.

"Morning, sweetheart." Blair skimmed her fingers over Diane's back as she passed behind her. She stopped abruptly when she felt Diane stiffen. "What is it?"

"This." Diane's normally sultry voice was scratchy from fatigue. She pointed to the newspaper spread out in front of her. "I don't understand this."

Blair peered over her shoulder and frowned at an article on the second page. *Noted Gallery Owner Assaulted After Gala.* She scanned the completely fictitious account of an assault, presumed to be a robbery, that occurred just outside the Boston Ritz Carlton the previous evening following a fundraiser for a noted research institute. The only thing in the article that resembled reality in the slightest was the fact that the victim, Diane Bleeker, *was* actually the owner of a trendy Manhattan gallery.

"Is this how things are done in your world?" Diane lifted her pain-filled and accusing eyes. "Are these kinds of lies necessary? I have friends, colleagues, family who will be concerned and what if...you know that Valerie will probably see this. Someone should have told me."

"I don't have any idea how..." Blair remembered a snippet of her conversation with Cam less than an hour ago. Cam had said she might have an idea about reaching Valerie. She had *also* said that Lucinda was involved, and this press manipulation had Lucinda's fingerprints all over it. Blair straightened, her mouth tightening. "I'm not sure what this is about, but I'm going to find out."

Grabbing the newspaper, she marched toward the dining room, now the security operations center, where she had last seen Paula and Mac. Mac was at the computer, studying what looked to be a floor plan. He swiveled on his chair to face her, his brows knitting.

"Where's Paula?"

"She went back upstairs to bed." Mac's expression was polite but guarded. "Is there something I can help you with?"

"How about this? Do you know anything about this?" She extended the newspaper. From Mac's quick glance, she knew that he was aware of the article.

"Ah, that might be something you want to ask the commander," he replied, obviously framing his reply carefully.

"She's in a briefing. Why don't *you* explain it to me?"

Mac regarded her with mute appeal. "I'm afraid I can't. I'm sorry."

"All right. Of course not." Blair turned and walked away. When she heard Mac rise she looked back over her shoulder. "Stay here, Mac. I'm not going any further than Cam's office. God, it's not like there's anywhere to *go*."

He grinned cautiously. "I've never known that to stop you. Respectfully, Ms. Powell."

She narrowed her eyes, then laughed. "Maybe it's time to rotate out my security team if you know me that well."

"It does take a long time to train the new ones," he said with a straight face.

"I suppose you have a point." Blair felt some of her anger ease. "I'll see you later Mac."

"Ma'am."

By the time she reached the guesthouse, her fury had abated enough that when Cam walked into the living room in response to her arrival, she managed to ask calmly, "Can I talk to you for a minute?"

Cam's gaze dropped to the newspaper she held tightly clenched in hand. "Ah." She slid her hands into the pockets of her black chinos. "I see that Lucinda is even more efficient than I anticipated. The article is in there?"

"Your doing?"

"Mostly. Lucinda made the necessary phone calls to the papers." Cam shook her head. "Even with the White House behind it, I didn't expect to see anything until this evening."

"Lucinda doesn't waste time or words."

"Apparently."

"Damn it, Cam. Diane doesn't understand this kind of thing. You should have told her, or let me tell her."

Cam gestured to the sofa. "Let's sit down for a minute."

"I don't want to sit, I want an explanation. I told Luce I wouldn't use my friendship with Diane like this. I didn't think I needed to tell you!"

"Just give me a minute and I'll explain." Cam sat down.

"Fine." Blair followed, but sat far enough away that they weren't touching. "You're using this to lure Valerie, aren't you?"

"Not entirely. It's a good cover story to explain all the official activity around the hotel last night. It keeps your name and Emory's out of the paper. And, yes," Cam said with a sigh, "it might draw Valerie out into the open. You can be sure she's scanning news sources for any available intel."

"Why didn't you tell me about this earlier?"

"Other than the obvious reason being that I was preoccupied?"

Blair smiled faintly. "Other than that."

Cam rubbed her eyes. "I didn't think we'd see any activity around this until later in the day. Diane was still asleep, and…" she met Blair's intent gaze. "I didn't want her trying to contact Valerie and telling her it was fabricated."

"Jesus, Cam. She's my best friend and she's hurting so much over this. How do you think she's going to feel if Valerie is…I don't know, trapped, because of her?"

"Blair," Cam said gently, "Valerie is in real trouble out there. The best thing for her is for us to be able to protect her. If she surfaces because she's worried that something might happen to Diane, or that something *has* happened to her, she'll be better off."

"Can I tell Diane?"

"It's going to put you in the middle. I hate to do that."

"I'm already in it. There's no middle ground left, Cam."

Cam moved along the sofa so she was closer to Blair, but did not touch her. "Can you tell her part of it, and leave out anything about Valerie for now?"

"She's not naïve, Cam—she might ask me about Valerie. What shall I tell her to do if Valerie calls?"

"Tell her to talk to her as long as she can."

"You're tapping Diane's phone?" Blair asked incredulously.

"We're tracing it back through her cellular provider. It's not perfect, but it gives us a starting place." Cam placed her hand flat on the sofa between them. "I'm sorry, Blair. It has to be done."

Blair was silent for a moment, then took Cam's hand and cradled it in her lap between both of hers. "This must be hard for you."

"I...not as hard as it is for you. I wish I could change that."

Blair shook her head. "No. One of the things I love about you is how clear you are about the right and wrong of things. About what should be done, no matter the cost. But there's nothing clear about any of this, is there?"

"Nothing has been clear to me since the moment I saw one of my own agents standing outside your door pointing a gun at your heart," Cam said bitterly. "I don't even know how to begin to think about that."

It was so very rare for Cam to voice her pain and disillusionment that Blair had to struggle not to pull her into her arms. Instead, she leaned close and kissed Cam's cheek. "I'll talk to Diane. It will be okay."

"I'm sorry."

"No. You shouldn't be. Not for doing what must be done." Blair rose. "You will be careful with Valerie, won't you?"

Cam stood. "She's a victim in this too. I'm sure of it."

"I trust your judgment. I do." Blair skimmed her fingers along Cam's jaw. "But you're the one thing in my life I can't do without."

"I'll remember that."

Blair smiled gently. "See that you do."

CHAPTER TWENTY

Cam tilted her chair back and scrubbed her face. A glance at her watch confirmed what she already knew. It was late, almost 9 p.m. Felicia and Savard looked just as exhausted as she felt, but neither had complained despite twelve hours of nonstop work at the computers. The rest of the guest house was dark, the only light coming from the computer monitors and a few muted lamps. She appreciated why so many government buildings had so few windows—the less intrusion from the outside world, the easier it was to become lost in the work to the exclusion of everything else. Even the important people in your life.

"Where are we?"

Savard deferred to Felicia, who had the most expertise in terms of computer investigation. Felicia shrugged.

"Between the files at Quantico I've been able to access and our own scans of Matheson's academy records, we have solid IDs on all four of the gunmen at the Aerie. We have names for the faces now and we're digging deeper."

"What does that give us in terms of Matheson's connection to the Company and Valerie's handler?"

Felicia shook her head. "Nothing yet. These men were all too young to be contemporaries of anyone who might have recruited Valerie."

Savard said, "If Valerie was recruited as a teenager, then we're probably looking at someone Matheson's age as her handler." She spread her hands in frustration. "He could be anyone."

"We have to work from the assumption that Valerie's handler and Matheson are tied together. It may turn out that they're not, but that's a more probable scenario than postulating that Valerie's contact within the Company reported the plans for the raid on Matheson's compound to someone *else* who then relayed the message to Matheson." Cam stood up and walked to the window, rolling her shoulders and trying to work out some of the stiffness from the previous week's injuries and the tension of poring through files all day. The first floor of the main house was alight, and she wondered what Blair was doing. "I don't believe in coincidences. The only person outside of our team who knew about the raid was Valerie. She reported to her handler and Matheson was tipped off. A plus B equals C."

"Matheson has had a lifetime to build up a network inside the system," Felicia said. "We're looking for a needle in a haystack."

"Maybe. But men like Matheson know that the most secure network is one that's small and built on personal loyalty." She turned away from the window and the reminder of the rest of her life to face her agents. "What creates the greatest loyalty?"

"Chain of command," Savard said immediately.

"Family," Felicia replied.

"Start with Foster and the other four men from the assault on Blair, and find their brothers, cousins, uncles, fathers, grandfathers— every male relative who might have been associated with Matheson or *Matheson's* brothers, uncles, father, whatever."

Savard frowned. "What about the women?"

Cam shook her head. "Not likely. Matheson runs a military academy for boys. All of the assailants were men. All of the paramilitary personnel at his compound were men. He doesn't entrust women with authority."

Felicia's eyes flashed. "One of his many mistakes."

"Agreed," Cam said with quiet satisfaction. "He's going to regret underestimating us."

❖

"I was wondering when you were going to surface," Blair said when Cam walked into the kitchen a little after 10 p.m. She pulled the red sweatband from her forehead and let her hair fall free on her shoulders. She'd just come from a run on the beach and still wore sweatpants and a cutoff T-shirt. "There's chicken in the oven."

"Thanks, but I'm good. Tanner had sandwiches sent in for us." Cam opened the refrigerator and extracted a beer. "Want one?"

"I've got wine." Blair waited until Cam sat down at the table and took several swallows of beer before moving behind her to massage her shoulders. "Long day."

Cam leaned her head back against Blair's body, briefly closed her eyes, and sighed. "Yeah. How was yours?"

"About the same. I painted a little this afternoon."

"Anything I can see yet?"

Blair smiled. "Soon. Maybe tomorrow."

"I won't forget. What else is new?"

"Tanner's people took Emory back to the city. Steph is going to stay with her for a day or so just to be sure she's okay."

"Good. How's Diane?"

Blair's hand stilled. "Upset."

"I'll talk to her as soon as I check in with Mac and Stark. Hopefully they had better luck sorting out what happened at the hotel last night than we had today."

"No progress?"

Cam sighed. "Some. I have no doubt that given enough time we could track the various threads back to the hub, but I don't think we have that much time. Not when Matheson can put together assault squads like he did at the Aerie, people who don't care if they die."

Blair went back to working on the muscles in Cam's neck. "You think it was a suicide mission?"

"I doubt they framed it that way, but the probability was overwhelming that none of the assailants would survive."

"You think he'll try again."

Cam fell silent, wondering if spelling out her concerns to Blair was fair.

"Don't try to decide what's good for me or not, just tell me what you think," Blair said.

Cam looked up into Blair's face. "Yes, I do."

"Well. He's not so smart, then, is he? I just hope he does it soon so we can get this over with." Blair kissed the top of Cam's head. "Why don't you take a shower and change into something more comfortable. Your back is one big knot."

"Are you going to come with me?"

Blair laughed. "No, not unless you intend on spending the rest of the night in the bedroom."

"Sounds good to me." Cam grinned, tilting her head further back against Blair's stomach. "I missed you today."

Blair traced Cam's eyebrows with a fingertip, then leaned over and kissed her mouth upside down. "I've been thinking of this morning all day. I love that position, but next time I want it to be your mouth under me."

Cam groaned and nosed Blair's T-shirt aside so she could kiss her bare middle. "Let me finish up a few more things, and I'll take care of that wish. I can shower later."

"I'll be waiting."

❖

"Anything?" Cam asked as she strode into the operations center. Stark, Mac, and—to her surprise—Wozinski were reviewing printouts. "Hi Greg. Things finished up in Boston?"

Wozinski shrugged. "The feebies are handling it. Need I say more?"

"Other than things are moving slowly?" Cam grinned. "What do you have?"

"Shooter's name was Allen Strassmann, and as we already knew, he was on Constantine's watch list. He's also on half a dozen other lists under watch—all right-wing, pro-Christian, pro-life, ultraconservative groups."

"On the surface," Stark said, "it looks like Dr. Constantine was the target."

Cam leaned against the door jamb and folded her arms. "You disagree?"

"If the doctor was the target, it seems pretty stupid to try to take her out when she's with Egret, who everyone knows would be heavily guarded."

"Maybe it was simply a matter of opportunity," Cam said.

"Possible. But how did they know that Constantine was in the hall with us? It was a spur of the moment decision to leave then."

"Maybe Strassmann was in the banquet hall or had someone watching Emory's movements who could alert him, the same as we postulated might be the case if Blair were the target."

Stark nodded, but she didn't look convinced. "If I were going to take a shot at Emory Constantine, I would plan to do it when she was leaving the hotel after the event—in the parking garage, maybe, or even in the crowd coming out of the banquet hall. There'd be a much better chance of getting away with it—and getting away, period."

"Do we have any indication that this guy Strassmann might have targeted Blair?" Cam joined the others around the table.

"We don't have anything in the files about this guy—or any organization he's involved with—contacting her, issuing statements, or posting inflammatory messages on any of their message boards regarding her. Nothing ties him to her."

"I'm not surprised. If I were going to choose an assassin, I'd want him, or her, to be someone anonymous." Cam shrugged. "That assumes there was someone behind this other than Strassmann himself."

"It would be a damn big coincidence," Mac said as he sat down with coffee, "if someone just happened to take a shot at Emory Constantine when she just happened to be with Egret. Despite the evidence, or lack of it, it's too big a coincidence for me."

Stark nodded. "I agree."

"So do I." Cam stood. "Keep working the Strassmann angle and assume his target was Blair. See if you can find a relationship between him and any known Matheson connections—maybe he's related to one of Matheson's men captured at the compound."

"Will do, Commander." Stark hesitated, as if she were about to say more, then fell silent.

"Chief?" Cam asked.

"Nothing, Commander."

"No," Cam said as if the question had been asked. "We didn't make a whole hell of a lot of progress, but we're still digging."

"We really need Valerie Lawrence to come in if we're going to find the link to Matheson," Stark said.

"I'm working on it." Cam surveyed the group. "Until then we carry on."

❖

Cam leaned into the living room and tapped on the partially open French door that divided it from the hallway and the first floor bedrooms. Diane was curled up on one end of the dark brown leather sofa in front of the fireplace. A half empty glass of wine sat on the end table beside her. She'd changed from the jeans she'd been wearing earlier into black slacks and a fitted, white scoop neck top with three-quarter length sleeves. She looked remote and very much alone.

"Can I talk to you?"

Diane glanced over her shoulder. "Of course."

Diane turned back to the fire as Cam sat down next to her.

"I'm sorry I didn't get a chance to warn you about the newspaper article before you saw it," Cam said.

"Would you still have released it if I had objected?"

"Yes."

"Thank you for letting me make the phone calls this afternoon. My sister and my office manager were very relieved to hear that I wasn't seriously injured." Diane added sharply, "Of course, I stuck to the script Stark provided me. The one you approved, I assume."

Cam winced. "I didn't mean to make you feel like a conspirator."

"Then why did you do it?"

"It's complicated—"

"That means it's about Valerie."

"Yes," Cam admitted. "She won't come in to protect herself, but she will to protect you. And we need her."

Diane shifted, studying Cam with no apparent trace of her previous anger. "That's emotional blackmail, don't you think?"

"Yes, it is."

"How do you make that all right?"

"It's better for Valerie, it's better for you. And it's better for Blair."

"That's the bottom line, isn't it? Blair."

Cam regarded her steadily. "Yes."

"No apologies? No elaborate rationalizations or arguments?"

"No."

"Clear and simple," Diane whispered to herself.

"Not clear and not simple," Cam said. "Necessary. Valerie will understand."

"And you're sure that this is the best thing for Valerie?"

"As sure as I can be," Cam said. "You have to trust me on that one."

Diane laughed harshly. "It seems that we all have to trust you for quite a bit, Cam. That's asking a lot, don't you think?"

"Diane," Blair said from the doorway. "Cam knows what she's doing. There's no one better to make these decisions."

"I hope you're right." Diane rose and strode abruptly toward the door, then paused to look back at Cam. "Because if something happens to Valerie because of this, I'll never forgive you for using me against her."

As Diane hurried from the room, Blair said, "She's just upset. I'll go talk to her."

"It's okay. She deserves to be angry. I didn't handle it well."

"Oh, don't be ridiculous, Cameron. You're not responsible for everyone, and she happens to be wrong."

Cam's lips twitched. "Thank you for coming to my defense. I think."

Blair grasped Cam's chin in her hand, and kissed her, a deep probing kiss. "I know how you get. I'm not letting you beat yourself up about this. You did the right thing even if your timing sucked."

"You don't usually complain about my ti—" Cam broke off as her cell phone rang. "Roberts." She held Blair's gaze as she spoke. "Where?...Tell them to intercept, but do not...I repeat...do *not* use deadly force. Alert Stark to secure the house. I'll be right there."

"What is it?" Blair asked anxiously.

"Intruder on the beach. I have to go."

"Let Tanner's people handle it. Cam—"

"Stay here, Blair. I'll be fine. I'll be back as soon as I can."

"Damn it, Cam—"

Cam ran toward the back of the house, punching in Felicia's number on her cell. "I need back up. I'll be on the path to the dunes."

"Roger, Commander. Savard?"

Cam pushed through the back door. It was dark with only moonlight to guide her, but she knew the route by heart. She issued orders as she ran, phone in one hand and weapon in the other. "No. Savard's not mobile enough. Tell her to take a position behind the guest house. No one approaches the rear of the compound except on my orders. Call Stark—red alert."

"Copy that."

Cam hit the beach running and saw a flurry of activity, dark shapes converging from multiple directions, a quarter of a mile up the strand.

Hearing muffled shouts, she closed the phone and shoved it into the pocket of her pants. As she drew closer, she saw three of Tanner's agents pointing assault rifles at a figure kneeling in the sand, arms outstretched. A slender figure with short blond hair in a dark jacket and pants. Cam skidded to a stop a few feet away and holstered her weapon.

Valerie looked up at her. "Hello, Cameron."

"Are you okay?"

"Perfectly, thank you."

Cam motioned the others away. "I've got this. Thank you. You can return to your posts."

Valerie rose and brushed sand from her pants.

"That was risky," Cam said. "They might have shot you."

"I knew your people would be better trained than that."

"Pretty trusting."

Valerie smiled softly. "I've always trusted you."

Cam wondered how long the trust would last. "Come up to the house," she said. "We've been expecting you."

CHAPTER TWENTY-ONE

I take it the newspaper item was fabricated?" Valerie asked as soon as they were out of earshot of the guards.

Cam grinned briefly, not surprised that Valerie had been suspicious of the cover story. Agents indoctrinated to clandestine work understood how often and to what extent the media was used to subvert the truth. Cam had hoped that Valerie would not take a chance on ignoring the report, even though she might not completely believe it. "Most of it was an embellishment."

"Is Diane all right?"

"Yes, she's completely fine."

"But there *was* some kind of an incident."

"Yes," Cam said, unwilling to discuss any further details until she had a better sense of Valerie's agenda.

As if understanding, Valerie didn't pursue it further. "I expected the guards to call Stark when they intercepted me," she said. "Are you running Blair's detail again?"

Cam shook her head. "No, but this entire operation is an OHS matter, and that puts me in charge."

"And you're going to take on the Company?"

"If need be."

"The Company's been around a long time," Valerie said. "Homeland Security is so fresh most people don't even know what it is."

"They'll find out soon enough."

"I guess we all will." Valerie pushed her hands into the pocket of her jacket and hunched her shoulders against the wind. "God, this is going to be a mess until people sort out their turf."

"Probably for a lot longer than that." Cam realized Valerie was shivering. "How far did you walk?"

"Four or five miles—I wanted to be sure to flank your guards so they'd have a good look at me as I came up the beach. I didn't want to come out of nowhere right on top of them and have them shooting at shadows."

"You said you thought they were too well-trained for that."

"Let's just say I prefer the odds to be solidly stacked in my favor when I'm unarmed in hostile territory."

"Sound procedure," Cam agreed. She'd find out soon enough just how Valerie had penetrated far enough into the island to get around the guards. She sensed movement in the shadows off to her right and slid her hand over her weapon just as Felicia stepped out of the cover of the dunes. Beside her, Valerie tensed.

"All clear, Commander?" Felicia asked.

"Yes. You can let Savard and Stark know to stand down."

"Yes ma'am." Felicia relayed the orders by radio, then regarded Valerie as the trio climbed the path toward the compound. "Good to see you."

"Thanks," Valerie replied. "I feel the same."

"You and Savard should take some down time while you can, Davis," Cam said. "We'll brief again at 0600."

"Yes ma'am." Felicia veered off the path toward the guesthouse. "Goodnight, Commander."

Cam stopped midway between the guesthouse and the main house at a point outside the visual range of the perimeter guards stationed at the rear of the house. She faced Valerie, who looked thin and pale in the moonlight. "Blair is inside. So is Diane. I know Tanner's men already frisked you, but I need to do it myself."

"Of course." Valerie unzipped her jacket, then held her arms out to her sides at shoulder level and spread her legs.

"Unbutton your blouse and unzip your jeans," Cam said. "I'm sorry it's cold out here."

"Just get it done, Cameron."

"I'll be quick."

Wordlessly, Valerie opened her clothing.

Cam swiftly checked for weapons, which she hadn't expected to find, and then more carefully skimmed her fingers inside the cups of Valerie's bra, over the bare skin of her abdomen and back, and underneath the top of her jeans in front and back looking for a microphone, which she hoped she wouldn't find. She didn't. "Thanks."

Valerie redressed. "Can I see Diane?"

"Yes, but just for a minute. You and I need to talk."

They resumed walking.

"I'll do whatever you want."

"For the record," Cam said, "I'm glad you finally got your ass here."

Valerie sighed. "I've done things I regret, Cameron, but I would never willingly have betrayed you. I didn't know how the intelligence I passed on was going to be used. I know it's not an excuse—"

"I know how the game is played. I know you didn't have any choice. We're okay on that."

Valerie briefly squeezed Cam's hand. "I'm glad."

"Let's get inside so you can warm up."

They climbed the stairs to the rear deck, and Cam nodded to Stark, who stood with her back against the kitchen door, an assault rifle held loosely in her arms. "All clear, Chief."

"Do you need me inside, Commander?" Stark asked.

"Not at the moment. Standard shifts tonight should be fine. We'll brief tomorrow."

Stark glanced at Valerie and stepped away from the door. "Yes ma'am."

Cam led Valerie inside. The kitchen was empty, as she knew it would be. Stark would have moved Diane and Blair to the center of the house as soon as she realized security had been breached. "Diane is probably in the living room with Blair. I'll wait for you here, if you want to tell Blair where I am."

"Thank you." Valerie met Cam's eyes. "I know you don't have to do this, any of this. I'm sure you were told to just turn me over to whoever's on top of the security heap at the moment."

Cam smiled grimly. "That would be me."

"I hope it stays that way." Valerie's tone was wistful. "Thank you, Cameron. I'll be right back."

❖

"Oh God," Diane whispered, rising slowly to her feet as Valerie stepped into the room.

Blair hesitated for a second, then rose and gave Diane a quick hug. "I'll see you later." She left Valerie and Diane alone in the dimly lit room.

Neither moved at first.

"Were you ever coming back?" Diane asked.

"I wanted to."

"Why didn't you?"

Valerie shivered. "I was afraid you'd get hurt."

Diane lifted a log and laid it on the ones already burning. "Come over here by the fire. You're cold." When she felt Valerie beside her, she turned to touch her face. "Are you all right?"

"A little tired." Valerie caught Diane's hand and brushed her lips across the palm. "I missed you so much."

"I don't know what to do first," Diane confessed. "I want to feed you. You look too thin. I want to hold you. Your hands are so cold. I want *you* to hold me. I feel...so empty."

"First things first." Valerie pulled Diane firmly into her arms.

Diane gave a small cry and slid both hands under the back of Valerie's jacket, then buried her face in Valerie's neck. "I don't care what happens after this, but you are not disappearing again."

Valerie caressed Diane's hair, sifting the sleek blond strands through her fingers. "I'd promise you that, if I could."

A tremulous smile countered the sadness in Diane's eyes. "Blair says you and Cam are the best at what you do. So the two of you should be able to figure something out."

"Cam's waiting to talk to me." Valerie couldn't bear the thought of leaving Diane again, especially knowing that it could be hours before she could return. And hours was the best she could hope for. Agents whose loyalties were in question had been known to be sequestered for weeks. Sometimes months. She had to believe that Cam would not do that to her, and she wagered everything that mattered to her on that belief. "I don't know how long I'll be."

"She's not going to take you away, is she?"

"I don't know."

"Why did you come? Was it because of the newspaper article? I didn't know—"

"When I first read it," Valerie said, instinctively pulling Diane closer, "I thought you were hurt and I nearly went crazy. I spent half a day frantically making calls and tapping into some old sources, but no one could find an accident or police report involving you. So I realized the article was phony, but I was still worried in case it was a half truth. I had to know you were okay."

"I'm so sorry," Diane said. "Cam didn't tell me what she'd done, or I would have found a way to call you."

Valerie smiled. "That's why she didn't tell you."

Diane's eyes darkened. "You're not angry at her?"

"I figured she had probably planted the article. Either that, or someone else trying to flush me out had." Valerie sighed and leaned in to Diane, more tired than she'd realized. "I was running out of options. It seemed like the time to come in. Besides, I missed you."

"Cam said you would understand what she'd done and why, and even though I don't approve of being used to trick you, I'm so very glad you're here." Diane brushed her fingers through Valerie's hair. "And I'm not letting Cam or anyone else take you away from me again."

"I need to go talk to her."

"I'll be upstairs. The last door on the right. Come to me."

"Are you sure?"

Diane put her arms around Valerie's shoulders and kissed her, a soft lingering kiss. "Never, ever more certain."

❖

"Scotch?" Cam closed the kitchen door after Valerie. "There's a good bottle in the cupboard over there."

"Now *that* I could use. Join me?"

Cam nodded. She watched Valerie take glasses down from the cupboard, add ice cubes, and pour the smoky liquor. She'd seen her do exactly the same thing dozens of times before, but more than just the circumstances had changed. Valerie looked different, too. It wasn't simply that her clothes were far more casual than anything Cam had seen her wear even when she wasn't working, or that her silky, platinum hair was far shorter than she had ever worn it. It would take more than jeans and a short haircut to hide Valerie's cool elegance. She wasn't just thinner, she was leaner and tauter, and she moved with a sense of suppressed anger and almost lethal purpose that Cam associated with caged animals. Valerie might not be caged, but she *was* being hunted.

"Just to be clear, I don't intend to turn you over to anyone," Cam said.

Valerie held out the Scotch. "You don't know what I have to say, yet."

"Who's after you?"

"Several different parties." Valerie sat down across the wide oak table from Cam and contemplated her Scotch. "The Company, for certain. My handler has been leaving messages at drop points for me to come in."

"Henry?"

Valerie smiled bitterly. "Well, that's what I've always called him."

"You don't trust him now?"

Valerie turned the heavy crystal glass slowly between her hands. Her fingers, much like the rest of her body, were long and thin, but not delicate. "It's unusual for him to insist on a face-to-face. In fact, in all the years I've worked with him we've only met a handful of times. Now he's making urgent requests for a rendezvous."

"A trap?"

"That's what it feels like," Valerie said with a shrug. "But a trap set by whom? Matheson because he's working with Henry? Or the Company, because they want me in for a debriefing? Because they think *I* tipped off Matheson."

"They want you for some reason."

"Yes, and if the Company's involved, I know what will happen if I go in. Believe me, I don't have any desire to disappear, even temporarily."

Cam saw no reason to protest what they both knew was possible. Agents suspected of turning were forcibly detained, debriefed, and sometimes, expunged. "Henry could want you to come in for protection *from* Matheson."

"I'd like to think that." Valerie took a slow swallow of Scotch and shook her head. "But I'd be foolish to assume that just because we've had a professional association for twenty years that we're friends. If he's Matheson's connection, I'm a liability now."

"That's why you're better off here." Cam finished her drink. "We had an incident in Boston the other night. An armed assailant penetrated our perimeter and got off a couple of shots before we contained him."

"Who was the target?"

"We don't know. Emory Constantine, a high profile and not so popular stem cell researcher, was with us. It might have been her. It might have Blair. It might even have been Diane."

"Diane?" Valerie's face became expressionless, as cool as carved marble. "What would be the point? If someone took her out, they'd have nothing to hold over my head."

"No one? Family? Old lovers?"

An old sorrow seemed to claim Valerie for a split second, softening her features. "You of all people should know that other than you, there's no one. Only Diane. You had someone guarding her?"

"Savard. We were lucky, there." Cam grimaced. "It's possible Matheson plans to clean house and take us all down."

"Then we need to get to him first."

"We might not be able to unless we force Henry to roll over. Do you have any idea how we can find him?"

Valerie shook her head. "I never once met him in an office. He could be stationed in California for all I know. God, Cameron, the man has run my life since I was a teenager and I don't even know his full name." She laughed harshly, her eyes bleak. "What kind of fool does that make me?"

"We both know that's not what it's about." Cam extended her hand across the table and Valerie clasped her fingers fleetingly. "You've done a job most of us couldn't do far longer than anyone should have to. That doesn't make you a fool in my book, it makes you a hero."

"Thank you," Valerie whispered.

"I take it you've tried to locate him some other way than through a meet?"

"I was hoping to discover his identity and I've called in every marker I have. Or *thought* I had." Valerie's disillusionment shone through beneath the composed façade she wore so effortlessly. "I've tried every source I know, but in the last few weeks, those have mysteriously dried up. Contact numbers are no longer in service, bank accounts are suddenly closed, drop boxes have new locks."

"You're being cut off."

Valerie nodded. "It could still just be to force me to make contact, or it could be the first step in removing me."

"I don't suppose you have a photograph?"

"No, and it's not like the Company keeps a roster of employees that I could go through."

Cam laughed. "Now, that would defeat the purpose of being a spy, wouldn't it?"

"A spy," Valerie said wryly. "Operative sounds so much better."

"Let's assume Matheson and Henry are working together—it's the most probable scenario. So, if we find one, we find the other."

"Any progress on your end?"

Cam scowled. "We're accumulating a file on Matheson's associates as far back as twenty-five years. It's slow going, but I'll want you to look through everything Felicia and Savard have put together so far. Unfortunately, some of the photographs are going to be of boys or much younger men than they're likely to be now."

"Perhaps Felicia can use age simulator software to project present appearances for any possibles."

"We might be able to do something even better," Cam said slowly as she stood. "It's almost midnight. I'd like you to brief with us in the morning. 0600 in the guest house."

"Are you sure? Savard and Felicia might not be quite as trusting as you are," Valerie pointed out.

"I disagree, but either way, it's not their choice."

Valerie rose. "You're taking a chance, Cameron, and I know that. I want you to know I appreciate—"

"Don't insult me, Valerie." Cam lightly touched her fingertips to Valerie's cheek. "Get some sleep." Then she dropped her hand and walked away.

Valerie waited until she heard Cam's footsteps disappear before following down the hallway and up the stairs. As she passed the room that she knew was Blair's, she recognized Blair's sensuous alto and then Cam's slightly deeper tones. The sound of Cam's voice in a phone message had once stirred her heart and her blood. Now, it filled her with a sense of comfort and safety. Wondering if that was fair, but being glad for it nonetheless, she continued to the last door on the right and knocked quietly before letting herself in.

The room was lit by a bedside lamp. Diane was in bed, a sheet pulled to her waist. Her breasts formed soft curves beneath a pale peach camisole. Valerie sat on the side of the bed and took her hand. "There's part of me that thinks I shouldn't be here."

"What does the other part think?"

"That it's the only place in the world I want to be."

Diane drew back the covers. "That's the part I'd listen to, if I were you."

"All right," Valerie whispered softly.

She stood and unbuttoned her blouse, unhooked her bra, and let them fall to the floor behind her. She unzipped her jeans, pushed them down along with her panties, and stepped out of them. Watching Diane watch her, she was surprised to feel her body quicken when for so long the only sensations she'd been aware of were fatigue and desperate sadness. She turned off the light and slipped into bed. Then she did something she'd never done before. She pulled Diane on top of her and guided Diane's hand between her thighs.

"Please make love to me. I need you."

CHAPTER TWENTY-TWO

Monday

A ny response from Lawrence on your request for a meeting?"
Matheson inquired via his disposable cell phone.

"Not yet."

Matheson sipped his coffee and watched the traffic on Main Street through the diner window in the small seaside town. A waitress slid a plate of scrambled eggs and toast in front of him. He made eye contact when he thanked her.

"You're very welcome." The brunette offered him a sultry smile as she lingered by the red leather booth made shiny by years of bodies slipping in and out.

He held her gaze for a few seconds, noting the invitation in her eyes while surveying her full breasts and curvaceous hips. His penis lengthened, reminding him that it had been some time since he'd satisfied his needs. He made a mental note to take care of that, then looked away, dismissing her from his thoughts. "Why do you think your operative is ignoring your direct order?"

"Because she's one of our best," the man snapped. Then, as if regretting his outburst, he added in a conciliatory tone, "The leak came too soon after her report to me for her not to be suspicious, but I didn't have a choice. If Special Forces hadn't moved on the compound so quickly, I might have been able to find another way to warn you, but Roberts's team was far more effective than we anticipated. I didn't have time for a cover story, and I didn't think you'd enjoy captivity."

"It's never wise to underestimate the enemy," Matheson said mildly, spearing a fluffy mound of egg. "It's unfortunate that eliminating her will cost us an inside link to several of our primary targets, but the longer she stays alive, the greater the likelihood you'll be compromised."

"I've warned her she's in danger, but she won't agree to a meet."

"You're not using the right enticement."

"What do you suggest?"

Matheson told him, disconnected, and punched in another number.

"He has forty-eight hours to take care of his mess, then we'll clean house ourselves, starting with him."

"Yes sir. It's a pleasure to serve you, sir."

❖

"Valerie?" Diane called urgently in the dark. The bed beside her was warm, but empty. The nightmare of the past few weeks instantly closed in around her, and she felt as if she were smothering. Bolting upright, she gasped, "Oh God."

"I'm here." Valerie hurried to the side of the bed and pulled Diane into her arms. "I found some clothes I'd left here last month, and I was trying not to wake you while I dressed."

"Where are you going?"

"A briefing with Cameron."

Diane held her tightly, running her hands over Valerie's back. She wore only a snug tank top and panties. "You're cold. Go finish dressing."

Valerie pulled the covers back and slid underneath. "I frightened you. I'm sorry."

Diane shook her head. "Just for a second. I wish you didn't have to go."

"I'll be back." Valerie stretched out above Diane and kissed her throat. "I wouldn't leave now except I might be able to help."

"You won't do anything foolish, will you?"

Valerie laughed softly. "There are times I think my whole life might have been foolish."

"No," Diane said with certainty. She feathered her fingers through the short hair at the base of Valerie's neck. "You're the most remarkable woman I've ever met."

"Diane," Valerie murmured, kissing her deeply. When Diane tightened her hold and strained beneath her, wrapping both legs around the back of Valerie's thighs, Valerie immersed herself in the heat pouring off Diane's body. Diane's passion was like nothing she'd ever felt. The fire burned effortlessly, searing into those dark, barren places where she'd learned to hide her feelings, not realizing that eventually that which was buried, died. Desperate not to lose the connection, Valerie tightened her grip on Diane's upper arms, digging her fingers into the firm, pliable flesh. When Diane moaned, she instantly pulled away. "I'm sorry. I didn't mean—"

"No. More." Diane dragged Valerie's head back down, her fingers twisting through Valerie's hair. She pressed her mouth to Valerie's ear. "You can't hurt me. Not by touching me. I'm dying to have you inside me."

Valerie sobbed out a cry of need and wonder. She pushed herself down until her face was pressed to Diane's stomach, then she cupped Diane's breast with one hand and filled her with the other. She squeezed and rolled Diane's nipple as she pushed into her, higher and deeper, thrust after thrust.

"God," Diane gasped, arching frantically to meet each stroke. "I don't want to come but you're going to make me."

"Yes," Valerie whispered urgently. She kissed her way lower, gliding her tongue over soft skin and trembling muscles and into the fragrant heat. She hummed as her lips found Diane's clitoris and she licked lightly.

"Oh no," Diane pleaded. "Don't make me come so soon."

"I want you," Valerie whispered, before sucking her even more firmly.

Diane gripped the sheets and pushed down hard around Valerie's fingers as her clitoris swelled to fill Valerie's mouth. "So good, so wonderful, so… oh, oh I'm…"

Valerie watched Diane's face reflect the pleasure that rippled around her fingers and pulsed between her lips, and thought she'd never seen anyone as beautiful. She didn't stop caressing her, inside and out, until Diane murmured a weak protest and twisted away.

"Love," Diane whispered. "I won't be able to walk today if you don't stop."

Tenderly, Valerie placed a delicate kiss at the apex of Diane's sex, then rested her cheek in the hollow adjacent to her hipbone. She continued to fondle her breast, smiling as Diane's mouth curved in obvious enjoyment. "That's what you *say*, but that's not what your body is telling me."

"My body is greedy." Diane gazed down through heavy lidded eyes. "Insatiable, in fact, for you."

"Really?" Valerie kissed low on Diane's belly, then nuzzled her face a little lower. "I can handle that."

"Oh, I know you can. Take your clothes off and come up here first," Diane murmured. "I want you, too."

Valerie shed her tank and panties and slid into Diane's embrace, easing her swollen center against Diane's leg. She kissed her lingeringly, slowly rocking against her. "I only have a minute."

"Can you come this way?"

"I think so, if you…help me."

"Anything."

"Play with my breasts," Valerie said thickly, already sliding faster up and down Diane's thigh.

"You're so wet. So beautiful." Diane pulled on Valerie's nipples. "Does it feel good, darling? Rubbing against me like that? Getting me all wet? Will you come for me?"

"Oh, yes. I'm almost…almost," Valerie gasped. "Kiss me. Kiss me…oh god, I'm so close."

"Soon," Diane breathed, capturing Valerie's mouth and squeezing her breasts rhythmically. As Valerie's motions grew more frantic, Diane plunged her tongue deeper, matching Valerie's frenzied thrusts. Sensing Valerie struggling to orgasm, Diane drove her hips up and forced her leg more tightly against Valerie's clitoris. "Harder, darling. Press yourself har—"

"I'm going to come." Valerie's head fell back, her eyes wide and fixed on Diane's. "God, I love you."

"I love you," Diane cried.

Shuddering, Valerie spilled onto Diane's welcoming body and collapsed into her arms.

❖

With several minutes to spare before the briefing, Valerie knocked on the door to the guesthouse. Savard answered.

"Hey," Savard said, holding the door wide. "You missed a good show at Matheson's compound a couple of weeks ago."

"So I hear." Valerie stepped inside but hesitated before going any further. "I'm sorry I didn't make it."

"Yeah, me too." Savard glanced toward the adjoining room where Cam and Felicia waited. "It could have been any of us in your spot. I'm glad it wasn't me."

"I appreciate that." Valerie grasped Savard's arm. "Listen. Cam told me about what happened in Boston. I owe you for taking care of Diane."

"No you don't," Savard said dismissively. "But if you really feel like you do, you can plan on sticking around here where your friends are for a while."

"Thank you," Valerie softly. "I'll do that."

"Good." Savard turned and started toward the command center. "Then let's go to work."

"Good morning," Cam said as Valerie came in. Felicia nodded to her. "Our priority for the day, and every day until it's accomplished, is to identify your handler. We'll work from the assumption that he's an associate of Matheson's, because otherwise we don't even have a starting place."

"All right."

"I want you to scan the files Davis has compiled of known Matheson associates, including the academy students. We might get lucky."

Valerie smiled ruefully. "We could use some luck."

"Before we get to that," Cam said, "I want Stark to join us so she can hear how you got behind our lines." She opened her phone and pushed several buttons. "Chief, can you come down for a minute? Thanks."

While they waited, Valerie and Felicia got coffee and opened several boxes of doughnuts that Tanner's day crew had delivered.

"It's good to have the team back together," Felicia said.

"It is." Valerie opened the refrigerator for milk. "How's Mac?"

"He's back on the team, too. He's up at the main house seconding for Stark. I'm sure you'll see him later." Felicia smiled and stirred her coffee. "He's...making a remarkable recovery."

Valerie studied her with interest. "Really."

Felicia met her gaze. "Quite."

"Well, good for you."

"Yes, it is." She sipped her coffee. "Ah, Diane?"

"Luckily, she's forgiven me."

Felicia shook her head. "I don't believe she ever thought there was anything to forgive."

"I hope you're right."

At the sound of the front door closing sharply, Felicia said, "Time for round two. Stark's not going to be happy."

"I don't blame her." Valerie followed Felicia back into the other room and sat at the table next to Cam. Stark sat stiffly across from her.

"Good morning, Chief," Valerie said formally.

"Agent Lawrence."

"Valerie will do," Valerie said softly.

Stark seemed to relax by degrees. "Sorry. That was quite a stunt you pulled last night. We could have killed you."

"I wanted to talk to Cameron."

"Did you ever hear of a phone?"

"I don't like phones."

"How about a car? You could have driven right up to the foot of this road and our people would have stopped you, checked your ID, and called me."

"Assuming they were all your people, and trustworthy."

"You don't trust us?" Paula flicked her gaze to Cam, who said nothing.

"I trust *you* and the other people in this room. And Mac, and Hara, and Wozinski. I don't trust people I don't know." Valerie's face was hard to read. "Besides, I might have been followed."

"How do you know you weren't?" Paula couldn't keep the anger from her voice. "You know you're a target, and you could have led whoever might be following you right here. *And* showed them a back door in."

"Number one," Valerie said, "anyone who might want me dead already knows where you are. I was extracted from here a few weeks ago, remember?"

Paula said nothing, but the muscles along her jaw tightened.

"Number two, no one followed me last night."

"How do you know that?" Paula demanded.

"Because I've been on the island since late last week. No one has been following me."

"The marina," Cam said, annoyed with herself for not having anticipating that.

Felicia laughed. Stark merely stared. Savard made a point of not looking at her lover.

Valerie smiled. "Yes."

"You came in by boat?"

"I rented a slip at the marina for my cabin cruiser a while ago."

Cam glanced out the window, realizing how far ahead Valerie had planned her moves. On some level, she must have been uneasy with her assignment from the beginning. "You set up an alternate identity when you were here working with us last month. So when we did a sweep for any newly registered guests last week, you didn't turn up. You were already there."

"I worried when the Company sent me in to infiltrate your team that it wasn't going to turn out well. It's always prudent to establish a new identity when you can't be certain that any of your old ones will be safe." Valerie spoke directly to Cam. "And I knew if you wanted to get Blair to someplace inaccessible, you'd come back here."

"Your handler doesn't know about any of this?"

"No."

Stark made an exasperated sound. "So last night you just circled around the tip of the island on foot and walked down the beach."

"Yes. Not exactly the route I'd use for a surprise attack, but it got me where I wanted to go."

"So we can assume," Cam said, "that Matheson *and* your handler suspect we're here. They know the general area since they were able to extract you undetected, but we hadn't established a perimeter that far from the houses at the time."

"Tanner has had reconnaissance boats on the water twenty-four hours a day since we've been here." Stark looked pointedly at Valerie. "Other than normal marina traffic, every vessel is monitored to ensure they aren't attempting a beach landing."

Valerie felt a mixture of gratitude, guilt, and relief at the disclosure. Stark trusted her or she would not be discussing their security measures. Valerie could tell her colleague was still angry with her for ignoring procedure the night before, but at least she was talking as if they were still on the same side.

"I'm sorry I put your team in an awkward position, Chief," she said. "To tell you the truth, I just wanted to get here."

"Well, we didn't shoot you, which is the main thing. It would have caused all kinds of hassles trying to come up with a cover story for that."

Cam gave Stark a nod, part affirmation, part prompt.

Stark rose. "If you don't need me any longer, Commander, I'll go back to the marina and look at everyone who has a slip or rents a room there."

"I think we're done, Chief. You intend to advise Tanner of the situation?" Cam struggled not to issue orders to secure the marina.

"Immediately, and I'll inform Egret and Ms. Bleeker that the marina is off-limits for the time being until we've secured it."

"Thank you."

Stark nodded to the group and left.

"What name have you been using here?" Felicia asked Valerie.

"Ingrid Klein."

"You realize you've just burned that identity if you want to disappear again," Savard pointed out.

"I seem to be limiting my options, don't I?" Valerie met Cam's eyes.

Savard smiled. "Looks like you'll just have to stay."

"Well then, put me to work."

Felicia turned a laptop in her direction. An array of photos filled the screen. "Start looking."

❖

Six hours later Valerie pushed away from the table in disgust. "If he's in here," she said, gesturing toward the computer, "I don't recognize him."

"When you met, did you ever get the feeling that he was disguised?" Felicia asked.

Valerie shook her head. "No. He always looked like a nondescript guy in an off the rack business suit.

"Which I'm sure is exactly how he wanted to look."

Valerie rubbed the bridge of her nose. "Maybe we should try military archives."

"And start where? What branch, what years?"

"Matheson served. Let's look at everyone he might have met from boot camp until the day he was mustered out."

Felicia nodded. "I'm working on it, but accessing those kinds of military files…I have to use a little finesse."

"Can't Cameron use her Homeland Security go-anywhere-free pass to access those records?"

"She could," Savard said from across the room where she worked at her own computer station. "But it would alert any number of individuals, and that's exactly what we don't want."

Valerie nodded. "I guess until we find out how deep this goes, it's safer to trust no one." She looked from one to the other. "So, when will I have more photographs to look at?"

"Later today," Felicia said.

"All right. Until then, if you give me a secure line, I'll try contacting some of my previous sources. I might be able to pick up a hint of what's happening out there."

"We should be able to arrange—" Savard tensed and swiveled toward the front door at the sound of it opening. She relaxed when Cam walked in.

"Stark says there's no one suspicious at the marina."

"Excellent," Savard said.

"Where are we?"

"I didn't get anywhere with the photographs. I'm sorry," Valerie said.

"It was a long shot with no reference point. Are you at a place where you can take a break?" Cam asked.

Valerie stood. "Yes, of course. Whatever you need."

"I thought we'd try to work up a sketch of your handler."

"We don't have a sketch artist here, do we?"

"No." Cam smiled. "We've got something even better."

❖

Blair closed the French doors to the living room and carried her supplies to the sofa. She pushed back the sleeves of her long-sleeved

T-shirt, kicked off her ankle high boots, and sat cross-legged on the sofa with her sketch pad propped on her knees. "Have you ever done anything like this before?"

"No." Valerie settled into an adjacent chair and crossing her legs. After waking with Diane and working with the team all morning, she felt almost normal again. "Have you?"

"No. It should be a challenge."

Valerie smiled thinly. "Well, what else is new?"

Blair glanced up. "I guess it's new ground for all of us."

"I thought I had learned to expect the unexpected a long time ago," Valerie said, draping her hands over the ends of the arm rests. "Apparently, I was wrong."

"Because of 9/11?" Blair asked, sketching Valerie's profile. It wasn't why they were there, but she couldn't help but be captivated by the classic lines of her face.

"That, and being asked to usurp information from an ongoing investigation and," Valerie said as Blair drew rapidly, "falling in love with Diane."

Blair's hand stilled. "Is that what happened?"

"Yes."

"Good."

"You approve?" Valerie inquired with a hint of surprise.

Blair turned over a fresh page in her sketch pad. "I could say it's not for me to approve or disapprove, but Diane is one of my two oldest friends and I love her. She didn't ask for my opinion, by the way."

"Which is?"

"I think you're a terrible choice for her. You're involved in dangerous work that requires you to lie to everyone, probably even yourself, about what you do and what you feel. Anyone with sense would find that scary." Blair met her eyes. "Speaking as her friend, I'd rather she got involved with someone who wasn't so likely to break her heart."

"I'm going to try very hard not to."

"I believe you, and like I said, that's good. Because you're the one she wants, and in the end, that's the only thing that matters." Blair picked up her pencil. "So, just off the top of your head, who does this guy remind you of when you see him?"

"Bob Hoskins, only thinner."

"Roundish face, broad eastern European features..." Blair sketched quickly and asked without looking up, "Hair?"

"Dark brown, thinning, no obvious balding spots. Subtle widow's peak."

"Good eye. That's great."

"Thanks," Valerie said. "For this and for looking after Diane."

"You're welcome." Blair continued to draw. "And by the way, I'm glad you showed up."

"Pale blue eyes, five o'clock shadow." Valerie sighed. "I should've thought to wear one of those little lapel cameras to one of our meets."

Blair stopped drawing and stared. "You actually use those things?"

"No, but I've always wanted to."

Blair shook her head. "Like I said. Scary".

CHAPTER TWENTY-THREE

Wednesday

Yes, that's correct. 777-3214. I'll pay by credit card." Valerie turned at the sound of footsteps behind her. Cam stood in the doorway watching her intently. "I'm sorry. Here it is." Holding Cam's gaze, she recited her account number. "And you'll be sure that goes in tonight. I understand. That's fine. Thank you."

Valerie closed her phone. "Did you need me?"

"Phone drop?" Cam asked neutrally.

"Yes. I change the contact number weekly and reprogram my cell."

Cam crossed the guest house kitchen to the window that looked out onto the wraparound deck. It was late afternoon and the sky was a solid blanket of hazy gray clouds. "Storm coming. I think it's cold enough to snow."

"Aren't you going to ask me if I'm planning on disappearing again?" Valerie joined Cam and their shoulders touched lightly. She might have imagined the heat that penetrated Cam's shirt and her own blouse, but she knew the sensation was real.

"No. That's not what I was thinking. I know you're not ducking out."

"Thank you."

"I do have a few questions, though."

Valerie smiled. "What do you want to know?"

"It sounds like you're anxious to get a new number to your handler."

"He won't use one more than once, and I ignored his last message a week ago."

"Any particular reason you want an open line to Henry right now?"

Valerie shrugged impatiently. "Cameron, in the last two days I've looked at hundreds, probably thousands of photographs. Felicia has worked on a regression image of the sketch Blair did. It's a good approximation of him when he was younger, and we've run that, plus an age-appropriate computer-generated image, through every database that exists, including Interpol. We can't find him, not this way."

"Eventually we'll sort out Matheson's other contacts, we'll find Matheson, and he'll lead us to Henry or someone else will." Cam turned her back to the window. She was inches from Valerie. "This is the tiresome part of investigative work."

"Believe me, I understand that some things take time. I spent five years creating my cover in DC before I'd even met you."

"Jesus." Cam was blindsided by a wave of anger and tenderness when she imagined Valerie being used as currency in the high-stakes game of international espionage. For an instant, the barriers of professionalism and personal restraint wavered, and she almost touched her.

Valerie shook her head, recognizing the change in Cam's expression. "It's all right, Cameron. Truly."

Cam's charcoal eyes darkened to obsidian. "It isn't, but it's done."

"Not quite." Valerie backed away. There was too much heat between them, there always had been. "It won't be done until I know that I can trust Henry or I can be sure the link is broken for good."

"You're planning to meet him."

Valerie smiled ruefully. "You're very good at this. The Company lost out when they didn't recruit you."

"They tried."

"I'm not surprised. What stopped you?"

Cam shrugged. "I was a little older than you by the time they approached me, and I already had serious trust issues. Seeing my father killed when he was supposedly being guarded made me wary of giving too much control to anyone. And I guess it made me want to do a better job than had been done for him."

"God," Valerie sighed. "I wish I'd had a little less trust when Henry first showed up in my life."

"How do you intend to determine if Henry can be trusted?"

"He'll either try to kill me, or he won't," Valerie said simply.

"And if he does try?"

"Then I'll know that my entire life has been more of a lie than I ever realized."

Cam stepped closer, but kept her hands at her sides. "Not all of it."

"No," Valerie whispered, her gaze gently caressing Cam's face. "Not all of it."

"You'll need backup."

"I'm not asking you or your team to put yourselves at risk because of my miscalculation."

"Bullshit," Cam said dismissively. "Number one, you're part of the team. Number two, it's not your miscalculation. Number three, I was going to suggest you meet with him myself."

"Really."

Cam rubbed her neck wearily. "Yes. I think we'd break this eventually, but I don't think we have the time. We can't stay here forever. Blair has public obligations. Diane has a life, and I think—no, I know—they'll try to get to you through her. We have to draw out your handler and Matheson on our terms."

"I agree. Besides, I never did enjoy waiting for someone else to dictate conditions."

"Then let's start calling the shots ourselves," Cam said fiercely.

"All right." Valerie hesitated. "May I ask you a personal question?"

Cam smiled. "There's something left about me you don't know?"

Valerie touched her sleeve, then dropped her hand. "Many things, I'm sure. This is about Blair."

"Go ahead."

"Do you tell her about these things?"

"Oh man, ask me something easy." Cam slid her hands into her pockets and walked the length of the room, then returned. "I tell her as much as I can because that's my part of what keeps us together."

"And what's hers?" Valerie asked.

"She tries to understand why I do what I do and doesn't ask me not to."

"She's going to be unhappy about this."

"Possibly, but not nearly as unhappy as Diane is going to be."

"I haven't decided if I'm going to tell her." Valerie returned to the window. "It will be beautiful here if it snows."

"You know, I'm the last person to give advice on personal matters," Cam said, standing beside her.

Valerie laughed softly. "But?"

"You should tell her."

"Why?"

"Because you owe it to her. You let her fall in love with you. You could have stopped it."

"I couldn't." Pain filled Valerie's voice. "I couldn't because I needed her so much."

"Then you forfeited your right to make unilateral decisions."

"Your approach to relationships is something like battle planning, Cameron," Valerie said.

Cam lifted her shoulder. "You use what you know."

"What *I* know is that I'm not going to run anymore. From anything."

"The only way we're going to know if Henry has turned is if he makes a move to take you out."

"Yes," Valerie said evenly. "In this particular instance, the length of our relationship works against him. He's used to thinking of me as a subordinate. He'll probably be suspicious, but I don't believe he'll truly see me as a threat."

"He'll still have the first shot."

"I'll just have to duck."

"Let's hammer out a plan with Felicia and Savard so you don't have to."

❖

"I'm not going to like this, am I?" Blair stepped away from the canvas she was painting and faced Cam, brush in hand.

Cam smiled crookedly. "Probably not at first, but—"

"Just tell me, and let me decide."

Cam moved a few more steps inside the door and studied Blair's new work. She'd never seen her paint a portrait before, and this one caught her by surprise. Blair had captured Valerie's innate loneliness in her remote expression and the faraway focus of her ice blue eyes. Cam found it hard to look away as she crossed the studio to her lover.

A roaring fire blazed in a large stone fireplace against the far wall. The only other light came from several spotlights that Blair had focused on her easel. Blair wore a faded red plaid flannel shirt a size too big, faded jeans, and moccasins. She had been engrossed in working on a small area of shading and hadn't heard Cam enter the room at first. Cam was sorry to have disturbed her.

She put both hands on Blair's shoulders and kissed her. "That's beautiful."

"So is she." Blair gave a quizzical smile. "I haven't been able to get her face out of my mind. I've seen beautiful women before, but it's not just that she's attractive. She's hauntingly sad and yet so strong."

"The sadness will disappear the longer she's with Diane." Cam rubbed her cheek over Blair's hair. "Mine did."

"Cam," Blair wrapped her arms around Cam's waist and caressed her back. "You sound a little sad right now."

Silently, Cam shook her head and kissed Blair's throat, then brushed her lips over Blair's ear. "I love you."

Blair leaned back, keeping her thighs tight against Cam's, and smoothed her palms over Cam's chest. "Oh, darling. I love you too. Now tell me the bad news. I know you didn't interrupt me just to remind me why I love you so much."

Cam winced. "I need to talk to you about an operation we're planning, and I need you not to tell Diane."

"Please Cam. I can't just stand by and watch Diane be used—"

Cam shook her head. "It's not like that. It's not that I don't want her to know, but it's not your place or mine to tell her about it. It's Valerie's."

Blair snapped off the spotlights, leaving only the fireplace to illuminate the room, and walked a few feet away to face the fire. Cam watched the red glow cast Blair in shadows and dreaded the distance that was about to come between them.

"Valerie is going to arrange a meet with her handler," Cam added.

"Is that safe?"

Cam said nothing.

"You don't know, do you? That's the reason for the meeting, to try to…what, make him show his hand?"

"Something like that."

"This was Valerie's idea?" Blair glanced back at Cam. Beyond her, through the window, the night sky was devoid of moon or stars. The ocean was a distant thunder that might have been the sound of bombs falling.

"Yes," Cam said, "but I was going to suggest it if she hadn't."

Blair shook her head wearily. "You two are far more alike than I ever realized." She paused, her expression rueful. "Appearances can sometimes be so deceiving. Valerie *looks* so much like the woman she was supposed to be—the kind of woman who would spend her time acquiring fine art and appreciating the company of a handsome woman like you in her bed."

"Blair—"

"And of course," Blair went on undeterred, "she is those things, isn't she? But she's also as single-minded and stubborn and...and reckless, in her way, as you and all the rest." Blair threw up her hands. "God, Cameron. Is there no other way?"

"We don't think so."

"I know there are things you're not telling me, but you don't need to spell it out for me to know how dangerous this is. How worried about you do I need to be?"

Cam kept her gaze steady but she flashed on Valerie, alone, with a man who very probably wanted to kill her. "I'll be backup. It's far more dangerous for her."

Blair tilted her head as if listening to something that hung in the air between them. "You're frightened. Frightened for her."

"I always worry about my team—"

"No, it's more than that." Blair closed the distance between them and settled her hands lightly on Cam's waist. "It's okay. I know how you feel about her."

Cam shook her head. "No. You don't."

Blair smiled wistfully. "You are everything in the world to me. And you love me perfectly, Cam. Perfectly."

"I wish I did." Cam frowned as she skimmed her fingers through Blair's hair. "But I swear I've never loved anyone like I love you, and never will."

"See what I mean?" Blair kissed her softly. "Perfectly." She traced the column of Cam's neck and slid her fingers underneath the collar of her blue button-down shirt. "I'd like to ask you a favor."

"I'll do it if I can."

"Let Savard lead the operation. You're too close to Valerie and I'm afraid of what you'll do if she's in trouble."

Cam rested her forehead against Blair's. "I have the most experience with operations like this. Savard is not a hundred percent. I can't let Valerie do this without the best backup possible." She looked deeply into Blair's eyes. "It has to be me."

When Blair framed Cam's face, her hands trembled. "Promise me that you will not sacrifice yourself for her. I don't care about your duty. I don't care about your honor. I care that you come home to me. So you promise me that."

"I…" Cam thought about what it meant to have Valerie and Savard and the others place their trust in her, to lead them into danger with the pledge that she would guard their well-being with her life. She thought about what it meant to ask for the love of a woman. She had asked for Blair's love, and her vow had been sworn the first time Blair had said *I love you* and she had not walked away. "I promise."

❖

Diane found Valerie on the beach.

"I'm sorry if you wanted to be alone." She kept both hands in the pockets of her coat, even though she wanted to touch her. "Savard and Felicia came up to the house for a late supper and said that you'd gone for a walk."

Valerie slid both arms around Diane's shoulders and kissed her softly on the mouth. "Don't apologize. I'm glad to see you. I'm sorry I lost track of time."

"It's cold and you don't have any gloves."

"I'm fine."

Diane pressed close to her. "You're not. You're shivering."

Valerie smiled. "Let's go inside, then. Have you eaten?"

"Not tonight. I was waiting for you."

"Sorry."

Diane kissed her lightly. "Stop saying that."

"All right." Valerie took Diane's hand. "Let's grab something quick to eat and warm up in bed."

"If I have a choice between you in bed or a meal, I'm not going to need dinner."

Valerie laughed. "Then let's go to bed first and have a midnight snack later."

"What I have in mind might take longer than midnight to accomplish." Diane drew Valerie's hand into her pocket as they climbed through the dunes. "I want to make love to you because I've been thinking about it all day."

"I think I hear a *but*," Valerie said gently.

Diane took a breath. "But I don't want to be with you while part of my mind is wondering what secret you're keeping. Is it something you can tell me?"

Valerie stopped on the back porch and pulled Diane into the shelter of her body, out of the wind. She rested her cheek against Diane's. "We're planning an operation. I'm preoccupied, that's all."

"An operation. You and Cam and the others?"

"Yes."

"Will it be dangerous?"

Valerie hesitated. "It could be if we're careless, but we're not going to be."

"I don't have any experience with this. I've known Blair most of our lives and I thought I had some understanding of what her life was like, but I was wrong."

Valerie stiffened. "I had no right to drag you into this. It might be better if I left."

Diane turned Valerie until she could see her face in the faint light coming through the windows from the house. "Is that what you want? To leave me—to leave us?"

"No," Valerie whispered faintly.

"Then don't ever say that again. Just give me time to get used to this. Can you do that?"

"Yes. God, yes. Anything." Valerie kissed her again, her fingers trembling as she cupped Diane's face. She buried her face in the warmth of Diane's throat. "Anything, anything as long as I don't lose you."

"You must be certain that I don't lose you either." Diane kissed Valerie urgently. "All right?"

Mutely, Valerie nodded, hoping that her silence would be taken as the promise she couldn't make.

CHAPTER TWENTY-FOUR

Thursday

Valerie grabbed the phone on the first ring and slipped from bed.

"Yes?" She moved to the window and peered out into a starless black night. She was barely silhouetted, but Diane could still make out the shimmering outline of her body.

"I'm ready...I had to be sure. Yes. Yes, but I don't trust her." She lowered her voice and Diane strained to hear. "Look, I can't talk... Where?...No, somewhere I can be sure you're alone. Trust?" She laughed harshly. "You might be followed...Look, forget it. I'll just... Yes, that will work. All right, if that's what you want...No, that's too soon. Because I don't want to alert anyone here to what I'm doing... Yes. Fine. The usual."

After breaking the connection, Valerie remained still in the silent room, listening to the echo of his voice and the breathing of the woman in the bed. Between those two people lay the boundaries of her world— past and future—bordered by truth and lies. Quietly, she made her way across the room and slipped back into bed. She drew Diane into her arms. "I'm sorry I woke you."

"How did you know?" Diane asked.

"I could tell from the way you're breathing."

"You're very perceptive."

Valerie grimaced. "It's funny, I was trained to do two opposite things equally well. To avoid intimacy with anyone, while at the same time being sensitive to every nuance of expression and movement. It seems I've spent my life watching, but never living."

Diane took Valerie's hand and drew it to her breast. "I'm alive and I'm very real. So is my love for you."

"Why?" Valerie murmured, cradling Diane's breast and brushing her lips over the nipple. "I can't imagine this is what you want."

"This? You mean being with you?"

"Everything that being with me means." Valerie sighed and rested her cheek between Diane's breasts, still softly caressing her nipple.

"Your phone call. That was the person you report to, right?"

"Yes."

"You're going to meet with him."

"Yes."

"You lied to him, about not trusting someone here. Cam, I guess."

"Yes, I lied to him," Valerie said, holding very still.

"Did he believe you?"

"I don't know. Probably not. One of the basic rules of our training is not to trust what people say, or sometimes even what they do, until they've proven beyond a shadow of a doubt that they're trustworthy."

"The two of you have known each other for a long time. Doesn't that count?"

Valerie gently kissed the curve of Diane's breast. "You'd think it would, wouldn't you? But it really doesn't. It's possible that he was telling me the truth at the beginning, and somewhere along the line his priorities or his orders changed. It's nearly impossible to tell."

"But you don't trust him any longer, do you?"

"No," Valerie said.

"Do you trust me?"

Valerie kissed Diane's throat, then her mouth. "Yes. Completely."

"Will you tell me what you're going to do?"

Valerie hesitated and the silence that closed in around them was more frightening than anything she'd ever known. "When I know, I'll tell you."

"Thank you."

"I know I'm asking a lot of you, but—"

"I have no idea why people fall in love," Diane said. "Or why we need to. But I do know this about you—you're strong but you're lonely, and you can survive without love, but you long for it. You need me, and I need you. None of the rest matters."

"You're the only person I've ever let myself truly need," Valerie said so softly Diane could barely hear her. "If I lost you now—"

"I'm not going anywhere, I promise." Diane lifted Valerie's face between her hands and kissed her, softly at first, then more deeply. She guided Valerie on top of her until their legs entwined and their bodies melded. Her kisses grew insistent as she urged Valerie's hips to move with hers, calling to her without words, marrying their bodies and hearts with the force of her passion and desire.

"I love you," Valerie murmured.

Diane's breath quickened as Valerie groaned and thrust harder. Wanting more, wanting everything, Diane twisted onto her side and forced Valerie onto her back. Still kissing her, Diane cupped Valerie's sex and found her already wet and open. With a soft groan she pushed inside her, rejoicing silently as Valerie arched and cried out in pleasure and surprise.

"Oh yes, that's how...there...I need you hard, please, harder," Valerie gasped.

Distantly, Diane was aware of her own building arousal, but all she wanted was to have Valerie with nothing between them—no secrets, no fears, no regrets. "I love being inside you. I love feeling your heartbeat under my fingertips. I love to please you."

With every word Diane thrust a little harder. Her teeth skated over Valerie's neck, and when Valerie tightened around her fingers, she sucked on the delicate skin of her throat.

"Oh my God," Valerie moaned, pushing against Diane's hand. "I'm coming. Oh God, it's so good."

Diane closed her eyes tightly, concentrating on Valerie's labored breathing, her soft cries, the pounding pulse that beat around her fingers. She carried her smoothly to a peak, and then again, until Valerie buried her face in Diane's neck and cried silent tears. Diane rocked her and caressed her face.

"It's all right, darling. Everything is just exactly as it should be."

"I'm not used to anyone touching me that way," Valerie whispered. "Sorry, I can't...my control..."

Diane laughed. "Oh, I hope you're not apologizing. You're beautiful when you come. I never want to stop making love to you."

Valerie laughed weakly. "That's one thing I'll never ask."

❖

When Cam walked into the kitchen at 5 a.m., she found Valerie seated at the table, her hands inert around a mug of coffee. "You're up early." Cam helped herself from the fresh pot on the counter. "What's on your mind?"

"Henry called."

"Are you ready?"

"More than ready."

"But?" Cam watched a litany of emotions flit across her face. Anger, unease, resolve.

"I know things are going to move quickly once we start planning the operation," Valerie said. "So I wanted to talk to you before the briefing, What I am going to say is just between you and me."

"I'm listening." Cam could guess what was coming. Valerie was used to working alone, being alone. She had never learned to lean on others—so like Blair that way.

"If something goes wrong, we both know it's very unlikely you'll be able to extract me," Valerie continued. "I don't want you to try. Collateral damage would be high, and..." She glanced down at her hands, which she'd folded on the tabletop, and then into Cam's eyes, "My life isn't worth yours or one of the others'."

A gasp cut across her words. "It is to me." Diane stood in the doorway. "Damn you, it is to me!"

"Diane!" Valerie jumped to her feet and caught Diane as she turned to flee. "Diane, wait, you don't understand—"

Diane whirled back, her cheeks pale and her eyes blazing. She knocked Valerie's hands away. "What do I not understand? I just heard you tell Cam she should let you die rather than risk someone else's life. Every single one of them risks their life every day protecting Blair. Is she so much more important—" She broke off and covered her face with her hands. "Oh God, I can't believe I'm saying this."

"That's enough," Cam said steadily, rising to her feet. "No one is going to die. And *no one*," she said, her eyes fixed on Valerie, "is going to be left behind. That's the last conversation I intend to have about this." She pointed to the clock. "We have a briefing in twenty minutes and we have a lot of planning to do. I expect you to be on time, Agent Lawrence."

Cam walked out without waiting for an answer.

"I'm sorry," Diane whispered, turning away.

Valerie gently caught her shoulders and embraced her. "No, *I'm* sorry. I'm sorry you had to hear that. I never should have talked to Cam about this here."

"But you're not sorry for asking her to leave you behind, are you. I thought you said you loved me."

"Oh God, I do," Valerie said desperately. "But can't you see, my whole life has been leading to this point, and I couldn't live with myself if Cam or one of the others suffered for the mistakes that *I* made."

Diane caressed Valerie's cheek. "You don't get it, do you? Loving someone means forgiving yourself for the past and living for the present. And the future. We all have regrets, darling."

"I've always operated with the knowledge that my life is expendable."

"Well, it isn't anymore." Diane kissed her softly. "Please try not to forget that."

Valerie took a deep breath. "All right. I'd better go."

"You won't…do anything without telling me, will you?"

"No. We've still got time."

"Of course we do," Diane said fervently. "Of course we do."

❖

"Yes?" Matheson said when his phone rang.

"We've arranged to meet."

Matheson smiled. "Run it down for me."

He listened, making a few notes on a notepad with the motel's name and logo stamped at the top. After a moment he said, "Nice work."

"There's still a chance we could bring her over. And she's got an inside channel to several targets."

"You might be right. Let's weigh the options."

❖

"Okay, let's get started." Cam walked briskly to the table, making eye contact with the agents already assembled. Stark and Valerie sat side by side across from Felicia and Savard. "Agent Lawrence, why don't you fill us in on your conversation with your handler."

If Valerie noted the formality, she didn't show it. "Henry and I made contact at 0330 and spoke for less than five minutes. We agreed to a rendezvous at 2300 tomorrow."

"That doesn't leave us a lot of time," Cam commented.

"I realize that, but he initially wanted to schedule the meet for tonight, and it would not have been unusual for us to rendezvous with such little lead time. Twenty-four hours was as much delay as I thought I could manage without rousing his suspicions."

"We'll work with it," Cam said. "Location?"

"The extraction point we used when I left the island the last time."

"The beach here?" Stark said sharply. "No way. We're not letting hostiles onto the island while Egret is on site."

"I'm sorry, I wasn't clear," Valerie said quickly. "Not on the beach, but where the extraction vessel was anchored."

"On the water," Savard said, making it a statement. "You're going to meet him at sea."

"Yes. I'll take my boat and we'll rendezvous approximately a mile out."

"So he knows you're at Whitley Point," Felicia said.

"He does. He asked if I had contacted Cameron. I said I had and confirmed my location when he asked." She glanced briefly at Cam. "I had to assume that he already knew. A lot of small planes pass over here every day, and he could easily have aerial surveillance photos. If he knows I'm here, or that you are, I didn't want to be caught lying to him."

"Whose idea was it to rendezvous at sea?" Cam asked.

"His."

"It's a trap," Felicia said. "He can sink you out there and make it look like weather or a mechanical problem."

Valerie shook her head. "Not before he meets with me. I told him I didn't trust Cameron. He'll want all the intelligence he can gather on Cameron's operation before he burns his connection with me."

"Smart," Cam observed. "He'll want to talk to you. He'll want to know what we might suspect about him or Matheson."

"That's what I think, yes," Valerie said. "That would be typical for this kind of situation. A brief verbal information exchange."

"What about putting me below deck on Valerie's boat, Commander?" Savard asked.

Cam shook her head. "He's going to search."

"Can you at least get him onto your boat?" Savard asked Valerie. "We can rig cameras and microphones to monitor you there, but if you have to board his, we'll be lucky to get audio."

"Will he search you for a mic?" Felicia asked.

Valerie shrugged. "I don't know. He never has before, but the rules have obviously changed."

Cam held up her hand. "We can't depend on him coming aboard Valerie's vessel. We'll need long-range satellite tracking. Mac can coordinate that from here." She looked at Stark. "You'll need to pull people from Tanner's day crew to augment your night shift. We can't be certain they won't try a dual assault, and you and Mac will be tied up coordinating communications."

Stark stiffened. "Mac doesn't need me to assist. I can go with the ground detail, Commander."

Cam shook her head. "Not with Egret on site. You need to be here. If something goes wrong, you'll have to evac her quickly. I'd suggest you make contingency plans to get her back to the White House, but that's your call."

"Yes, ma'am."

"We'll have to go without visual if Valerie boards Henry's vessel," Cam said with a nod to Savard, "but I want audio surveillance that Henry won't catch even if he looks. Wires are too risky if he does a body search."

"He's not going to have the equipment to look for an implantable," Valerie said. "If we get it in by tomorrow morning, the puncture site should be very difficult to spot as little as twelve hours later."

"A transdermal receiver?" Savard said, her eyes brightening with anticipation. "How are we going to get it? That's the kind of stuff only the DOD has, and even that's just a rumor."

"It's not a rumor," Valerie said.

"What's the range?" Felicia asked.

"1000 yards." Valerie glanced at Cam. "He may see you at that range."

"Possibly," Cam said. "But we're close enough to fishing and shipping routes that there will be plenty of water traffic, even at night. We'll run without lights as much as we can."

"That's quite a distance if we have to extract quickly," Savard said.

"Once Valerie and Henry rendezvous, he'll be occupied and we'll be able to drift in closer." Cam cut her eyes to Valerie. "A minute. That's likely to be how much time we'll need to get aboard if you signal. Two, tops."

"Understood," Valerie replied with a faint smile. "That's a very acceptable margin."

"With respect, Commander," Savard said, "that's a long window."

Cam didn't disagree. Even sixty seconds could be a death sentence if the operation went bad. "We've got thirty-six hours to cut the margin. Let's get working."

CHAPTER TWENTY-FIVE

Friday

Y ou don't have to leave right away, do you?" Diane sat on the
bed watching Valerie dress. "It's not even nine o'clock."
Valerie hesitated, still not used to disclosing the particulars of an
operation to anyone. Of course, before Diane, there had never been
anyone close enough other than Cam. Now, even though she would
trust Diane with her life, she felt uneasy discussing the work she did.
She had only just returned from spending the day finalizing the last
details of the plan with Cam and Savard, and her mind was completely
engaged with what was to come. It occurred to her then that there were
reasons intimate relationships were discouraged for agents such as
herself. The needs of others were a distraction. *Life* was a distraction.

Forcing herself to focus on Diane, Valerie found her looking more
pale than usual. She knew Diane hadn't slept the night before, even
though she had tried to pretend she was sleeping. Eventually they'd
both admitted they were awake and had made desperate love until
morning, when Valerie had silently slipped away while Diane slept.

"I want to be at the rendezvous point well before he arrives,"
Valerie said.

"What about the others? They'll be with you, won't they?"

"They'll follow a short time later. Don't worry, they'll be there
long before anything happens."

"Can I come with you to the marina?"

Valerie shook her head as she tucked her long-sleeved T-shirt
into her jeans. "I'm riding down with one of Tanner's crew and they
won't be coming back here." She kissed Diane softly. "I don't want you
getting marooned out there in the middle of the night."

"I don't mind waiting." Diane rose and clasped Valerie lightly around the waist. "I'm going to go slightly stir crazy waiting here."

"You need to stay here," Valerie said gently, pulling Diane close. She brushed her mouth over Diane's ear. "It's important that you stay close to Blair in case you have to leave quickly."

Diane stiffened. "You mean if something goes wrong out there."

"There are any number of reasons why Stark might want to move you both, and it won't necessarily mean that anything has gone wrong. Just promise me you'll do whatever Stark says."

"I'm not leaving here without you."

"You may have to. Please, love, I need to know that you will do what Stark says." Valerie cupped Diane's cheek. "I need to know you're all right so I can concentrate on doing this thing. Can you help me?"

Diane took a deep breath. "Yes. But promise you'll call me or come find me as soon as you can?"

Feeling Diane tremble, Valerie murmured softly and kissed her. "I won't disappear. I won't do that to you again. No matter what."

Diane nodded. "Where's your gun? You're taking your gun, aren't you?"

"Yes." Valerie released Diane and went to the dresser where she kept her weapon. She clipped the holster to the waistband of her jeans. "He'll expect me to be armed." She didn't add that he might also ask her to relinquish it as a show of good faith. Diane didn't need more to worry about.

"I'm sure there are things I should be doing or saying, but I forgot to ask Blair for pointers," Diane said shakily.

Valerie gathered her close again, drawing deeply of her scent, imprinting the shape and feel of her body and the way she fit so seamlessly into her own waiting places. "You don't require any advice on giving me exactly what I need. I love you."

"I love you too. I'll see you soon."

"Yes you will," Valerie said gently. She kissed her and was careful not to make it feel like goodbye. She would not leave Diane with that memory.

❖

Cam reached for her shoulder holster but Blair got to it first and held it up so Cam could shrug into it. She pressed against Cam's back, caressing the tops of her shoulders and down her arms. When she reached her hands, she slid her fingers between Cam's.

"Tanner was here earlier. I think she wanted to come with you."

Cam shook her head. "We're using more civilians than we should already, but since I *know* I can't keep Tanner from sending her people out on the water to do perimeter surveillance, I asked her to head up that part of the operation. But there's no way I'm letting her get anywhere close to Henry."

"I wish you didn't have to get close either," Blair said, meeting Cam's eyes in the mirror over the dresser. What she saw made her tighten her hold on Cam, wrapping their joined arms around Cam's middle, as if she could keep her safe within her embrace, forever. "You're worried about something. What is it?"

"The problem is we can't really get close *enough*," Cam said, "so we're going to be relying on some pretty dicey technology. That's not the way I like to do these things."

"No, I know," Blair murmured. "You like to be right there yourself. Is it selfish of me to be glad that you're not going to be able to stand in front of her if someone starts shooting?"

Cam eased out of Blair's embrace and turned. "No, it's not selfish. I wouldn't feel any differently if the positions were reversed. This is just one of those times when it's actually better to be close to the line of fire." Cam kissed her before walking to the closet to retrieve her windbreaker. "But we have an experienced team, and with Stark and Mac here coordinating and Tanner's people on the water, we've got all the bases covered. It'll be fine."

"Where's your vest?" Blair said sharply.

"In the truck."

"Tell me you're going to wear it."

"I will." Cam grabbed Blair and kissed her again, harder this time. "We'll need to debrief as soon as we're done, so it might take awhile before I can call. Don't worry, okay?"

"I'll try."

She stepped back, but kept a grip on Blair's forearms. "If for any reason Stark wants to evacuate, it might be tomorrow or the next day until we reconnect."

Blair narrowed her eyes. "Why might Stark want to evacuate?"

"We don't think Matheson will try to hit here, but it's not beyond the realm of possibility."

"Is that the only reason?"

"Blair," Cam said pleadingly.

"Cameron. When will you stop trying to protect me?"

Cam shrugged ruefully. "Probably never."

Blair stroked her face. "All right. Good enough. Then just answer when I ask, if you're not going to volunteer the information."

"If Stark loses communication with us for any reason, we've agreed that she will get you out. It might be something as simple as the satellite link going down, so there's no reason for you to worry if it happens."

"You can't honestly believe that."

"The only person at risk here is Valerie," Cam said. "That's the truth."

"Don't think I don't care about what happens to her, Cam," Blair said, "because I do. I like her. Diane loves her. I don't want anything to happen to her." Blair tangled her fingers in Cam's hair. "But *you* are my lover, and you come first, before anyone. Before Diane. Before my father, before this country."

Cam held Blair's face as gently as she could and caressed her mouth with her lips. As she kissed her, she whispered, "The same is true for me. I'll be back as soon as I can."

❖

"How's the leg feeling?" Paula asked as she buttoned her shirt.

"Good. Steady." Renée slid an extra clip of ammunition into her jacket pocket. "Did you post extra people on the beach?"

"Yeah." Paula threaded her belt through her holster and snugged the buckle down. "We tightened the perimeters and doubled the guards. Matheson is not coming ashore without us knowing it."

"What about the road?" Renée sat on the bed to lace her boots. It still hurt to squat down or bend over. Fortunately, she wasn't going to be doing much moving once they got on board the boat.

"We put up roadblocks diverting everything except local traffic, and we've got two people there to check any cars coming through. Fortunately, island traffic is really light this time of year."

"Yeah, I know. If this had been summer, it would've been a nightmare." Renée walked to Paula and snaked her arms around Paula's shoulders. "Don't take any chances, okay? I don't have to tell you how good Matheson's people are."

Paula thought back to the attack on the Aerie and the insane few moments when the automatic weapons fire was all she could hear. It seemed almost incomprehensible that six short weeks ago an attack like that had been beyond imagining, and now she was preparing to protect the first daughter of the United States against a possible assault by a group of US extremists as if it were business as usual.

"The commander was right moving us here. It's more defensible than if we were almost anywhere else. But don't worry, at the first sign of any problem, I'm moving her."

"Good." Renée kissed her quickly. "I'll see you in a little while."

"Hey," Paula said, stopping Renée with a hand on her arm. "I know you want this guy. We all do. Just…just don't take any chances, okay?"

For the first time, Renée recognized that Paula was worried. Worried and trying not to burden her by saying so. For the last two days, they had both been so caught up in planning the operation that they'd barely had a moment alone together. When they had taken a break, they'd had little energy to do more than fall into bed to catch a few hours' sleep before getting back to work. And, she had to admit, she was excited about another operation and thinking about nothing else. She was eager to get back into the field, and hungry, *aching*, for payback. Ever since 9/11 she'd felt impotent, and the thwarted raid on Matheson's compound had only added to her sense of helplessness. Now she had a chance to settle the score, and that was all she'd been thinking about.

"Hey, sweetie, I'm sorry," Renée said. "I've been running on autopilot since yesterday morning. God, I want this guy so bad."

"Do you think you'll be able to take Henry alive?" Paula asked.

"That's going to be Valerie's call, I think," Renée said, sitting down on the edge of the bed and patting the space next to her. "Sit with me for a minute."

Paula sat beside her and slipped an arm around her waist.

"If Valerie reads Henry as still friendly, she's going to recommend a meeting between the three of them—her, Cam, and Henry—someplace on neutral territory. If she doesn't trust Henry or if Matheson shows, I think Valerie is going to make a different call."

"That's got to be tough after all the time they've worked together," Paula said.

"She's ice." Renée said it respectfully. "She'll do whatever needs to be done."

"I know. We all will." Paula kissed Renée and squeezed her hand. "Try not to mess your leg up again tonight."

"I won't." Renée smiled, tightening her grip on Paula's hand. "By the way, I love you like crazy."

"Same here," Paula whispered. "Same here."

❖

"All set?" Cam asked as Valerie joined her and Savard in the kitchen.

"Yes. Where are the others?"

Cam tilted her head toward the closed doors of the adjoining room. "Operations center. Do you want to look at the setup?"

"No," Valerie said. "I'm sure Mac has everything under control." Valerie stood next to the table where Savard was drawing a clear solution from a 50cc glass vial into a 1cc syringe and unzipped her jeans.

"How does your neck feel?" Savard asked as she opened a foil wrapper and extracted an alcohol swab.

"A tiny bit sore," Valerie said, rubbing a fingertip lightly over the spot just below her ear where the transdermal microphone had been inserted that morning. "How do you read it?"

"Loud and clear," Savard said, pointing to the wireless receiver that was barely visible in her ear. "Right leg or left?"

"Left."

Savard pulled on gloves, swabbed Valerie's upper thigh with the alcohol, and palpated for the femoral pulse. When she found it, she inserted the needle half an inch away, drew back until she saw venous blood, and injected the Neosynephrine. "You're going to feel your heart race in a few minutes, but the peripheral vasoconstriction won't be maximal for an hour and a half to two hours." She met Valerie's eyes. "Once this starts working, your skin is going to be damn cold and if he touches you, he'll know."

"If he touches me it will only be for a second and I don't think he'll notice," Valerie said as she zipped her jeans.

Savard gathered her equipment. "Wear as little as you can on the boat on the way out to drop your core temperature even more. I don't know how well this is going to work. I'm just guessing on the dosage."

"I dressed light and I'll take my jacket off. I'd go in the water, but he'll notice if I'm wet."

"We can't risk you getting that cold," Cam said, shaking her head. "If you have to go into the water for any reason later on, and you start out with a core temperature that low, you won't last thirty seconds."

Valerie smiled. "You'll be there before that."

Cam said nothing.

"See you later," Savard said, touching Valerie lightly on the arm before leaving.

"There's a car outside to take you down to the marina," Cam said as she and Valerie walked toward the front door. "I'll ride with you."

Valerie stopped. "No. Stay here. I know how many last-minute details there are to check. I'm all right, Cameron."

The hallway was dimly lit, and Cam thought Valerie looked almost ghostlike in the shadows, as if she were already gone. It made her uneasy, and she unconsciously reached out and touched her cheek. "You're not going to be alone out there."

"I know. I'm not worried." Valerie covered Cam's hand for a brief second. Then she drew it away from her face, but kept Cam's fingers in her grasp. "There are many things unsaid between us. You should know that there were times that your presence in my life was the only thing that mattered to me. There was never a single moment when I felt anything but cared for by you."

"Valerie," Cam murmured. "You're—"

"Let me finish, because we've got work to do," Valerie said gently. "I've been happier these last few weeks, despite everything, than I've ever been in my life. Diane means everything to me, and if it weren't for having met you and realizing that I could love someone, I don't think I would have been able to love her the way I do. Take care of her for me, if anything happens to me tonight."

"All right," Cam said roughly. "I'll make you that promise because I don't want you thinking about anything tonight except the operation.

Do your job, and I'll do mine, and you'll be back here before sunrise."

"Thank you, Cameron." Valerie leaned close and kissed Cam lightly on the mouth. "Happy hunting, Commander." Then she turned and walked out the front door.

Cam listened to the engine start and the vehicle pull away before heading back to the operations center. The ache in her chest eased as soon as she walked in and saw Mac and Stark sitting before computer consoles. Felicia stood just behind Mac, her hand on his shoulder. These were her people, the best at what they did of anyone in the world. She trusted them to keep Blair safe. To keep Valerie safe.

"How's the feed?" Cam asked.

Without turning around, Mac said, "Excellent. Our friends in the Pentagon have great toys."

Cam leaned down to look at the satellite image of the sector of ocean where Valerie would rendezvous with Henry. It was so clear, she could feel the spray. "Amazing. Why didn't we have this before we hit Matheson's compound? We might not have dropped into a hot zone."

"Because it wasn't their action." Mac looked over his shoulder at Cam and grinned. "And, you weren't a deputy director of Homeland Security. If you had been, who knows what kind of cool equipment they would have pulled out for you."

"Hopefully Henry doesn't have the same toys." Cam glanced at Stark. "Exit strategy in place?"

"Yes. We've got choppers standing by at Bradley."

"Do they know why?"

Stark shook her head. "No, only that it's priority one."

Stark's phone rang and she pulled it off her belt. "Stark. Send him in." She closed the connection. "Tanner's man is here."

A moment later, Wozinski entered with a thin, sandy haired young man dressed in black BDUs.

"This is Jeff Donaldson," Wozinski said.

Cam held out her hand. "Donaldson."

"Ma'am."

"Tanner tells me you're a good shot."

"Sniper duty in Somalia, ma'am."

"Good." Cam watched his eyes as she spoke. They were clear and calm and steady. "Comfortable with infrared targets?"

"Yes ma'am. If it's hot, I can hit it."

"That's what we're counting on." Cam thought of the injection she'd just given Valerie. "And we're hoping that one hot target is all you'll have."

CHAPTER TWENTY-SIX

They're leaving." Blair rose from the living room sofa where she had been waiting with Diane.

"If you don't mind, I'll stay here," Diane replied, her voice subdued.

"I'll be right back."

Blair caught up to Cam just as the team reached the front door. She smiled briefly at Savard and Felicia, then turned to her lover. She ran the edges of Cam's windbreaker through her fingers as she leaned close and kissed her softly, far more quickly than she wanted. "See you soon."

"I'll call you," Cam murmured. "I love you."

Blair stepped away and in the next instant, Cam and the others were gone. When she turned, she saw Diane halfway down the hall, standing in the doorway of the living room. She forced a smile and went to join her.

"What now?" Diane asked.

"It's going to be quite a while before we hear anything," Blair said. "I'm too restless to sit, and if you'll be all right, I'd like to check in with Mac and Paula. I'll feel better if I know what's going on."

"I don't know what I want to do." Diane made an angry sound. "But I don't need to tell you, sitting around and waiting is not my style. Can I come with you?"

Blair hesitated, remembering the horror of seeing Cam on the video monitor after she'd been shot—lying on the ground, bleeding—and literally watching her die. She doubted that they would have that kind of communication link tonight, but even if they couldn't see or hear exactly what was happening, she still wasn't certain that letting Diane listen to Paula and Mac monitoring the events was such a great idea. If something went wrong, Diane would never be able to forget it. Blair didn't want that kind of nightmare for her.

"I may be new at this," Diane said as if reading her mind, "and I'm hoping this is the last time I have to wait while she's out doing something like this, but if she's willing to go out there and do it, I can at least be a part of it here. Then I'll feel like she's not alone."

"Okay," Blair said, shaking her head ruefully. "I don't know why I even questioned it. You wouldn't have fallen in love with her if you couldn't handle who she is."

Diane smiled. "Thanks."

Blair knocked on the closed door to the dining room before opening it a few inches and sticking her head in. "Can Diane and I come in?"

Paula swiveled in her chair, her expression distracted but her tone polite. "Of course. We're not going to be able to explain much once things get going, but you're welcome to stay."

"Thanks," Blair said. "You don't need to worry about us, Chief."

Blair and Diane moved up behind Mac and Stark.

"Can you tell us what we're looking at?" Blair asked.

"This is a satellite relay of ten square miles surrounding the meet point," Paula said, turning back to the computer monitor, which showed a smattering of small blips on a grid surrounding a dark circle in the center. "The majority of the vessels in the area are fishing boats, commercial ships, and the occasional recreational vehicle." She pointed to a glowing dot in the middle of the circle. "That's Valerie."

"How do you know that?" Diane asked.

"We have GPS transponders in all of the vessels, including Valerie's, the command ship with Renée and the commander and Felicia, and Tanner's surveillance boats." Paula skimmed her finger in a semi circle along the border of the screen. "These are Tanner's people here."

"When will we be able to see Cam?" Blair asked.

"They're just leaving the marina now." Mac adjusted the wireless receiver in his ear and spoke using a throat mic, keeping both hands on the keyboard of his computer. "Commander? How do you read?"

A few seconds passed, then Mac spoke again. "Loud and clear, Commander."

Paula said without looking at him, "Can you put that on audio, please, Mac."

"Yes ma'am." Mac keyed a series of commands into his computer and then spoke again. "Ready for camera scan."

"Sending image…now," Felicia's voice announced from the speakers.

Yellow, red, and blue images vaguely resembling human forms flickered on Mac's screen and then stabilized.

"How do you read?" Felicia asked.

"Four hots." Mac opened a small window within the larger screen and a fluctuating bar-graph appeared. "Temperature variation less than two degrees. Give me a coordinates check."

Savard rattled off a list of figures.

"What are they doing?" Blair asked, not really expecting an answer.

"Checking the variance on the infrared thermal detector camera," Paula said. "The lower levels of thermal radiance are due primarily to two things—either larger body mass and high body fat, which blunts the reading, or a true depression in body temperature."

"You're the warm one, Renée," Mac said.

Savard laughed. "That's what they tell me."

"Mac, can you correct for body mass using the limited readings we have?" Felicia asked. "Valerie is thin and her core temperature is going to skew the thermal readings. Can you factor for that?"

"Working on it," Mac said, inputting figures as he spoke.

"You're in visual range, Commander." Paula straightened and her voice took on an edge. "We have an approach vessel closing on ground zero, bearing…"

Blair sensed Diane trembling beside her and slid an arm around her waist. She kept her voice low so as not to disturb Mac and Paula. "Just remember that we're only getting part of the picture here, so don't worry, no matter what seems to be happening."

"I know. I'll remember. It's just…she feels so far away," Diane whispered.

"She isn't. And Cam and Renée and the others are right there."

"Savard, hold us here," Cam's voice said.

The words were so clear that Blair almost looked over her shoulder to see if Cam had miraculously returned. Even miles away over radio, the sound of Cam's voice eased the tension that had been slowly clenching her muscles and squeezing around her heart until she felt as if she were a piano wire tightened to the point of snapping. She forced herself to take a breath and let it out slowly.

The red numerals in the lower left-hand corner of Paula Stark's monitor read 2258.

❖

Cam opened the priority one channel to Valerie. "Lawrence?"

"I'm here, Commander," Valerie said.

"Approach vessel on its way."

"Roger that."

"If you're forced to board his ship and we lose our audio link to you, I want you to bail at the first sign of trouble. Are we clear?"

"Clear, Commander," Valerie replied.

"Confirming scan now," Cam said. "Switching to open channel."

"Roger that. Greetings, team," Valerie said. "Glad to see you."

"We're right behind you, Valerie," Savard said.

"Do we have her?" Cam asked Felicia, bending down beside Felicia's computer array against one wall of the ship's cabin. Behind them, Savard eased the engine down to idle and the ship rocked in the swells.

"I've got her," Felicia said. "I'm just adjusting the feed to Donaldson's video goggles." She opened up the com link in her head set. "Donaldson? Target on screen?"

"Sweet and hot, ma'am," he radioed from his position outside on the bow.

"Not too hot, I hope," Cam murmured. "Where does she fall on the thermal range?"

"Five percent below mean."

Cam frowned. "That's not much to distinguish her from Henry."

"She's cold, I can guarantee you that," Savard said. "Much colder and her reaction time will be so slow she won't be able to protect herself."

"Here he comes." Valerie's voice filled the cabin. "Switching to transdermal mic."

Savard linked to Mac. "Anyone else out here with us?"

"Lots of someones," Mac radioed, "but no one in critical range."

"Okay, let me know if anyone moves within the strike radius."

"Roger."

A minute of silence passed until broken by Valerie's voice, muted by the shielded microphone.

"Toss me your tie line," Valerie said, *"and come aboard."*

"Here you go. Catch," a deep male voice responded. *"Drop your ladder."*

Savard glanced at Cam in surprise. Cam shook her head, thinking it wasn't necessarily a good sign that Henry was so willing to board Valerie's boat. It meant they had an open channel to Valerie if they needed one, but if Henry's plan was to eliminate Valerie, he wouldn't want to do it on his own vessel. He'd want to do it on hers.

"Are you armed?" Henry said.

"Of course."

"What about the others?"

"What others?"

"Don't tell me you came without backup."

"Do you see anyone?" Valerie asked.

Henry laughed. *"Only about two dozen boats out there."*

"I told you I don't trust them. No one knows I'm out here. Search the boat if you want."

"Not necessary. I agreed to this meet under these less than optimal circumstances," Henry said, *"so you'll believe me when I tell you that you need to come in. You're in danger."*

"From whom?"

"From Roberts. The White House sent her after you."

"Why?"

"They need a scapegoat. How long do you think they'll be able to keep the attack on the president's daughter quiet? Add to that they botched the assault on Matheson's compound and let him escape."

"He had help."

"The country needs accountability, especially after 9/11. Someone needs to pay for that," Henry said. *"Washburn and the security adviser and a fair number of other people have decided it will be you, for starters. It's out of our hands."*

"And if I come in?"

"We'll help you get lost for a year or two. There's work to be done elsewhere."

"Convincing, isn't he," Felicia muttered. "Bastard."

"What's the temperature register look like?" Cam asked.

"There's a three degree difference between them." Felicia keyed Donaldson. "Can you distinguish the primary from the friendly?"

"Yes ma'am, as long as they don't move around too much."

"On my mark," Cam ordered on the same channel.

"Yes ma'am. Locked and loaded."

"Who tipped Matheson?" Valerie asked.

"We think he has friends in the Special Forces."

"Do we have a name?"

"Several possibles. I'll brief you as soon as you are secure."

"Where do you want me to go?"

"I want you to come with me now."

"Tonight?"

"If you go back, Roberts may lock you down and we won't be able to extract."

"What about my boat?"

"We'll sink it. It's a good cover."

"He came prepared." Cam checked the digital readout on the electronic timer running in one corner of Felicia's monitor. Henry had been on board almost five minutes. That was a long time for this kind of rendezvous.

"If she goes with him, he sinks the boat and she'll disappear," Savard said. "If she doesn't agree to go, and he's bad, he'll sink the boat and she'll disappear. Either way, he wins."

"I need at least 24 hours to create a plausible cover with Roberts," Valerie said. "I didn't spend all that time getting close to her to lose my connection to her now. Even if I have to go deep undercover, I'll still have a link to her."

"She'll never give you anything."

"She already has."

"What?" Henry's voice rose.

Listening, Cam tensed. Valerie was playing a dangerous game. If Henry thought she already had important information, he might not let her go even if he wasn't working with Matheson. If he *was* Matheson's front man, all the more reason to take her now, or eliminate her.

"They're close to identifying..."

Two miles away, Stark's satellite image showed a new blip at the same time as Mac picked up a thermal flair five miles from Valerie's boat.

"Christ," Mac blurted. "It's an SSM!"

Stark jumped to her feet. "Target?"

"Tracking!"

Stark grabbed her radio. "Hara, this is command one. Stand by to evacuate."

"No!" Blair exclaimed, grabbing Stark's arm. "What is it?"

"Missile." Stark turned sharply to Mac. "Target. I need it now, Mac!"

Mac was already opening the comm channel. "Savard! Ship to ship missile, targeting Valerie's boat. Forty seconds to impact!"

❖

"Donaldson, mark," Cam snapped.

"Roger."

Cam switched to the open microphone on Valerie's boat. "This is Cameron Roberts. You are targeted for a direct hit by an SSM. You have thirty-seven seconds. Evacuate your vessel."

"She's lying," Henry shouted. *"Stay right there!"*

"No," Valerie said, *"she's...Henry, we have to...why are you drawing your weapon? There's no one..."*

❖

"Thirty-two seconds," Savard called. "She'll never disengage from Henry's vessel in time, Commander."

"Fire!" Cam ordered and Donaldson's rifle cracked from just

outside the cabin. Cam spun toward Savard. "Get us in there *now*."

"It's going to get hot," Savard noted even as she powered up the engine and shoved the throttle to maximum.

Cam didn't answer, stripping off her windbreaker and vest as she ran from the cabin. She'd been wrong. They didn't have thirty seconds.

❖

Blair pressed close to Paula's back, unconsciously gripping her shoulders. "What's happening?"

"Time?" Paula shouted to Mac.

"Five... four... three... two... one..."

For a millisecond, the blip in the center of Paula's screen doubled in size. Then it winked out.

After a minute of silence, Diane asked unsteadily, "Where's Valerie?"

"We've lost the signal," Paula said tightly.

"What about Cam's?" Blair's fingers dug into Paula's shoulders.

Paula shook her head.

❖

"Fine shooting, Colonel." Matheson leaned against the rail of the boat, feeling a swell of satisfaction as a tower of flame climbed into the sky on the horizon.

"Thank you, General."

"We've eliminated both problems at once," Matheson said. "It's time to rejoin our men and re-dedicate ourselves to our true mission. We have a war to win."

CHAPTER TWENTY-SEVEN

Is she...are they...Oh, God," Diane whispered.

"Get me a narrow-field, real-time image!" Paula ordered. She keyed her radio. "Hara, standby. Close the roads. No one in or out. Call in the backup units and position them on the shore and the perimeter."

Blair realized she was still gripping Paula's shoulders and forced herself to let go. She couldn't move her eyes from the screen in front of her. She stared at the dark circle, willing an image to appear.

"Cam's boat," Blair asked hoarsely. "Cam's boat should still be there, shouldn't it? Paula?"

For the first time in her life, Paula ignored the first daughter. Renée was on the boat that had suddenly disappeared. The thought sent a momentary surge of panic through her and she went completely blank. Then, as if changing a channel in her mind, picture after picture snapped into view and came sharply into focus. Beirut, the Cole, the World Trade Center, the Pentagon. A field in Pennsylvania. Not one life. Not hundreds of lives. Thousands and more to come, she knew. And her part to play was here, today, and it would never be about one life again. Not even the life of the woman she loved.

"They're there, somewhere, and we'll find them," Paula said steadily, because she had to believe it. "Mac, get me a picture of what's going on out there and an open line to Renée Savard."

"Yes ma'am," Mac said, his voice rough with strain. "I'll do that."

❖

"There's debris in the water," Savard shouted over the roar of the engine.

Cam leaned over the railing, narrowing her eyes against the icy spray and staring at the shiny black surface of the water. "Who's got the wheel?"

"Donaldson. I need to be out here." Savard raised the radio cradled in her hand. "I'll direct him."

Cam didn't argue. She doubted she could get Savard to go back inside, and she didn't have the time or inclination to persuade her. One hundred feet in front of them a geyser of flame spouted into the air, the engine fuel from Valerie's and Henry's boats burning. She should have expected something like this. Matheson would be a fool to leave a weak link like Henry alive, and Matheson was no fool. Henry had underestimated him, and so had she. She would not let Valerie pay for her miscalculation. She kicked off her shoes, shrugged out of her holster, pulled her badge off her belt, and pushed everything into a bench locker.

"You can't…the water is 40 degrees—Commander?"

"Tell Donaldson to head for the flames and to get all the lights focused off the bow. Move ahead slowly. Christ, we don't want to hit her."

"Commander—"

"She's in the *goddamn water*, Renée, and I'm going to get her out."

Savard shouted orders into the two-way. As the boat corrected course, Cam flung her head back, furiously trying to clear her vision. Oily smoke roiled from the flaming hulls, obscuring the surface of the water. The boats were no longer tethered to one another and huge sections wallowed in the waves. Burning fragments the size of refrigerators drifted as they slowly sank.

"There!" Savard pointed off to their right. "The dinghy!"

Cam jerked around and followed Savard's arm. A capsized inflatable rubber dinghy bobbed on the water.

"The explosion probably upended it," Savard cursed.

Cam stepped up onto the railing and dove into the water.

❖

"I'm getting something now, Chief," Mac said urgently as he continued to rapidly type. "It'll just take a second to redirect the satellite focus."

"Get me in as tight as you can." Paula turned at a sound behind them. Hara stood in the doorway. "All clear?"

"Yes ma'am. Everything is quiet." She glanced toward the monitors but said nothing.

"Run status checks every five with the team leaders," Paula directed.

"Yes ma'am. I'll take point on the shore."

"Good." Paula bent forward, peering at the monitor as if that would make the fuzzy images clearer. Without warning, the screen cleared and a sharp black-and-white image of a burning boat came into view.

Blair caught her breath, momentarily disoriented by the eerie sensation that she was watching news footage, the kind of images that were ubiquitous and somehow mind-numbing. But she felt anything but numb. Her nerve endings burned, and it felt as if her entire body were twitching. A red haze of fury and panic threatened to skew her vision, and she had to blink to focus.

"Can you tell whose boat it is?" she asked.

"Not yet," Mac answered. "We'll have a slightly wider field in just…there, there's another vessel." His voice drifted off as a partially submerged, smoking boat came into view. "We've got at least two vessels hit." He touched his ear and frowned. "It's Tanner requesting permission to begin search and rescue."

Stark shook her head. "No. We don't know that whoever sent the first missile doesn't have another one ready to go. The commander's boat is out there somewhere. Until we contact her, we keep this locked down. Tell Tanner to maintain her position. She is not to pursue any unknown vessel."

Mac relayed the order.

"They might need help, Paula," Blair urged. "What about the Coast Guard?"

"No. This is a Homeland Security operation. We don't involve anyone else."

"What if Cam's boat was hit too?"

"If we confirm that," Paula said, "I'll send a team out from here."

"How long can they last out there, if they're in the water?" Diane asked.

Paula didn't answer. Instead she said, "Find them for me, Mac."

❖

Cam didn't think she'd ever been so cold. It was the kind of cold that went so deep it was an ache inside of her. She didn't think about the pain but just swam arm over arm in the direction where she'd seen the dinghy. Valerie had been in it, she knew that she'd been in it. Henry was dead. She'd ordered him shot. Valerie was the only one who could have launched the dinghy.

Her clothes were sheets of ice dragging her down. Her arms and legs were heavy. It was hard to move. So much smoke. Black acrid stinging smoke that singed her already swollen throat and clouded her eyes with tears and salt. Cold.

Her hand struck an object and she tried to grab it, but it floated away. She rubbed her face against her frozen sleeve. The dinghy. A wave crashed over her head and she went under. It was a relief to be out of the smoke. Her throat felt momentarily soothed until she reflexively took a breath and water flooded her lungs. She gagged, vomited, then clawed her way to the surface. She broke through and sucked in a lungful of tainted air. Coughing, she tried to swim and managed only to keep her head above water. Then she saw it again. The dinghy. From somewhere deep inside, she found another ounce of energy. Valerie was there, she knew she was there. Valerie had launched the dinghy.

Cam pushed herself toward it. She had sent Valerie out here alone. She would not let her die alone. She found the nylon rope that circled the dinghy and tried to hold on to it with frozen fingers. When it popped away from her she gave up trying and sluggishly circled it, her muscles slowly turning to lead.

For an instant, she thought she imagined the white form floating next to the dinghy. When she reached out, her fingers were too stiff to grasp the ghostlike figure. Closer now, she could make out Valerie's wrist wedged underneath the encircling rope on the rubber life raft. She had tethered herself to it somehow.

"Valerie," Cam croaked. She got a mouthful of water and spat it out angrily. "Valerie!"

Cam struggled to release Valerie's wrist from the twisted lines. The instant Valerie's arm slid free, she started to sink beneath the surface. Cam couldn't grip her clothing, but she managed to get an arm around her waist and pulled her against her body.

"Valerie, it's Cam. Swim. You have to swim."

Cam couldn't tell if she was breathing or not, and for a fraction of a second she felt the way she had when Blair had been exposed to a potentially deadly toxin. The floodgates she kept securely locked against loss and despair broke open and the pain was so crippling she was momentarily paralyzed. They went under together, Valerie clasped in Cam's arms.

❖

"Command One, do you read," Felicia's voice filled the room.

"Felicia," Mac cried. "Status. Status report. Are you—"

"… engaged in search and rescue. Any sign of incoming?"

"Negative." Mac switched channels and the original wide-angle view came into focus. "Advise evacuate area as soon as possible."

"Roger, as soon as rescue is complete. Do you have visual?"

Mac turned to Paula who was staring at the speakers as if she were trying to see through them to Felicia and the others.

"Felicia, this is Stark. We have debris from two vessels…no survivors identified."

"Thermal scans?" Felicia asked sharply.

"Nothing," Mac said, "but if Valerie's in the water, she's probably too cold already."

"We have two in the water. Do you read? Two."

"Who?" Paula inquired urgently.

Blair didn't need to hear the answer. She already knew.

❖

Cam didn't have the energy to fight. The cold in her bones had dissipated, and so had the pain. Her body was strangely heavy, yet weightless at the same time. She couldn't see, but the sharp smoky sting in the air was gone. She wasn't in the air. She was underwater.

She was underwater, and Valerie was with her. Valerie wasn't moving. What had Blair said to her? She'd made her promise something. Cam was so tired and it was so hard to think.

Promise me. Promise me you won't sacrifice yourself for her.

That's right. She had promised Blair. Promised her not to die for Valerie.

A surge of adrenaline shot through Cam, electrifying her. She'd promised not to die for Valerie, but she hadn't promised to let her die. What had she said? *No one was going to die.* She tightened her grip on Valerie and kicked. The surface seemed very far away.

And then she felt it—Valerie was kicking too. Neither one of them was going to give up without a fight.

❖

"Mac's got a thermal body pattern in the water," Felicia announced, hurrying from the cabin to join Savard on deck.

Renée strained to see through the smoke, arcing the floodlights back and forth. "Over there—two in the water, twenty yards off to the right. Help me lower the life raft."

"I'm coming with you. Donaldson can handle the boat."

Renée nodded and between the two of them they unlashed the life raft from its deck moorings, disengaged the lock on the pulley, and swung the small boat out over the water. Felicia hit the switch for the motor and as the inflatable raft lowered automatically, she grabbed two PFDs from a nearby locker. She tossed one to Renée and pulled hers on.

"There are two more clipped inside the raft for them." Felicia swung her leg up and over the railing. "Let's get them the hell out of the water."

"Great idea," Renée shouted and followed her over the side and down the ladder.

Felicia started the motor and propelled the boat toward the area of the last sighting. "Do you have them?"

"No!" Renée leaned as far over the front of the raft as she dared, gripping the handholds. "Head further to your right. There…wait. Yes! There!"

"Be careful," Felicia shouted as Renée braced her legs against the side of the raft, released the handholds, and leaned over the side. Felicia set the motor to idle and clambered forward, joining Renée. Together, they grabbed for Cam, whose head and shoulders were just visible above the water next to the raft. Even in the flickering red light from the scattered fires still burning amongst the debris, her face looked deathly pale.

"Commander," Renée shouted as she reached down with both arms. "Can you grab on to me?"

"No," Cam gasped. She pushed Valerie forward. "Take her first."

Felicia and Renée grasped Valerie's inert body under the arms and pulled her into the raft. She wasn't moving and appeared unresponsive. When Renée looked back into the water she saw Cam go under. She dove in, grabbed Cam around the waist and pulled her back to the surface. Shaking water from her eyes, she saw Felicia leaning down and pushed Cam into her arms. Then she fumbled for the rope around the edge of the raft and finally managed to hold onto it. Together she and Felicia pushed and pulled Cam into the raft. Finally, Felicia grabbed Renée's arm and Renée managed to lever herself up and onto the floor of the life raft.

"Commander," Renée gasped. Cam lay curled up against the opposite side of the raft. Valerie was stretched out between them.

"The commander's conscious, but I don't think Valerie's breathing," Felicia shouted, hurrying back to rev the engine. "We need to get them to the boat."

Renée scarcely noticed as the small, crowded raft tossed and spun from crest to trough and back up again. Kneeling beside Valerie, she opened her blouse and pressed an ear to Valerie's breast. She heard a distant heartbeat but she couldn't detect any movement of her chest. Cupping Valerie's chin, she tilted her head back, covered her nose with her opposite hand, and sealed her mouth to Valerie's. As she blew into her lungs, all she could think was that Valerie was cold. Cold as ice. Cold as death.

"Come on, Valerie. Come on." Renée blew another breath. "Breathe. Goddamn it. Breathe." She felt the barest flicker as Valerie's chest rose beneath her hand and she hurriedly pressed her cheek to Valerie's breast again. This time the heartbeat was slow and even fainter than before. Far slower than it should be. Frantically, she yelled over her shoulder, "She's breathing, but I'm not sure for how long. Hurry up or we're going to lose her!"

❖

"This is Staff Sergeant Donaldson reporting," Donaldson's voice announced through the speakers.

Paula straightened up abruptly. "Where is everyone else?"

"The agents are engaged with resuscitation efforts, ma'am. I have the conn, and we are returning to base."

"Status?" Paula snapped.

"Two casualties."

"Put that launch right up on the beach below our location. Do you copy?"

"Loud and clear."

Paula signaled to Mac as she spoke and he nodded, murmuring instructions into his radio. "Donaldson—ETA?"

"Ten minutes."

"How badly are they hurt?" Blair said, standing so close to Stark she could hear her rapid breathing. "Are they burned?" Behind her, she heard Diane groan softly.

"What's their condition?" Paula asked.

"Major hypothermia. That's all I can tell you, ma'am."

"Roger that. Bring them home, Donaldson."

"Yes ma'am. I'll be pleased to do that."

As Paula instructed Mac to call the marina for additional resuscitation equipment, Blair grabbed Diane's arm and dragged her toward the door. "Come on. We need to get fires going in the bedrooms and fill the bathtubs. We're going to have to get them warmed up."

"Shouldn't we call for an ambulance or something?" Diane asked, hurrying along beside Blair.

"No time," Blair said, taking the stairs to the second floor on the run. "The most critical thing for an exposure victim is to get them warm as quickly as possible." Blair stopped outside Diane's bedroom. "Are you okay?"

Diane stared at her as if she were insane. "This is a nightmare and I keep praying I'll wake up. But until I do, I'll do anything I have to. I'm not going to let her die."

"Don't worry," Blair said grimly. "No one is dying tonight."

CHAPTER TWENTY-EIGHT

It was too dark for Blair to see exactly what was happening on the beach, even with the floodlights on the boat spotlighting the people swarming all over it. When she had attempted to run down in search of Cam, Paula had informed her that both she and Diane were confined to the house until further notice. Blair would have argued, but that only would have delayed Paula in organizing the teams to get Cam and Valerie up to the house. She was acutely aware that Paula was doing everything possible to take care of the injured, even though she had to be crazy with worry over Renée.

Despite understanding the reasons behind the protocols, Blair couldn't control what she felt, which verged very close on panic. She just wanted to see Cam, and waiting was agony. She alternated between stalking out to the rear deck and pacing in the kitchen. Diane waited at the window, watching the activity on shore in pale silence.

"Here they come, finally," Blair said when she was able to make out a clutch of figures transporting a still form on a stretcher toward the house. Only a single stretcher. Her chest tightened. What did that mean? Where was the second casualty? Where was *Cam*?

"I'm sure they'll take them right upstairs," Blair said, concentrating on what she could do rather than letting the terror swallow her. "Let's go up so we can help."

Within minutes, Felicia and Wozinski half-carried Cam into the bedroom. She was wrapped in an emergency thermal blanket and, other than her shoes, appeared to be naked. Her face was gray and her skin looked rubbery from the cold, but Blair was nevertheless enormously relieved to see that she was conscious and making some effort to walk. Blair pushed back the covers on the bed. "Over here."

"I'll get the IV set up," Wozinski said, as Felicia and Blair helped Cam into bed.

"No," Cam rasped. "You and Felicia give Savard a hand with Valerie."

"Stark had supplies brought over from the emergency aid center at the marina," Blair said, replacing Cam's damp blanket with several layers of dry ones. "I heated four liters of saline in the microwave. Greg, I can help you get Cam's line started while Felicia assists in the other room."

"Yes ma'am," Greg said.

Cam shook her head weakly. "I can wait—"

"No, you can't," Blair said firmly. "Go ahead, Greg."

Felicia said, "I'll be next door with Valerie."

When Greg left to get supplies, Blair sat on the edge of the bed next to Cam. She cupped her cheek, shuddering inwardly at the icy touch. "Are you injured anywhere?"

"Bumps and bruises." Cam's teeth chattered. "Fire feels good. Maybe I can sit closer."

"As soon as you get some warm fluids into you." Blair stroked her face. "You know that rapid external rewarming can cause problems." Blair had skied in enough remote areas to know the protocol for exposure and hypothermia. So did all of her security staff, and every shift contained at least one agent who was an EMT like Savard and Wozinski. Many hypothermia victims died during the initial resuscitation attempts because warming the outside of the body without raising the internal temperature led to cardiac collapse. "We'll get you warmed up as fast as we can, but we're not taking any risks."

"Right now I'd take my chances," Cam said, shivering violently. "Christ, I'm cold."

"I'll get some more blankets."

"No," Cam said, grasping Blair's hand. "It won't help. Just…stay close."

"I can do better than that." Blair kicked off her shoes, shed her jeans, and got under the covers. She cradled Cam's head against her shoulder and wrapped her arms and legs around her. "I'm not going anywhere."

Cam had drifted off by the time Wozinski returned. He silently and efficiently started an IV in Cam's right arm and hung a liter of warm saline. "That will run for about ten minutes. I'll be back to hang the second liter then."

"Thanks, Greg." Blair said, stroking Cam's hair. "For everything."

"It's an honor, ma'am."

Alone, Blair closed her eyes, even though she wasn't tired. She wasn't planning on sleeping. All she wanted was to listen to Cam breathe.

❖

"Glad you're here Greg," Renée Savard said, applying EKG pads to Valerie's chest. "Start another IV in her left arm, would you. We need to get another bag of the hot stuff into her. Her temp's ninety-two."

"Got it."

"Tell me what I can do," Diane urged, pressing close to the side of the bed near Valerie's head, trying not to interfere but wanting desperately to do something. Valerie looked so white, so still…so lifeless. "Please."

"Here." Felicia tossed Diane a thermal towel from the emergency kit brought over from the marina. "Dry her hair and when that towel gets cool, I'll get you another hot one."

Valerie moaned, her body twitching reflexively when Diane touched her. Diane blocked out the sound and concentrated on doing anything she could to get her warm and dry. "Is she going to be all right?"

"Yes." Renée placed an oxygen mask over Valerie's face. "Here, hold this on. It's really important. The warm air will heat the blood in her lungs and help raise her core temperature."

"I've got it," Diane said, taking the mask from Savard. When Valerie moaned again and jerked her head away, threatening to dislodge the mask, Diane leaned down and whispered in her ear. "Valerie, darling, it's Diane. You're all right. You're safe. Let us help you."

Valerie's eyelids, so bloodless that the blue of her irises shone through the skin, flickered and opened. Wordlessly, she stared into Diane's eyes.

Diane smiled and caressed her forehead above the re-breathing mask. "You're going to be all right. I love you."

Valerie nodded almost imperceptibly and closed her eyes again. Diane shivered, not from cold, but from the pain of losing that brief connection. "Tell me what to do. Tell me how to help her," she said desperately.

Renée slid an arm around Diane's shoulders and hugged her briefly. "You're here, and she knows it. That's exactly what she needs."

❖

"Do we know yet what happened out there?" Renée said, slumping into a chair in the command center. Mac and Paula hunched over the monitors. Printouts spewed from several nearby machines.

"Theories—no confirmation." Mac said, looking over his shoulder. "How are they doing upstairs?"

"Both stable. Valerie's in for a rough ride for a while."

"Mac," Paula said, pushing away from the computer console, "take over here for a second."

"Sure thing, Chief," Mac said.

Paula grasped Renée's hand and gently guided her to her feet. Then she wrapped an arm around her waist and led her toward the hall. "You need to change your clothes. They're wet."

Renée looked down as if realizing for the first time that her shoes and jeans and shirt were dripping. She shivered. "Yeah. Good idea."

Once upstairs in their bedroom, Paula took Renée into the bathroom. "Are you okay?"

"Yeah." Renée kissed Paula and brushed her fingers through her hair. "I'm fine, sweetie."

"Okay," Paula said shakily, wondering why she always seemed to lose it *after* she knew Renée was safe. "Stand there." She pulled off Renée's T-shirt and unzipped her jeans. "Take your shoes off and get out of these pants."

Renée steadied herself with a hand on Paula's shoulder. "What a cluster fuck. Who targeted Valerie's boat, do you know?"

"No," Paula said with disgust. "We've got satellite images of close to a dozen boats, not counting Tanner's, that were in missile range. It will take a while to sort through them, but at first glance, they all look civilian or commercial."

"It's got to be Matheson." Renée leaned against the vanity and closed her eyes, moaning with gratitude as Paula wrapped her in a huge towel. She burrowed her face in the curve of Paula's neck. "You feel so good I never want to move."

"Works for me." Paula held her tightly and kissed the top of Renée's head. "Scared me there for a while."

"I thought we were going to lose both of them out there."

I thought I might have lost you, Paula thought, and tightened her grip.

"I was pretty scared for a few minutes," Renée whispered.

Paula finger-combed Renée's tangled golden-brown hair. "Me too."

Renée raised her head. "I'm sorry, sweetie."

"Not your fault. You were doing your job, and I'm glad you were." Paula kissed her. "I love you."

"Yeah, me too." Renée stroked Paula's face. "Big-time."

"And yeah," Paula said grimly. "I think it was Matheson or one of his people. Who else could it have been? Henry must have told Matheson about the meet and Matheson decided to eliminate both of them at once."

"Makes sense. Who would have figured he'd have that kind of firepower?" Renée shook her head. "We're playing in a whole new league, now, aren't we? Domestic terrorism is just another name for war."

"We thought we had everything covered," Paula said. "We were monitoring for air and water assaults, except we were looking for aircraft or boats. Who would have expected a missile launch off the New England coast?"

"I don't suppose there's any chance of intercepting him?"

Paula snorted. "Zero. I called Tanner's people back in. Besides the fact that they're civilians, he could have fired that missile from fifty miles away and been gone before it even hit."

Renée stepped away, toweled off, and pulled the robe from the back of the door. Shrugging into it, she grasped Paula's hand and walked back into the bedroom. As she opened the dresser and extracted clean clothes, she said, "Did someone contact the Coast Guard about Valerie's boat?"

"Mac is doing that."

"What's our cover story?"

"We're telling them it was a DEA surveillance operation and the engine on one of the boats caught fire. All personnel evacuated to another vessel, and there were no casualties. Because of the 'sensitive nature' of the operation, we can't provide any further details."

Renée grinned and pulled on dry jeans. "Nice. Your idea?"

Paula flushed. "Yeah."

"I never knew you were so sneaky." Renée found a dark green cable-knit sweater and pulled it over her head. Then she wrapped her arms around Paula's shoulders and kissed her. "I'll have to remember that in the future."

"I didn't want you to discover all my tricks before you were in too deep to escape me."

"Oh, you needn't worry," Renée murmured. "There's no chance of me going anywhere."

❖

Blair jerked awake and bolted upright. Cam was no longer lying next to her but sat with her legs dangling over the side of the bed.

"Where do you think you're going?" Blair asked sharply.

"I want to check on Valerie."

"Get back in bed, Cameron." They were alone. A fire burned vigorously in the fireplace, throwing a hot red glow throughout the room. Blair gripped Cam's wrist. "I mean it—and I'm not in the mood to argue."

Cam, nude except for the sheet bunched at her waist, shifted to look down at Blair. "Just for a second. I only need—"

"You need some decent rest and to recover from nearly drowning out there." Blair grasped her shoulders. "You don't get it, do you? You're not indestructible. And you won't be any good to them, any of them, if you're too weak or injured to function. If you don't care about me, think about *them*."

Cam blinked, her face registering her shock. "You think I don't care about you? Is that what you think?" Gently, she tangled her fingers in Blair's hair and kissed her, softly, first her mouth, then the angle of her jaw, then her eyes. "I thought Valerie was dead. I thought I was dying, too. But I knew I couldn't, because of you. You're all I thought about. You're everything I live for."

"Don't." Blair pulled Cam down on top of her and drew the covers over them. She caressed Cam's back with both hands, slowly stroking the sleek skin and elegant curve of muscle and bone. "Don't try to melt my heart. It's not going to work this time."

"All right," Cam said softly. "I'm sorry. I'm sorry for frightening you." She kissed Blair's neck and settled her head on Blair's shoulder. "I couldn't let her die, Blair."

"No," Blair whispered. "Of course you couldn't." She sighed. "What happened to Henry?"

"He's dead. I ordered Donaldson to take him out."

Blair stiffened. "Are you all right?"

"It had to be done. The boat was about to go up and he was in danger of shooting—"

"Darling, you don't have to explain that to me. If you gave the order, it was the right thing to do."

"You believe in me that much?"

"More." Blair cupped Cam's jaw. "I trust your judgment, just like all of them do. I can only imagine what it takes for you to make those decisions and give those orders, and maybe everyone else needs to believe that it's easy for you to do, but I know differently." She cupped Cam's chin, tilted her head up, and kissed her firmly but gently on the mouth. "If you hurt, I want to know. If you need a shoulder, I have one for you. I can't be on the front line the way you are, but I'm part of this fight just the same."

"Thank you," Cam whispered. "I've never understood more clearly than I did tonight that you are my strength."

Silence ensued, then Blair said with a sigh, "Five minutes, Cameron."

"What?" Cam said.

"You can see Valerie for five minutes."

Cam stirred, raising herself on her elbow to study Blair's face. "Why?"

"Because you won't rest until you do, and because the others need to see that you're all right. As wonderful as each of them may be, you are the force that holds them together." Blair pushed the covers aside. "Let's get up. I'll help you dress."

❖

Diane finished settling a log on the fire and turned at the sound of the door slowly opening. Absently she cinched the sash on her robe.

"We didn't knock because we didn't want to wake her," Blair whispered as she and Cam stepped inside.

"That's all right. It's good to see you." Diane touched Cam's arm. "Are you all right?"

"Fine. How's she doing?" Cam asked quietly. She wore old khakis and a sweatshirt, and loosely clasped Blair's hand.

"I'm not sure," Diane admitted, pushing her hair away from her face. "She's still asleep."

"Diane?" Valerie muttered, twisting from side to side and dislodging the blankets that covered her. "Diane?"

"I'm here, darling," Diane said and hurried to the bed. She leaned down and stroked Valerie's face. "Everything is all right. You're safe now."

Valerie opened her eyes and after a few seconds appeared to focus. "Am I really in bed?"

Diane smiled. "You most definitely are."

"I'm almost warm."

"Yes," Diane whispered, her voice breaking as the tears she hadn't had the time or luxury of shedding finally filled her eyes. "You're going to be fine."

"Is everyone all right?"

Diane glanced over her shoulder. "Cam? Maybe you should talk to her for a second."

Cam joined Diane by the bed. "Hi. Bit of a rough ride out there. Everyone's fine, but you had quite a swim."

A smile flickered across Valerie's face. "I remember some of it. Thanks."

"Don't mention it."

"Henry…" Valerie frowned. "Henry." She closed her eyes briefly, and when she opened them, they were clearer. "I don't think he knew what was coming."

"No," Cam agreed.

"He didn't set me up tonight at least," Valerie said faintly. She held Cam's gaze. "Thanks for getting me out of there."

"I'm sorry about Hen—"

"No, it was a good call on your part. Just…not on mine."

"You don't know that," Cam said gently. "People change."

"I wonder." Valerie shivered violently and Diane quickly took her hand.

"You need to get some sleep, darling. No more talking right now." Diane glanced at Cam. "Thank you for everything."

Cam nodded and backed away from the bed. "Let me know if there's any problem."

"I will," Diane said.

Blair slid her arm around Cam's waist. "Let's go. You're shaking."

"I want to check downstairs with Stark and—"

"Nice try," Blair said, laughing gently. "You're all out of options tonight. Might as well surrender."

Giving in to the fatigue, Cam leaned on Blair. "Terms accepted."

CHAPTER TWENTY-NINE

Saturday

Just before noon, Cam tapped on Valerie and Diane's door. When Diane answered, looking as if she hadn't slept all night, Cam whispered, "Sorry. Is she awake?"

"On and off, yes." Diane grimaced. "She woke up a few hours ago and wanted to get dressed for the morning briefing. Fortunately, she can't get out of bed by herself, and I won't help her."

Cam smiled, but at the flash of fire in Diane's eyes, she quickly smothered it. "I'll only be a few minutes."

"Do you want to speak to her alone?"

"If you don't mind."

Diane gestured to her robe. "Give me a second to throw on some clothes. I need coffee, anyhow."

"Thanks."

"Cam," Diane said, partially closing the door, "I want to apologize for some of the things I said to you before. I know Valerie went out there because she wanted to, and you risked—"

"Diane," Cam murmured, shaking her head. "There's nothing to be sorry for. We've all been under a lot of strain."

"You saved her life."

Cam glanced across the dimly lit room to the quiet figure in the bed, thinking of where they had begun. "Then we're even."

"What happens now?" Diane asked.

"We take back control of our lives."

❖

Five hours later, Blair and Cam walked into Lucinda Washburn's office. Lucinda's only concession to the fact that it was a weekend was that she wore a gray sweater, casual black trousers, and low heels instead of a suit.

"I'd like to hear your preliminary report before I send it on to Averill," Lucinda said, referring to the security adviser.

In other words, Lucinda would put in writing whatever she wanted the official story to be after she'd heard the facts. Cam sat on the sofa with Blair beside her and waited while Lucinda gave someone instructions to hold her calls before taking her customary seat across from them.

"I take it this unscheduled visit means something important broke?" Lucinda said.

"We've located Valerie Lawrence," Cam replied. "Her Company handler, known to us at the moment only as Henry, is dead. I'm confident that he was the source of the security breach and not Valerie."

"Excellent," Lucinda said. "When will we be able to debrief Lawrence?"

"You won't," Cam answered.

Lucinda showed no change in expression when she shifted her gaze to Blair. "Would you mind excusing us for a few moments."

"You know," Blair said, leaning back and crossing her legs, "I really would."

"Blair," Lucinda said with the merest bit of heat.

"Luce," Blair snapped, "you were the one who suggested using my best friend to lure Valerie out into the open. You wanted me involved then, and now I am. So I'm not leaving."

Cam decided it might be wise to forestall the fireworks that were sure to come. "Valerie Lawrence is a member of my homeland security team, and any information she may have will be relayed by me if I feel it necessary. My agents will not be debriefed by anyone else."

"Since when is Ms. Lawrence part of your team?" Lucinda asked.

"Since noon today."

Lucinda folded her hands in her lap and appeared to be lost in thought. "How secure is her identity?"

"I'm not certain," Cam said, "and neither is she. Henry has always been her only personal contact, but undoubtedly there are records of her somewhere in the Company system. However, the right word in the right place can take care of that."

"What do you propose?" Lucinda asked.

"I propose that Valerie Lawrence died at sea in the same unfortunate boating accident that killed her handler."

"I think you'd better fill me in on the details."

Cam gave her a rundown of the events, and as she spoke, Blair shifted closer and took Cam's hand.

"You *executed* a CIA handler?" Lucinda said incredulously.

"Jesus, Luce," Blair said.

"I did, yes," Cam said evenly.

"And you're certain it was warranted?"

"Yes," Cam said. "He was a traitor and he was about to kill Valerie Lawrence, or cause her to be killed."

"What about this missile you described?" Lucinda's eyes narrowed as she visibly assessed, ordered, and prioritized information. "Can we trace it back to Matheson somehow?"

"Doubtful. The boats and whatever might remain of the SSM are in several hundred feet of heavily trafficked waters. Salvage would draw unwanted attention. I don't think it's worth the risk."

"All right." Lucinda tapped her fingers soundlessly on the arm of the chair, an action that nevertheless had the impact of a gavel falling. "The official line is that Agent Lawrence died at sea during a meeting with her handler. And now what?"

"We'll arrange for her to have a new identity," Cam said, "and she'll join my team as the counterintelligence chief."

"I know we told you to pick your own people," Lucinda said, "but—"

"You did." Cam leaned forward, tucking Blair's hand against her middle. "If you've changed your mind, then I resign."

"Not many people try playing hardball with me, Deputy Director Roberts."

"I can appreciate why. But I'm not playing. I didn't ask for this job, and if I'm going to do it, I'm going to do it the way I see fit."

"You'll continue to report to me and, through me, to the security adviser."

Cam nodded. "Agreed."

"How do you assess the danger to Blair?"

"Currently, I don't see her as a target. Matheson needed to eliminate his contact in the Company because he knew we would be searching for it. Who knows how much Henry knew about Matheson and his operation? Matheson risked exposure and possible capture to deal with Henry, but it was a calculated risk and for the time being, it's paid off for him. Now, I think he'll go underground and consolidate his power base."

"Makes sense. What about the long term?" Lucinda asked.

Cam grimaced. "Eventually, once Matheson has rebuilt his forces, I think…" she hesitated and glanced at Blair. "I think he'll make another attempt on Blair."

"To what end?" Lucinda said.

"Blair is as much a figurehead as her father, and striking at her would not only privately undermine the president, but also publicly demonstrate that he is incapable of protecting the American people, even his own daughter."

"Interesting theory," Lucinda said, rising and beginning to pace. "That makes Blair as important to national security as—"

"Blair's sitting here," Blair said, giving a little wave with her free hand.

"Sorry," Cam said.

Lucinda laughed and regarded Blair with her hands on her hips. "You wanted to stay, Blair. I never said we weren't going to talk about you."

"Including me usually works better." Blair shifted her focus from Lucinda to Cam. "Just how long have you been working on this hypothesis?"

"Since the attack at the Aerie. There had to be some compelling reason to risk something like that—for Matheson to send his best men on a suicide mission. Why you? Why not the president?"

"Because," Blair said slowly, "if my *father* were killed, he would become a martyr. The people would demand an explanation, if not retribution. Congress would rush to allocate money and personnel to find out what happened. But if he remains in office while his ability to lead is called into question and his authority is eroded, just the opposite happens. The political and economic ramifications would be devastating."

"Yes." Cam brushed her thumb over the top of Blair's hand, which she cradled between both of hers. "All this means is that you have to be careful and we'll all have to be vigilant. That's nothing new."

Blair smiled and skimmed her fingers over the edge of Cam's jaw. "Thank you. I know what it means."

"How close are you to getting Matheson?" Lucinda asked impatiently.

"Not close enough." Cam frowned. "We won't find him through any direct channels. He's not going to return to his home base, or call upon men he served with, or contact remaining family members. He's going underground. And the only way to find someone who has done that is to uncover a link to potential associates."

"And that is the slowest route," Lucinda said with a sigh. "Just ask the FBI. How many people have been on their Ten Most Wanted list for a decade or more?"

"Exactly. We're compiling extensive profiles of known or possible contacts, but we need to expand our investigation to include paramilitary organizations. We might just stumble over him or someone who can lead us to him."

"You'll need more people for that."

"We'll need information analysts and data collectors based here in DC, but none of them will require critical security clearance. I want to keep the core investigation with my personal team working out of New York City."

Lucinda sat back down. "Who don't you trust here?"

"The better question is, who *do* I trust." Cam shrugged. "I trust you, but there are too many eyes and ears in this building and all over this city." Cam laughed bitterly. "Hell, the CIA put people inside an escort service. You can bet they have them in the White House."

"It's unorthodox to work that far outside the system."

"Matheson came after Blair," Cam said flatly. "I'll do whatever I have to do with or without anyone's approval."

Lucinda glanced at Blair. "It boggles my mind that you haven't killed her."

"It was touch and go for a while when we first met." Blair smiled softly and entwined her fingers with Cam's. "Once you get to know her, of course, you discover…she's just as dangerous as she sounds."

"And what about the wedding," Lucinda said dryly. "Considering recent events, have you two decided to take the prudent course and delay?"

Cam eased back against the sofa and said nothing.

"We're getting married Thanksgiving weekend in Colorado," Blair said. "You can try to keep it a secret if you want to, but it's going to leak and we all know it, so you might as well go ahead and announce the details."

Lucinda shook her head. "You're sure?"

"We've been sure for a long time," Blair said.

"And until then?"

"We're going back to Whitley Point," Cam said, "to finalize details for purchasing the house. We'd also like to arrange for renovation of the Aerie."

"I thought we'd decided that the security breach was too severe to risk Blair returning."

"We need a place to live in Manhattan if Cam's base of operations is there," Blair said. "And that's my home."

"Blair and I talked about it on the flight down here," Cam said. "The breach wasn't because of an inherent problem with building security, but because Matheson had an inside person providing him with details and access. Instead of reinventing the wheel somewhere else, we'll correct for weaknesses there."

"I'll discuss it with the president." Lucinda held up her hand when Blair started to protest. "You can save the damn declaration of independence, Blair. There are some things he wants to know about, and your security is one of them. That's the way it is."

"Okay," Blair said quietly. "But I'll talk to him about it, okay?"

"I suppose it *is* a father-daughter thing." Lucinda smiled fleetingly. "So, where are we then?"

"Well," Cam said, "we know our enemy, which is the critical element necessary to win any war. We have the best people anywhere in the world working for us. And we have every reason in the world to prevail, so eventually, we will." She smiled at Blair. "As to the immediate future, Blair and I have a wedding to prepare for."

Blair pulled Cam to her feet and slid an arm around her waist. "Finally, a plan I can't find anything to argue with."

Lucinda laughed. "Will wonders never cease."

"No," Blair said, kissing Cam tenderly, "not in this lifetime."

About the Author

Radcly_ffe_ is a retired surgeon and full time author-publisher with over twenty-five lesbian novels and anthologies in print. She is the recipient of the 2003 and 2004 Alice B. Readers' award for her body of work and has been short-listed for the Lambda Literary Awards and Golden Crown Literary Society Awards multiple times, winning the 2005 Lambda Literary Awards with *Erotic Interludes 2: Stolen Moments* ed. with Stacia Seaman and *Distant Shores, Silent Thunder* and the 2006 Gold Crown Awards with *Justice Served*. She has selections in numerous anthologies including *Call of the Dark*, *The Perfect Valentine*, *Wild Nights*, *Best Lesbian Erotica 2006 and 2007*, *After Midnight*, *Caught Looking: Erotic Tales of Voyeurs and Exhibitionists*, *First-Timers*, *Ultimate Undies: Erotic Stories About Lingerie and Underwear*, *A is for Amour*, and *Naughty Spanking Stories 2*.

She is also the president of Bold Strokes Books, a publishing company featuring lesbian-themed general and genre fiction.

Her forthcoming works include *Winds of Fortune* (Oct 2007), and *In Deep Waters: Volume 1*, an erotica collection written with Karin Kallmaker (2007).

Books Available From Bold Strokes Books

Red Light by JD Glass. Tori forges her path as an EMT in the New York City 911 system while discovering what matters most to herself and the woman she loves. (978-1-933110-81-3)

Honor Under Siege by Radclyffe. Secret Service agent Cameron Roberts struggles to protect her lover while searching for a traitor who just may be another woman with a claim on her heart. (978-1-933110-80-6)

Dark Valentine by Jennifer Fulton. Danger and desire fuel a high stakes cat-and-mouse game when an attorney and an endangered witness team up to thwart a killer. (978-1-933110-79-0)

Sequestered Hearts by Erin Dutton. A popular artist suddenly goes into seclusion; a reluctant reporter wants to know why; and a heart locked away yearns to be set free. (978-1-933110-78-3)

Erotic Interludes 5: *Road Games* eds. Radclyffe and Stacia Seaman. Adventure, "sport," and sex on the road—hot stories of travel adventures and games of seduction. (978-1-933110-77-6)

The Spanish Pearl by Catherine Friend. On a trip to Spain, Kate Vincent is accidentally transported back in time...an epic saga spiced with humor, lust, and danger. (978-1-933110-76-9)

Lady Knight by L-J Baker. Loyalty and honour clash with love and ambition in a medieval world of magic when female knight Riannon meets Lady Eleanor. (978-1-933110-75-2)

Dark Dreamer by Jennifer Fulton. Best-selling horror author, Rowe Devlin falls under the spell of psychic Phoebe Temple. A Dark Vista romance. (978-1-933110-74-5)

Come and Get Me by Julie Cannon. Elliott Foster isn't used to pursuing women, but alluring attorney Lauren Collier makes her change her mind. (978-1-933110-73-8)

Blind Curves by Diane and Jacob Anderson-Minshall. Private eye Yoshi Yakamota comes to the aid of her ex-lover Velvet Erickson in the first Blind Eye mystery. (978-1-933110-72-1)

Dynasty of Rogues by Jane Fletcher. It's hate at first sight for Ranger Riki Sadiq and her new patrol corporal, Tanya Coppelli—except for their undeniable attraction. (978-1-933110-71-4)

Running With the Wind by Nell Stark. Sailing instructor Corrie Marsten has signed off on love until she meets Quinn Davies—one woman she can't ignore. (978-1-933110-70-7)

More than Paradise by Jennifer Fulton. Two women battle danger, risk all, and find in one another an unexpected ally and an unforgettable love. (978-1-933110-69-1)

Flight Risk by Kim Baldwin. For Blayne Keller, being in the wrong place at the wrong time just might turn out to be the best thing that ever happened to her. (978-1-933110-68-4)

Rebel's Quest, Supreme Constellations Book Two by Gun Brooke. On a world torn by war, two women discover a love that defies all boundaries. (978-1-933110-67-7)

Punk and Zen by JD Glass. Angst, sex, love, rock. Trace, Candace, Francesca...Samantha. Losing control—and finding the truth within. BSB Victory Editions. (1-933110-66-X)

Stellium in Scorpio by Andrews & Austin. The passionate reuniting of two powerful women on the glitzy Las Vegas Strip where everything is an illusion and love is a gamble. (1-933110-65-1)

When Dreams Tremble by Radclyffe. Two women whose lives turned out far differently than they'd once imagined discover that sometimes the shape of the future can only be found in the past. (1-933110-64-3)

The Devil Unleashed by Ali Vali. As the heat of violence rises, so does the passion. A Casey Family crime saga. (1-933110-61-9)

Burning Dreams by Susan Smith. The chronicle of the challenges faced by a young drag king and an older woman who share a love "outside the bounds." (1-933110-62-7)

Fresh Tracks by Georgia Beers. Seven women, seven days. A lot can happen when old friends, lovers, and a new girl in town get together in the mountains. (1-933110-63-5)

The Empress and the Acolyte by Jane Fletcher. Jemeryl and Tevi fight to protect the very fabric of their world: time. Lyremouth Chronicles Book Three. (1-933110-60-0)

First Instinct by JLee Meyer. When high-stakes security fraud leads to murder, one woman flees for her life while another risks her heart to protect her. (1-933110-59-7)

Erotic Interludes 4: *Extreme Passions* ed. by Radclyffe and Stacia Seaman. Thirty of today's hottest erotica writers set the pages aflame with love, lust, and steamy liaisons. (1-933110-58-9)

Storms of Change by Radclyffe. In the continuing saga of the Provincetown Tales, duty and love are at odds as Reese and Tory face their greatest challenge. (1-933110-57-0)

Unexpected Ties by Gina L. Dartt. With death before dessert, Kate Shannon and Nikki Harris are swept up in another tale of danger and romance. (1-933110-56-2)

Sleep of Reason by Rose Beecham. While Detective Jude Devine searches for a lost boy, her rocky relationship with Dr. Mercy Westmoreland gets a lot harder. (1-933110-53-8)

Passion's Bright Fury by Radclyffe. Passion strikes without warning when a trauma surgeon and a filmmaker become reluctant allies. (1-933110-54-6)

Broken Wings by L-J Baker. When Rye Woods meets beautiful dryad Flora Withe, her libido, as hidden as her wings, reawakens along with her heart. (1-933110-55-4)

Combust the Sun by Andrews & Austin. A Richfield and Rivers mystery set in L.A. Murder among the stars. (1-933110-52-X)

Of Drag Kings and the Wheel of Fate by Susan Smith. A blind date in a drag club leads to an unlikely romance. (1-933110-51-1)

Tristaine Rises by Cate Culpepper. Brenna, Jesstin, and the Amazons of Tristaine face their greatest challenge for survival. (1-933110-50-3)

Too Close to Touch by Georgia Beers. Kylie O'Brien believes in true love and is willing to wait for it, even though Gretchen, her new boss, is off-limits. (1-933110-47-3)

100th Generation by Justine Saracen. Ancient curses, modern-day villains, and an intriguing woman lead archeologist Valerie Foret on the adventure of her life. (1-933110-48-1)

Battle for Tristaine by Cate Culpepper. While Brenna struggles to find her place in the clan, Tristaine is threatened with destruction. Second in the Tristaine series. (1-933110-49-X)

The Traitor and the Chalice by Jane Fletcher. Tevi and Jemeryl risk all in the race to uncover a traitor. The Lyremouth Chronicles Book Two. (1-933110-43-0)

Promising Hearts by Radclyffe. Dr. Vance Phelps arrives in New Hope, Montana, with no hope of happiness—until she meets Mae. (1-933110-44-9)

Carly's Sound by Ali Vali. Poppy Valente and Julia Johnson form a bond of friendship that becomes something far more. A poignant romance about love and renewal. (1-933110-45-7)

Unexpected Sparks by Gina L. Dartt. Kate Shannon's attraction to much younger Nikki Harris is complication enough without a fatal fire that Kate can't ignore. (1-933110-46-5)

Whitewater Rendezvous by Kim Baldwin. Two women on a wilderness kayak adventure discover that true love may be nothing at all like they imagined. (1-933110-38-4)

Erotic Interludes 3: *Lessons in Love* ed. by Radclyffe and Stacia Seaman. Sign on for a class in love…the best lesbian erotica writers take us to "school." (1-9331100-39-2)

Punk Like Me by JD Glass. Twenty-one-year-old Nina has a way with the girls, and she doesn't always play by the rules. (1-933110-40-6)

Coffee Sonata by Gun Brooke. Four women whose lives unexpectedly intersect in a small town by the sea share one thing in common—they all have secrets. (1-933110-41-4)

The Clinic: Tristaine Book One by Cate Culpepper. Brenna, a prison medic, finds herself drawn to Jesstin, a warrior reputed to be descended from ancient Amazons. (1-933110-42-2)

Forever Found by JLee Meyer. Can time, tragedy, and shattered trust destroy a love that seemed destined? Chance reunites childhood friends separated by tragedy. (1-933110-37-6)

Sword of the Guardian by Merry Shannon. Princess Shasta's bold new bodyguard has a secret that could change both of their lives. *He* is actually a *she*. (1-933110-36-8)

Wild Abandon by Ronica Black. Dr. Chandler Brogan and Officer Sarah Monroe are drawn together by their common obsessions—sex, speed, and danger. (1-933110-35-X)

Turn Back Time by Radclyffe. Pearce Rifkin and Wynter Thompson have nothing in common but a shared passion for surgery—and unexpected attraction. (1-933110-34-1)

Chance by Grace Lennox. A sexy, funny, touching story of two women who, in finding themselves, also find one another. (1-933110-31-7)

The Exile and the Sorcerer by Jane Fletcher. First in the Lyremouth Chronicles. Tevi and a shy young sorcerer face monsters, magic, and the challenge of loving. (1-933110-32-5)

A Matter of Trust by Radclyffe. When what should be just business turns into much more, two women struggle to trust the unexpected. (1-933110-33-3)

Sweet Creek by Lee Lynch. A celebration of the enduring nature of love, friendship, and community in the heart-warming lesbian community of Waterfall Falls. (1-933110-29-5)

The Devil Inside by Ali Vali. The head of a New Orleans crime organization falls for a woman who turns her world upside down. (1-933110-30-9)

Grave Silence by Rose Beecham. Detective Jude Devine's investigation of ritual murders is complicated by her torrid affair with pathologist Dr. Mercy Westmoreland. (1-933110-25-2)

Honor Reclaimed by Radclyffe. Secret Service Agent Cameron Roberts and Blair Powell close ranks to find the would-be assassins who nearly claimed Blair's life. (1-933110-18-X)

Honor Bound by Radclyffe. Secret Service Agent Cameron Roberts and Blair Powell face political intrigue, a clandestine threat to Blair's safety, and the seemingly irreconcilable differences that force them ever farther apart. (1-933110-20-1)

Innocent Hearts by Radclyffe. In a wild and unforgiving land, two women learn about love, passion, and the wonders of the heart. (1-933110-21-X)

The Temple at Landfall by Jane Fletcher. An imprinter, one of Celaeno's most revered servants of the Goddess, is also a prisoner to the faith—until a Ranger frees her by claiming her heart. The Celaeno series. (1-933110-27-9)

Protector of the Realm, Supreme Constellations Book One by Gun Brooke. A space adventure filled with suspense and a daring intergalactic romance. (1-933110-26-0)

Force of Nature by Kim Baldwin. From tornados to forest fires, the forces of nature conspire to bring Gable McCoy and Erin Richards close to danger, and closer to each other. (1-933110-23-6)

In Too Deep by Ronica Black. Undercover homicide cop Erin McKenzie tracks a femme fatale who just might be a real killer...with love and danger hot on her heels. (1-933110-17-1)

Erotic Interludes 2: *Stolen Moments* ed. by Radclyffe and Stacia Seaman. Love on the run, in the office, in the shadows...Fast, furious, and almost too hot to handle. (1-933110-16-3)

Course of Action by Gun Brooke. Actress Carolyn Black desperately wants the starring role in an upcoming film produced by Annelie Peterson. Just how far will she go for the dream part of a lifetime? (1-933110-22-8)

Rangers at Roadsend by Jane Fletcher. Sergeant Chip Coppelli has learned to spot trouble coming, and that is exactly what she sees in her new recruit, Katryn Nagata. The Celaeno series. (1-933110-28-7)

Justice Served by Radclyffe. Lieutenant Rebecca Frye and her lover, Dr. Catherine Rawlings, embark on a deadly game of hide-and-seek with an underworld kingpin who traffics in human souls. (1-933110-15-5)

Distant Shores, Silent Thunder by Radclyffe. Dr. Tory King—along with the women who love her—is forced to examine the boundaries of love, friendship, and the ties that transcend time. (1-933110-08-2)

Hunter's Pursuit by Kim Baldwin. A raging blizzard, a mountain hideaway, and a killer-for-hire set a scene for disaster—or desire—when Katarzyna Demetrious rescues a beautiful stranger. (1-933110-09-0)

The Walls of Westernfort by Jane Fletcher. All Temple Guard Natasha Ionadis wants is to serve the Goddess—until she falls in love with one of the rebels she is sworn to destroy. The Celaeno series. (1-933110-24-4)

Erotic Interludes: *Change Of Pace* by Radclyffe. Twenty-five hot-wired encounters guaranteed to spark more than just your imagination. Erotica as you've always dreamed of it. (1-933110-07-4)

Honor Guards by Radclyffe. In a wild flight for their lives, the president's daughter and those who are sworn to protect her wage a desperate struggle for survival. (1-933110-01-5)

Fated Love by Radclyffe. Amidst the chaos and drama of a busy emergency room, two women must contend not only with the fragile nature of life, but also with the irresistible forces of fate. (1-933110-05-8)

Justice in the Shadows by Radclyffe. In a shadow world of secrets and lies, Detective Sergeant Rebecca Frye and her lover, Dr. Catherine Rawlings, join forces in the elusive search for justice. (1-933110-03-1)

shadowland by Radclyffe. In a world on the far edge of desire, two women are drawn together by power, passion, and dark pleasures. An erotic romance. (1-933110-11-2)

Love's Masquerade by Radclyffe. Plunged into the indistinguishable realms of fiction, fantasy, and hidden desires, Auden Frost is forced to question all she believes about the nature of love. (1-933110-14-7)

Love & Honor by Radclyffe. The president's daughter and her lover are faced with difficult choices as they battle a tangled web of Washington intrigue for...love and honor. (1-933110-10-4)

Beyond the Breakwater by Radclyffe. One Provincetown summer, three women learn the true meaning of love, friendship, and family. (1-933110-06-6)

Tomorrow's Promise by Radclyffe. One timeless summer, two very different women discover the power of passion to heal and the promise of hope that only love can bestow. (1-933110-12-0)

Love's Tender Warriors by Radclyffe. Two women who have accepted loneliness as a way of life learn that love is worth fighting for and a battle they cannot afford to lose. (1-933110-02-3)

Love's Melody Lost by Radclyffe. A secretive artist with a haunted past and a young woman escaping a life that has proved to be a lie find their destinies entwined. (1-933110-00-7)

Safe Harbor by Radclyffe. A mysterious newcomer, a reclusive doctor, and a troubled gay teenager learn about love, friendship, and trust during one tumultuous summer in Provincetown. (1-933110-13-9)

Above All, Honor by Radclyffe. Secret Service Agent Cameron Roberts fights her desire for the one woman she can't have—Blair Powell, the daughter of the president of the United States. (1-933110-04-X)